GIVE IT A MONTH

Other Titles by Mairi Louise

My Fake Fiancé

Betting on You

(Online only)

Witches in Suburbia

My Summer Affair

My Royal Romance

a Birch Lake novel

Give it a Month

Mairi Louise

First paperback edition September 2024

Cover design by Mairi Louise

ISBN 979-8-9905370-5-7 (paperback)

Published by Lakebound Love Publishing

This is a love letter to my favorite place and a thank you to my Gammie for putting me in the position to be able to accomplish my dreams, and my family for supporting me along the way.

GIVE IT A MONTH

Chapter 1

Dylan

"Lyn, have you heard the good news?" Mary, the front desk associate, sidles up next to me with a mischievous look on her face. She matches my pace as we head to Meeting Room 3, affectionately named "The Doom Room". The thought of going to another meeting there is frustrating but Mary seems to think it's a good thing.

"What is it, Mary?" I ask, slowing down to hear the information before the meeting. I smile at my coworkers as we pass them, most offer polite smiles in return.

"Oh, I shouldn't say," Mary teases me as we enter the conference room. "But it is good news, I promise."

Mary winks at me as she goes to take her seat along the wall with the rest of the associates. I head to the main table in the center of the room and take a seat beside my other coworkers. The table is unofficially divided by our levels in the company. I sit toward the back of the room, away from the giant screen, with the rest of the Financial Advisors while the FAs with a Vice

President and above title sit further toward the front of the room, and the Associates in chairs around the edge of the room.

"Thank you all for joining us today," Marvin, the CFO of the Southern District says as he walks into the room. The room falls quiet besides a few of the other FAs saying hello and joking with the CFO as if they are friends, which they probably are.

"Alright, let's cut the noise," our office's Managing Director, Kevin, barks out with a grumble before turning the floor back over to Marvin.

"Thanks, Kev," Marvin says, stepping into the center of the room. "Okay, let's see. What is on the agenda?"

Marvin looks down at the tablet in his hand and clicks around on the screen. His tablet is reflected on the giant screen in the conference room and we all watch as he finds the agenda for the day.

"It looks like we have a promotion in the mix!" Marvin looks up with a big smile.

I look at the screen and see my name is on the agenda, right under 'promotion'. My heart starts to beat a little faster as I get excited. I sit up, ready to receive the good news.

"But first!" Kevin steps in before Marvin can announce my promotion. He looks at me with a smirk before turning back to the group. "We have a very special birthday today. Gary! You didn't think we'd let this one sneak by, did you? The big 6-5."

"Aw, come on guys, you didn't need to do anything for me," Gary, one of the FAs closest to the front, protests even with a smile on his face, enjoying the attention.

Kevin leads everybody in a quick singing of 'Happy Birthday' to Gary and I join in before we all turn our attention back to Marvin. Marvin clears his throat, clearly a little annoyed at the interruption. His time is valuable and singing wasn't worth adding a few extra seconds to this meeting and his schedule. Marvin checks his watch while the room settles.

"Yes, Happy Birthday Gary. Now, back to the agenda. Our only promotion this month is Dylan Monroe. Dylan, sir, where are you? Stand up so we can congratulate you," Marvin says as he looks around the room for a male Dylan.

I awkwardly stand up and give a little wave. There is a look of surprise on Marvin's face, even though we have met three times now.

"Ah, yes, Lyn, sorry. Congratulations on the promotion! I know the team will be happy to have your experience and leadership. I'm sorry they couldn't be here to meet you but I'm sure they'll welcome you with open arms on Monday," Marvin says with a curt nod.

Monday? I wonder why they aren't here today.

"Thank you so much for the opportunity. I can't wait to continue to grow my career here," I start to give my thanks and a little speech that I had had prepared for almost a year now, but Marvin claps his hands when I pause.

"Of course, and we look forward to watching you grow with our company!" Marvin says again. I can tell he is moving on from the conversation so I sit back down. "Congratulations, Lyn," Marvin says again. "It looks like you have had a great year and the promotion is well deserved."

The meeting goes on a little longer but I can barely concentrate. I am very excited about my promotion. I start to think about which office I will get to move to, hopefully, it will have a nice view of downtown. I'm ready to move out of my cubicle and have my own space. And I'm excited to meet my new team. Although, I'm a bit surprised the team wasn't shared during the announcement but maybe Marvin is just too busy and Kevin will tell me after the meeting.

When the meeting ends, Marvin gestures for me to get up and come shake his hand so I do. I awkwardly make my way between all of the chairs and let him wildly pump my hand before pulling away and smiling at the coworkers clapping for me once again.

"Thank you so much for this opportunity. I have worked hard to obtain all my licenses and am up to date with trends in the market," I start to explain my credentials but Marvin has started looking at his phone so I trail off.

"It was great to meet you, Lyn. Mary should be able to get everything set up for you for your move to the office. We'll take care of all the travel arrangements, of course," Marvin states and I chuckle a little. What travel? The journey across the hall or even to a new floor in the building shouldn't cost too much.

"Well, thank you. I shouldn't expect it will be a pricey journey," I say in a teasing manner but Marvin just raises his eyebrows at me.

"Right. Okay, I have to get going. It was nice to meet you, Lyn," Marvin says, shaking my hand once again before turning to Kevin. "I'll check in with you later in the week about those tickets, alright?"

"Sounds good!" Kevin grins and shakes his hand. I step up to ask more about the promotion but Marvin isn't interested anymore. "Alright, birthday cake time!" Kevin jumps at the opportunity to take away my spotlight once again. "We went all the way to Eatzi's for you, buddy."

Kevin claps Gary on the back and the smile on my face falters but I don't want to ruin the mood. The coworkers around me congratulate me before quickly moving off to get a piece of the birthday cake.

Once the excitement of the birthday cake has settled down, I take my plate over to my little group of friends and munch on the cake. It is delicious so I can see why everyone was so excited about the cake rather than my promotion.

"Wow, I can't believe you're going to be moving to Minnesota, Lyn. That is crazy, and it's going to be so cold especially right now," Mary tuts, and I look up from my cake with a confused expression on my face.

"What are you talking about? Minnesota?" I ask, my heart starting to beat faster and my breath becoming more shallow.

"Yeah, that's where the job is. Didn't they tell you?" Mary asks, faux confusion on her face. She is clearly amused by this whole situation.

"No! Of course, no one told me. Of course," I say with a huff then quickly leave the room, dropping my half-eaten cake into the trash.

I march down the hallway and barge into Kevin's office. He is on the phone while simultaneously shoving cake into his mouth. He holds his finger up to indicate that he needs a minute. I cross my arms and tap my foot impatiently. Finally, after what seems like way longer than necessary, Kevin finally hangs up the phone and looks up at me with a barely contained smirk.

"Yes? How can I help you?"

"Kevin, how could you not think to mention that the job was in Minnesota!" I practically shout at Kevin who dares to look surprised by my outburst. "You were the one who brought the job to my attention. You helped me apply and sent in recommendations. How was it never mentioned that the job was not here in Dallas, Texas but is instead in Minnesota?"

"Okay, first, lower your voice," Kevin crosses to the other side of his desk and shuts his office door even though it is glass and people can still see through to our argument.

"I didn't think you were ready for this job in a big city," Kevin says with a shrug as he goes back to his desk.

"That doesn't exactly answer my question now, does it? It also brings up another question; Where in Minnesota is the job? You just said you don't think I'm ready for a job in a big city so where is the job, Kevin?" I interrogate him, unfalteringly questioning him because I am tired of being jerked around by his incompetence and jealousy.

"Okay, again, calm down, Lyn," Kevin says, waving his hand in a gesture to get me to sit down. I hesitate but then feel my energy deflating so I drop into the chair across from his desk.

"There is another job coming up in this office, in another month or so. Just stick it out in Minnesota, show everybody you can kill it out there and then I promise I will get you the job here," Kevin says. He sets his folded hands on his desk, looking over them at me. "There weren't any promotions immediately available in our office or in Dallas in general anyways so this is the best I could do for you unless you want to wait it out until one of the old guys on the floor retires, but you know they've all got a few more years at least. They don't do anything except make a few trades once or twice a week but they are raking it in. Whew."

Kevin looks like he admires their lack of effort and it annoys me, but he is right. There is no position here for me unless I want to remain stationary. I don't, I want to keep going up in the company. I sigh, resigned.

"Kevin, where is the job?"

"A small town in Minnesota," Kevin says, then he looks at his computer to find the name of the town. He searches his email for a few minutes before finding the paperwork for me. "A small town called….ah, there it is, Birch Lake."

"Birch Lake," I repeat, mulling the name over in my head. I had never heard of it. "A small town?" I clarified.

"Yep."

"Great. This coming Monday?" I check, hoping I'm wrong but the smirk on Kevin's face confirms otherwise.

"Yes, ma'am," he confirms, his grin growing. "Mary will send your itinerary to your email by the end of the day."

"I would hope so," I grumble. "Seeing as how today is Friday. You couldn't have given me anymore notice?"

"Nope." Kevin grins.

I roll my eyes and head back to my desk to get as much done as I can while packing my things.

Chapter 2

Dylan

"So, you're moving to Minnesota?" Max asks as I toss more of my clothes onto the bed. He takes each item, folding it carefully before sorting everything for me into random stacks.

"Only for a few weeks, I think. I hope," I say softly. "Maybe I shouldn't go."

"It is a long distance," Max says, sounding a little put out as he thinks it over but he shakes his head. "No, babe. You have to go. You've been talking about this next step in your career and this is it. I'll be fine here without you for a few months."

"Are you sure?" I sit down on the bed next to him, pushing my clothing aside so I don't wrinkle anything. "I don't have to go. I like my job right now."

"No, you don't," Max points out and I shrug. I don't *not* like it but he's right. I've been talking about the next steps in my career and this is a good one.

"I'll just go for a couple of weeks. Kevin said there is a new position opening up in the Dallas office soon and I just have to stick it out in Minnesota until then. Well, excel there, not just 'stick it out'," I say and then hang my head, dropping it into my hands. "In Minnesota, in February!" I half grumble and half whine. Max rubs his hand over my back to comfort me.

"It'll be good. And you know what they say; distance makes the heart grow fonder," Max says and I lift my head to glare at him. He chuckles but holds his hands up. "Too soon?"

"Yes, much too soon. Speaking of soon. I have to get to the airport." I sigh and stand up. "I can't believe they sprung this on me last minute."

I shake my head, annoyed as I continue to pack. I take the neatly folded piles and place them into my suitcases, all of them.

"You know what, babe?" Max says and I glance over at him. "It's pretty good timing."

"How so?"

"I've got a lot of studying to do," Max says.

"Are you saying I'm a distraction?" I tease, moving toward him with a smirk.

"I'm saying we should hurry because we really shouldn't have spent so much time saying goodbye to each other," Max teases me. I blush a little. I was excited about the promotion but annoyed about the location and I had so much built-up energy and adrenaline that I had practically jumped on Max when I got home.

"Yeah, that's fair," I relent. "Okay, I guess that makes me feel a little better."

"Good. You almost ready?" Max asks as he checks his phone once again before he sets it aside and grabs one of my coats.

"Oh, be careful with that one. That one was not on sale but when you're in Armani Exchange and see a beautiful leather jacket, you have to get it. Especially if it is the last one in the store and it's your size. I mean, come on, it was meant to be," I say as I take the coat to hang it up on the door. I breathe in the delicious scent of the leather and Max chuckles.

"Okay, that is everything. Are you bringing that coat?" Max asks as he stands up and finishes zipping all of my suitcases.

"Yes, it is going to be cold when I land so I think I will bring it on the plane with me," I tell him and he looks skeptical.

"Are you sure that is going to keep you warm enough? It may be in the 70s here but I doubt it'll even get up to 50 in Minnesota. You are going in the dead of winter," Max reminds me and I groan.

"Is it really the dead of winter there? It's February," I contemplate, looking over the jacket. "But it's so cute," I pause to look at the jacket again and make my decision. "No, I'm bringing it. This is my coat for the winter. It is perfect and stylish. I need to bring some of this Dallas style to small-town Minnesota."

"That is true. Alright, well, I'll go start to load the car. It will take a couple of trips," Max says before kissing my cheek and taking two of the huge bags with him.

It does take a couple of trips for both of us before the car is loaded. We are both sweaty messes and the car ride is mostly silent as we drive to the airport. As we get closer, I find myself doubting the trip more and more. The anxious feeling in my stomach growing.

"Babe, it'll be fine. Text when you land, okay?" Max takes my face in his hands and wipes the tears off my cheeks. I nod sadly and we kiss one more time. This time it's just a peck and a little disappointing. I'm going to miss him so much.

We finish unloading the car at the airport and are saying our final goodbyes. Well, not 'goodbye', just a 'see you later'.

"Do you need a cart for all your things? Let me see if they have anything." Max releases his grip on me and looks around for a cart. He finds one eventually and we load all five of my bags onto the cart, setting my medium-sized carry-on on top.

"I'm going to miss you," I say, choking back another sob. Max takes my hand and squeezes it.

"I'll come visit you soon. Okay, baby?" Max kisses my lips softly and pulls me into a hug. I snuggle against his chest and hold onto him tight. "You've got this," he reassures me.

We finally pull apart after a car behind us honks, wanting to get around us but they didn't leave room to pull out.

"Thanks for dropping me off," I say, not wanting to end the conversation so I don't have to leave yet. Max shakes his head at me, seeing right through my tactics.

"Go, Dylan. It is going to take you forever to get all those bags checked," Max says with a chuckle. He turns the cart toward the door for me and gives me a pat on the behind. I pout a little but start to push the cart inside. I look back as the doors are closing and see Max getting in the car to drive away.

I fight the tears in my eyes as I walk over to the counter to check my bags. After only a few steps, the front wheel of the cart pops under the weight of my bags, and my cart droops. It takes my best effort to hold back more tears. I maneuver the cart carefully to the counter and struggle to heft all of them onto the scale. Only one is free and it doesn't matter the weight of the rest because they're already going to cost extra. Thankfully, I have a company card I can use. I pull out the card and hand it to the woman behind the counter.

The card is new, for my promotion to the new office and I know I'm supposed to use it for clients or the office but this is part of the job too. They're sending me out here so the company can pay for my bags, that is part of my travel expenses and Marvin promised to pay for it.

"Alright, you are all set. You're going to be flying out of Gate 8 and it looks like boarding begins in…half an hour almost exactly," the woman at the front counter informs me. "Security has been moving quickly today so you should be fine."

The woman's reassurance does little to settle my nerves. She hands me my boarding pass with a smile. I thank her and then grab my carry-on bag and head for the security line.

Thankfully, the lady at the front desk is right and the line moves pretty quickly. I make it to my gate just in time for them to call the first group to board. I take someone's seat as they stand to join the group. My boarding group is group 3 so I have a few minutes to sit and catch my breath. I pull out my phone to make sure I have an audio book loaded up on my phone to listen to during the flight.

When my group is called, I jump up and take my place in line. The line moves slowly but before I know it, I am on the plane and shoving my carryon into the overhead bin. I drop into my seat and let out a sigh of relief.

I pull out my headphones as the plane takes off and try to listen to a few chapters but it's been a long, exhausting day and my eyelids are getting heavier. I pause my book, switch to soft music, and then bundle up my sweatshirt and put it on the seatback tray before putting my head down to sleep.

Chapter 3

Shawn

Watching the snowfall through the giant bay window in my mother's living room, I debate going outside to get a head start on shoveling the driveway. Technically, I don't need to shovel the driveway because Mom tends to walk to work, even in this weather.

The snow has been falling for a couple of hours now and is glistening under the moonlight. It's a cold night tonight but with the fire burning and the heater on, Mom's house is toasty and I am starting to overheat in my knit sweater.

I roll up my sleeves and kneel before the fire, stoking it and tossing in another couple of logs of wood. I stand up to admire my work and put the fire poker back. Wiping my hands on my jeans, I go over to the couch to sit down for a few minutes. I debate turning on the TV but I know my Mom would kill me if it came on before dinner. She stuck to her habits and it was a rule she had implemented when I was a young boy. My dad sometimes struggled with the rule but Mom was persistent and after a few scoldings from her, my dad had learned it was best to wait until after dinner.

So, instead of turning on the TV to see what game is on, I sit quietly staring at the fireplace while my mom works diligently in the kitchen. I often try to join her but I mostly get in her way. The kitchen is small and with the two of us in there, I only slow her down. I learned to stay out of her way while she works.

"Honey, come sit down for dinner," Mom calls over to get my attention. I walk away from the window and find her setting a big dish on the dining room table. I follow her back into the kitchen to help carry in the sides.

When we've finished bringing out all the dishes, I drop into my usual chair and we both look at the empty chair at the head of the table. I still haven't gotten used to my dad being gone. Four years later, we both still expect to see his smiling face each time we sit down for family dinner.

Mom bows her head for a few seconds offering a silent prayer before she looks up at me with a smile. She takes her plate and starts serving herself, taking the biggest piece of meat from the pile. She slaps the thigh on her plate with a satisfied look.

"So, how was work today?" Mom asks before taking a huge bite of the delicious meal she prepared for us.

"Steady. Even with this weather we still have lots of work," I inform her and take my own giant bite. "We just lost Benji. He and his family moved to Minneapolis, so we're stretched a bit thin. But it's okay, it keeps me busy."

"That's good. I heard Benji and Natalie found an apartment in the city. I just can't imagine moving from all this beautiful acreage and a big home to an apartment in the city. I mean, I know it's closer to her family for the kids but still," Mom goes on, chattering away.

I eat silently while she continues talking. She tells me about the bookstore and a new shelf she needs help building. Her old handyman retired and I've been around to help more, it also helped save a little money.

"You know, you don't have to come over every Friday for dinner," Mom says after a few minutes.

"It's a force of habit. Plus, I missed so many Fridays while I was living in Minneapolis," I point out and Mom shakes her head but laughs.

"That's true. I am very glad you moved back. However, there is nothing wrong with Minneapolis. Having you back home has been such a blessing," Mom prattles on with a loving smile on her face. "You have been such a big help around the house and at the store. I know everybody is so glad that you're back in town. All the ladies love seeing you."

I shake my head at her while I take another bite of dinner.

"Ladies both young and old," Mom says with a chuckle. "Ms. Whitney was asking about your status the other day when she stopped into the store."

"Ms. Whitney? Isn't she, like, your age?" I ask after clearing the shock out of my voice. Mom shoots me a stern look, her eyes narrowed in disapproval.

"Watch your words, Shawn. She is old enough to be my mother," Mom scolds me with a shake of her fork. "But she is single," Mom points out and I stifle another laugh.

"Oh, is she?" I ask, pretending to entertain the idea.

Mom swats at me with her napkin but continues talking.

"Yes, Ms. Whitney has been single for almost two decades now. I guess she's ready to get back out there. Her husband was the love of her life and I can understand why it has taken her so long to be ready to move on," Mom says with a knowing smile but then she looks at me again. "And that is not me saying I'm ready to move on. It's barely been four years since your father passed away, I'm not ready to move on. Plus, I have been so busy lately. I wouldn't have time for a new man in my life."

"Alright, thanks, Mom," I say to get her to stop talking about it. She chuckles a bit and then we fall into a comfortable silence, the only noise the crackling of the fireplace and the sound of our utensils scraping our plates.

When dinner is over, I help Mom pack away the leftovers. I wash the dishes off and put them in the dishwasher while Mom packs up some of the leftovers for me to take home.

"Oh, dear?" Mom taps my shoulder and gestures to the package of food for me. I nod a quick thanks. "I think I told you that I have a new renter coming in tonight?" Mom tells me and this is the first I am hearing about it. I wasn't aware that the apartment above the bookstore was ready for a renter yet. I was sure there would be issues I would have to fix but she never called me about anything.

"Are you sure? The apartment is pretty old," I start but she cuts me off.

"Oh, no. It's fine. You checked it out when you got back and I just went over today to make sure everything was clean," Mom says and now it is my turn to interrupt her.

"Mom, I lived there when I first moved back, four years ago. And I only lived there for a year. I'm sure some things need to be updated or fixed since I moved out," I point out and she shrugs.

"It's fine. I've had a few people sleep there after some late nights," Mom says and I raise an eyebrow. She laughs and winks at me. Wow, must be some wild nights at her famous book club. "Plus, you're around to fix them if it's needed." Mom smiles and she looks happy about having a new renter so I brush it off.

"Okay, that's fine. Do you know who the renter is?"

"Ah, no. It's someone who is being transferred here from work. Dylan Something, but they don't get in until this evening so I won't get to meet them. I left the key for the apartment in the planter out front of the store and all of that information should have been passed along to the renter and my phone number for future needs," Mom says. I fight the urge to argue, it's frustrating to have almost zero information.

"Do you need me to swing by the apartment tonight to make sure everything is okay?" I ask as I pack up the Tupperware containers and pull on my coat. I shove my hands into my gloves, it's a short ride back to my place but my fingers take forever to warm up after being outside in the cold.

"Oh, no. I wouldn't want you to scare the new renter." Mom chuckles and pats me on the back once. Then she pulls me into a hug. "Thank you for coming over for dinner."

"Thank you for dinner." I release her and go out to my car, turning it on as I hit the driveway.

I jump into my car to the heater already blasting. I pull out of the driveway and glance back at it. I almost turn around to shovel the driveway but instead, I keep the car straight and head back to my house.

Chapter 4

Dylan

When my plane lands, I am still drowsy and even more so because it is late in the evening now. I look out the plane window while waiting to deboard the plane and see that there is a light layer of snow covering the tarmac but the workers are moving quickly to keep the runways clear.

Once at baggage claim, I find a cart and wait patiently for my luggage to come down the conveyor belt. I struggle with most of the bags but finally, have everything loaded onto the cart and make my way outside to find my ride.

The wind and cold hits me as soon as the airport doors open. The burst of freezing cold air shoves me back into the building and thankfully, the doors close between me and the tundra outside, and the heater blows down on me furiously.

"What the-!" I catch myself before I curse but I still get a few judgemental looks. I wince and offer a polite smile. One woman smiles and shakes her head with pity as she heads out into the wind without a second thought, setting off the heater once again.

I pull the cart to the side of the exit and dig through my carry-on to find my leather coat. I pull it on quickly and it hits just above my knees. Hopefully, this will help. I wore my leggings and a sweatshirt on the plane so the layers should help keep me warm.

Once I'm all buttoned up and have hyped myself up to face the cold again, I check my phone and see that my driver has arrived. It took quite a while to find someone willing to come to the airport and then drive three hours to get to Birch Lake. I start to stress out about it but the car pulls up so I feel the relief setting in. I brave the cold and make my way to the car, waving at the driver for confirmation. The driver pops out of the car and jogs over to help me load my bags into the car.

"Is that your biggest coat?" He asks, looking me up and down. I wince a little as my body begins to shiver. He gestures for me to get in the car while he finishes loading the rest of my bags.

Climbing into the car and shutting the door behind me brings me almost instant shelter from the cold. I sit back and close my eyes. Today has been such a rush from the minute I woke up. Work was crazy and then I had to immediately pack up my life in only a few suitcases to move from Dallas, Texas to Birch Lake, Minnesota. I have not had a second to breathe today aside from the plane ride up, that I slept through most of. Now, I have an equally long car ride to the town and hopefully, all I need to do is go inside, take a hot shower, and climb into bed.

"You ready to go?" The driver asks, making me jump a little because I had not heard him get back into the car. He smiles at me in the rearview window and I nod my head.

"Yes, thank you so much," I reply as he pulls out of the loading/unloading zone and heads away from the airport.

"Is the heat enough for you?" The driver asks and I can tell that he is sweating but I'm still trying to defrost even though I was only outside for a few minutes.

"Yes, thank you!" I point both of the backseat vents directly at me and let the heat overwhelm the whole car, fogging the windows.

I try to stay awake on the drive to Birch Lake but I find my eyelids drooping once again. The driver checks in about halfway there to see if I need to stop for anything and we do stop for a quick bathroom/gas station break before heading back out on the road again.

"So, are you visiting family for break?" the driver, Cain, asks once we are back on the road. "Spring break for some colleges right?"

"Ah, no," I chuckle, sitting up so I can talk to him through the plastic divider. "I actually just got a promotion but no one told me it was out here in the middle of nowhere. No offense," I add at the last second and then sit back in the seat.

"None taken." Cain chuckles. "Where did you fly in from?"

"Dallas."

"Dallas? Like Dallas, Texas?" Cain practically chokes on a laugh before it gets out. He coughs a little to clear his throat and I roll my eyes. "Now, I know why you don't have the right coat."

"Hey, this coat is in season," I point out. "And I look amazing in it."

"That may be true, but being in season doesn't matter up here. That coat isn't going to protect you from the weather," Cain tells me and I huff.

"I have boots that I can wear with it too. I'll be fine. Layers, you know?" I say which makes Cain laugh again and shake his head at me.

"Layers, sure, lots and lots of layers. You remember that." Cain looks at me in the mirror, fixing me with a stern look. I nod my head to let him know I understand. "Good. Okay, we are almost there. It says we are a mile out and pulling into the town now."

"Oh, really?" I turn to look out the window and watch the town go by as Cain slows down so I can see what the town looks like. It's dark out by now but the town still has a few lights on so I get to see the storefronts of many of the buildings. "Oh! There's the bookstore! 'Bookbound', that's a cute name."

"Ah, I see it," Cain says as he pulls up in front of the store. A few cars are lining the street but for the most part, the town looks asleep. "You go find the key while I unload your bags, okay?"

"Yes, thank you, Cain."

Cain stops the car and we get out together but Cain goes to the trunk of the car while I make my way carefully up the sidewalk to the flower pots in front of the bookstore. I shiver as I search the pots until I find the one with the key in it.

"I got it!" I call back to Cain who has unloaded all of the bags and is trying to stack them in a way that he can bring all of them to the base of the stairs in one trip. That's definitely a bad and dangerous idea so I run back over to him and try to help drag my bags up the stairs.

I unlock the door and it opens after a shoulder check then we push inside. Cain helps me get all the bags inside.

"Anything else you need?" Cain asks, looking around the apartment and nodding with approval.

"I should be good. Let's hope I survive the first night," I say with an awkward chuckle that turns into my teeth chattering and a shiver wracking my body. "It is pretty cold in here. I hope they have spare blankets."

"Ah, let me see something," Cain says as he walks into the living space. He finds the heating system and fiddles with the settings, "Okay, there. You should start heating up soon. Looks like it was set for a lower temperature, which you should do while you're out of the house."

"Thank you, Cain. I appreciate all your help this evening," I tell him as we walk back to the door.

"Of course. Don't forget to give me a five-star review," Cain says with a wink.

"Oh, Cain, I would give you 10 stars if they'd let me," I point out and he chuckles then jogs down the steps back to his car. I write a glowing review immediately and add a large tip, annoyed I didn't have any cash to give him.

Once I am alone in the apartment, I take a few minutes to look around. It's a cute little apartment, it will do for a month or so. The bedroom is small but fits a queen-sized bed, with a cute, comfy-looking comforter. There are two nightstands on either side of the bed and a dresser that looks antique and not very roomy. Thankfully, there is also a large closet, or else I would have to have racks of clothes in the living room.

I drag my bags into the bedroom and shove all of them into the closet for now. I will have to unpack over the weekend, most of my clothes need to be hung up sooner rather than later. Once all of the bags are out of the way, I grab my carry-on and pull out my robe and toiletries bag. I strip down and toss my dirty clothes in a corner of the room and then pull on the robe and head off to find the bathroom, shivering still but I can feel the heater working.

The bathroom is off of the hallway, outside of the bedroom. It's a quaint space. Enough room for one person to comfortably get ready but I'm not sure Max and I would be comfortable knocking elbows to get ready in the morning. It's not something I need to worry about yet but I like to consider all scenarios and plan ahead.

I set my toiletries on the counter and start unloading the things I will need and stacking them in the shower. Everything is travel-sized for now but they won't last long so I'll have to pick up full-sized bottles soon. I find a towel already hung up for me and make a note to buy fresh ones for the long haul but this one will do for tonight.

Then I reach for the shower handle. I turn the handle and the pipes make an unusual noise. I jump back a little, worried that the water will spit out at me, but nothing happens. I lean into the shower again, twist the handle once again, and pull the little tab on the top of the faucet.

Still nothing.

"Seriously?" I twist the handle again and this time it pops off and I groan in annoyance. "Come on, I just wanted a nice hot shower before bed, but no. Of course not."

I set the handle on the counter and storm out of the bathroom. I grab my phone and debate calling the landlady but it's almost midnight and I'm not that cruel so I sigh and set my phone back down. I go into the kitchen and make myself a glass of water from the tap and almost immediately spit it out.

"Ew! Why?" The water tastes disgusting so I make a note on my phone to get a filter for it when I go grocery shopping tomorrow. Then I go to rummage in my carry-on and find the water bottle I picked up at the airport after I got off the plane.

I chug the water as I walk back to my room. I set the bottle on the nightstand and look at the bed. It is very inviting and looks quite comfortable. The bed has a large, plush yellow comforter with matching pillows and a couple of white pillows as well. I drop my robe to the floor and climb into bed. It is as comfortable as I thought it would be.

I fall asleep quickly, I don't even have time to stress about the big move.

Chapter 5

Dylan

When I wake up in the morning, my nose hurts and I immediately begin shivering. The heater must have kicked off and I am freezing. I breathe out and see my breath in the air.

"Crap," I mumble as I wrap the comforter around me and run across the cold wood floor to check out the heater. I need to add slippers to my shopping list. I adjust the settings once again and the furnace immediately kicks on. I stand in front of the hot air for a few minutes to warm up before returning to the bedroom, replacing the comforter, and making the bed for the day, even though part of me wants to crawl back under the covers.

It's still early but my growling stomach reminds me that I didn't have time for dinner last night. I walk into the kitchen and find nothing to tide me over so I decide to get a start on the day. I go and sit on my bed while I search for the local grocery store on my phone. I wasn't sure if I had seen one when we were driving through the town last night. Thankfully, the store pops up on my phone, and looks like it is only a couple of blocks down the road.

"Perfect, this should be a quick trip," I say, finding comfort in talking to myself.

Getting ready for the walk to the store takes a few minutes. I layer up, putting on a tank top then a longsleeved undershirt, and then a sweater. I start sweating almost immediately and start to regret my choices. I go to my suitcase and pull out a couple of my reusable grocery bags, three of them should be enough as I don't plan to load up today.

My boots sit waiting for me at the front door and I yank them on. Before leaving, I grab my leather jacket and pull it on. I open the door and jog down the stairs, bracing myself for the cold.

My first step outside sends a shiver up my spine. Once the initial wind dies down, I step out onto the sidewalk. My foot slips on the sidewalk but I steady myself before I can land on my butt in the cold snow. I try to take careful but quick steps. I keep my head down on the walk to the store, not to be rude but because I am trying to make sure I don't slip again and to protect my face from the wind. There aren't that many people out but I do see a few cars drive by, expertly traversing the freshly plowed street.

Walking slowly to admire the storefronts is not something I am capable of today. It is too cold and I am starting to regret leaving my car in Texas. Although, I think I would be scared of driving in the snow. I hate driving in the rain so the snow would probably be much worse and a lot harder.

I hustle as quickly as I can to get to the grocery store and when the doors open, I am greeted by a burst of hot air welcoming me into the store. I sigh in relief, I made it. I take my coat off and lay it gently over the handles of the cart and start going down the aisles. The store is small but they have a wide variety of options. I pull out my phone and start gathering things from my list. The cart begins to fill and I realize I need to cut my list in half and make another trip because I don't think I will be able to carry anymore.

"Oh, the filter. That is something I definitely need today," I say to myself, leaving my cart at the end of the aisle and searching the shelves for a Britta filter.

Then, I run into a wall. Not literally a wall, there is some give, but it sure is painful. The force is enough to stop me in my tracks and even push me back a little. The wind gets knocked out of me as I grip the wall to keep from tipping over.

"Whoa," a gruff voice comes from the wall and strong hands grip my arms to keep me from losing my balance as well.

"Oh, my god. I am so sorry," I ramble at the same time that he says, "Watch where you're going."

I take a step back and look up at the wall and come face to face with a tall, rugged, full-bearded, very large man. His brown beard matches the hairs poking out from under his knitted hat. I take a minute to admire the mountain of a man but I notice him mumbling under his breath.

"Excuse me, what did you say?" I ask, narrowing my eyes at him.

"I said…" He starts but then changes his mind. "You know what, forget it. Just watch where you're going."

He looks me up and down and I see something flash in his eyes but I don't feel creepy about it. It makes me blush a little. He opens his mouth to say something else but then he shakes his head and walks off grumbling. I have to step aside to avoid him plowing through me.

"Hey! I said I was sorry. Jeez," I shout after him and scoff at his behavior. I hope his behavior doesn't reflect the rest of the town. If it does, this is going to be a very long couple of months.

The man turns around to look at me and a little smirk appears on his face. I want to shout something else to wipe the look off his face but before I can think of anything, he has disappeared around the corner. Now, it is my turn to grumble to myself. What a rude man. A rude but very attractive man. Wow.

The interaction keeps trying to force its way into my mind but I push it aside and get back to the list on my phone. I find the filter a few paces away and snatch up the closest one before going back to my cart and wheeling it over to the checkout line.

"Hey, you new in town?" The young man at the register asks when I step up to load my things on the conveyor belt.

"Yeah, how can you tell?" I ask with a laugh.

"Well, I've never seen you around before," the young man points out.

Looking at his nametag, I smile. "Well, Cam, that is because today is my first day. I got in late last night."

"Oh, okay. Where are you staying?" Cam asks while he finishes scanning my items. I hand my bags over and he shoves all of the items into each bag, filling them up.

"Ah, at the apartment above the bookshop," I comment, struggling to put my coat back on and then load my arms with my heavy bags.

Cam sets the final bag on top and holds his hands out to make sure it doesn't fall. When it stays for a few seconds, he nods his head, proud of the accomplishment. He walks with me to the door, chatting away about the owner of the bookstore, my landlady. He says she is very nice and her husband was his shop teacher in middle school, who also owned a local business. And he had, unfortunately, passed away a few years ago. I make a mental note of all of the information he is sharing with me.

"Do you need a ride home?" Cam asks, looking at me with a skeptical expression. He is doubting my skills to carry everything back to the apartment.

"Thank you for all your help, Cam, but I think that I can handle it," I say with waning confidence but I need to learn how to do everything for myself.

Cam eyes me but then nods and heads back to the register where the wall I ran into is waiting to be checked out. With one last glance back at the warm interior of the store, I turn toward the doors and head outside once again. The wind isn't as painful this time and the sun certainly helps but the cold is still ridiculous. I slip and slide my way back to my apartment but make it with everything still intact and in the bags.

Chapter 6

Dylan

Stomping my feet on the mat by the front door helps discard some snow before I walk further into the apartment. I set all the groceries on the kitchen counter and take off my boots, tossing them back to the door only a few feet away from the kitchen.

The first thing I do is clean the filter and put the newly filtered water into the fridge. Then I start to put the rest of the groceries away. The kitchen is pretty small but easily holds all of the items that I picked up. My stomach growls a little, reminding me that it is still empty so, while I put the groceries away, I leave out a few things to make lunch. Once everything is put away, I search the kitchen to find a cutting board and knives. The sandwich I make is delicious and huge, I may have gone overboard in my hunger. I feel like I have to almost unhinge my jaw to take a bite of the sandwich, but it is worth it. The sandwich is amazing and settles my hangry stomach.

With newfound energy, I head into the bedroom to tackle the task of unpacking my wardrobe. One suitcase holds my essentials, including velvet-lined hangers for my clothes. The closet has plastic ones and I push those aside to make room.

It takes me about 2 hours to unpack everything and when I'm done, the closet is almost overflowing. Thankfully, the room also has a dresser so I fold a few things that won't crease, or it won't bother me if they crease, and place them into the dresser. Which mostly means night outfits and undergarments.

I step back to admire my work and notice a sweater out of place. The sweater still has a tag on it, it is one of my only sweaters but Dallas winter hasn't required it's weight and now I finally get to wear it. I pull the tag off and go to the bathroom to toss it in the waste bin. The sight of the shower handle sitting on the counter annoys me, I still need to take a shower. I can probably go one more day but I would rather shower now. Hopefully, the shower will be fixed before my first day of work.

After unpacking my bathroom products, I go back to the kitchen to grab my leftover chips from lunch. I bring the chips to the couch with me and flop down. The couch is a big oversized loved seat but somehow I fit perfectly. I scrunch myself down prop my feet up on the arm of the couch and place the bowl of chips on my belly. I've barely closed my eyes for a few seconds, just taking a minute to slow down, when there is a knock at the door.

I groan but put the chips on the coffee table and haul myself off of the couch. With a quick sweep of my eyes around the room, I decide that the place doesn't look too messy so I won't pretend I'm not here. It takes about six steps to get to the door and I open it to find a woman around my mother's age, smiling at me.

"Hi! Dylan?" I nod in confirmation. "I am your landlady and resident owner of the bookstore right downstairs," the woman in the doorway grins at me. "Oh, sorry, I'm Vivian."

"Oh, hi, Vivian." I smile back and shake her hand then step back to invite her into the apartment, ready to close to door to the chilly hallway. "Please, come on in."

"Well, thank you. I won't stay long but I just wanted to come over to introduce myself and see if you're settling in alright," Vivian says as she walks passed me into the apartment.

"So far, yes. I just got back from the grocery store and met one unsavory character but the young man at the register was very friendly and spoke highly of you and your husband," I report to her and that makes her laugh. Her laugh is bright and airy and reminds me of bells. The laughter is infectious and I smile.

"That sounds like Cam, right?" Vivian asks and I nod. "Ah, of course. He is a good kid. So, is there anything you need while I'm here?"

"Oh, yes. Thank you for reminding me. Yes, the shower is…well, the shower isn't working. You can probably tell by how messy I look," I laugh, but Vivian waves her hand, dismissing the idea.

"You look gorgeous. And honestly, I was expecting a man so it was a bit of a surprise to see a nice young woman here," Vivian says and this time, I laugh.

"Ah, yeah, I get that a lot," I chuckle. "I think my parents wanted a boy," I add which isn't true but it makes her laugh once again and I love the laugh. It reminds me of my mother's laugh. I think she and my mother would be good friends. But I don't know if I will be here long enough to cajole my parents into coming out for a visit. I wouldn't want to disturb them with the cold weather either.

"Alright then, Dylan, it is lovely to meet you. Now, what is the deal with the shower?" Vivian puts on her game face and heads toward the bathroom. I follow behind her and wince when she picks up the shower handle off of the sink where I left it last night. "Ah, so this popped off?"

"It did, yes. Although it popped off after the pipes started making funny noises and then nothing happened so I tried to twist the handle again and it…popped off," I say, explaining the issues I faced last night and trying to not sound stupid.

"I'm going to be honest with you," Vivian starts and I get nervous. "I have no idea what the issue is. *But* I do have an amazing handyman who will know exactly what to do, my son." Vivian winks at me with that last comment and I chuckle, hopefully, he knows what he's doing.

"I might be a bit biased but he is a very skilled young man," Vivian adds to my amusement and sets the handle back on the sink. "I will send him a text right now but he should be coming to my place tonight so I will remind him then as well."

"Okay, thank you very much. I definitely need a nice hot shower," I comment as I follow her back to the living room.

"I'm sure. It seems like you've had a busy schedule. If you need a shower today, feel free to stop by," she offers much to my surprise. My reaction must be obvious because she chuckles. "That's a small town for you. Instant family," she winks. "But it seems like you've had a busy schedule so no rush, stop by whenever you have time. And I'll try to get my son out as soon as he can."

"Okay, thank you. And yeah, I didn't realize this job promotion was in Minnesota and they only informed me of the promotion yesterday so I had to go home after work and start packing and then hop on a plane and now here I am." I am exhausted just telling her everything that went down.

"Wow, that sounds exhausting," Vivian says as if she is reading my mind. I want to wrap my arms around the woman and give her a big hug. We are going to get along splendidly. "Well, I am glad you're here and made it in safely. But I will get out of your hair and make sure my son comes over as soon as he can to fix your shower."

"Thank you so much, that would be greatly appreciated," I say with a sigh of relief. Vivian pats my shoulder and then pulls me into a hug and I lean into her, squeezing her back gently.

"Welcome to Birch Lake, dear. Let me know if you need anything else. Most days, I will be in the bookstore so any time you need anything, come stop in and say hello." Vivian releases me from the hug and says goodbye, leaving me alone in the apartment again.

Hopefully, she can send her son over today but we'll see. The couch calls to me once again and I sit down with my bowl of chips. Everything has been moving so quickly that my situation is finally starting to sink in.

I just moved halfway across the continent, in the dead of winter to a small town where I know nobody, except now Vivian. What am I doing?

Yikes.

Chapter 7

Shawn

"Hey, Mom, I'm in the kitchen," I call out when I hear the front door open.

A few seconds pass before she comes into the kitchen. She drapes her coat over a kitchen chair and helps me unload all the groceries.

"You know, you didn't have to pick up the groceries, I was going to do that later in the week," Mom points out as she puts things in the fridge. She eyes me when she picks up a bag with a couple of bottles of Gatorade. "Also, these are not my favorite flavors," she teases.

"Yeah," I chuckle and take the bag back from her. "That is because some of these groceries are for me. I just knew you were out of a few things so I figured I'd be a good son and pick up the items while I was already at the store."

"Well, that is very nice of you. Oh, speaking of, why don't you be a good son and go fix the plumbing over at the apartment." Mom eyes me as she brings up the request, or rather, order.

"What's wrong with the plumbing?" I groan and run my fingers through my hair. I knew there would be issues at the apartment, she should have told me a renter was coming so I had time to check out the place.

"Mm, it seems like our new renter had a little trouble with the shower. It won't turn on, and the handle popped off," Mom informs me and I groan again.

"Wow, okay. Well, I have to get these groceries home but I can stop by tomorrow. Will that work?" I ask, not wanting to wait too long to get over there but also needing to do some errands for myself as well.

"Yeah, that should be okay. I will send notification to expect you sometime tomorrow. Preferably earlier in the day," Mom says as she pulls out her phone to send the message, a small smile on her face as she taps away at the screen. "Not too early though. I assume both of you would enjoy sleeping in."

Mom chuckles and puts her phone away then pats my arm.

"Thanks," I say with a shake of my head, chuckling as well. "You opening the shop tomorrow?"

"No, Sundays are my day off." Mom smiles.

"Alright, I should head out. I just wanted to stop by to drop off the groceries," I let her know.

I pack up the rest of my grocery items and then pull on my coat. Mom grabs a couple of my bags and walks me to the door.

"Thanks for stopping by, and for bringing those groceries," Mom says as she pulls me into a hug and then hands me the rest of my bags so she doesn't have to walk out to my car in the cold.

"Of course. I didn't get much. I just saw you were low on some essentials," I say with a shrug. Mom smiles and shakes her head.

"Such a good son, my boy." Mom pinches my cheek, a gesture she knows I don't enjoy so she does it occasionally to annoy me. "Don't forget the tenant's shower handle!"

"Yeah, yeah. Stay inside, it's cold out tonight," I tell her, opening the door. Mom nods her head and steps back but waits in the window to watch me leave.

When I get back home, I kick off my boots and shuck my coat. Then I go to the kitchen and shove most of the groceries into the fridge. I save one Gatorade and crack the lid open, chugging about half of the bottle as I walk into the living room. Dropping onto the couch, I kick my feet up on the coffee table and switch on the TV. I flip through different channels before finding a good movie playing.

Leaning my head back on the couch, I close my eyes. Thoughts of the grocery store girl fill my head. Her long blonde hair was sleek in her ponytail. I remember the smell of her shampoo when she accidentally whipped me with her hair as she ran into me. She smelled airy and fruity. I was so close to her that I could smell the hints of citrus in her hair. Her deep blue eyes reminded me of Birch Lake in the summer, her eyes were almost swimmable. She must be new or visiting someone because I've never met her. And I would remember meeting a woman like her.

I scold myself for thinking about her like that. I don't even know her but one interaction has left me wanting to. Thinking of her makes me feel flustered. I feel like the apartment is too warm for the layers I have on so I sigh and stand back up, going to my room to change. My sweater, henley, and Long Johns land in the basket and I pull on my favorite pair of old sweatpants then head back to the couch.

I probably could have gone to help the renter today but I've had a long week and want to use my Saturday to relax. The renter can wait another day before taking a shower, hopefully.

Chapter 8

Dylan

Sunday morning, I wake up feeling nervous but excited. The previous night had ended with me trying to come to terms with my situation. It was rough but I welcome the new challenge. I had a call with Max last night and was able to relieve some of the tension. It was good to see his face. It helped put me at ease and relax a little.

This morning is beautiful. I look outside and the sun is shining but it still looks way too cold to go outside so I decide to stay in today. I also decided to stay in because when I looked at the town on my phone, it showed that most of the places around here close early on Sundays, if they are even open at all.

I make myself a big hearty breakfast and bring everything to the coffee table to watch TV while I eat. I desperately need a shower but the landlady's son hasn't shown up yet. Vivian did say he would be coming over today. So, I need to be sort of prepared for a visitor.

Shoveling food into my mouth, I grab the remote to turn on the TV. I flip through the local stations but decide to sign into my streaming accounts on the smart TV. I find one of my comfort shows and start it where I left off.

In the first scene, the group of girls are sitting out on a restaurant's patio, chatting and sipping mimosas. It makes me miss my friends in Dallas. They're probably doing the same thing right now. Once a month, we got together at our favorite restaurant and brought each other up to speed on our lives. We used to hang out more but as our jobs got busier, we weren't able to hang out as much. When I texted our group chat about my promotion and needing to miss our monthly check-in, everyone was very understanding and congratulated me. They offered to call me while at the restaurant but I knew it would be too loud and a hassle so I just told them to have fun. It makes me a little jealous to think about all of them sitting outside and enjoying the weather.

Thinking about my friends distracts me from the giant bite of food and I end up dropping some cheesy scrambled eggs. They fall onto my tank top and then bounce off and land on my sweatpants. I groan and scoop the wasted bite up with a napkin and set it on the coffee table. I start to stand to change my clothes but decide against it. I didn't get too messy.

I take my plate and trash to the kitchen and start to clean up after myself. Thankfully, this apartment has a dishwasher. It is very small but I'm just one person, so I probably won't be using that many dishes. It doesn't take me too long to finish cleaning up. I open the fridge to look for a snack but then force myself to close the door. I just ate, I don't need anything else for now.

The couch calls my name and I hurry back. My show is still playing but I didn't miss much, and what I did miss, I've seen a hundred times before. I check my phone and see a picture of all of my friends at brunch. I like the picture then toss my phone onto the couch.

I should go out and make friends here. It is only my second day though. And it's so cold out. Plus, a lot of places are closed. And who knows if anyone else would be out in this weather.

A boundless barrage of excuses swirls through my mind. The excuses win out so I find myself sinking into the couch.

My show plays in the background while I pull out my laptop. I have a few emails from work that I quickly respond to. I didn't have much time to say goodbye to everybody and I have a few messages from my close coworkers asking me tons of questions and saying how much they'll miss me. I also have a message from Kevin telling me that I need to have some portfolios printed and bound for a meeting on Monday. The message makes me roll my eyes. He knows I won't be in the office on Monday. He is just doing it to rub it in my face that I'm not in Dallas anymore, and instead am freezing my ass off in Birch Lake, Minnesota.

Kevin's message annoys me enough that I shut my computer and set it aside. I responded to most of my friends and Kevin's message does not deserve a response right now so he can wait and be fake shocked when I don't show up on Monday.

Once I settle in to watch more of my show, there is a knock at the door.

"Oh, thank you," I mumble as I hop off the couch.

Hopefully, this is Vivian's son and I will be able to take a shower in no time at all. Of course, I will wait until he leaves but still, the thought of a shower brings back some of my energy.

When I open the front door, the smile is wiped off my face and I feel a touch embarrassed thinking about showering right away. Not that I was thinking about showering with him.

Although, now that I was thinking about it side by side, the thought starts creeping into my mind.

Wait, why is he here?

"You!" I gasp, seeing the man from the grocery store standing in front of me.

"Me?" He asks, confused. "You?"

"What are you doing here?"

"I'm here to fix the shower," he informs me and I take a step back. He takes a step forward, thinking that I am inviting him in. I hold my hand up to stop him and he stops short of touching my hand.

"Wait," I say, hesitating. I'm not sure I should let this man into my apartment.

"Why? Do you need to clean up before I come in?" He asks with a teasing smirk.

"I resent that. I literally just got here Friday night, the apartment's not that messy yet," I say in response, thinking it's a good comeback.

"I wasn't talking about the apartment," he says, his smirk growing as he looks me up and down.

I feel blood rushing to my face and know my cheeks are turning bright red. I cross my arms under my chest, which in turn boosts them up and that draws his eyes so I drop my arms and put them on my hips instead.

"You know what," I start.

"What?" He questions with his smarmy smirk.

"I would look much better if the shower actually worked," I point out. His eyes go wide but he just shakes his head and chuckles under his breath. His chuckle is deep and rumbles through my body.

"So, you going to let me in?"

"Yeah, I guess I have to," I respond quickly, moving aside to give him room to come inside before I stop him. "Wait, I don't even know your name."

"My name is Shawn," he says, holding his hand out. "Nice to meet you."

"Shawn, hi. My name is Dylan." I slide my hand into his, and it practically disappears. He shakes my hand, holding it gently before releasing it. When he lets go of my hand, I can still feel where his calloused hand rubbed against mine. I try to shake off the feeling, a feeling I liked, as I step back to let him into the apartment.

Chapter 9

Dylan

As Shawn walks past me, the smell of wood, sweat, and clean laundry fills my nostrils. I almost find myself leaning in toward the intoxicating smell but I pull back and clear my throat awkwardly. Thankfully, Shawn did not notice how I practically inhaled his smell. Even Max didn't smell as good.

I used to think Max smelled amazing, it was one of the things that initially drew me to him. But lately, he hadn't smelled as good. He didn't smell bad per se. He was clean and showered every day, but there was something different. I had heard a theory that women dislike their partner's body odor during the breakdown of a relationship. I hoped it wasn't true though. I didn't think Max and I were falling apart, exactly, we had just gotten busy.

"So, you know Dylan is a guy's name, right?" Shawn asks with a laugh as he comes into the apartment, pulling me out of my thoughts.

"Maybe." I shrug, too flustered to engage further.

"Alright. So, Dylan, the issue is in the bathroom?" Shawn nods his head in that direction and I nod in agreement.

"So far, the only issue has been with this shower," I say as I follow Shawn into the bathroom. "I read this book where the Female Lead was named Jack and her last name was Daniels. So her name was literally Jack Daniels." He laughs at my ramblings, or at the character's name, I'm not sure. "So I think Dylan is a little better."

Shawn shoots me an amused glance over his shoulder before he turns back to the task at hand.

"So, do you like the name Dylan?"

"I do. Some of my friends and coworkers call me Lyn, though," I say and make a face. Shawn catches the look in the mirror and chuckles.

"Not a fan of that nickname then?"

"No, definitely not. I'm not sure why but it has never sat right with me. I love it for other people, I do. I have nothing against the nickname itself but it just doesn't work for me," I tell him and then shrug.

"Yeah, you seem more like a Dylan to me," Shawn teases me and I roll my eyes. He just met me. Shawn swipes the shower handle off of the counter and tosses it into the air before catching it and spinning it in his hand.

"So, this popped off, huh?" Shawn asks, dubious.

"Yes, it did. The shower pipes were clanging but nothing came out so I tried to handle again and it just… popped off," I explain, using hand gestures to show him what happened. He watches me with an amused look on his face. I narrow my eyes at him. "I didn't break it, I swear."

"No, you didn't. Don't worry," Shawn reassures me as he pushes the shower curtain back to get in the tub for a better angle. "I used to live here and there were some issues which is why I wanted to get everything fixed before Mom had a renter move in," Shawn grumbles while he works on the shower.

"It was kind of last-minute notice. I didn't even know I was moving here until Friday," I tell him and he almost drops his wrench in surprise.

"Seriously? Wow, your bosses must hate you," Shawn says jokingly.

"Why? Because they sent me to some little town in the middle-of-nowhere, halfway across the world with six-hour notice, oh, and in the middle of freaking winter?" I scoff. "Oh, no. They love me. I am for sure their favorite."

"Hey, this place is great," Shawn says with an annoyed grunt, either at me offending his town or because of the shower.

"Right, sorry. No hate to Birch Lake but I'm from Dallas, Texas. It's a lot different than this. And sure right now the weather might be chilly but that means, like, 70s. Maybe down to the 50s if it gets really cold. At night," I add.

I lean against the sink and watch Shawn work. His biceps flex as he works the wrench and his tank top lifts, exposing his midsection as he reaches up. His side is tight and glistening with sweat from the work. I can almost see the V in his side, going down to his… I cut the thought short and force myself to look away from him.

"So, is this, like, your job?" I ask, awkwardly.

"Ah, no," Shawn grunts. I look over at him just in time to see him flexing extra hard, sweat drips down his arm and I realize the bathroom is pretty hot. The heater is running on high to keep me warm but with two of us in a small space, it is getting hot very fast. I step away from the bathroom and go to turn the heat down a bit.

When I head back to the bathroom, I pause. I don't want to get in his way but I also don't want to awkwardly disappear. Before I can think about it too much, Shawn comes out of the bathroom.

"Hey, come here," Shawn tells me and then disappears back into the bathroom.

I follow him immediately and find him waiting for me in front of the shower. I stop short but he gestures for me to come closer. I take a couple of steps closer but still try to stay about a foot away.

"You can come closer, I won't bite," Shawn teases with a chuckle. "I just wanted you to do the final touches and put the handle back on." Shawn laughs as he holds up the handle for me. I roll my eyes snatch it from him and step in close, showing I'm not scared to get close to him. I brush against him, looking up at him under my eyelashes before turning toward the shower.

"Just push it on?" I ask. Shawn doesn't respond right away but I can feel his eyes on me. "Shawn?" I ask to get his attention, looking back at him.

He clears his throat and forces his eyes to meet mine. "Yeah, just push it back."

I turn back to the shower and pop the handle back into place.

"Yay!" I cheer a bit which makes Shawn chuckle.

"Don't celebrate yet. We still have to see if it will turn on," Shawn points out and I automatically reach out to grab the handle, popping it out gently and with ease this time. "No!" Shawn shouts but it is too late and Shawn is too good at fixing things.

The shower crackles to life and instead of pouring out of the tub faucet, it comes flowing out of the shower head. I forgot to push the tab back down from when I first tried to turn the shower on. I jump back, slamming against Shawn's chest which causes both of us to stumble and slip in the tub. We end up on our asses in the tub, with me in Shawn's lap, plastered against his hard chest.

"Turn it off, turn it off!" Shawn shouts as the cold water pours over us. He tries to reach for the shower handle but he's stuck behind me so I use his momentum to push myself up enough to shove the handle in to turn the water off. I fall back into his lap and he lets out a loud 'oof'. The noise is a bit embarrassing. I scramble to stand up but I can't so instead, I pull myself over the edge of the tub and land on the bathroom mat.

"I am so sorry!" I bury my face in my hands and shake my head, completely mortified. "I did not mean to do that."

"Which part; falling on me twice or turning the shower on while we're in it?" Shawn says after a beat, taking a more comical route. Shawn pushes himself up in the tub and slips a little but regains his balance and offers his hand to help me stand up off of the floor as well.

"Ha-ha, thanks," I mumble sarcastically but take his hand and let him haul me up. He steps out of the bathtub at the same time and we end up chest to chest. We stay pressed together for a few seconds, Shawn's hand still gripping mine.

"Uhm, thanks. And sorry for getting you wet," I say, stepping back from him but bumping into the counter. Shawn steps back to give me space, bumping into the wall.

"It's okay. At least we know the shower works." Shawn looks down at his soaked t-shirt. Thankfully, he took off his jacket when he first got to the apartment but I still feel bad because it looks like his jeans got wet too.

"I can't let you go back outside like that," I tell him. "You'll freeze in all the wrong places."

My comment makes Shawn laugh. He shakes his head and then sighs. "You're right, that wouldn't be ideal."

"I probably have a pair of sweats you can borrow. They might be stretchy enough to fit." I quickly leave the bathroom to go find them, even though I doubt they'd fit. If they do, it would be like a second skin.

"Actually," Shawn says, and I jump realizing he followed me into the bedroom. Shawn gives me a strange look and then moves past me to the box in the back of the closet. I hadn't opened it when I unpacked because it wasn't mine, I just shoved it into the back of the closet. "Sorry about this. Like I said, I was planning to come back before my mom rented this place out. So, I left a few things behind."

Shawn squats in front of the box and pulls it open, taking out a shirt and a dry pair of jeans. I catch myself staring at his backside while he digs through the box. When he stands up, I back out of the closet to give him space. He holds the clothes up, asking where he can change.

"Oh, yes. You can change in here. I will give you some space," I mumble and quickly leave the bedroom, shutting the door behind me.

I pace the living room, my heart racing. I just let a very attractive, random man into my apartment, his old apartment, and then I soaked him and now he is probably naked in my bedroom.

"You okay?" Shawn's voice makes me jump again. I put my hand on my heart to calm down the speed. "Jeez, you're very jumpy. Is that normal for you?"

"No, gosh, no. This has just been a very busy, and very confusing week," I explain as I look up to see him in an old Harley-Davidson shirt and a tight-fitting pair of jeans. I must have made a little strangled noise because Shawn looks down at himself.

"Yeah, I think I remember why that box was still here. It was meant to be a box for donation," Shawn admits with a chuckle. "Alright, so the shower is fixed. Is there anything else that needs attention while I'm here?"

The question elicits a spark inside me and I shiver a little. Shawn drops his wet clothes on his toolbox and looks around the apartment.

"Ah, no. I think everything is all good. But I will let your mother know if anything comes up," I say and Shawn pauses, looking at me before he nods.

Shawn picks up his things and walks to the front door. "Well, if that is everything, I should head out."

"Yeah, thank you for coming over on a Sunday. I appreciate it," I say, pulling his jacket off the hook near the door and handing it to him. The jacket is heavy and smells just like him, I almost hesitate to hand it back to him but release it instantly when he grabs it.

"No problem," Shawn says and then pulls the door open to leave but before he does, he turns back and points at my coat hanging on the wall. "Hey, is that your heaviest coat?"

"Uhm, yeah. It's beautiful," I point out, annoyed. I put my hands on my hips, narrowing my eyes at him.

"Well, I didn't say it wasn't but that's not going to keep you warm out here," Shawn says as I roll my eyes.

"Why do people keep saying that? I'll be fine," I insist, feeling stubborn.

"We'll see," Shawn says with a shrug.

That comment boosts my annoyance and I usher him out the door.

"Yeah, we'll see," I say and then shut the door on him to make sure I get the last word. I hear him laughing as he jogs down the stairs.

Chapter 10

Dylan

Monday morning comes sooner than I want it to but I picked out my outfit on Sunday night so I'm ready. I get out of bed almost an hour before my alarm is set to go off, and take another shower, grateful for the working hot water and pipes. The shower helps me relax a little but my nerves are still strong.

Since I'm awake early and doubt I can go back to sleep, I grab my laptop and climb back into bed. I pull the covers up to my waist, trying to stay warm since I already turned the heater down for when I leave.

My laptop roars to life and the screen flashes on. I sign in to my work desktop and begin to research my new office co-workers. It's a small office, with only two other people but it takes a while to find anything on either of them. This office doesn't have a very large online presence. That is something I will have to help them with.

I don't do a deep search on them but instead, I just look up their credentials and titles within the company. I start to navigate their website and make notes about how I could improve it. I will, of course, add my profile on the website for now and that will help boost the site but there are other things I can do as well.

When I have the beginnings of a plan worked up, I shut my computer and get up to change. In my closet, my outfit choice for today is hanging neatly, waiting for me. I chose a brown leather skirt with tights underneath to be paired with a longsleeved, cream-colored mock turtle neck shirt. I also grab my black blazer to go with it. The blazer will make the outfit look professional and will give me another layer for the walk to work.

I get dressed quickly and then style my hair, curling my blonde hair slightly. My hair is already curly but I use the curling iron to make more defined curls. Then I pack my bag for work and pull on my knee-high boots for added warmth. Then I pull on my leather coat and check myself out in the bathroom mirror one more time before pulling my bag onto my shoulder and heading out the door.

The wind hits me as I walk down the stairs and open the door to the outside. The sun is out and shining but the doorway creates a wind tunnel and I almost get blown back inside when I open the door. Once I make it outside, it is still freezing but the wind isn't as intimidating.

I pull my coat tighter around me and head down the sidewalk. I pass the giant front window of the bookstore and look inside. I see Vivian walking around with her head down, reading something. She looks up as I pass and a big smile comes over her face. I smile back and wave when she does but I don't have time to stop this morning. I keep walking and a few more people smile from inside stores as we pass each other on the sidewalk.

Everybody looks at me and I try to be polite and smile at everyone I see. They must be shocked to see a newcomer.

As I walk to work, I start to shiver. The leather coat does not keep the cold from sneaking in. I pick up my pace, still walking as carefully as I can in the snow. The sidewalks are nicely cleaned but are still icy with patches of snow. I breathe out and see the fog in front of my face. It entertains me for a little but soon my lips feel chapped and I hustle to get to work.

I only slip a couple of times, luckily none of the slips result in me taking a tumble. My fingers are freezing and I try to put them in my pockets but then the slipping makes me worry so I walk the rest of the way with my hands out of my pockets and I realize I need to get some cute mittens. They might not go with my cute outfit but my fingers are practically begging for them. Even my feet started to get cold, I knew I should have put on another pair of socks but I opted not to.

By the time I end up at work, I am almost 45 minutes early. There is someone already in the office so I don't have to worry about standing out in the cold because I don't yet have my key to the office. I tug on the door handle but it is still locked. When I knock on the door, the older woman inside looks up and waddles over to the door with a smile on her face. She unlocks the door and ushers me inside, locking the door behind me.

"Come in, come in! Whew, it's a cold one out there today, huh?" The woman says. She looks familiar and I realize this must be Michelle. One of my two new coworkers.

I take a minute to try to warm up before engaging with her, blowing on my fingers as she goes back over to the coffee maker and pours herself a glass.

"Yes, wow. That physically hurt," I say as I touch my fingers to my face. My nose and fingers sting and my cheeks feel numb from the cold.

"Oh honey, come here and warm up." She brings me over to her desk, the one in front of the entrance, between the two offices, and helps me settle into her spot. She reaches under the desk and clicks a few buttons on her heater to get it to full power.

"Thank you," I say through chattering teeth.

She pats my shoulder and smiles with sympathy. "Of course. I'm Michelle, by the way. Nice to meet you, hun." Michelle squeezes my shoulder instead of offering her hand to shake but I am thankful because I have both of my hands close to the heater to warm up.

"Hi, Michelle, I'm Dylan."

Chapter 11

Dylan

Once I finally get warmed up, I vacate Michelle's chair. "Thank you so much. That was very helpful," I tell her as I move out of her way.

Michelle chuckles and waves it away. "Don't worry about it. I will order you a heater for your desk too." Michelle winks at me and then claps her hands. "Alright, Lyn, welcome to Birch Lake. How are you enjoying your stay so far?"

"Actually, if you don't mind, I would prefer to just be called Dylan," I say, trying to be polite about the correction.

"Oh, dear. I'm sorry. How silly of me," Michelle apologizes and explains how Kevin and Mary told her my name was Lyn. I try not to roll my eyes.

"Really, it is no worries. I'm just not a Lyn," I explain awkwardly.

"You know, I completely understand. It won't happen again, Dylan," Michelle says with a wink and it makes me smile. Michelle seems like she is going to be a great friend and coworker.

"Thank you, Michelle."

"Of course. So how are you settling in?" Michelle asks again and I shrug a little, unsure of how to answer. There is a lot to unpack.

"Ah, well, it has been a whirlwind, that's for sure. And the weather has been a huge shock to my system. Hey, are you always this early?" I ask as Michelle leads me to my office. I take a hanger out of my bag and hang up my leather coat, then I straighten out my blazer and look around the office.

"I usually get here about half an hour before our doors officially open. I know that must be a little different than your big city office but since there are only three of us here, we tend to open the office around 7:30 am, but feel free to come in as early as you want. Noah usually isn't in until 9 am but I told him he should arrive earlier today to greet you on your first day," Michells tells me with a smile. "I set up your office with everything basic so let me know if there is anything else you need. Obviously, you can order things on your own but if you're ever too busy or just need me to order something, I am here to do so."

"Thank you, Michelle. I'm guessing this office wouldn't run well without you," I comment with a laugh and Michelle nods her head proudly.

"Oh, that's for sure," Michelle says and it looks like she is about to say something else but then there is a knock on the glass door to the offices and we both look out to see a young man standing in the cold. The man looks like a chilly version of the coworker I looked up online, Noah. "Ah, he must have forgotten his key." Michelle checks her watch as she walks to the front door. "Looks like it is time to unlock the doors for the day anyway."

Michelle unlocks the door and lets Noah in. Noah shivers a little as he steps into the office, he sheds his coat and I find myself admiring him. He's around my age and in great shape, but not as muscular as Shawn. I find myself comparing the two, Noah looks like the typical Finance guy. He looks smart and fit, bordering on nerdy and wirey. I don't think he would win in a fight against Shawn, maybe against Max though. Not that Max would ever fight anyone, he's never been a violent or very passionate guy.

Whoa, all of these thoughts are very uncalled for.

"Dylan, this is Noah. Noah, this is our new FA, Dylan," Michelle introduces us. Noah hangs up his coat before turning his charming smile on me and holding out his hand.

"Nice to meet you, Dylan. Welcome to Birch Lake," Noah welcomes me and I shake his hand with a polite smile. "You are the prettiest Dylan I have ever seen," Noah comments and I laugh but Michelle rolls her eyes and elbows Noah in the side.

"Noah! She is your coworker," Michelle scolds with a shake of her head.

Noah winces a little and rubs his side where her elbow made contact, acting as if she injured him. Michelle just rolls her eyes again at his antics.

"I have heard that before though so it wasn't quite as charming as you think it was," I tell him and he raises his eyebrows, pleased at my willingness to banter with him. I might have to put him in his place later but for now, I want to have a great first impression with both of them.

"So how are you liking Birch Lake? You're coming from Dallas, right?" Noah asks, walking to the coffee maker and pouring himself a big mug of it. Michelle rolls her eyes again and takes it from him to make a new pitcher. "The weather must have been a shock."

"That is exactly what I said to Michelle," I say with a laugh. "Yeah, the weather is something else. I mean, I've spent some time in cold weather, for winter holidays but this is the worst."

Noah laughs and nods his head. "I was born here so I'm pretty used to it but it is colder this year. I even had to break out my thickest pair of wool mittens for today."

"Oh! I need to get some mittens, thanks for reminding me. Great to meet you," I say and then rush to my office to make a reminder for myself for later. I debate going back out but it's getting closer to 8 a.m. so I decide to sit down to get some work down.

There is a window in my office that looks out into the lobby of the office and I can see Michelle and Noah chatting for a few minutes before Noah goes into his office and sits down to get to work. Michelle sits at her desk and after a few minutes, I get an email saying I now have access to her schedule and Noah's. I scan both of them and see Noah has a few meetings this week. I share my calendar with them and then switch over to my IMs. I find a new message from Kevin from a few minutes ago.

Kevin: Oops, ignore my earlier messages since you won't be in Dallas today.

The message annoys me and I know he would have added a laughing emoji if his associate, Donna, one of my friends, didn't monitor his messages. She would have torn him a new one for teasing me. A new message pops up before I can exit the chat.

Kevin: How's Minnesota?

Dylan: Lovely.

Kevin: Oh, I'm sure. How are you liking the weather out there? It's a stunning 73 degrees here in sunny Dallas.

I sit back in my chair and groan. Of course, Kevin is trying to bait me into arguing over messages. He probably is laughing his butt off right now. Instead of responding, I close the chat and pull up my email to respond to my clients.

A few hours pass and at lunch time Michelle knocks on my door. "I'm running out to grab lunch. Can I get you anything?"

"Oh! Yes, please," I say, looking up from my computer. "I completely forgot to make something for lunch today. Wow, yes, thank you. Here, please take a company card." I start to dig in my purse to find my card for her but she just smiles and holds up a card of her own.

"Don't worry, I already have one," Michelle smiles mysteriously and I laugh. "Any preference? I'm just running next door to the diner but they have a lot of options."

"Ah, surprise me," I tell her, sitting back in my chair.

"Alright, any allergies or dislikes I should know about?"

"Nope, anything and everything is good for me." Michelle starts to leave but I call her back quickly. "Actually, preferably no fish. It's a small office and I don't want to stink it up on my first day."

"Good idea. No fish for anybody," Michelle says in agreement. "Alright, I will be back in a few."

When Michelle is gone, Noah comes over to my office. He knocks on the doorframe since I left the door open. I look up as he enters.

"What can I do for you?" I ask, setting my hands on my desk to give him my full attention.

"Nothing about work," Noah says as he sits down in the chair across from me. "I was just coming in to invite you to drinks after work."

"Oh, Noah," I start but Noah cuts me off.

"I'm not asking you out, Dylan. I am just inviting you to meet some of the town's people and get to know the locals a bit," Noah explains and I hesitate. "Come on, it'll be good. You can ask for advice about dealing with the weather and you can also see how amazing the one bar in town is." Noah chuckles and I think it over. "It's pretty much the only place that stays open late this time of year," he adds.

"Yeah, okay. That sounds good. It might be nice to make friends while I'm here," I say and Noah nods and then stands up. The interaction was quick but he got what he wanted.

Michelle comes back with our lunch soon and luckily no one got fish so the office is stink-free. I eat at my desk while I work, trying to get caught up on tasks I had set for myself before I knew about the transfer.

The hours at work pass by quickly and we only had one visitor who had a meeting scheduled with Noah. Soon, Michelle is getting up and packing away her desk items. She goes around and closes down the office, closing the blinds in each room and setting the timer on the coffee pot to schedule it to start brewing a few minutes before she arrives.

I start packing my things as well when I noticed Noah packing up to leave too. We all meet out in the lobby and Michelle hands me a key.

"Normally, I will always be the first one here so you don't have to worry about being locked out but just in case," Michelle says as I slip the key onto my keyring. It clangs against the apartment key when it slides into place. "Alright, kiddos, you two have fun. But remember it is a work night so don't stay out too late."

Michelle laughs joyously at her own motherly nature as we all walk to the front door together. She opens the door for us and we step outside.

"This weather is too much," I comment with a sigh. I don't know if I can last out here for very long. I am already missing my home in Dallas.

"Ah, just give it a month. You'll see. The weather grows on you, and it doesn't hurt that our town is probably the cutest small town in the world," Michelle says with a wink before she leaves me with Noah out front. She locks the doors behind us and then heads out the back to her car.

"You ready to go meet the other five people our age in this town?" Noah teases. I shrug and follow him down the street to the local bar.

Chapter 12

Dylan

"Hey!" Noah walks up to the bartender as he sheds his coat, laying it over a stool at the bar. "Billy, two Tito's and Cranberry, please." Noah orders for both of us but I don't stop him. I look around the bar and notice it is quickly becoming packed. I guess this is the place everyone hangs out at after work. It's a dark, dimly lit, and pretty typical-looking bar.

Billy makes the drinks quickly and sends them across the bar to us. He winks at me as I pick mine up and I smile at him.

"You the new girl?" Billy asks, leaning onto the bar.

"Yeah. Word travels fast around here, huh?" I take a sip while conversing and Billy chuckles, nodding in agreement.

"A stunning woman comes to town with plans to stay? Yeah, word gets around," Billy says the compliment with a wink and I blush a little. The heat of the alcohol burns sliding down my throat but I take another sip.

"Come on, let me introduce you to some of my friends." Noah gestures for me to follow him away from the bar to join his group of friends closer to the dance floor where they're all gathered around high tables.

"Let me know if you need anything while you're here, whether it's a drink or something else," Billy says with a smirk, looking me up and down, I just chuckle and lift my glass in a 'cheers' to him.

Noah leads me over to his friends and introduces me to a group of people all around our age. I try to make a mental note of their names as he goes around the group.

"Dylan, this is Marlee. Marlee and I went to high school together. We are the group of friends who didn't make it out of this small town," Noah introduces us with a laugh at himself, and Marlee throws her arms around me, pulling me into a big hug, already a few drinks deep.

"Dylan! Omg, what a cute name. You're the cutest Dylan ever!" Marlee says with a squeal and I have to detach her carefully so she doesn't spill her glass all over me.

"That's what I said!" Noah says with a laugh but Marlee gives him a quick side eye before her smile returns, bright and light. Noah turns his attention to the rest of the people standing around the tables. "This is the rest of the group; Kayson, Xander, Conrad, Bella, Eloise, and Di."

"'Die'?" I ask, and she shakes her head with a laugh, almost choking on her drink.

"Her name is Diana but everyone calls her Di," Eloise informs me with a southern accent almost as thick as mine, while Di is busy recovering from choking on a big sip of her drink, unable to answer.

"Oh, okay. That makes sense. Wow, I love your accent, but I might be biased," I chuckle and the group agrees. "Where are you from?" I ask, knowing she's not from Texas but trying to place the accent.

Eloise grins while her friends laugh. "I am from Savannah, Georgia. Born and raised. Then I went to school at Bemidji and shortly after, I found my way here. I've been in love ever since. Not with any man unfortunately but with this town," Eloise informs me with a bright smile on her face. "And my job," she says dreamily. "I love my job."

"Oh? What do you do?" I ask, taking a sip of my drink.

"I'm a teacher," she tells me. "2nd graders. It's the best. They are so cute. Hard not to love this place when I get to spend the day with the best residents. I'm sure you will fall in love too." Eloise winks at me and I chuckle.

"Well, it is nice to meet y'all," I say once everyone has been introduced.

"Hey, do you think Shawn is coming tonight?" Conrad asks Xander as the group breaks off into smaller conversations.

"I don't know. He was a little stressed at work today so I suggested that he come out but we'll see," Xander answers with a shrug. I try not to listen in but I'm curious.

"I'm so excited," Eloise chirps with a grin on her face, ignoring the guys and addressing the girls. "I just got in these cute little bookmarks, they have the school's logo on the bottom and then little cute cartoons."

"Oh, I love that!" Marlee gushes.

Bella frowns and shakes her head. "I'm so jealous. I'm finally in a higher position, enough to give my opinion on the Spaghetti Supper, and I swear, it's still going to be the same boring decorations as it always is. Year after year," she grumbles.

"I'm sorry," I jump in. "What are y'all talking about?"

Marlee laughs loudly and the rest of the girls join in.

"I guess we should explain, although, I'm surprised Michelle hasn't mentioned it to you?" Marlee asks and I shake my head.

"Oh, wow. Okay, it's the best," Eloise starts, getting excited.

"It's called 'Around the Town'," Marlee adds.

"We hold the event twice a year," Bella continues. "'We', meaning the town. I work for our City Hall and we basically reach out to businesses around the town and…" She trails off as Di cuts in.

"And basically it's like an open house for our town. You get to visit different stores throughout the day and then we have a 'Spaghetti Supper', which isn't just spaghetti since everybody likes to bring a dish like a town pot luck party," Di explains and the rest of the girls nod along.

"Oh, but the best part," Bella says, tapping the counter with excitement. "The best part is that we made these little 'passports' for everybody to pick up at City Hall and then at each business that is participating, you get a little stamp. And the top three people with the most stamps, get a prize! Which, of course, we have not figured out what those are yet but I'm really pushing for some good ones this year."

"Not that the previous years have been bad," Marlee says, patting Bella's arm in a reassuring manner. Bella gives her an appreciative smile.

"Are you sure Michelle didn't mention this to you today? She's always so excited each year. She makes her famous apple pie to bring to the supper," Di informs me with a dreamy look on her face. "I would have thought it'd be the first thing she said to you, besides 'hello'," she adds with a chuckle.

"I don't think she's mentioned it," I say with a laugh. "But I'll make sure to ask her about it tomorrow. I'd love to help out anyway that I can, it sounds so fun! I've been to open houses for businesses before but not one where you can walk around town and collect stamps. When is this event?"

"It's the last weekend in March. So, like 5 weeks." Eloise taps on her phone to be sure then nods when she finds it.

"Oh," I mumble, biting my lip. I'm not sure if I'll still be here by then. Thankfully, no one catches on to my sudden quietness. Instead, the topic has turned back to the guys, and me apparently.

"So, what's your deal?" Marlee asks, turning to me.

"Uhm, what? What do you mean?" I ask, letting her lead me over to a tall table with the other girls in the group. Eloise pulls me onto the stool next to her and maneuvers a shot glass in front of me. I take the shot with her and the other girls.

"Like your deal, like status," Marlee tries to elaborate.

"Are you interested in Noah? That's what Marlee is trying to ask," Eloise leans in to tell me. Marlee smacks her arm and blushes but doesn't deny it. "Marlee and Noah have a thing. Well, it's not really a thing. They just hook up every so often."

"Ah, sounds like a great relationship," I say with a grimace. Eloise cackles at my response and Marlee looks a little upset but she takes another shot and shakes it off.

"See! That is what we've been trying to tell her," Bella joins in, pointing at Marlee with her drink. Marlee rolls her eyes and waves her hand dismissing their thoughts.

"But no, I am not interested in Noah. I just work with him,"

"Ooo, speaking of unattainable guys," Eloise says with a nudge and she gestures toward the door. "Look who just walked in."

"He is so attractive," Bella mumbles before biting down on her straw. She stares at Shawn, sipping on her drink, as he walks in the door.

Shawn walks over to the bar and orders a drink with Billy. He gives a nod to his group of friends and then his eyes land on me. He stares at me for a few seconds and I can't help but stare back. Our eyes stay locked until Billy puts his drink on the bar. Shawn breaks eye contact and grabs his beer before heading over to the table of guys a couple of paces away from us.

"Is there something going on between you and Shawn?" Bella squeaks when she notices our prolonged eye contact. I turn to face her, feeling my cheeks heat up.

"No," I say a little too quickly. "No, no. I'm staying above the bookstore. His mom is my landlord. She sent him over to fix the shower," I comment awkwardly.

"Oh? The shower?" Eloise wiggles her eyebrow, teasing me. I can feel my cheeks heat up even more, very aware that they are bright red now.

"Oh my goodness," I mumble, looking down at my drink and taking another sip. "Next subject."

"Ooo, someone has a little crush," Eloise says with an elbow to my side, nudging me.

"Oh, no. No, I have a boyfriend," I admit, coughing a little to clear my throat.

"Doesn't mean you can't admire the gorgeous man in front of you," Eloise says with a shrug and Bella nods eagerly in agreement.

"Gorgeous, absolutely gorgeous," Bella says while Marlee hasn't taken her eyes off of Noah. "Marlee just go ask him to dance. We all know you two have a thing, no one is going to be shocked when you two start grinding."

Di laughs at Bella's comment and I chuckle too. Marlee rolls her eyes but goes over to Noah and he lets her pull him out onto the dance floor. The other girls start pairing off as well and before long, Shawn and I are the only ones left behind. We're still at separate tables and he hasn't made a move to join me, he is actively avoiding eye contact. So, I let the energy of the night influence me and I pick up my drink and start to head toward him but before I can, Billy slides in front of me.

"Hey, I just got off my shift," Billy says and he hands me a refill. I hesitate to accept, I should probably switch to water but since he brought it to me, I would feel bad saying no. I accept the drink with a smile. "Do you want to dance?" Billy asks after I've taken a sip of the fresh drink.

Once again, I hesitate but I figure it's my first night so I might as well have some fun. I don't want everyone to think that I'm not fun. I can dance with some friends while still respecting Max. I set my drink down and follow Billy to join the rest of the group. Billy dances close to me and we dance together but I try to focus on dancing with the girls. They seem like best friends and have eagerly welcomed me to the group. Marlee even breaks away from Noah to come dance with us.

When I finally look up, I notice that Shawn isn't at the table anymore. I look around the bar, searching for him but I don't see him anywhere. I do see that he left some money on the table and it looks like enough to cover a round for the whole group.

"Hey, where's Shawn?" I ask Eloise, shouting above the music. She leans in to hear me and then looks around the room, all while she continues to dance.

"Probably went to check on his Momma!" Eloise shouts back. She dances closer so we can hear each other. "His daddy passed about four years ago and ever since he goes to check on his momma any chance he gets. He's left early from a few late nights," Eloise informs me. "He's even skipped out on a few day trips to stay and help his Momma at the bookstore."

"That's sweet," I say still looking around for him.

"It is. Very sweet, but it does make him a little unattainable. Or at least noncommittal," Eloise says with a shrug. "Not that that keeps people from trying."

"So he's not dating anyone?" I ask and then almost scold myself. It was none of my business, I shouldn't be acting so nosey.

"Nah, but like I said, doesn't stop people from trying," Eloise repeats with a laugh and a wink that makes me blush.

We dance for another few songs before the exhaustion of the day starts to seep in. I step away from the group and get a glass of water. After I drain the glass, I close out my tab and say a quick goodbye to everybody before bundling up and braving the cold to head back to the apartment.

Chapter 13

Shawn

On my way to my car after work, Xander comes jogging up to me. He slaps his hand on my back and I grunt as a greeting. I've had a long day and just want to go home, take a shower, and relax. I might stop at my Mom's house on the way home. She probably has dinner all ready and she always makes extra in case I stop by.

"You should come out tonight. Jamie gave me the night off," Xander adds, still walking beside me on the way to our cars. "She opted to stay home with the kiddos, for some reason. But the rest of the gang is getting together at Reynold's."

"It's Monday," I point out. Xander just shrugs.

"Yeah, hence why Jamie is staying home. She's got this show on TV she loves and it's growing on me, but I can't let her know that," he adds with a laugh. "Anyway, Noah has a new coworker and suggested we all get drinks to welcome her to town," Xander tells me and my ears perk up.

"New coworker?" I ask as we reach my car. I unlock the car and open my door but I don't get in yet. I need to know if he's talking about Dylan.

"Yeah, this girl just moved here and today was her first day of work so Noah thought it would be nice to introduce her to us," Xander informs me, patting the hood of my truck. "So, you should come out for a drink. You need it after today."

"Ah, you know, I will think about it," I admit. I still want to go home but the thought of seeing Dylan again is tempting. I know I should avoid her, I don't have time for anything that a girl like her would want.

"Okay, man. Hope to see you there," Xander calls out as he walks over to his truck. He pulls out of the parking lot and heads into town toward the bar.

The truck roars to life beside me as I hit the start button on my keyfob. I should have turned it on as I was leaving the office but it's a new truck and I'm still getting used to these new features. When I get in, the heater is on full blast so I punch it down to half the power. Leaning my head back, I close my eyes.

Dylan pops into my head and the image has me opening my eyes, putting my car in drive, and heading toward home. I shouldn't be thinking about her and since I am, I clearly need to distance myself. So, going to the bar would be a bad idea.

I pull into my garage and take off my shoes before entering my house. The house is quiet until the heater noisily kicks on at my entrance. I hang up my coat and move into my house, heading straight for the bathroom. I shower quickly, just to rinse off after a long day.

Once I'm cleaned up, I head into the kitchen to find something to eat. I pull out some leftovers from my mom and toss them in the microwave to reheat. I lean against the counter while I wait, thinking about Reynold's. It would be fun to go see my friends. I don't get to spend that much time with them lately, or really ever since I came back. And I could use a drink.

The bar seems to be calling my name so after I finish eating the dinner out of the container, I pull my jacket back on and head to my car. The snow is falling gently but I tell myself I will stop by my Mom's house on the way home and do a light bit of shoveling.

It's a quick drive to Reynold's and I soon find myself parked in their back parking lot. It takes me a second of hesitation, wondering if I will regret my decision to come tonight before I turn off the car and head into the bar.

The first person I see is Dylan. I don't even have to look for her. She looks stunning. Even after a full day of work, she still looks incredibly hot and put together. She is wearing the same jacket I teased her about yesterday. I almost smile but I see the way Billy is looking at her. I walk over to the bar and bark out my drink order. Billy gives me a look but walks away to get my drink. I slap a bill on the counter, not planning to stay for more than one drink.

When I turn around to wait for my drink, I find myself staring at Dylan again. This time, she is looking at me too. I don't know what to do. I want to walk over to her. Her refusal to look away makes me think she wants that too. But I shouldn't. I don't have time to entertain her. And I would probably bore her anyway.

Billy sets my drink on the counter and I look away from Dylan. I grab my drink and say a quick thanks to Billy as an apology for barking my drink order at him. Then I head over to the guys' table. They always split up when we first arrived at the bar. The girls like to get together to chat and catch each other up on their days, while the guys do the same but mostly play in the bar's arcade. Although tonight, it looks like the guys are staying close. Probably wanting to get to know the new girl.

I join their table and let myself be pulled into the meaningless chatter. The other guys talk about their days and Xander tells them about our day so I sit quietly, sipping my beer and trying not to look at Dylan.

I notice the girls keep glancing in my direction, including Dylan, and I try to listen in but the bar is too noisy.

Marlee breaks away from the group and comes over to talk to Noah. The pair have been an item for a while now but neither of them has made it official. Although, I think Marlee is trying to. She takes his hand and leads him out to the dance floor. The worn floor welcomes them and calls to the rest of the group as well. The girls abandon Dylan to come steal my friends from around me, pairing up to hit the dance floor as well.

Soon, Dylan and I are the only two left at our tables. She looks over at me but I stare out at the dance floor, immaturely ignoring her. I can feel her staring at me before she makes a decision and stands up. She walks toward me and I look up just in time to be blocked by Billy sliding between us. The scowl on my face comes quickly and I wish Billy would keep moving. Dylan was coming to talk to me, maybe even to ask me to dance with the rest of the group.

"Do you want to dance?" Billy asks her, my scowl growing. I want her to say no but instead, she takes a drink and goes out onto the dance floor with Billy.

I watch them dancing together. The annoyance bubbling in my stomach as I watch her hips sway to the music. Her hair glimmers under the seedy lighting in the bar. She almost looks out of place in this bar but the smile on her face and the laughter that I wish I could hear, makes her seem like this is home for her. She is probably one of those girls who can make herself comfortable anyway.

Watching her dance with Billy is irritating though. I'm not sure why I feel so jealous watching them. My stomach is knotted and I can feel a headache growing. I set my beer down on the table and turn my back on the dance floor. It's getting late, I should go.

I pull on my jacket, tossing cash on the table before I head toward the door without glancing back. I don't need to see Dylan flirting with Billy anymore.

I park on the curb at Mom's house and stalk out of my truck. The night didn't go as I planned, but I wasn't sure what I wanted to have happened at this point. I just know that I don't like seeing Dylan with Billy. Billy isn't good enough for her. He was one of our town's players. For a small town, we had a lot of them. At one point, I would have been considered one as well but not since I came back, not since my father passed.

A shovel is waiting for me in my dad's old tool shed in my mom's backyard. Mom made him get one after all his belongings started taking over the garage whenever he tested a new tool for work. I grab the shovel and walk back around to the front of the house. I'm sure Mom would scold me for not telling her I was here but she is probably asleep and I don't want to wake her up. Plus, I'm not in the mood for any interaction, I just want to shovel the driveway in silence and sweat all my anger out.

Chapter 14

Dylan

I wake up the next morning with my head throbbing and my throat begging for water. I try to chug the water on my nightstand but it does little to help.

"Ugh," I groan, rubbing my temples. I didn't think I had that much to drink last night.

My stomach growls, reminding me that I went to bed without any food for dinner, that is probably another reason why I have such a bad hangover. Tossing the covers back, I hoist myself out of bed. My head throbs for a few seconds so I stand in place until it passes. When I'm clear to walk again, I hurry to the kitchen make some toast and fruit, and pour myself a large glass of juice.

I choke down my food, my stomach needing something in it but also threatening to send it back up. This is one of the worst hangovers I've ever had to deal with. Even brushing my hair gives me a headache. I give up and pull my hair up into a ponytail. I add extra layers to my outfit today then head out to work, the blistering weather not helping my headache.

When I arrive at work, Michelle has the coffee pot on and is making a fresh batch. She sees me coming and hustles over to unlock the door before I get there.

"Thank you," I say as I walk past her into the office, shivering slightly.

"How was your night out?" Michelle asks with a wink. She follows me into my office picks up my coats and sets them on the hangers in my office seconds after I set them down on the chair across from my seat. Michelle then takes a seat in the same chair that the coats just vacated and watches me as I sign in on the computer.

"Ah, it was good," I admit. I sit back and look at her after I've signed in and wait for the screen to load.

"Noah has a great group of friends," Michelle tells me. "I will admit that. He might be the worst one out of the lot. Not that he's bad, of course. Just a bit of a know-it-all and loves to think he's a ladies' man. But everyone knows he's smitten with Marlee and she is obsessed with him too."

I chuckle at all of the information but nod in agreement. I could tell Noah was trying to act tough in front of his friends and the rest of the group but he folded easily when Marlee asked him to dance. For the rest of the night, they didn't leave each other's sides until it was time to leave the bar and even then, I think they went home together.

"Oh, hey," I call out as Michelle starts to leave my office. She stops, turning back to face me. "Last night 'Around the Town' was mentioned. Some of the girls seemed surprised that you hadn't brought it up before," I add with a chuckle and a little sniffle. Michelle smiles, nodding her head as she hustles back into the office and plops down in the chair across from me.

"Oh, yes!" She claps her hands excitedly. "So end of March, and end of August, our town holds a fun event called 'Around the Town'! So the upcoming one is end of March, couple weeks out but I've already started prepping."

Michelle goes on to tell me most of the details I learned about last night and how she's so excited to add my information to the brochure she doctors up for the event. Then she pauses and frowns.

"Well, if you'll still be here by then?" She poses it as a question and I blow out a breath, my face twisting in uncertainty. "You don't have to answer that right now. But I do hope you'll be around for the event. It's a lot of a fun. Noah and I like to take shifts so we can also explore the other shops."

"It sounds like fun," I offer since I'm not sure what else to say. I'm not certain I'll be around for it, so just like last night, I'm hesitant to confirm my involvement. "Let me know if there is anything I can help with."

"I'll have to show you our stamp for the passports." Michelle sits up excitedly. "Oh, do you need me to get a passport for you? Bella will have some if you have time to run over to City Hall but I can always get one for you." When I hesitate, Michelle waves her hand. "I'll get it for you."

"Thank you," I say, even though I'm not sure if I'll need one.

"Hey, your nose looks a little red, are you getting sick?" Michelle asks and then she hands me a tissue as I sniffle a bit. I take the tissue with a thankful smile and turn to wipe my nose before responding.

"Thank you," I say before addressing her comment. "I don't think so. I hope not. I think I just have a hangover from last night, and still defrosting from the walk to the office."

Michelle chuckles and shakes her head at me, with her eyebrows raised. There's no judgement, just amusement.

"Oh, I probably shouldn't have told you that I'm hungover, huh?" I ask halfheartedly which makes Michelle laugh more. She waves her hand, dismissing the concerns.

"Oh, no worries. When I was your age, I came into work hungover all the time. But then again, most people did. Or they were drinking on the job," Michelle says with another laugh that grows when she sees my reaction. "I don't do that so much anymore. I can't handle getting drunk enough to even have to deal with a hangover."

"I really shouldn't have gone out last night but it was good to meet everybody and get to know the town a little," I say with a shrug and Michelle smiles at me.

"Well, if this is how you look after one night out with those kids, I can't wait to see what Noah looks like. He usually has a few too many but I think he has a night and morning plan," Michelle says and I give her a confused look. "He likes to make sure he's taken care of so he doesn't suffer the consequences. Like water, antacid, a bit of food before bed, and then this whole elaborate meal for breakfast. Apparently, it is usually quite effective. I think he has a shower routine too."

"Ah, that's good to know. I might have to ask him to share."

Michelle and I chat for a little bit until it's time for her to unlock the doors. She looks like she is about to head back to my office after unlocking the doors but the phone rings, she sits down at her desk, answering incoming calls and other work.

An hour or so later, Noah comes strolling into the office with a grin on his face and a thermos in his hand. He waves to me but doesn't stop to chat, instead going straight to his office. Michelle catches my eye and grins at me, raising her shoulders. I chuckle.

I work for a few hours but soon the screen gives me a headache so I go to the water cooler to refill my water bottle and chug half of the bottle. Michelle eyes me from her desk but doesn't say anything since she is on the phone.

When closing time comes around, Michelle eyes me as I gather up my things.

"Alright, Dylan. You have a nice evening, don't stay outside too long. I'm not entirely sure that hangover is the only thing you've got," Michelle advises me and I try to push the thought aside as I head back to the apartment.

The next day, I don't feel any better but I persevere. I get up, chug a glass of orange juice, and take a nice warm shower.

"How can I have a hangover again?" I question myself in the mirror until it hits me and I groan in misery as I stare at my red nose and puffy eyes.

"Oh, no. No, no, no, no," I mutter to myself, shaking my head which doesn't help the pain at all.

I push aside the nagging pain and pull on my work clothes. I trudge to work once more and find myself using up a whole box of tissues. Michelle eyes me as she brings me a fresh box.

"Honey, you should go home," Michelle says as she sprays disinfectant on my desk. I grumble at her and narrow my eyes, she isn't helping. "You're not feeling well. Just go home, we've got this. If it makes you feel better, you can still work from home," she adds but from her look, she expects me to go home and pass out immediately.

"No, no. I'm fine," I say then cover my mouth to stifle a cough. Michelle narrows her eyes at me and takes a step back.

"Mhm," Michelle hums but she doesn't say anything else. She puts her hands on her hips and stares at me for a few seconds before she leaves my office. When she returns, she places a big jug of water on the desk. "Make sure to drink."

"Thanks," I choke out, once again trying to hold back a cough. Michelle makes a face of disgust but it soon morphs into sympathy. She shakes her head, points to the jug, and then to me before she leaves the office again.

I suffer through the rest of the day but I make it until the office closes and then I head home. I tell Michelle I will be back tomorrow and she looks worried but she waves goodbye.

When I wake up on Thursday, I feel even worse. There is no way the hangover lasted this long. I sit up in bed and my head spins. I pull my knees to my chest and place my forehead on the top of my knees.

"I can't be sick. There's no way," I try to convince myself but I have to face the facts. Everyone was right about me being ill-prepared to live in the North. I don't have the right attire to walk to work like I have been doing the past week.

"No, I won't be sick. I can't be," I say out loud.

I get out of bed, moving slowly, and head to the bathroom to get ready for work. It takes longer than normal to get ready for work since I am moving slowly but eventually, I am at the office and even Noah is eyeing me suspiciously.

"I'm fine!" I protest and Noah just raises his hands.

"I didn't say anything," he comments which annoys me.

"Your expression says it all," I grumble in retaliation.

"Alright, alright, kids, let's not get into a fight. Dylan, we are just concerned," Michelle says, stepping in to intervene.

"Yeah, concerned you're going to get ME sick," Noah comments with another disgusted look at me. I glare at him which makes him chuckle.

"I'm not sick, so therefore, I couldn't make you sick," I point out much to his amusement.

"Yeah, alright," Noah says, clearly not believing me. That's okay. I don't need to convince him. I need to convince myself.

When I finally make it home after another long day that I can't seem to remember doing anything during, I drag a chair over to the heater and sit in front of it trying to warm up. I eventually get too hot and strip down to take a cold shower and then I start freezing again and pull my robe on after the shower.

I point to myself in the mirror. "You are not sick. You will drink a bunch of vitamins then go to sleep and then tomorrow you will wake up feeling perfect."

The affirmation makes me feel a little better, I am usually able to talk myself out of some things. I take a deep breath and then drink more juice and take some vitamins before brushing my teeth and climbing into bed. I set my alarm for work tomorrow with the highest of hopes. Then my eyelids get heavy and I drift off to sleep, only to be awoken an hour later and spend the rest of the night tossing and turning, coughing and running to pee, and using up a whole roll of toilet paper for blowing my nose.

Chapter 15

Dylan

When my alarm goes off, I groan in misery still. I don't feel any better this is the worst I've felt all week.

"Dylan, is that you, dear?" Michelle says when she hears my grumbling voice over the phone. "Wow, I could hardly tell it was you."

"Yeah, I'm sick," I admit and Michelle lets out a laugh but tries to cover it with a cough.

"Oh, honey, I'm sorry. You staying home today?" Michelle inquires and I nod before I remember she can't see me. I clear my throat to answer her and end up coughing. She waits until I recover.

"Yes," I eventually choke out.

"Okay, that's very good, dear. Do you need me to swing by and bring you anything?" Michelle asks and I can hear her keys jangling as she opens the office to get inside early.

"No, Michelle, thank you. I think I am just going to go back to sleep," I tell her and I hear her nodding, her earrings tingling as she jostles her head.

"That sounds like a good idea. Alright, well let me know if I can do anything for you. Noah and I will hold down the fort while you are gone, and hopefully, we will see you Monday but if not, do not worry about a thing," Michelle reassures me and my heart swells with love for her.

Whenever I am sick, I miss my mother desperately. I know she would hop on a plane to come take care of me in an instant but I know she's busy and I am a grownup but it still makes me feel better knowing I have a maternal figure nearby that is willing to help me when I'm in need. I debate sending a text to my parents but I know they'd send me a care package ASAP and I'm too exhausted to get out of bed to get whatever will be delivered to my door.

The thought of my parents helps me fall back asleep and this time I fall asleep for hours. I don't wake up until I hear someone knocking on the apartment door. I groan and grab a blanket off of the bed, wrapping it around me as I walk toward the door, coughing a little.

"I'm coming," I choke out, in case the person is still there even though I haven't heard another knock since I started toward the door.

When I get to the door, I open it to find Shawn walking down the stairs. I clear my throat and he stops walking, turning to face me.

"I said I was coming," I tell him and he looks at me.

"Oh, I didn't hear," he admits and now it's my turn to stare at him. "Ah, I brought you some soup." Shawn points to the medium-sized crockpot on the floor in front of me.

I tilt my head in confusion at the whole contraption.

"Well, my mom made it. She heard you were sick, from Michelle," Shawn explains. "And she made lots of soup and made me bring it to you. Not that I protested, or put up a fight," Shawn starts to ramble but I turn around to go back into the warmth of my apartment, leaving the crockpot where he set it.

I look over my shoulder at him. "You coming?'

"Uh, yeah," Shawn says, and then I hear him jogging back up the steps.

I leave the door open for him as I go to the kitchen to get a mug for the soup. It smells amazing and I want a bowl immediately. I haven't eaten much these last few days and I can't wait to feel the soothing soup going down my throat.

"Here, I can do that," Shawn says as he comes into the kitchen. He sets the crockpot on the counter, plugging it in to heat the soup. Then he comes over to where I'm standing and gently removes me since I've seemed to have forgotten how to move.

"Oh, no, don't touch me!" I say at the last minute, jumping back. Shawn regards me with an amused look.

"Why not?" Shawn asks with a smirk on his face. He reaches for a mug and sets it on the counter then digs around in the drawers for a spoon to serve me. "Afraid you'll fall in love with me?" Shawn teases but I'm not amused.

"No, because I'm sick. Obviously," I point out and Shawn just chuckles. "I wouldn't want to get you sick."

"I can handle myself," Shawn says, stubbornly. I cough a little, rubbing a tissue on my nose. "Unlike somebody," Shawn adds, giving me a look.

"Hey! I can too take care of myself. I was doing just fine before you got here," I say, equally stubborn. Shawn looks at me and then looks around the apartment which is now littered with tissues, with blankets and pillows strewn about. I frown, I didn't realize I had made such a mess. I hardly remember making the mess.

"Yeah, I can tell." Shawn laughs and then hands me a mug full of soup before I can protest. "Go sit on the couch, I will clean up a bit."

"Well, since you offered," I say before making my way to the couch. I sit curled on the couch, a blanket pulled over my legs, and watch him over the top of my mug. I let the steam from the mug fill my nostrils and am pleased that I can smell the soup quite clearly, that must mean my nose isn't too stopped up anymore.

"How are you here?" I call out after a few minutes. Shawn walks into the living room and hands me a new, warm mug, taking the other half-empty mug. "Hey, I wasn't finished with that," I protest but Shawn ignores me, taking the old mug back to the kitchen.

When he returns, he has a trash bag in hand and he goes around the room using a paper towel to pick up all of the tissues strewn about the room, tossing them into the bag. I watch him, admiring his backside each time he bends over.

"Stop watching me," he grumbles without looking my way.

Instead of listening to him, I spoon some soup into my mouth and continue to watch him clean up after me. That is something Max would never do for me. Every time I was sick, he complained that I was being too loud or too messy and he never wanted to clean up after me. He was always afraid of getting sick and made me stay in the guest room, even a day longer than needed, just in case.

Max isn't an uncaring boyfriend but he certainly has his limits. So, watching Shawn clean up after me with no hesitation makes my heart swell. Shawn came off as arrogant and cold when we first met but now here he is feeding me soup and cleaning up after me.

"How are you here?" I ask again.

"I told you, my mom told me you were sick and gave me some soup to bring over," Shawn explains again and I sniffle. I rub a tissue under my nose and Shawn comes over with the trash bag for me to throw it away. I smile up at him, my lips feeling chapped as they stretch. Shawn frowns when I wince and reaches into his pocket. He pulls out a giant chapstick and hands it to me. "Here. It's fine. Come on, use it." Shawn wiggles it in my face and I reluctantly accept it.

"Thanks," I mumble, applying the huge stick to my lips. Shawn watches me closely as I wipe the stick off with a clean tissue when I'm done. When I hand it back to him, he shoves it back into his pocket. "But don't you have work?" I redirect back to the original question.

"My schedule is flexible," Shawn says with a shrug. "If you're all set, I guess I should head out."

"Wait," I say as Shawn heads to the door.

"I brought an extra coat for you. I don't wear it anymore, it was going to the donation soon, so I figured you could keep it until you can get something for yourself," Shawn says, not hearing my weak request for him to wait.

"Shawn." I start coughing and he rushes back over to me. His warm hand settles on my back and he rubs gentle circles, trying to relieve the coughing.

"Breathe, just breathe," Shawn speaks softly to me.

He holds the warm soup up to my nose to let me breathe in the steam. He removes his hand from my back to scoop some broth for me to drink. The coughing subsides enough to drink some of the broth and it helps my burning throat.

"You okay?" Shawn asks after a few seconds of us sitting in silence. I nod, not wanting to speak yet, in case I have another coughing fit.

Shawn gets up again but looks down at me with concern on his face. He looks hesitant to leave me. I reach out slide my hand into his palm and hook my thumb around his. He looks down at our hands locked together and I can feel his pulse picking up.

"Will you stay, please?" I manage to croak out. Shawn bites back an amused smile and I frown. "It's not funny," I rasp much to his delight. A chuckle escapes and I glare at him, only making him laugh more.

"It's a little funny," Shawn admits but he settles onto the couch beside me and it makes me happy, even though it's a tight fit. I set my feet in his lap. The blanket shifts off my legs slightly and his hands automatically go to my socks, adjusting them back into place before he pulls the blanket over us. The gesture makes me smile. "Even through your socks, I can still feel your freezing feet."

"Well, quit complaining and start warming them up," I suggest and Shawn rolls his eyes at me.

"It seems like you're feeling better already, so I should probably get going," Shawn teases, starting to get up off the couch. I frown and wiggle my feet like a child, making him lose his balance and sit back down with a smile.

"Let's watch a movie," I suggest after the silence takes over again. It's not an uncomfortable silence but it is a tad awkward.

"Okay, what do you want to watch?" Shawn reaches over my legs to get the remote off of the coffee table, careful not to jostle me too much.

"You can pick," I say but he hands me the remote.

"I'm going to get you more soup," he tells me, delicately moving my legs so he can get up, then he sets them, gently on the couch.

"Thanks. Oh, while you're up, will you please bring me my phone?" I ask and Shawn nods then looks around the room for it. "It's in the bedroom. Bedside table."

Shawn leaves and comes back into the room but the look on his face has changed. He no longer looks happy or content, he looks a touch annoyed. His eyebrows are furrowed and he doesn't look at me, as he heads into the kitchen.

I check my phone and find that Michelle has sent a text checking in to see how I am doing, and I also have a couple of messages from Max as well. I hadn't told him I was sick, he was just sending me memes and pictures of him out with our friends. I smile as I scroll through his messages. Shawn grunts a little and I look up to see him walking away from me.

"Did you find something to watch?" Shawn gruffly asks as he returns to the living room with a fresh mug of soup for me.

I set my phone on the arm of the couch and queue up one of my favorite movies. "Is this okay?" I ask.

Shawn nods curtly, and I click the volume up as the movie starts. I rest my head back on the couch and stretch out a little. Shawn is stiff as my legs stretch over his lap but he doesn't ask me to move them. He doesn't touch them either though.

I stare at him for a few minutes until he flicks my leg and gestures to the TV. "Watch the movie, Dylan."

He doesn't look over at me but his hands move to rest on my shins lightly. I turn to face the TV and try to follow what is on the screen but I can feel my energy draining. Shawn must notice too because he takes the mug from me and sets it on the coffee table.

"Don't leave, okay?" I say when I feel myself drifting. I plump up the pillow under my head as I snuggle down onto the couch. With my movement, I push my ass against the side of his thigh, the small couch not leaving much room for me to lay down comfortably otherwise. The small space makes me not worry that we're so close, pressed against each other. The couch is tiny, that's the only reason.

Shawn's warmth helps me fall asleep not even half an hour into the movie. When I wake up, the credits are rolling and I shift on the couch, finding plenty of room to turn over. Shawn has disappeared and I look over at the coat rack by the door and find that his coat is gone. He must have left while I was asleep. Even when I asked him not to. I'm going to have to speak with him about that if I run into him again. But for now, all I want to do is curl up and fall back asleep.

Chapter 16

Dylan

The next few days pass in a blur and on the 3rd day, Monday, I finally wake up feeling halfway decent, until I open my eyes and the sunlight streaming in through the half-opened curtains and shining off of the TV hits me straight into my face. I groan and shift out of the light. I sit up and look around the living room in a daze. This is the second morning I have woken up in the living room. The couch is relatively comfortable and has become my new bed over these last few days. I even dragged in the comforter and made up the couch to be my bed.

Finally, I am feeling well enough to get up and moving. I step into the bathroom and take a nice long, hot, steamy shower. The shower helps my body and throat feel even better, well enough that I get dressed for the day. I pull on a pair of leggings and then put on my sweatpants over them. My top half is covered with multiple layers as well and as I head toward the door, I spot a new coat hanging on the hook. It must be Shawn's, I barely have any recollection of him placing the coat there but I think I recall him saying that he had a coat I could wear.

The coat is massive as I slide my arms into it. It hangs heavily on me but warms me instantly. I zip it up to my chin and bury my face in the soft but worn material. The coat smells just like Shawn. I close my eyes and imagine him wearing the coat.

The images fill my head but I quickly open my eyes. I don't have time to be daydreaming about another man. I barely have time to dream about the one I already have. I need to get to the store and load up on some appropriate winter wear.

Leaving the apartment is less painful now that I have Shawn's coat on. I feel stronger today as I head out to go to the store. I had already spoken to Michelle this morning and she told me not to come in too soon, so even though I was feeling better, I still took the day off and decided to go shopping.

When I arrive at the town's bait and gear shop, I am greeted with the smiling face of Marlee. She rushes to the door and pulls me inside, giving me a big hug once the door shuts.

"Dylan! It is so good to see you," Marlee comments once she releases me. "How are you feeling? I heard you were under the weather." Marlee eyes my attire but doesn't say anything.

"Yeah, I guess I wasn't fully prepared for this winter," I admit with a shrug. My voice sounds better today, less stopped up but still a little hoarse. Marlee nods in understanding.

"Oh, Eloise had the same problem when she first moved up here." Marlee leads me over to the clothing section of the store.

"So, you work here?" I ask, trying not to sound too shocked as she pulls out different sweatshirts and knitted caps for me to try on.

"You can sound surprised, most people are," Marlee says with a delighted laugh as she hands me a bundle of clothing. She keeps her hands outstretched and I realize she's telling me to take off the giant coat I'm wearing. I reluctantly shrug it off, instantly missing its warmth and the smell of Shawn.

"But anyway, yes, I work here. Well, I actually own it. Or my parents do but they retired early and left all of this to me. This is my kingdom," Marlee says, spreading her arms out and gesturing around her. "I don't mind it. This is where I met Noah. For such an uptight, preppy-looking dude, he sure comes in a lot. But I think he has ulterior motives." Marlee winks at me as I pull off one sweatshirt to try on another one.

"Oh, he definitely does. I haven't known him for long but I cannot picture him fishing or hunting," I add, my voice muffled by the sweatshirt I yank down over my head.

Marlee chuckles. "One day in high school, I was working a shift after school, he came in with Xander to get some gear for ice fishing!" Marlee cackles at the memory. "Xander is very outdoorsy, hence his job. He works with Shawn," she adds before continuing. "But I have no idea how he dragged Noah into it. Although, I am glad he did because I might not have met him. Well, I'm sure I would have met him at some point, I did know of him. Small school and all but…oh hey!"

Marlee gets distracted and rushes off as the door to the store opens, a little ding from the bell indicating a new customer has entered. I pull off the last sweatshirt and make a pile of the ones I want and the ones I need to put back. I look up as I sort the piles and see Marlee talking to the new customer, chatting away vibrantly while the man nods along. Marlee shifts on her toes and I see she is talking to Shawn.

Seeing him again so soon brings a smile to my face, but then I frown, remembering that he left me when I asked him to stay. It must have been awkward for him to stick around after I passed out practically on top of him. But, I'm still annoyed that he left without saying anything and I haven't heard from him since.

I pick up my bundle of sweatshirts and head over to the two of them. Shawn looks over Marlee's shoulder at me and his face flushes with a mix of emotions.

"Hey," Shawn mumbles when I refuse to say anything. I eye him and then decide to ignore him, petty as that may be.

Turning to Marlee, who has a confused look on her face, I hand her the sweatshirts I want to buy along with one knitted cap. "I am ready to check out."

"Alright," Marlee says as she takes the clothes from me. She looks between me and Shawn and then takes a step out of the firing zone. "I'll go get you rung up at the counter."

Marlee scurries away and Shawn looks back at me. "Is that all you're getting?"

"Yeah, so?" I cross my arms, staring him down but he doesn't budge.

"You need more than a few sweatshirts," Shawn says.

"I got a hat too," I point out, feeling more stubborn than usual.

"It's a great hat," Marlee calls out from behind the counter. I make a face at Shawn.

"See?"

"Marlee, stay out of this," Shawn grumbles in a deep voice. I stand up a little straighter and smirk. I'm getting to him and he doesn't appreciate Marlee being on my side.

"Don't talk to Marlee that way." I narrow my eyes at him and walk over to the counter. I hear him sigh but he follows me.

"Yeah, don't talk to me that way," Marlee adds on, clearly enjoying this interaction. She scans all the items, gives me a total, and then looks between the two of us again. "You know, he's kinda right though. You need more than this. I remember your outfit from Monday and while it was beyond amazing, it will not keep you warm while you are here and you seem more stylish than wearing sweatshirts to work," she laughs. "Hey, here's an idea," Marlee says with a mischievous glint in her eyes, "Why don't you two go into the town over to shop? They have more options than our store, especially for work. We don't really have work clothes here. Well, not corporate wear anyway."

Marlee's idea makes both Shawn and I start to protest but she holds up her hands to stop us. "Hey, you were complaining about her not having the appropriate clothing, and you," Marlee turns to me, "you definitely need something stylish to wear to work but also not suffer in the cold on the walk there anymore. It's a win-win scenario."

"How so?" Shawn asks, the annoyed look on his face growing.

"I just explained that." Marlee shoots him a look and then turns to me with a smile. "Shawn will drive you into Fallon Falls. They have a couple of really good stores for winter wear and for work too. So, that settles it. Here are your items. Thanks for shopping, please come again," Marlee says with a delighted smile on her face. She hands me the bag with all my things and then shoos us away from the counter as another guest comes in.

We both step away and stand awkwardly together.

"So," Shawn starts, shifting awkwardly. "I guess I can drive you if you want."

"If you don't mind. It would be good to get some winter work clothes. I didn't realize how ill prepared I was."

"Well, it sounds like you didn't have much time to prepare," Shawn sympathizes.

"Yes, exactly. I had zero time," I say, nodding my head, feeling better about it.

When we start to head toward the door, I realize he must have come into the store for a reason and Marlee immediately accosted him. Between that and our interaction, he didn't have time to do what he needed to when he came in. "Hey, wait. Did you come in for something?" I pause before the exit to ask.

Shawn shrugs. "I can get it later. Let's go."

There are only four cars in the parking lot of the store and Shawn heads toward the truck that roared to life the minute we stepped outside. I admire the truck and am a bit shocked when Shawn walks over to the passenger side door to open it for me. I say a quick thank you as he shuts the door on me and walks around. I take a few seconds to look around the cab of the truck, trying to learn more about him but the space is clean and I get a whiff of that new car smell.

We drive mostly in silence, not discussing his time at my apartment or his sneaky departure when I fell asleep. I turn on the radio to fill the silence between us and then fiddle with my phone while he keeps his eyes on the road.

"What are you doing?" I ask when Shawn pulls up in front of a building that must be Fallon Falls' shopping mall.

"I'm dropping you off," Shawn states, looking equally confused as we idle in front of an entrance.

"Oh, are you going to go find a spot and then come in? I can walk a short distance, you know," I say with an amused chuckle. "I won't freeze."

"No, I was going to drop you off and come back in a few hours," Shawn says and then he laughs at the horrified look on my face. "What? Why does your face look like that?"

"Because you're coming in with me."

"No, why would I?" Shawn retorts.

"Uhm, because you are the one who is so concerned about my attire," I point out, and Shawn stutters, trying to find his words. "So, you need to come in with me to make sure I find everything that I need," I say before he can speak.

"I-," Shawn starts and I raise my eyebrows, waiting for him to complete a sentence. "Fine," Shawn relents and puts the truck into drive, taking us back into the parking lot to find a decent spot.

Chapter 17

Shawn

Going shopping with Dylan was not on my to-do list but I can't seem to say no to her, especially seeing her practically swimming in my old coat. Even when she loads my arms with clothes, I follow her around like a helpless puppy. My arms start to ache, I didn't realize clothes could be this heavy but the stack continues to grow.

"Dylan, don't you think you should try some of these on," I point out, grumbling under the clothes. Dylan looks back at me and assesses the pile. She breaks out into a grin and starts laughing. I grunt at her reaction and she puts her hand over her mouth to stifle the laughter.

"Sorry," Dylan giggles. "No, you're right. Let's go find a dressing room."

We walk around the store to find the fitting rooms, with Dylan finding a few more items before we finally find them. A woman is waiting nearby and ushers us into one of the biggest rooms.

"Here, your boyfriend can go with you, but no funny business," the woman adds with a wink. I start to protest but

Dylan just says thanks. She starts unloading my arms, hanging some things up, and setting others on the long bench.

"I'll just wait out here. Any of these would work for keeping you warm," I tell her, stepping out of the room with a nod as the curtain swings shut. I'm about to tell her that the curtain didn't close all the way but she starts to take off her many layers and I can't find any words as I watch her through the gap. When she gets to a tank top, I turn around to give her privacy but find myself face-to-face with a mirror. I see Dylan behind me in the mirror and she is on her last layer. I quickly avert my eyes but not before I see her matching floral bra and panties. Great, I will never be able to get that image out of my head now.

"Hey, you can turn around," Dylan says a few minutes later. I turn to face her and see that she has pushed the curtain back for the grand reveal. I can't help but look her up and down, admiring how amazing she looks. She strikes a pose for me and I chuckle. "So? What do you think?"

The dress she has on is sweater material in a brilliant cream color. The color makes her look tan and hugs every curve perfectly. The end of the dress hits right below her knees and I look down at her exposed legs but quickly pull my attention up to her face. She is waiting for my response. I clear my throat but before I can speak, I glance back down at the outfit.

"Okay, what? Is it good? Do you approve?" Dylan turns to look at herself in the mirror.

"It's good, great. Did you pick up thermal tights to wear with it?" I ask since the whole point of this shopping trip was to make sure she had the right attire. "And maybe a henley or two for underneath," I add, even though the material looks thick.

"No, but thank you for the reminder. I think I saw tights by the checkout counter though so I can grab some when we're done here," Dylan comments and I nod in approval.

Dylan steps back into the dressing room and closes the curtain again with a flick of her wrist, once again leaving it an inch or two from fully closed. I might have to mention to the sales woman about the curtain's malfunction. A second later, Dylan strips off the dress and hands it over the top of the curtain for me to hang up.

I busy myself with the hanger while she tries on another sweater dress. This one is a deep green with flowy sleeves that tighten around her wrists. The skirt is a little short, only landing mid-thigh. I can't take my eyes off her thighs, they look strong and luscious. I want to wrap my fingers around them and press my mouth all over them. I snap out of the thought when the curtain flies open again.

"This is cute, but it might not be appropriate for work. Maybe for a date night though," Dylan adds, looking at herself in the mirror behind me, twisting to see her backside which I can confirm for her how amazing it looks.

"Wait, date night?" I ask, realizing what she said, detaching my eyes from her ass to look up at her in the mirror.

"Yeah, my boyfriend is coming to town next week," Dylan says and my heart drops into my stomach.

"You have a boyfriend?" I mutter, she doesn't hear me.

"This is the longest we have been away from each other, ever," Dylan states. She shimmies out of the dress and I quickly turn around to give her privacy, annoyed now that she can't seem to get the curtain closed all the way. Maybe she's doing it on purpose.

"I didn't know you had a boyfriend," I say, trying not to sound too shocked. Dylan nods, popping out of the stall quickly as she tries on a couple of pantsuits, all of which look stunning on her and once again I can barely form sentences.

"Yeah, we've been together a few years, friends for years before that," she comments, her voice garbled by the curtain and the strain of putting on a new outfit.

"Why were you dancing with Billy if you have a boyfriend?" I ask, my question coming out more accusatory than I had intended.

"I was just dancing with a new friend." Dylan shrugs. "It was nice. You have great friends, you know."

"I know," I say. "Billy isn't really a friend, though," I add.

Dylan opens the curtain again and shrugs. She pulls on the blazer for one of the velvet pantsuits she picked up. The whole suit is neon pink which would make her stand out in our small town but she is smiling at herself in the mirror so I think she loves it.

"He was nice. Gave me a free drink, and didn't ask me to go home with him at the end of the night," Dylan says with a laugh.

"You get a lot of guys asking you to go home at the end of the night?" I ask, my voice once again sounding more bitter than intended. I clear my throat trying to cover it up.

"More than you'd think." Dylan laughs another beautiful, melodic laugh. "No, not really. Just Max, that's my boyfriend."

She shoves all her chosen items against my chest and I accept them in silence, following her out of the changing room.

"Did everything work for you?" The sales lady says once we are back on the floor. Dylan hands her the things she decided not to get but the smile on the sales lady's face indicates that the amount she has to put back is worth it when she sees the load I am still carrying.

"We need scarves, and mittens too," I suggest and Dylan nods reluctantly. "And henleys," I add.

"Oh, perfect. The accessories section is right against the wall over there. I will come and check on you in a few minutes," the woman says, pointing us in the right direction before she goes to put the unwanted clothes away.

Dylan walks over to the wall without talking to me and I can tell I really hurt her by questioning her flirtations. Part of me is hurt too, I shouldn't be though. It should not bother me that Dylan has a boyfriend.

I let Dylan have space while she picks out a couple of scarves and gloves too. She comes back with her arms full and I can see her debating if she could get away with adding her items to my arms. I narrow my eyes at her and shake my head, this makes her laugh a little.

"Don't even think about it," I tease.

Dylan rolls her eyes but I think I can see her holding back a small smile as she heads over to the checkout counter, setting her items there. She barely has time to step aside before I unload onto the counter too.

"Hey, watch out," Dylan protests as she jumps back.

"You watch out," I reply. Dylan laughs at my witty comeback. She seems to have cooled down and gotten over my absurd interrogation.

"Alright, did you find everything you needed?" The sales lady says when she comes over to help us check out.

"Yes, thank you so much for all your help," Dylan says sweetly and I have to refrain from scoffing. What help? I was the one who helped her pick out everything.

"Of course. I'm so glad you were able to find so many amazing items. You are all set for the winter!" The sales lady grins at the two of us and I try not to roll my eyes.

"I am, yes. Finally," Dylan says with relief. She doesn't bother to look at the total price before shoving her card in the machine.

"Ah, wait," I say and Dylan yanks her card back out of the machine, narrowing her eyes at me.

"What?"

"What did we forget?" The sales lady chimes in, peeking into the multiple sets of bags we've already filled.

"You need a parka," I remind her.

"Crap," Dylan says, smacking her forehead. "Of course. The most important thing probably."

"Oh, definitely," the sales woman replies.

A few minutes later, we return to the counter with a heavy parka. The parka will go down to her ankles, so she should be good for the worst of the weather. Although, she's missed a great deal of it by coming up so late. But you never know.

When the items are all bagged up, there are so many bags that Dylan has to carry a few as well. We load all the items into the back seat of my truck. Dylan shoves them into the space, grunting dramatically which makes me chuckle. She shoots me a glare and that sets me off even more. She rolls her eyes and pulls herself into the passenger seat with a huff, tugging my coat tight around her to warm up.

"You hungry?" I ask once I'm in the truck too. Dylan grumbles in response and I pretend to not understand. "What? What was that? No?"

Dylan grumbles and crosses her arms, almost pouting. "I said yes, very clearly. I know you understood me."

"Oh, definitely not," I say, trying to hide my grin.

I put the truck into drive and stop at Taco Johns on the way back to Birch Lake. Dylan is thrilled by the introduction to Taco Johns and she happily munches on a large bowl of Potatoe Olés as soon as they hand us our bag. Dylan opens up a little once she has food in her system. The rest of the drive home, she is quite chatty.

When we pull up to her apartment, I notice my mom is still working at the bookstore and I decide to stop in when I'm done helping Dylan. We unload my truck and it feels like the hardest workout I have done in a long time. The bags weigh a ton and my biceps start to ache as we walk up the stairs to the apartment.

"Thank you for your help today. Sorry to take up most of your day," Dylan says as we enter the apartment. She sets her bags on the couch and gestures for me to do the same. I set most of my bags there but have to set some on the floor when I run out of room.

"Sure, no worries. I didn't have much planned today," I admit with a shrug, rolling out my shoulders and flexing my arms a little to stretch them after carrying such a heavy load.

"I'm sure your boss wasn't too happy, though," Dylan adds and I chuckle.

"Like I said, my job is flexible," I remind her and she watches me for a few seconds before nodding.

I'm sure she's wondering how my boss would allow for such a flexible schedule. Little does she know that I am the boss. With Benji moving to the city, leaving us with more work, I shouldn't have taken the day off but I couldn't say no to spending more time with Dylan.

"Okay, well. I will leave you to get acquainted with your new clothing. You should be all set for your walk to work now," I point out and she looks at all the bags with a laugh.

"Yeah, I might have gone overboard but I really was starting from scratch," Dylan admits and I have to agree. "Oh, here, you should have your jacket back."

Dylan strips off the jacket and holds it out to me. I look at it and then look at her.

"Nah, you can keep it. I was going to donate it anyway. It looks good on you," I add and try not to immediately regret it. Dylan blushes a little but retracts her arm, holding the jacket against her front.

"Thanks," Dylan says with a soft voice.

"Yeah," I say. We stand in silence for a few seconds before I clear my throat. "Well, I was going to stop by the bookstore to talk to my mom before heading home, so I should probably catch her before she leaves too."

"Oh, yeah, definitely." Dylan escorts me to the door. "Thanks again for all your help today."

"Of course. Well, I'll see you around," I say as I awkwardly shuffle out the door. Dylan shuts the door behind me and I jog down the stairs to go to the bookstore.

Mom spots me exiting the doors to the stairwell and waves to me. I open the front door, making the bell jingle. I shake my head at the noise. Someone's brilliant idea was to get every store in town the same bell for Christmas one year and the rest of the town has been suffering ever since.

Chapter 18

Shawn

"Hey, hun. How was your day?" Mom kisses me on the cheek as a greeting.

Instead of stopping her work, she continues walking around the store, expecting me to follow her. I do, I trail after her as she brings her clipboard to another shelf of books.

"It was good," I comment, nonchalantly and pluck a book off the shelf. Mom swats my hand and gives me a stern look. "What? I was going to put it back in the right place," I defend myself. Mom shakes her head and pulls out the book next to it instead, checking it before putting it on her clipboard, she must be pulling an order for someone.

"Right. Also, just good? I thought I saw you coming home with Dylan and going up to her apartment," Mom says, looking back at me with a knowing smile on her face. I groan and feel my face flushing.

"Mom." I close my eyes, rubbing my hand over my face. "That's so weird. Don't, don't do that."

"Do what?" Mom asks with an innocent shrug.

I give her an annoyed look. "If you saw me bringing her home then you also saw me leaving her apartment five minutes later and coming in here."

"There's a lot you can do in five minutes," Mom says much to my embarrassment and I choke on the air I just inhaled.

"Mom! Seriously!" Turning, I knock my forehead against the shelf a couple of times before Mom puts her hand between my head and the shelf to cushion the impact.

"Shawn, stop it," she says with a chuckle.

After I stop, I look over at her with narrowed eyes. "Then stop humiliating me, jeez."

"You're my only son, I have to keep you on your toes." Mom grins at me and reaches out to pinch my cheek but I dodge just in time. "So, you two are getting close?" She persists but walks off to continue checking the shelves, pretending just to make casual conversation even though I know she is dying to know.

Most girls I dated or hung out with, I did not bring home. Often because I wasn't with them long enough to warrant it. My last relationship was in college and that ended when I came back here to help out around the house and store after my father died. The 'long distance' was too much for her and she met someone else that was only 10 minutes away rather than the three hours that I was. I didn't blame her but it did leave me heartbroken.

"Shawn?" Mom asks, drawing me out of my head. "Dylan seems like a nice girl."

"Yeah," I admit and then sigh. "She has a boyfriend."

"Oh? I didn't know that." Mom seems a little saddened by that news. I didn't know she had taken to Dylan so quickly. "But you spent the whole day with her."

Running my hand through my hair, I shrug. "So? We're just friends."

"Okay," Mom says and I think she is going to drop the conversation. "Did you take her that soup I made for her?"

"Ah, yeah. She loved it. She had five huge mugs of it while I was there." I chuckle thinking about it. Then I catch my mom looking at me and I roll my eyes, knowing more questions are incoming.

"You were there a while then?"

"Not really, she ate a lot of refills in a short amount of time. I mean, I guess I was though. She wasn't taking very good care of herself so I offered to help clean up and she asked me to stay," I inform Mom and she smiles at me again with the same knowing smile. I shake my head and go to put the book back.

Distancing myself from my mom doesn't stop her from shooting glances over at me. I know she wants to ask me more questions but I don't have any answers and I don't want to talk about Dylan anymore. We've only hung out a couple of times but I can already feel myself growing attached to her. Whenever I see her, my heart beats faster and I feel happier. When she told me that she had a boyfriend, I felt my heart drop to the bottom of my stomach and I knew I had developed feelings but I've been trying to shake those off as best I can. I haven't made much progress but it has only been a couple of hours so I don't blame myself.

"Well, since you're here," Mom says, coming back over to me, and patting my back. "Might as well put you to work."

Mom gestures for me to follow her once again so I do. She takes me to the back office and hands me a couple of empty cardboard boxes. She looks around the room but decides the two boxes will be enough so she walks back out onto the floor.

"Okay, so. I'm donating some of these books to the local school and library. I have some of them tagged so all you have to do is pull them and put them in the right box," Mom explains. "Those four shelves and then the one on the back wall as well." She points out the different shelves and I nod when I see the little tabs marking which books to grab.

"I can do this by myself if you need to do something else," I offer but she shushes me.

"I know you're just trying to get rid of me so you don't have to answer any more of my questions," Mom says with a smirk. She is very astute.

"No, of course not," I lie, badly.

Laughing, Mom shakes her head at me but we work side by side, plucking the books off of the shelf and gently placing each into the right box.

"So why are you donating so many? Not that I don't think it will be appreciated," I add as I pull another book down. I look at the cover, turning the book in my hand. It is a used book but in great condition. I think I read this in middle school.

"They needed some nicer copies and most of these books are not popular in the store aside from teachers buying them, so it really isn't a big loss to try to help them save a few bucks. Plus," Mom clears her throat, pulling down another book and holding it to her chest, "the school goes through me to order bulk copies, and even with the discount I get it's not cheap for them. I figured they could use a few good books for free. They won't be able to read these in class since I don't have enough copies but it will give them a bigger library to choose from. And of course, we always donate books to the library when it's time to pass them on."

"Do you need me to drive them over when we're done?" I ask, nodding at her response, loving that she makes these types of donations whenever she can.

"That would be great, thank you. They aren't expecting them until next Monday so you have a week but you can take them over whenever you have time." Mom gives me a grateful smile then turns back to the shelves to continue pulling books.

We work in silence for a few minutes but I can see her looking over at me every so often. I roll my eyes and let her stew for another few minutes. She starts huffing and sighing dramatically as she pulls the book and a smile creeps onto my face.

"Fine," I say after a while. She pauses and looks over at me, raising her eyebrows. "I said, fine. Go ahead and ask me anything you want."

"Really?" She asks, a little apprehensive. I laugh and nod, hoping I won't regret my decision immediately. "Okay, so you like Dylan, right?" Mom asks way too loudly and my eyes widen as I shush her.

"Mom," I scold.

"What? It's not like she can hear me. It's not like our vents are connected to her vents in the apartment and the very one I'm standing under, goes up into her apartment and directly to her living room," Mom says, her smile growing.

"Jeez, you have a great imagination," I say with a chuckle but glance up at the vent, considering if it's possible. Mom laughs, amused with her own antics. "Wait, that's not really a thing, right?" I ask and she just shrugs like she doesn't know. "Ha-ha, you are hilarious."

"I know I am, I'm hysterical," Mom says confidently. "But seriously, I can tell. You like her."

Sometimes, I wish my mom wasn't able to read me as well as she can. I could try to lie to her but she would see the truth and that might make her sad that I lied.

"It doesn't matter how I feel. I barely know her and I'm too busy to get to know her," I say. Mom opens her mouth to protest but I continue before she can say anything. "And, she has a boyfriend, let's not forget that important piece of information."

Mom chews on her lip, thinking it over. "Well, where is he? Is he planning to move her to be with her?"

"I don't know. We didn't talk about him that much. Although, she said he is coming soon though," I inform her and she nods thoughtfully. "Don't do anything embarrassing," I plead.

"Who? Me?" Mom teases and I groan. "I would never do anything to embarrass my beautiful, baby boy."

Mom approaches me as she talks and I back away from her, shaking my head. "Ugh, Mom, even that was embarrassing."

She backs off with a delighted laugh. I roll my eyes at her but can't suppress the smile spreading on my face. I love seeing my mom so happy. For a long time after my father passed, she had this dark cloud hanging over her. It was rare to see her smiling for more than a few seconds before the darkness crept back in. Lately, things have been looking up. I think having a tenant in the apartment adds excitement to her life. Or maybe she just likes this specific tenant.

"Oh hey," I say, checking my phone after working for a while. "I need to head out. I didn't get as much work done today as I would have liked so I want to get an early start tomorrow."

"Okay, thank you for stopping in," Mom says and she walks me to the door.

We finished pulling all of the books but haven't scanned them out yet so, I promise her I will be back tomorrow after work to help finish up or help with anything else. "Do you need me to wait around while you close up?"

"No, it's okay. I think I'm going to stick around for another hour or so. You go ahead and go home. Let me know when you're on your way tomorrow. I might have a delivery arriving that I could use your help with," Mom informs me and I nod.

"Will do. See you tomorrow."

Chapter 19

Dylan

Waking up this morning was much easier than the last few days. I wake up to my alarm as usual and get out of bed without feeling dizzy or ill. The hot shower almost puts me back to sleep so I have to make it colder at the end just to wake myself up.

Now, I'm trying to decide which outfit to wear for my first day back. My new collection of clothes is massive and I spent almost two hours putting everything away last night and it is making it extremely difficult to choose what to wear today.

I want to look stylish but I also want to remain comfortable and warm. Michelle texted me last night to say that my heater should be arriving today so I will be warm in the office but that doesn't help me on the walk to work. The maroon pantsuit is calling to me today so I pluck it off the rack and bring it over to my bed. I lay it down on the bed to admire it.

Shopping with Shawn yesterday was a lot of fun. It was a little awkward when Max came into the conversation and I did feel a little guilty about having Shawn around to give his opinion.

The whole interaction almost put a damper on the day but I liked hanging out with Shawn. After he left my apartment yesterday evening, I called Max to talk to him about my day and he didn't seem too worried about the situation so that helped me feel better. The conversation was a touch awkward and he seemed to brush right over the fact that I had been sick the past few days. Instead, after our serious conversation about Shawn, Max switched his moods and asked for phone sex. I was not in the mood so I told him I was still recovering, and he ended the conversation shortly after.

I sigh, trying to push the phone call out of my mind. I need to concentrate and get back into work mode. The pantsuit certainly helps.

Admiring myself in the mirror by the closet, I spin around slowly. The pantsuit works perfectly and looks amazing paired with a black turtleneck underneath the blazer.

When I get to my front door, I hesitate to take my new parka. Shawn's old coat hangs beside the bright, shiny, new coat. His coat wouldn't work with my outfit though. My hand reaches out as if thinking on its own, heading toward Shawn's coat. I felt comfortable and warm in it. But I just got the new coat, I should probably wear it.

At the last second, I switch directions, grab the new parka, and zip it up over my pantsuit. The end hits the top of my new winter boots, right above the ankle. I slide my kitten pumps into my work bag and am excited to start the day.

This time, when I leave the apartment, I feel prepared for the cold. I pull the hat down over my ears and wrap the scarf around my mouth and nose as I walk down the stairs. I might look silly but I will be warm the whole walk to work, especially with my thick knitted gloves keeping my fingers nice and warm. Shawn tossed a couple of hand warmers on my pile of clothes at the last minute yesterday so those are now stuffed in my pockets. I open the door to the street and the gust of wind barely affects me. My eyes water a little but for the most part, the cold no longer stings my body.

I've barely taken ten steps when I look up to see Vivian waving at me in the window of the bookstore. I chuckle. She likes to get to work earlier than I do. I've always liked starting work early. I get a lot done before people start to show up in the office. So far, Michelle's presence in the office has not stalled my work any more than I let it. And I have found myself loving being distracted by her. She is such an angel and reminds me a lot of my mother.

Vivian gestures for me to come in and I hear the bell jingle as I step into the bookstore. The delicious smell of books fills my nostrils and I'm surrounded by warmth. Vivian comes over to greet me, pulling me into a hug. I'm a bit stiff but I manage to hug her back.

"Thank you so much for the soup, it was amazing," I tell her when she releases me from a tight hug, one that I can barely feel through all the layers I have on.

"Of course, dear. I am glad to see you looking better. I hope Shawn wasn't a hindrance to your recovery," Vivian says with a wink as she goes behind the counter.

"Oh, no. Shawn is great," I say and she looks up with a smile. I feel my cheeks heating up but I tell myself that is just from the heat of the store and all the layers I am wearing.

"Good. He is, isn't he?" Vivian hums delightedly. She continues before I can respond, not that I would know what to say to that. "So, the reason I waved you over, is because I got the official word that the delivery is arriving a little later this afternoon. Your book should be ready for pickup before we close. Or any day after. I just wanted to let you know since I saw you walking by."

"Thank you. That's great. I completely forgot about it," I admit with a chuckle.

I start sweating from all my layers and Vivian smiles at my quickly reddening face. "Alright, well, I should let you get to work. I didn't mean to keep you for so long," Vivian says with a chuckle as she walks me back to the door.

"Oh, no worries. Thank you for ordering the book for me," I tell her. "I had already forgotten I'd asked you about that. I reached out about it while I was on the plane and it's completely slipped my mind since."

"Of course! I ordered a few extra copies because some of the other ladies in town have mentioned wanting to read it," Vivian says with a wink.

"Oh, good. I'm glad I could help out," I say and feel a bit of relief when she opens the door and the cold air hits me. I was heating up pretty badly because I didn't think I needed to take all my outerwear off while talking to her for a few minutes.

"I'll stop by on my way home. What time do you close?"

Vivian rubs her arms, getting chilly from the wind. "I will be here until 6 pm but I can stay later if you need me to. Just shoot me a text."

"6 will be fine. I should be here before then," I say then give her a quick wave and strut the rest of the way to work. I think I have finally gotten a hang of this cold weather.

"Oh look at you," Michelle says when she lets me into the office. "Someone went shopping."

"What do you think?" I ask, giving her a show of the whole outfit. I show off the parka, scarf, and hat layer before shedding the layers to show her my new pantsuit. I show her my new boots too as I pull them and my layers of socks off to put my heels on.

"I love it, all of it. It is amazing, fashion-forward, stylish, comfortable, warm," Michelle looks like she can keep going which is only making my smile grow. "Overall, fabulous."

"Why, thank you, Michelle." I bow for her and she chuckles, watching me walk to my office. "Oh, hey, did you get that message I sent you last night? No worries if you didn't. I realize I sent it pretty late."

"Yes, I just saw it when I got in this morning." Michelle stands in my doorway while we talk.

"Great, I had a few ideas I wanted to run by you, if you have some time today." I look up from my desk and Michelle nods.

"Let me go unlock the doors and grab my laptop and then I will be right back." Michelle leaves me to settle in while she goes about opening the office and gathering her items before she comes back to sit down in my office to strategize.

Chapter 20

Dylan

Michelle and I are still holed up at my desk, munching on lunch after a few hours of planning for a prospective client. Noah popped in to see if he could contribute but he kept trying to hit on me instead of helping, so Michelle kicked him out.

"What's up with him? I thought he and Marlee were a serious thing," I lean across the desk, lowering my voice so he doesn't hear. 'Serious' might be the wrong word but I still thought they were a pair.

Michelle shakes her head. "I don't know. These kids these days, no offense."

Michelle chuckles and I roll my eyes. "Yeah, thanks. But, I just saw Marlee yesterday and she was still...," I trail off and Michelle raises her eyebrows at me.

"What?"

"I don't know. Maybe I encouraged her to go for it?" I grimace and Michelle rolls her eyes. "I swear I didn't say anything dramatic. She said she likes him, he likes her. I don't know what could have happened to have him hitting one me extra hard today."

"Boys are stupid. And yes, Noah is still a boy. Marlee probably said something that scared him. He's never been huge on commitment. But he is harmless," Michelle adds, looking back at him pouting in his office. "He does like Marlee. I don't think him hitting on you is meant to go anywhere."

"Hm, should we freak him out?" I ask and Michelle turns to face me again, with a mischievous look on her face. "Maybe it'll nudge him in the right direction."

"Oh, I think we should," Michelle agrees with a wink.

"Oh, Noah!" I call out.

Noah pops up from his desk, eyeing us from the other side of the window. He narrows his eyes, suspicious but I wave him over. Noah walks over slowly and I roll my eyes, casting a look at Michelle who returns the gesture.

"Yeah? You called for me?" Noah leans against the doorway, trying to look smooth and not nervous at being summoned.

"Yes," I say, getting up from my chair on the other side of the desk. Noah watches me move around the desk, and I make sure to sway my hips more dramatically than I normally would. I look down at Michelle who looks impressed with my antics.

"What can I help you with?" Noah asks, his face heating up a bit, his cheeks turning pink as I move closer to him.

"Well, I was just wondering what you're doing after work?" I ask slyly, stopping a few inches in front of him.

Noah stands up straighter, his back almost against the door frame as he tries to maintain a respectful distance from me. "Oh, uhm. I don't know, why?"

He seems perplexed by my question. I hear Michelle chuckle behind me. I try to hold back a smile. I put my hand near my hip and wave my hand frantically behind me at Michelle to stop laughing before I break character too.

"I need a big, strong man to help me at my apartment," I say, stepping closer to him. "And of course, I thought of you."

I can hear him gulp as he tries to keep his eyes on mine. I'm starting to feel like I am harassing him but after his behavior, I think this little game will make us even.

"Wh-what do you need help with?" Noah stutters now, still trying to maintain his composure. I can't stop a little giggle from escaping. "What? Why are you laughing?"

When he asks that question, Michelle and I both burst out laughing. I back away from Noah and press my hand to my stomach, doubling over with laughter. Michelle wipes her eyes as she cackles away.

"What is going on?" Noah asks.

I look up to see him frowning at the two of us, clearly pouting, not enjoying this as much as Michelle and me. I try to stifle the laughter, handing Michelle a tissue to wipe her eyes as I go back to my seat. I sit down, leaning back in my chair, and let out a heavy breath.

"That was too good," Michelle gasps through her laughter and it sends me into another fit of giggles.

"Seriously, what is going on?" Noah looks incredulous now and it makes me giggle harder. Michelle wipes at her face, her laughter subsiding. "Oh, I get it. You guys were just messing with me," Noah says, narrowing his eyes at us and shaking his head but I can see a small smile quirking up the side of his mouth.

"Yes, yes we were." I grin at him and he rolls his eyes before turning to leave.

"And you deserved it," Michelle points out. Noah waves his hand at us but doesn't look back. Michelle chuckles some more and then tosses her tissue in the trash and claps her hands. "Alright, we should get back to work."

"Right." I look at my monitor and drum my fingers on my desk. "So this client," I start and Michelle nods, finishing my sentence for me.

"He's pretty important. I think the proposal is great so far. Do you want me to print and bind a copy of it and we can run through it in the conference room?" Michelle asks. I mull over the idea before nodding.

"I think that would be helpful but I'm not sure if he is the type of client I want to just bring into the conference room, you know? I think we need to go above and beyond in this case." Michelle nods in understanding.

"He needs a little bit more than that, I agree," she says then bites her lip thinking about what to do. "Oh, okay. There's this great restaurant in Fallon Falls. It's fancy but not too fancy where it would be considered too much for a business dinner. But fancy enough that a man like him would feel at home but also let him know his business is important to us." Michelle hums while thinking over the idea.

"Yes, that sounds like the right idea. What is the restaurant?" I ask, pulling up Google on my computer to check the place out. Michelle rattles off the name of the restaurant and I pull up their website. "Oh, yeah. He will love this."

Michelle smiles, pleased with herself. "I'll go print the proposal for you to practice then I will call the restaurant and his assistant to get something set up. This is so exciting! I've heard he's very handsome. And obviously, he is well off," Michelle makes another pleased face and wiggles her eyebrows at me.

I chuckle. "I've heard that about him too. Wow, I don't think we've said his name at all during this proposal planning session. Are we too scared to jinx it by uttering his name?"

Michelle cackles at that and stands up to go get the proposal from the printer. "Mr. Richard Bonoventure is a mighty fine client," her eyes twinkle at the double entendre, "and I know this proposal will convince him to hire us, you specifically."

"Thank you, Michelle, but Lord knows you Associates do most of the leg work," I reply with a wink. She grins at me and waves her hand, dismissing the compliment but I can tell she appreciates it. "I'm not expecting him to hand us his whole portfolio but a few accounts would be great!"

Michelle nods eagerly, then disappears to get everything set up. When she comes back, she has a thoughtful look on her face.

"What is it?" I ask.

"I think Eloise is his daughter's teacher," Michelle says and I sit back, surprised at the news.

"He has a daughter?" I ask.

Michelle chuckles. "Oh sorry, I forgot to mention it. That's probably something you should know for your meeting."

"Yeah, probably." I laugh. "Wait, so he lives in town?"

"Well, I think he lives here for part of the year," she explains. "He owns that big blue house across from the former Sanitarium, Asylum," she adds. "Come to think of it, I think he owns that too."

"Oh, the giant one with those massive statues at the end of the driveway and the flower bed along the fence?" I ask and she nods.

"You should have seen the flowers during the spring," Michelle chuckles. "His wife must have hired the best gardener because it was always so beautiful. Well, it's beautiful year round but it was always fun to see what she did with it."

"She doesn't keep up the garden anymore?" I ask and Michelle's smile turns sad.

"No, unfortunately Mrs. Bonoventure passed a little over a year ago," Michelle tells me with a soft shake of her head. My heart breaks for Mr. Bonoventure and his daughter.

"Oh, wow," I say.

Michelle nods. "I know. It's such a sad story. They were a beautiful family but the Mrs. really held them all together. With Mr. traveling so much, she was home to take care of the child and property. Thankfully, she had help and when she fell ill, Mr. Bonoventure was home by her side every day."

"Oh, Michelle. That's horrible." I put my hand over my heart as it aches. "How are they doing now?"

"I think he's closed himself off but the town has really rallied around his little girl. He's here more often than he used to be but he's still not really here, you know?" Michelle sighs, shaking her head. "Grief is a difficult thing, and a long process."

"I can only imagine." I sit back in my chair and look down at the picture of my family on my desk.

"Oh, but please don't let this ruin your meeting. It's good you have this information about him but don't go in with the 'I'm so sorry for your loss'," Michelle instructs me and I shake my head, agreeing with her.

"No, of course not. This is a professional meeting. Of course, I will be pleasant and ask about him personally while remaining professional," I explain and Michelle nods her approval.

"Here." Michelle hands over the paperwork for the meeting. "I'm sure we'll have changes to make before the meeting but I've always liked having physical copies to hold and look over at every stage of the process."

"I agree. Sorry, trees. I know how bad that is for the environment," I grimace.

"Don't worry, dear, we recycle." Michelle winks at me as she leaves me alone to run through the presentation.

Chapter 21

Dylan

"Okay, I'm heading out!" I call out to Michelle and she waves to me from Noah's office, who left about an hour before.

"See you tomorrow!" Michelle straightens Noah's wild desk, cleaning up a bit before she heads out.

Bundled up in my coat, I brace for the wind when the door opens. I'm pulled out into the cold and shiver a bit but feel mostly protected in my new outerwear. I trek down the sidewalk, keeping my head ducked in the wind.

When I approach the bookstore, I see Vivian in the window display setting out new books and knickknacks. I pop in and give her a quick wave.

"Hey! I'm just going to drop my things in the apartment and I'll be right back!" I let her know before backing up and hurrying up the stairs to my apartment.

I drop my things on the couch and change into more comfortable clothes then pull my heavy jacket back on and make my way back to the bookstore.

Vivian is still in the window display area so I join her after slipping my coat off and hanging it by the door.

"Sorry," I say since I took longer than a few minutes. "I decided to change." I gesture to my sweatpants and new bait and tackle sweatshirt with a laugh.

"No worries. I am just finishing up here." Vivian flicks on the light in the display and steps back to admire her work. "What do you think?"

"It looks good. Is that…the book I ordered?" I ask with an embarrassed chuckle.

"Yes!" Vivian's response is bright and she claps her hands excitedly. "I mentioned the book to one of my friends who stopped in and she seemed interested so I offered to order her a copy too. Well, it turns out that she spread the word around about the book so I had a few more people stopping by to ask for a copy. I decided to order more than enough to cover the five who asked for it and whoever else might hear about it."

"Oh, okay. Well, I hope we all love it." I shrug and laugh a little.

"Come on over to the counter. I set aside the best one for you." Vivian winks and leads me over to the counter. She pulls out the book dramatically and places it on the counter for me.

"Ah, beautiful." I pick up the book and examine it. The cover is stunning, with bright colors and a curving font for the title.

"Right?! I love the cover. Are all books like this now? Most of the covers here are a little outdated, but that's because the books are older." Vivian laughs, looking thrilled at the new designs.

"Yeah, the covers lately have been amazing. I think a lot of them are from Indie authors, but there are some good ones from the big publishers too." I hand Vivian my credit card and she swipes it through her system and then neatly packages the book for me even though I'll just be bringing it upstairs.

"I looked up some other popular books too but haven't ordered anything yet because I want to get a couple of other opinions. Yours included." Vivian spins the computer to face me and pulls up a website that shows all the books she can order. My eyes grow wide and I lean in.

"Wow," I gasp.

"Right? There are a lot of options. If you see anything that you like or think would sell well here, please add it to my cart," Vivian implores, pushing the computer mouse toward my hand.

"Oh, I couldn't…" I trail off as I spot several books that I have read or want to read and tap each to add them to her cart. "I mean, you can always look at them to approve before buying them, right?" I justify my actions while adding another book to her cart.

Vivian chuckles. "Exactly." She watches me scroll through books for a few minutes, intrigued. "I know you're probably pretty busy but…"

"I have a big meeting in a couple of weeks but I think I'm pretty much caught up on everything, back to the normal workflow," I tell her then set the mouse aside and look over at her. "What's up?"

"Well, I was wondering if you wouldn't mind helping revamp the store." Vivian regards my hesitant face and quickly continues talking. "Of course, we'd work around your schedule."

"It sounds fun but I'm not sure how much help I would be." I consider the ask but I don't have too much time on my hands yet and know very little about interior design, aside from personal opinions, so I wonder what help I would actually be.

"Oh, you can just come up with the ideas and I'll send them to Shawn to put together. He's quite handy. And if he has any questions, I'll just direct him to you. Or if I can answer any of them, I will." Vivian smiles at me, excited by the idea.

"Can I think about it for a few days?" I ask and Vivian's smile falters a bit. "Oh, no sorry. I just mean I need a few days to see if I have any good ideas." I reassure her with a chuckle and her smile grows bright again.

"Of course! Take all the time you need. It will be necessary to have a fresh perspective on the shop. Add some of that big city, Texas spirit." Vivian looks so excited that I decide I will help her in any way possible. "So, how has your stay been so far?" She asks, moving on to the next conversation.

"Besides freezing?" I say with a chuckle. "It's been alright. I have been so busy at work and then I wasn't feeling well, so I haven't had much time to miss home yet. Although, it is starting to sink in now."

Vivian nods in understanding but doesn't say anything.

"Thankfully, my boyfriend is coming to visit in a few days. It's only a short visit but he's a little piece of home so I'm very excited."

"Oh, honey. That's great! I have to admit, I was a bit surprised that he didn't come up while you were sick. You were out for almost a week," Vivian says with a frown.

"It was silly, my own fault, really, for getting sick. I wasn't prepared. I just got the transfer on such short notice, I didn't have time to do any research on the climate here. Which, I should have known the basics, it is the dead of winter, but I thought my cute little coat for Dallas winters would have been okay. I was way wrong," I chuckle, embarrassed.

"Mm, still." Vivian looks disappointed and I want to defend Max.

"Really, Max is a sweet guy. I'm sure he would have come up to take care of me if I had asked," I tell her but I don't think either of us is convinced. Max was never very good at taking care of me while I was sick. "I just didn't want to bother him and make him come out for only a few days…" I trail off to stop myself from listing other defensive reasons as to why I hadn't asked Max to come out.

"Right, dear. I'm sure he's lovely," Vivian replies with a small smile.

Chapter 22

Shawn

Stopping by the bookstore after work grants me a pleasant surprise. I see Dylan leaning against the counter chatting with my mom. Her smile is bright and I can hear her laugh from outside.

I don't want to bother them so I head around the building to enter from the back. The back door does not have the same bell that the front door does so I slip in silently. Their voices grow louder as I walk through the backroom.

I stop when I hear Dylan speak again.

"Thankfully, my boyfriend is coming to visit in a few days. It's only a short visit but he's a little piece of home so I'm very excited."

My eyebrows furrow and I feel something stirring inside me. I don't want it to be jealousy but I've felt this way before and as ugly as it is, it's jealousy.

Her boyfriend is coming to visit? I still can't believe she has a boyfriend. I thought she felt the same connection that I felt whenever we hung out but I know now that she was just being friendly.

I putz around in the backroom for a few minutes to give them privacy to finish their conversation and give myself time to cool down.

When I make my presence known a few minutes later, they both look up at me with a smile. Dylan's cheeks are a little red but I ignore them and move to hug Mom.

"Hey, Shawn. I wasn't sure if you were still planning on stopping in today." Mom kisses my cheek in greeting, giving me a tight squeeze before releasing me.

"I thought I would stop by to see if you needed help with the delivery and then wanted to grab some dinner after. But it looks like I'm interrupting." I turn my attention to Dylan and offer her a polite smile and nod.

"Hi, Shawn," she squeaks out before clearing her throat and lowering the package in her hands off of the counter to hide it from my view.

I narrow my eyes at it but don't say anything.

"You're not interrupting anything," Dylan continues. "I should get home, start on dinner, and start this book."

Mom winks at Dylan, who blushes a bit more before taking a step away from the counter.

"Oh! Before you go, let me go grab something for you." Mom hustles around the counter and into the backroom, leaving Dylan and me alone.

We stand in silence for a minute but when Mom doesn't return right away, I clear my throat. "So, what are you trying to hide from me?"

The question seems to shock her because her head whips up and the flush on her cheeks grows darker. I gesture to the bag she was trying to hide.

"Oh," Dylan lets out a breath of relief. "This." Dylan holds up the bag and a little smile grows on her face. "None of your business," she says and bites her lip to keep her smile from growing.

"Oh? Is that right?" I can't help the smile growing on my face as well. I step closer to her and hear her breath hitch. I place my hand on the counter, leaning toward her, trapping her between me and the counter. She steps back and gasps a little when she bumps into the counter. I move closer, almost enough to press my hips against hers but I don't. I hover mere millimeters in front of her, watching her breathing pick up and her eyes widen. She's flustered.

Before she can say or do anything, I take the opportunity to swipe the bag from her hand. She lets it go without a fight and then blinks as I step back from her, triumphant.

"Hey!" She shouts when she realizes what I've done. Dylan tries to reach for the bag but I keep it out of her reach as I work the book out of it. When my eyes land on the cover, she stops struggling and bites her lip. I look over at her with wide eyes, my lips once again curving up in a smirk.

"What do we have here?" I chuckle looking at the book. "Is this a discrete cover?"

Dylan gasps. "How do you know about those? Never mind, give me the book back." She puts one hand on her hip, holding the other one out to me, pouting a little. I chuckle and hand the book and the bag back to her. She slips the book back into the bag and rolls her eyes. Her hand stills when I take a step closer to her. She looks up at me from under her eyelashes. Her cheeks are pink again as I brush a piece of hair out of her face. She sucks in a breath as my fingers brush across her cheek. Dylan looks up at me and I try to convince myself that there isn't desire in her eyes.

I want to kiss her. I shouldn't.

Leaning in and sliding my hand behind her head to cup it gently, I can practically hear her heartbeat. She stays still, doing nothing to stop me as my lips hover in front of hers.

I'm about to give in when I hear noise from the back of the store.

"Found it!" Mom's voice breaks Dylan and me out of a trance. Dylan looks down, no longer giving me access to her lips. I drop my hand and step away from her as Mom comes back out to the front.

Mom is oblivious to the tension in the room as she hoists and rolled up paper into the air triumphantly. "I found it!" She says again and pushes her way between us, causing me to take a couple of steps back.

Dylan gives me a long, thoughtful look before turning to face my mom. "What did you find?"

Mom sets the paper on the counter and rolls it out for us to see. I step a bit closer and notice Dylan shifting away from me, leaving Mom between us.

"What is that? Is that the floor plan for this building?" I narrow my eyes at the paper, noticing the familiar layout.

"Yes! I wanted Dylan to have a copy of it while she thinks about ways to revamp the store," Mom explains before rolling the paper up again and handing it to a reluctant Dylan. I raise my eyebrows in question but she just shrugs. "I would have tried to find a digital copy but that would have taken a few days. I can still," Mom starts but Dylan waves her off.

"Oh. No, this is fine." Dylan slips the paper into the bag with her book.

"Take your time with it. I'm excited to see what you come back with." Mom grins at her and pulls her into a tight, short hug.

"Okay, will do." Dylan smiles and makes her departure, looking back at me for a second too long before pulling on her jacket and heading out the door.

"Did you scare her off?" Mom tsks, catching me staring after Dylan.

"What? No, of course not. Do you need help with the deliveries of are you ready for dinner?" I ask to redirect the conversation.

Mom narrows her eyes at me for a few seconds before shrugging. "Go lock the front of the shop and flip the sign while I finish up here."

I nod and swipe the keys from the counter. "Is this a new display?" I toss over my shoulder as I make my way to the front of the store.

"It is! Looks good, doesn't it?" Mom calls back, sounding proud of herself.

"Looks great," I agree. I lock the front door, flip the sign on the door with a flick of my wrist, and turn off the lights in the front window displays.

"Okay, I'll have to finish this tomorrow." Mom shuts off her computer and takes the keys back from me when I saunter over.

"What is it you're doing?"

"Well, I'm probably getting a little ahead of myself but I asked Dylan to recommend some books. I'm not big on social media, as you know, so I figured she might have better ideas than

I do for new books, popular books," Mom tells me and I raise my eyebrows. "Which, as I said, is a little soon since we haven't even begun to redo the store so I should probably hold off on ordering new things but I figured my big, strong, amazing son would make quick work of the renovations needed."

Mom grins at me with a sweet, innocent smile. I roll my eyes and rub my hand over my gruff beard, shaking my head at her.

"Oh, is that what you two were talking about?" I ask. Mom smiles innocently. "When were you going to ask your son about this work?" I try to ask politely.

"Hm, how about over dinner?" She offers with a smile and once again I shake my head, sighing at her.

"That was my idea," I say and she starts to protest but I keep talking. "But, I will consider what you have to say, and what you want me to do, over dinner. Let's go."

"Have I ever told you that you're my favorite son?" Mom grins at me, hanging onto my arm as we walk out the back door of the store. She locks up the door and slides into my truck so we can drive together.

"I'm your only son, Mom."

Chapter 23

Dylan

The next few days go by in a blur. I'm glad to get a couple of uninterrupted days at work but that's all it is, work, nothing special. And I do my best to try to avoid Shawn. After the "almost kiss" in the bookstore the other day, I wasn't sure how to face him. I feel guilty thinking about it now.

Max is arriving later today and as I clean the apartment, I can't stop thinking about Shawn.

I trip on the edge of the rug but catch myself before I fall. Serves me right, thinking about another man with my boyfriend on the way to see me.

Looking around the apartment, there's not much else to do but I know I need to keep busy so I bundle up, grab my grocery list and a couple of reusable bags, and head to the grocery store.

Cam greets me with a smile as I step into the store, the hot air pounding on my face when the doors open. I smile and give a little wave as I strip off my coat and set everything in a cart.

I slow my pace down the aisles, looking for each ingredient. I want to make Max his favorite meal for his first day here. I doubt it will convince him to move but it might at least appease him after a long flight.

Plucking the items off the shelf, I toss them into the cart absently. Still thinking about Shawn's lips. The way he moved in closer.

"Dylan?" A familiar voice jolts me out of the memory and I turn to see Vivian strolling toward me. "Ah, Dylan, I thought that was you."

"Hey, Vivian," I greet her and she joins me walking down the aisle.

"Have you had time to look over the plans?" Vivian asks, reaching for a box of bread crumbs. I grab a similar product as well.

"Oh, gosh. No, I'm sorry, Vivian. I haven't had a chance to," I apologize but Vivian doesn't look upset.

"No worries, hun." Her northern accent comes out strong when she calls me the little nicknames.

"I will get to it next weekend," I assure her. "I've just had a lot on my mind." Admitting it doesn't relieve any of the guilt I feel, about forgetting to look at the plans and thinking about Shawn.

"Oh, that's right, your boyfriend is coming to town. When is he arriving?" Vivian asks as we shop side by side.

"Later today actually."

"Are you excited to see him?" Vivian pauses to gauge my reaction. I try to paste a genuine smile on my face but I know she can sense some turmoil.

"Of course! It's been a few weeks. I miss him, I miss Dallas. It'll be nice seeing him again, like a little piece of home." I sigh softly. I grab another ingredient for Max's favorite meal, placing it in the cart.

"Oh, that does sound lovely. Hey, if you two are available this week, I would love to have you over for dinner. I can't believe I hadn't thought of this before. Of course, you are welcome to come over for dinner any night," Vivian adds with a big smile.

"Thank you, Vivian. Actually, that would be great. I'm not a big cook so I can probably only handle a couple of meals during his trip. I would love for you to meet Max too, he's a great guy," I promise. I still think highly of him even though we've been drifting apart for a while.

"Oh, I'm sure. He would have to be to date you," Vivian says with a wink. "Oh, do you need a ride to the airport?"

"Oh, my gosh. I didn't even think about that!" I rub my hand over my face. "I'm so used to having my car."

"You can borrow Shawn's truck," Vivian offers.

That thought gives me pause. I probably shouldn't, but I do need a car. "He wouldn't mind? Are you sure?"

"Oh, it's not a problem. What time do you need the truck?" Vivian and I finish shopping at the same time and head to the front where Cam is finishing up with another customer.

"He texted me a few minutes ago that he had just arrived at the airport in Dallas." I check his flight status on my phone. "The status shows they're boarding in half an hour. The airport is, what, three hours away?"

"More or less depending on traffic," Cam chimes in, helping Vivian unload her cart. She nods, agreeing with him.

"I should probably leave in about an hour, right? That will give him time to land, go to the bathroom, get his luggage. All of that," I say, looking to both of them for confirmation.

"That sounds about right," Cam agrees. "Never too much traffic at the airport."

"I'll let Shawn know. He can swing by the bookstore and drop his truck off. He can use my car the rest of the week if you need to keep his truck," Vivian offers. "I would let you borrow my car but I wouldn't trust it so much on the highway."

I chuckle. "Are you sure he won't mind?" I ask again. Vivian waits while Cam finishes bagging my things.

"Oh, no. He'll be fine." Vivian waves away my concerns.

We walk to her car together and I can see why she wouldn't trust her car going more than 45 mph. I help her load her car and she offers to drive me home but I think the walk will do me some good.

Part of me is looking forward to seeing Shawn again but another part is reminding me that I am only borrowing his truck to pick up my boyfriend from the airport.

Chapter 24

Dylan

"Are you sure you're fine with this?" I ask Shawn for the tenth time. He smiles and shakes his head at my constant need for reassurance.

"Dylan, it's fine. My Mom promised you my truck, my truck you shall have." Shawn smiles as he hands me his keys.

Our fingers brush against each other with the exchange of the keys. A spark flies up my arm and I pull back from him. We stand in silence for a few seconds and I notice Shawn looks confused and shocked, he must have felt something too.

"You should get on the road." Shawn steps back from his car and holds the door open for me.

"Thank you again, so much," I say, swinging into the cab of the truck.

"Please don't hurt her. She's still pretty new," Shawn says, patting the car affectionately. I roll my eyes but agree with a grumble.

Shawn steps back from the truck and watches as I drive off. The ride is smooth but it takes me about half an hour on the icy road to feel comfortable. The government here knows how to take care of the roads, they're used to the weather and know how to treat it and clear it. That should make me feel more comfortable but I'm still nervous.

On the drive, I listen to an audiobook, pulling up to the airport right as the climax comes over the speakers. And I do mean 'climax'. I blush and turn down the speakers. I feel like everyone waiting outside can hear what I'm listening to and they're judging me. I look around, trying to spot Max.

Putting the car in park, I pick up my phone and scroll through my texts with Max. He said he was waiting for his bag a few minutes ago. He should be coming out soon.

I turn off my audiobook the second I see him. My cheeks are flushed as I hit the hazard lights and jump out to greet him. Max looks a little put off by the weather but he breaks into a smile when he sees me. He catches me in his arms with a grunt. He spins me around. I immediately feel the chill of the wind and dry cold seeping through my sweater.

"Come on, let's get back to the truck," I insist as I shiver in the cold. Max releases me and grabs his bag in one hand and my hand in the other.

"You okay driving? I'm so tired, I might take a nap on the way to your place," Max tells me after putting his things in the bed of the truck.

"No worries." I lean into him as he wraps his arms around me. "Hi," I say with a smile. "I missed you."

"I missed you too, Dyl." Max leans down and gives me a soft peck on the lips. There's no passion to it but I don't think anything of it, it is cold outside and other people are waiting for us to move so they can pick up their loved ones.

We separate and climb into our seats. I pull out and merge into traffic.

"Why don't you get some rest now? I will wake you when we get closer so you can see the town. It is so cute, I think you'll like it," I tell him, checking my mirrors before merging again to get onto the right road back to Birch Lake.

I look over and see Max has already leaned the seat back and is pulling his baseball cap over his eyes. "I'm sure it's great, Dyl." He yawns and is soon snoring softly.

I wait a few minutes before turning my audiobook back on. Occasionally, I glance over at him to make sure he hasn't woken up to the sounds of my surprisingly spicy audiobook.

When we get close to the town, I start getting excited. The town has started to grow on me and I am excited to show Max around.

"Max, honey," I say softly, wanting to rouse him so he can see the sign at the beginning of town. But then I get distracted as my book takes a turn and I become wrapped up in the characters.

"What are you listening to?" Max asks with a chuckle.

I practically jump out of my skin at his voice. My hand flies out and I slap the volume button, shutting the system off. "It's just a book."

"Mhm, seems like you've definitely missed me," Max teases, sliding his hand over my thigh and giving it a firm squeeze.

My cheeks flush with embarrassment. "Oh look! There's the town sign!" I point out, grateful to change the subject.

"Mm, cute. It's a *really* small town, huh?" Max kneads my thigh with his hand. I want to swat his hand away to make him pay attention but the feel of his hand on my leg is not unwanted.

"There's where I work," I point out, my voice rising with delight. Max barely glances over but I chalk that up to it being too dark to see much. "I can show you the town tomorrow before dinner."

"Are we doing something special for dinner tomorrow night?" Max sits up in his seat, his hand slipping further between my thighs.

"Actually, yes. My landlady, who's becoming a good friend, invited us over to dinner." I pull into the parking lot behind the bookstore and my apartment, park the car, and help Max with his things. He seems impatient.

"Do we really have to? I came up here to visit you. I don't want to go to dinner with… someone random, like your landlady," Max complains, pulling his bag out of the truck bed.

I lead him up the stairs to the apartment and can feel him closing in on me, pushing against my butt as I pull out my key.

"Max," I scold him even though there is no one around to see us. "We're going to this dinner, okay? I want you to meet her and get to know the town a bit. Who knows, if everything goes well, you might be joining me here."

Max grumbles in response as I get the door open. He barely glances around the apartment before shedding his many layers of clothing. It takes so long that by the time he's done, he's switched gears, especially with the aroma in the air.

"Is that my favorite?" Max asks, walking into the kitchen toward the delicious smell.

"Yes!" I skip after him, proud of my effort. I'm not a great cook but I figured I could make Max his favorite meal. Thankfully, it's easy to throw in a crock pot so the meal was cooking while I went to pick him up.

It smells good and when I lift off the lid it even looks good. I send a quick picture of the pot to my mom who immediately responds but an excited thumbs-up emoji and heart eyes. I set my phone aside and get bowls out for both of us.

While I serve us and make drinks, Max tells me about the day he had before he even got on the flight. The office, where he works as a paralegal, is in the process of hiring a new lawyer and he's upset because he thinks he should be promoted to the position but since he's only in his second year of law school, he hasn't been offered the position.

He goes on to complain about the other students in his classes. He's one of the older ones in most of his classes because he didn't decide to go to school until after he had been working for a couple of years. Which is working out for him in some ways since his office is paying for most of his school.

Max goes on about both the job and his classes. I sit, eating silently, listening to him go on and on. I forgot how much he likes to talk, he seems to love the sound of his own voice.

That was rude. I can't think like that. I should be excited that he's taking the time out of his schedule to come visit me.

When we finish dinner, Max dumps our bowls into the sink and pulls me back to the bedroom.

"I really should clean the dishes," I protest as Max plants little kisses along my neck, his hands groping at my body.

"It can wait, baby. I've missed you," Max's voice is husky as he pushes his hand up my shirt. Then a second later there is a rumble from his stomach and his hand stills.

"What was that?" I ask but he doesn't answer. His stomach gurgles again. "Are you okay?"

"Where's your bathroom?" Max detaches from me and looks around the room.

"Back in the hallway." I point toward the hallway and he dashes out of the room.

I give him a few minutes while I bring his bag into my room and get changed for bed. I pass the bathroom on the way to the living room and can hear him struggling in there.

"You okay, hun?" I knock on the door. He just grunts so I leave him be.

When I am done washing the dishes, I plop down on the couch to scroll through TV channels. There's nothing on TV tonight so I find an old movie in one of the baskets by the TV. I put in the movie and distract myself.

I hope he isn't sick because of the food I made. But I think I would be getting sick too and I feel fine. The movie is about a third of the way through when Max, after multiple flushes, gives one final flush and finds me in the living room looking a little worse for wear.

"Hey, you okay?" I offer him a glass of water that he accepts gratefully, chugging down the first glass and moving to the kitchen for a refill. I follow him in.

"I think I had some bad food on the plane," Max says, rubbing his stomach with a grimace. He gulps down another glass of water. "I got a meal on the plane, first class, I guess I shouldn't have trusted it." He groans.

"Let's go get you into bed." Taking the glass from him, I refill it and then lead him back to my room. I help him strip out of his clothes and climb into bed.

"Hey, this is pretty comfortable," Max grumbles, snuggling into my pillows.

I climb into bed next to him and he loops his arm over my stomach, pulling me closer. His hand rubs over my skin, he starts kissing my shoulder and moves into my neck.

"Are you sure you're up for this?" I ask, trying not to giggle as his kisses grow sloppier, tickling my neck.

"Shhh…" His shushing tickles even more which sets off more giggles. He shifts in the bed and tries to position himself on top of me but then his face pinches in pain and he groans, rolling off of me.

"Are you okay?" I check in.

"No, I don't think I can…" he trails off.

"Do you want me to…?" I ask and gesture with my hand. "Get on top? Or start?" I gesture to his crotch ungracefully.

"Would you?" Max asks and I nod, pulling my hair back. I move in bed and kneel next to him, touching the waistband of his boxers. I start to pull them down but he groans again.

I pause and look up at him, noticing a sheen of sweat on his brow. "Are you okay? Should I not?"

"Maybe it's better if we just get some sleep. It's been a long day." Max pulls me back up to him and makes himself comfortable, using me as a pillow. "We can try again tomorrow."

"Right. Okay." I stare up at the ceiling, slightly relieved as Max gets heavier against me. His snores are loud because his mouth is right near my ear. I inwardly groan, trying to turn my head but not wanting to suffocate him with my hair. I huff and lay still, hoping sleep will find me soon.

Chapter 25

Dylan

After letting Max sleep away most of the day to recover from whatever food poisoning he had, all he wanted to do was sit on the couch and occasionally try to feel me up. He finally felt better in the evening, just in time for us to get ready for dinner at Vivian's house.

"Come on, Max. We need to go or else we'll be late," I complain as Max procrastinates leaving. He doesn't like the weather here and wants to stay in tonight, he is also milking this food poisoning thing even though I know he's feeling better. And I am looking forward to having dinner with Vivian so I'm not going to let him sit around complaining.

"Are you sure she's actually expecting us?" Max asks again, from the couch, where he has yet to get up. He is dressed but hasn't layered up yet.

The stern look I give him elicits a groan out of him but he pushes off the couch and grabs his coat. He snuggles in close to me while I wait by the door. His nose nuzzles my neck.

"What if I just wanted to stay in with you tonight? I haven't seen you in a while and we didn't really get to enjoy each other,"

Max comments, his hands sliding around my waist. I lean back against him and entertain the idea. I have missed him and I don't want him to feel otherwise.

"No, no." I step away from him. "She's expecting us."

Max tries to nuzzle in close again but I put my purse between us. "Fine," he sighs.

We opt to take Shawn's truck to dinner so we don't have to deal with the weather on the walk over. Part of me hopes Shawn isn't there, but another part of me wants to see him again. When we pull up to Vivian's house, I can't tell if Shawn is there or not. We're in his truck so there is no obvious sign that he's here.

"You coming?" Max asks, already out of the truck. I nod and climb out as well.

The front door flies open and Vivian greets us with a big smile. "Dylan! And you must be Max." Vivian ushers us into her house, directing us where to put our shoes and coats before hugging me. She turns to Max and pulls him into a reluctant hug too, he looks a little overwhelmed but I love Vivian's energy. Max's trip has not been great so far so I appreciate her energy and hope it will bring more life into his trip.

"Hi, Vivian. How are you doing?"

Vivian brings us into the living room as she tells me about the books she ordered, the ones I picked out. Then we move into the kitchen to talk about the bookstore a bit while Vivian finishes preparing dinner. When talk of the bookstore falls off, Vivian turns her questions to Max and his interests. Max looks slightly disinterested but he answers Vivian's questions politely and my apprehensions about tonight start to fade away until Vivian brings up a topic that I was slightly worried about coming up tonight. Max and I still haven't discussed the timeline of me living here, and I honestly haven't made a decision so when Vivian brings up 'Around the Town', I start to get a little nervous again.

"Are you coming back for 'Around the Town'? Michelle told me you asked her about it," Vivian addresses the last comment to me, and she looks so excited about the event that I feel a twinge of guilt. I smile politely but squirm in my seat a bit. "I know it's a couple of weeks out but you two must hate being apart for so long."

"I've never heard of this 'Around the Town'," Max snarks, shooting me a look. "You've never mentioned it."

"I only found out about it recently and have been so busy, I haven't had time to think about it let alone tell you about it," I tell him, blowing out a breath and shrugging.

"When is it?" Max asks, still staring at me.

"Oh, uhm. Last weekend in March," Vivian offers with an apologetic grimace on her face.

"Oh, well," Max starts and I can tell he's going to say something inappropriate. "Dylan probably won't be around for that anyway," Max says with a nonchalant shrug. Vivian looks like she wants to say something but she holds back.

We are just sitting down to dinner when the front door opens. Although we can't see the front door from the dining room, there's only one person I can think of who would show up here. My guess is proven accurate when I hear a familiar voice.

"Mom?"

"Oh honey, you made it! I wasn't sure you would. Come in, come in. We just sat down to eat." Vivian gets up to usher Shawn into the room. He stops short when he sees Max and me.

"I told you they were coming, didn't I?" Vivian asks with a mischievous smile.

"No, I don't think you did," Shawn says through tight lips.

"Hm," Vivian hums as she makes a plate for Shawn as well. "Dylan you know, but this is Max, her boyfriend."

"Nice to meet you, man," Max stands up to shake Shawn's hand. Shawn takes his hand stiffly and nods in greeting. Max looks a little more interested now that there is another man here. But once he takes in Shawn's appearance, dirty jeans, and tight henley, his smile falls, and the look of annoyance returns.

I tug him back down into his seat. "Be kind," I whisper, leaning into him. I look over to see Shawn watching us, Max must notice too because he leans in and kisses my lips before returning to the meal.

"This looks delicious, Vivian. Thank you," I say to return to the conversation. Vivian beams at me.

"Thank you, dear. So, Max, what do you do?" Vivian asks Max, redirecting the conversation to her guest. I try not to watch Shawn stab at the broccoli on his plate. He's glaring at Max and I have no idea why.

"I'm a lawyer. Well, I'm a paralegal but I am in law school right now," Max starts and Shawn grunts a laugh.

"So, you're not a lawyer?" Shawn says as more of a statement than a question.

"I will be. I am in my second year of law school," Max goes on about his classes and his job which makes Shawn roll his eyes and grunt every so often. Max tries to ignore him but sends him a few glares mid-sentence.

Vivian is sweet enough to ask him follow-up questions even though I can tell she is not super interested in this topic. In the middle of another story, and after a few passive aggressive comments from both Max and Shawn, I stand up suddenly. I need to get away from the table.

"Where's the restroom?" I ask when all the eyes at the table turn to me.

"I'll show you," Shawn grunts as he stands quickly and I have no choice but to follow.

Shawn leads me out of the dining room and down a hallway, he's silent but I can't help it when I blurt out, "What's your problem?"

His steps falter and he pauses. "What are you talking about?" He dares to act like I'm crazy.

"That," I say, waving my hand toward the dining room, "back there. Why are you being so snotty to Max?"

"Oh, I'm sorry. Did I hurt your poor little boyfriend's precious feelings?" Shawn says with a sarcastic smirk.

"Seriously, what the hell did he ever do to you?" I step closer to him, trying to keep my voice low so Vivian and Max can't hear us.

Shawn's face changes, he's no longer smirking, and he looks pained and annoyed. He steps closer to me and I back up until he has me backed up against the wall. It reminds me of the other night at the bookstore when he trapped me against the counter.

"Shawn," I whisper.

"What do you see in him?" Shawn asks, his voice low, his head tilted to look down at me. "He's a tool. He hasn't talked about you at all tonight."

"Why would he talk about me? Vivian was asking him questions about his job."

"She asked him about his life," Shawn points out. "You should be a big part of his life. Yet, he didn't mention you."

"What are you doing?" I question him. My body is confused, I'm angry at him for questioning our relationship but his closeness makes my heart beat faster and I feel my legs starting to tingle. I should be angry at myself, at my body for feeling this way around Shawn, especially since Max is just in the next room but I can't help the excitement his closeness elicits.

Shawn looks down at my lips and leans in. "He should talk about you, a lot. I would." Shawn's words leave me speechless. I can't move my feet but I don't have to because Shawn reaches passed me, grabs the handle of the door, and pushes the door open.

"There's the bathroom," he says, stepping back from me. He waits, looking at me for a few seconds, leaving me to decide what I want to do.

"Thanks." I chicken out, duck my head, and shuffle into the bathroom. Closing the door between us is hard but it's the right thing to do.

Splashing water on my face, I look in the mirror and tell myself to get it together. Just because Max and I have been having issues for a while, does not mean that I can be this excited about Shawn flirting with me.

When I exit the bathroom, I hear raised voices. I quickly return to the dining room where Shawn and Max are standing up, arguing over the table. Vivian looks over at me when I enter the room, her eyes wide.

"What's going on?" I look at Max, then at Shawn, then back to Vivian.

"That's what I would like to know!" Max huffs, his voice almost a shout and his tone accusing.

"What are you talking about? Can you please sit down?" I walk over to the table and take my seat beside Vivian. She gives me a worried and apologetic look.

"I won't sit down," Max's voice raises again. "I just found out that this guy was in your apartment, taking care of you while you were sick!" Max points an accusing finger at Shawn, who in turn rolls his eyes but his stance remains defensive.

"I told you that I was sick and that he brought me some soup," I explain to him slowly, a headache starting to form in my temples. I eventually told Max, a bit after the fact but I told him. Maybe I didn't tell him how long Shawn stayed but it was an innocent friendship thing.

"Right, okay," Max huffs, his anger fizzling but he's trying to hold onto it and prove he's not wrong for feeling that way. "And what about the day you two spent together shopping? Hm?" Max narrows his eyes at me, his face turning red with anger. I raise my eyebrows because that was also something I told him about and he had no issue with it then.

"Sorry," Vivian leans in to apologize quietly to me. "I was just making conversation and told him how you got sick because of the weather and then went to get winter clothes." Vivian's face scrunches up and she looks so guilty that I feel bad for her.

I shake my head and touch her hand gently. "It's not on you. He knew all of this." I turn back to face Max and Shawn. "Where is this coming from?"

Max turns his glare back to Shawn. Shawn holds his gaze with a glare of his own.

"I knew this was a mistake," Max says, rubbing his hand down his face and turning back to me.

"What?" I ask, cautiously.

"Letting you come out here. It was a stupid idea. You should have just toughed it out in the Dallas office," Max starts but I interrupt him.

"You encouraged me to go! I even asked if you were okay with it, and you said I should go!" I'm starting to get worked up now and feel my heartbeat picking up. We shouldn't be having this fight here, not in front of Vivian and Shawn.

"Yeah, well I was just trying to support you. Clearly, that was the wrong decision." Max shoots me a look that tells me he is done with this conversation.

"You should always support her," Shawn's low voice is practically a growl. I look over at him and see that his fists are clenched at his sides. "If she wants to move to pursue an advancement in her career, you should stand behind her. Why were you so eager to get rid of her?" Shawn asks, suspicion filling his voice.

"Why the fuck do you care, dude?" Max rounds the table, getting closer to Shawn. I jump up to be nearer in case I have to separate them, even as Shawn's words make me question Max's initial reaction and compare it to how he's acting now.

Max gets up close to Shawn but he must realize that Shawn is much bigger than he is so he stops a foot away and tries to puff up his chest to look intimidating. Shawn smirks, standing up tall and cracking his neck from side to side. I roll my eyes at their antics.

"You're an idiot, *dude*," Shawn mocks him, his smirk growing more prominent.

"What? Do you want to say that to my face?!" Max takes another step toward Shawn, getting up in his face.

"I quite literally did say that to your face," Shawn points out which makes Max even angrier. His mouth opens to speak but I step between them and put my hand on his arm.

"Max, stop," I implore him but he doesn't even glance at me. Instead, he takes another step forward which pushes me back into Shawn's chest. Shawn's hand lands on my waist to steady me. Which, of course, sets Max off.

"Get your hands off of my girlfriend," Max practically snarls.

"You pushed her into me," Shawn points out with a roll of his eyes.

I push against Max, to get him away from Shawn but also to get myself away from Shawn. The feel of his chest on my back and his hand on my waist elicited more butterflies than I want.

"You need to start treating her right," Shawn states. Max narrows his eyes at Shawn.

"Why? You think you would treat her right? Because you think you have a chance to steal her away from me? You don't." Max laughs and it is not a pleasant sound. I flinch at his harsh words.

"I could do a hell of a lot better than you're doing. Couldn't even check on her while she's sick," Shawn throws that back in his face but Max doesn't look offended, he looks pissed. "And it's not my fault the curtain didn't shut all the way while she tried on clothes."

The revelation shocks me a little. I hadn't noticed the curtain while I was changing but I feel my cheeks flush with heat. Shawn smirks and Max glowers.

"Are you saying you were creeping on my girlfriend?" Max sounds like he is about to fly off the handle, his hands ball into fists at his sides.

Before either of them can make a move, Vivian stands up and clears her throat. Shawn turns to look at her and I can see the anger in his eyes soften a little.

"Shawn, sweetie, I think maybe you should step out and cool off," Vivian says in a sweet yet stern voice.

"Me?" Shawn questions but Vivian gives a tight nod. Shawn huffs but turns on his heel and stomps out the door, slamming it shut behind him. A second later a blast of cold air hits us and I shiver.

Chapter 26

Shawn

Starting a fight and slamming the door probably wasn't the most mature. And Max wanted to rile me up. But he deserved the shit I told him. He doesn't deserve Dylan, but she certainly didn't deserve how I acted tonight. Jealousy reared its ugly head.

I'm such an idiot. I shouldn't have mentioned the curtain thing. It probably was creepy that I kept looking. Dylan's face when I said it made me regret it immediately but it was too late to take it back.

I kick a snow pile as I walk down the driveway. My truck is sitting there looking so tempting but I know it would be petty of me to take it now. And I don't want Dylan to be stuck walking home in the cold. So instead, I trek into town on foot.

The lights of the dim bar are welcoming and look just about as moody as I feel. The door swings open and a patron comes stumbling out.

"Hey! Shawnie-boy!" Billy grins when he sees me. Ah, not a patron, the bartender.

"Hey, you not tending bar tonight?" I ask as he holds the door wide open, ignoring the groans and jeers of the people inside to bar, annoyed that he's letting in the cold air.

"I am," Billy confirms. Billy leans in to whisper to me, "People have been buying me shots."

"Whew, yeah. I can smell that." I take a step back and wave my hand in front of my face. Billy laughs a big, hearty laugh.

"Close the door, man!" Someone shouts from inside the bar.

"Hey, I need another drink!" Someone else calls out.

"Yeah, yeah. Hold your horses." Billy rolls his eyes and then turns back to me. "You going in?"

"Might as well. After you." I step around him to hold the door open. "Maybe drink some water, eat something," I suggest.

"You're so smart, man. Just the smartest. I always wonder why you came back to this little podunk town. You were destined for great things.' Billy's heartfelt words catch me off guard. He's not usually this friendly to me.

"Thanks, man." I pat his back, pushing him back inside the bar.

"Let me get you a cold one." Billy pops back behind the bar and rattles around a few bottles before grabbing one and setting it on the counter for me. I take a seat on the stool in front of the beer and shrug off my coat.

"Thanks." I lift the bottle in a salute before taking a sip.

"Hey, where's my drink?" Noah, the one who asked for a refill earlier taps on the bar. He's not drunk yet but he looks like he's getting close.

"Coming up," Billy tuts, disappearing to the other side of the bar. Noah frowns.

I should probably talk to him but before I can say anything, Bella sidles up next to me, putting her hand on my arm.

"Hey, handsome." Bella grins at me, hopping onto the stool next to me and swinging to face me. "I was hoping you'd show up tonight."

"Thanks, Bella." I shouldn't entertain her antics tonight but after the fight at my mom's house, I could stand to let off a little steam. "You look good."

Her dark hair is pulled back in a low ponytail and her black shirt is a tight fit, hugging her body. She's not curvy like Dylan but she's still attractive.

"Thank you. That's high praise coming from you," Bella teases me, leaning in a bit closer. "Can I buy you a fresh drink?"

I should hesitate or say no but I agree quickly. I want to forget tonight, I want to forget this growing attraction to Dylan.

Bella isn't boring but I constantly find my thoughts turning back to Dylan. I should leave the bar and go apologize.

"Shawn, this is my friend, Jessica," Bella interrupts my thoughts as her friend comes over to the bar. "She lives in Fallon Falls."

"Hi, Shawn." Jessica's eyes twinkle as she shakes my hand, lingering longer than necessary.

The two rope me into a couple more beers and another hour or so of mindless flirting. I try not to lead either of them on but I do indulge in a little banter, it makes me feel a little better.

Bella announces that she has to pee so they excuse themselves to use the restroom and leave me alone at the bar. I take another gulp of my beer and look around. I spot Noah still sitting a couple of stools away from me. The frustrated look on his face hasn't changed in the hours we've been here.

"What's wrong with you tonight?" I ask him. We're not good friends either but there are only so many of us around the same age that we all know each other. And I think I'm drunk enough to hear whatever bullshit he's contemplating.

"Woman problems," Noah grumbles, not bothering to look in my direction.

"You mean 'Marlee problems'?" I chuckle before taking another sip. Noah's expression darkens. "Oh no, what did you do?"

"Nothing!" Noah protests. I narrow my eyes at him and he sighs. "I think I love her." He lifts his shoulders with a shrug like it's no big deal, but clearly it is.

We sit in silence after his revelation until I clear my throat. "Wow, that's a big thing to admit."

"You ever have a girl that you can't get out of your head? She's on my mind 24/7." I automatically think of Dylan. Noah studies my face. "You got one too?" He nods, knowing it's true.

"Have you told her?" I ask, instead of responding to his question.

"It's Marlee. How do I approach this with her? All she wants to do is hook up with me," he grumbles.

"Uh, yeah. That is very much not true." I chuckle and finish another beer.

"What?" Noah asks, looking uncertain but hopeful. "What do you mean?"

"Hey, we're back. Did you miss us?" Jessica slides her arm over my shoulder, leaning into me as she interrupts my conversation with Noah. He looks pained and annoyed but he turns back to his drink, not wanting to join the girls and I. Bella giggles and tugs on her friend's arm.

"Thank you for the drinks," I tell them as I drop a couple of bills on the counter anyway. My mind has been made up and it is time to go home. I can't keep leading these girls on. I like Dylan and I need to go home to figure out some things.

"Oh, are you leaving already?" Bella pouts but it doesn't dissuade me. I nod and stand up, putting my coat back on. "Do you want some company?"

"Thank you," I say and they both smile but eye each other, trying to figure out who will stay behind. I quickly put an end to that argument, "Thanks but no," I clarify. "I have to get home and get some rest. I have a big project tomorrow."

"Oh, okay. Well, it was nice getting to hang out with you," Bella sounds a little dejected but she puts on her bright smile and I know she'll recover quickly.

"It was nice meeting you, Shawn." Jessica smiles politely and gives my arm another squeeze before they leave me to head onto the dance floor.

I don't look back as I head out the door, letting the cold wind sober me on the walk home.

Chapter 27
Dylan

"Dear, don't worry about it," Vivian reassures me as I apologize for the umpteenth time since Shawn stormed out. She accepts the dish I've just washed and wipes it dry. "Shawn has always had a bit of a temper. It seems to flare around pretty girls he thinks deserve to be treated better," she says with a knowing smile.

"Oh," I try to brush over her statement. "Max isn't usually this jealous…" I trail off as other memories of him getting upset pop into my mind. "Or maybe he is. I don't know. I'm sorry it ruined dinner."

I keep my voice low even though Max excused himself to use the restroom a few minutes after Shawn left. He had stiffly apologized for his raised voice, to Vivian, not to me, and then excused himself from the table.

"Oh, it wasn't ruined. It was quite entertaining," Vivian says with a smile, her eyes twinkling. She is quick to forgive and I want to give her a big hug for how she is handling this very confusing situation. "We have lots of leftovers if you want to take some home with you," she offers.

"I don't think Shawn got to eat anything, I wouldn't want to…"

Vivian waves her hand, cutting me off. "Don't worry about Shawn. He's a big boy." Vivian goes quiet like she wants to say something to me but is hesitant.

"What is it?" I ask, handing her another clean dish to dry.

"Shawn's temper… He just lets it build. He doesn't show a lot of emotions," Vivian tries to explain. "Ever since his father passed away… Well, he seems to bottle everything up. Not that he was very open with his emotions before." She chuckles. "He was the typical teenager but his dad always made sure he knew he was safe here. Safe to express his emotions, safe to be happy, to be sad. When his father passed, he shut off. I was a wreck which probably didn't help. I think he was trying to be strong for both of us."

I nod in understanding, not wanting to speak, my heart aching for both Vivian and Shawn.

"I'm doing much better now but Shawn hasn't returned to his old self. But these last few weeks, I have seen some of that old Shawn returning," Vivian admits with a little smile.

"Oh? That's great." I can feel myself smiling too. Vivian looks over at me and her smile grows. "What?

"I'm just glad you came into town," Vivian admits with a shrug and a mischievous smile. I narrow my eyes at her but her smile is contagious.

"Thank you, the town is really growing on me. And the people too." I grin at her and bump her hip gently with mine. "Are you sure Shawn won't mind me taking all these leftovers?" I ask again as Vivian loads me up with multiple Tupperware containers.

"Oh, yeah it's fine. I think you could do anything and he wouldn't mind." Vivian laughs handing me another container. "Don't worry about him."

"Yeah, stop worrying about Shawn. How about you worry about your boyfriend who just got humiliated in front of complete strangers?" Max comes into the kitchen, full of attitude before I can respond to Vivian.

"Max," scolding him seems childish but he's acting childish right now. I look over at Vivian to start an apology but she just smiles, a soft, sympathetic smile.

"Why don't you two head home? Thank you for your help cleaning up. It looks like we got most of it done so I can handle the rest from here." Vivian gives me an out but I hesitate. I don't want to let Max and Shawn's attitude ruin the evening but this is something Max and I need to handle in private.

"Okay. Thank you for dinner, it was delicious. And thanks for all the leftovers." I hold them up with a smile. Vivian pulls me into a side hug and whispers good luck.

"I'll be in the truck," Max grumbles. Before he can leave I shove the containers at him. He takes them reluctantly and then stalks out of the house.

"Don't tell him it's Shawn's truck." Vivian's eyes light up as she lets out a loud laugh. I shake my head but smile as well. Max would be so mad he might even walk home in the cold.

When I get to the truck, Max is silent. He's given me the silent treatment before but this time, I'm not in the mood to talk either. His outburst was embarrassing to me too.

We drive home in silence but as we park the truck, Max tries to cozy up to me. He wraps his arm around me as we walk to the building and walks side by side up the stairs with me. He brushes my hair back and presses his lips against my neck.

"Max," I whisper. I don't hate the sensation but I'm still upset about how tonight went.

I get the door open and Max sets the leftover containers on the table near the door then starts to unzip my heavy jacket. I let him help me take off my outer layers and kiss on my neck but I can't get out of my head enough to enjoy it.

"Max, we should talk about what happened tonight." I try to extract myself from his embrace but he has gotten over his anger and has turned his emotions elsewhere.

"It's okay, I forgive you," Max mumbles into my neck, his hands wandering over my body.

"What?" I push his hands off of me and take a step back.

"Yeah, baby. I forgive you. Now, let me show you how much I've missed you." Max returns his hands to my waist and he walks me back toward the bedroom.

"I really think we should talk first," I protest.

"What's there to talk about? I've already said I forgive you. I trust you going forward, plus, you'll be back in Dallas soon enough," Max explains, pulling off his shirt and tossing it to the floor.

"Well, I hope so. But I don't know yet," I admit, bracing my hand on his warm chest. His strong hands know where I enjoy being touched so I'm starting to give in. It has been a few weeks since we saw each other last and I have missed him.

"What do you mean you don't know?" Max steps back. "I thought the plan was to only be here for a month or two?" He's getting angry again. I take a step back, the back of my knees hitting the bed.

"Well, that's what I thought too but I haven't heard anything about the job in Dallas," I tell him and he huffs, annoyed.

"So, what does that mean?" He backs up, frustrated. Max looks down at my body and I can see his thoughts fighting.

"I really don't know. I'll check in with Kevin when I get back to the office," I promise. Walking away from him, I hear him huff at my back but I don't think either of us is in the mood anymore.

"I'm going to take a shower," Max states before leaving the room. I hear the bathroom door shut firmly behind him.

I walk to the kitchen, grabbing the Tupperware containers on the way. After storing them in the fridge, I debate joining Max in the shower but decide against it. We both need to cool down, away from each other.

Instead, I sit on the couch and wait for him to finish in the bathroom. When he comes out, he joins me on the couch. We don't talk, but we put in a movie and he pulls me close. Neither of us bring up the fight or the dinner but I can still feel a shift in our relationship.

We go to bed without addressing anything.

Chapter 28

Dylan

When we wake up on Max's last day here, I feel a little disappointed by the trip. We went to bed with a lot of tension between us last night and I don't know where our relationship stands.

Today should be a bit sad, Max is leaving and I won't see him again for a few weeks. But instead, I feel a bit relieved. He has spent most of this trip complaining about Minnesota and complaining about my absence from Dallas, and of course, complaining about Shawn's behavior last night.

This morning, I want to have a little bit of fun so I convince Max to come into town with me. I want to show him where I've been living and working and making friends. We head out around 10 am, bundled up in our warmest clothes. The wind isn't too bad today but Max looks in pain almost immediately after we walk down the stairs and into the cold.

I expect him to start grumbling but instead, he keeps his mouth shut and tucked into a wool scarf I let him borrow. His gloved hand holds mine tightly to show we're still a team.

As we walk toward my office, people in town that I've met wave and say hello as we pass. Max plasters on a fake smile but keeps hold of my hand and doesn't let me stop to chat with anyone. When we reach my office, I unlock the doors to let us in. Since it is the weekend, neither Noah nor Michelle are in today.

I show him my office space and he grumbles when I mention Noah, but I graze over the topic and gush about how great Michelle is.

We're only in my office for a few minutes before Max grows bored and expresses his disdain out loud. "You really prefer this tiny office over the one in Dallas?" He practically scoffs at the idea. "I've seen your office in Dallas. The building you work out of is incredible, and the view? Amazing. And you'd rather work here instead?" Max laughs; a cruel, cold noise.

"I didn't say that. I love Dallas, and the office there. This was just the next opportunity for me," I explain, even though we have talked about it a few times.

He just huffs, shaking his head.

"Max, you said that you would consider moving here with me if this is the way my career went," I point out, needing him to remember that at one point he was a supportive boyfriend.

"Hm, why don't we go back to your apartment and you can remind me why I said that." Max steps closer to me, pulling me into his arms and kissing me softly.

It feels a bit awkward to be kissing in my place of work so I lean away from him. I try to keep a smile off of my lips but sometimes he can be very charming.

"Why don't we go get some food first?" I offer and Max nods eagerly. "I want to show you a couple of other places before we have to head out to the airport."

"Can we do this tour of town quickly? I want to spend some time together in your apartment before I have to leave." Max winks at me and I chuckle.

"Depends on how good you act during this tour," I comment as I lock the office door behind us. We walk hand in hand to one of the town's restaurants and I feel the mood picking up.

"Baby, I am always on my best behavior." Max pulls me close, smirking down at me.

"Mhm, except at Vivian's dinner," I point out.

Max rolls his eyes. "I was provoked," he protests, annoyed but the smile remains.

We have a quick lunch, and our energy gets better. Flirtatious leg taps under the table have both of us smiling and me giggling. Max tips well for lunch and raises his eyebrows at me, knowing it pleases me when he is kind to the waitstaff.

"One last stop, I promise." My words are met with a groan. Max tries to sneak his hands inside my coat and I squeal at the cold. He chuckles but lets me zip up and follows me back to the apartment. He looks pleased but his smile falters as I stop at the bookstore, spotting Vivian inside.

"Your apartment is right there," Max protests, tugging my arm playfully, trying to get me to keep moving.

"It's just going to be a few more minutes," I say with a laugh. He mock whines, pouting a little bit as he follows me into the bookstore.

"Dylan, how are you, dear?" Vivian asks when she looks up from the counter. Max recognizes her and tries to keep the pleasant look on his face but I can tell he is thinking about last night.

"Hi, Vivian. I'm alright. It's Max's last day so I wanted to show him around town a bit. And of course, I had to show him my favorite shop in town."

Vivian beams at my declaration. "Ah, lovely girl."

"Actually, I wanted to come over to apologize for last night."

"Dylan, you've already apologized enough. It really was not that big of a deal. I just hope it didn't mess up your trip," Vivian directs toward Max who offers a tense smile.

"It already wasn't such a great trip," I say softly, but Max can't hear since he has already wandered away from us.

"I'm sorry to hear that, dear." Vivian squeezes my arm.

"It's okay. Today has been better."

"Good. Oh, can I help you with anything? Do you need another book?" Vivian asks, shifting back into work mode.

I chuckle. "Oh no. I have barely had any time to read. But thank you though. Okay, I guess we should head back to my apartment. We're leaving for the airport soon."

Max comes over to join us again as I say goodbye to Vivian. Vivian moves to hug Max too, which he accepts reluctantly.

"It was lovely to meet you. I hope you like our little town. We've certainly enjoyed Dylan's presence here," Vivian tells him. Max gives another tight-lipped smile.

"Mhm, she sure is great." Max pulls me against his side and starts pulling me back toward the door. I wave to Vivian and giggle as Max pulls me out the door and upstairs to my apartment.

I barely get the door shut before Max has stripped most of his clothing. I giggle at his eagerness and allow him to relieve me of a few layers of clothing as well. He leads me over to the couch this time and sits down, pulling me onto his lap. I place my knees on either side of his hips, straddling him. I put my hands on his shoulders and smile at him.

"You look hot," he says and leans in to give me neck kisses.

I wish he would say something more romantic but lately, he only gives these short shallow comments.

I put my hand on his chest and push him back against the couch. I lean down and capture his mouth with mine. His kissing grows frantic, I can feel something else growing under my ass.

"Have you packed yet?" I ask, breathless from our kisses.

Max groans. "That's not hot, babe."

"I'm being practical," I protest. "That is very hot." Max chuckles. He wraps my hair around his hand and brings my head back down to kiss me again.

He leans back and sighs. "Shit."

"What?"

"I have not packed," he admits. "It won't take that long," he tries to reason as I plant little kisses along his shoulder.

"What won't? The packing or the sex?" I ask with a laugh. Max grumbles a bit, not appreciating my joke. "Go pack!" I scold him, teasingly with a smile on my face.

"Stop moving on me then," Max grumbles, his hands still firm on my hips. I giggle as he squeezes them gently before helping me get off of him. "I'll be quick," he promises.

"I'll be waiting," I reply and blow a little kiss at him as he looks back at me, sprawling on the couch. I lean my head back on the couch to wait for him. I'm still contemplating our relationship but this day has been better.

Max comes back with his bags half an hour later and sets them by the door. He comes back over to the couch and sits next to me, pulling me into his lap.

"That was quick." I smile at him, wrapping my arms around him once more.

"This won't be," Max promises as his mouth finds mine.

He kisses me deeply, starting soft then he gets stronger and pushes his tongue into my mouth. He flips me over so my back is pressed against the couch. I giggle at the movement, loving it. Then I catch sight of something over his shoulder.

"Oh no," I say quietly.

"What?" Max murmurs, leaving a trail of kisses down my neck, throat, and clavicle.

"It's snowing," I point out.

"So?" Max's hands grip my sides, moving up my body.

"We're going to need to leave early for the airport," I tell him, bracing for his response. He huffs and then lets out a low sigh against my chest.

"Soon?" He asks, and I nod. "Now?" He clarifies and I grimace but nod again. I haven't had much experience driving while it's snowing so it's better to leave now so I can take my time and he won't miss his flight.

"I'm sorry," I say as Max pushes off of me. He looks a little pained as he adjusts himself in his pants.

"It's fine. I'm going to use the restroom then I'll be ready to leave." He disappears before I can say anything.

I try to make small talk on the way to the airport to break the tension that's grown back. But I really want to ask how he liked the town if he has any desire to move here. I want to tell him that I've started to like it here. But I also miss Dallas.

When we pull up to the airport, Max doesn't get out. We sit in silence for a few seconds before he turns to look at me. I can feel the distance between us even though we're less than a foot apart.

"Dylan," Max starts. My heart begins to race as I look at him. He has this dumb little look on his face. Like he's annoyed but also trying to look sympathetic. "I think that we should take a break."

The statement throws me off and my heart skips a beat, in a bad way. "What?" I finally choke out. I can fear tears pricking the corner of my eyes.

"Just while you're out here," he hurries to say. "You only have a couple of weeks left up here, hopefully. So when you come back to Dallas we can talk about everything and see how we will move forward with this relationship."

"I don't understand. Are you breaking up with me?" I ask, shocked, stunned.

Max sighs. "No, we're just taking a break. When you come back to Dallas, my apartment and I will be there for you."

I notice he doesn't say that they will be waiting for me, just that they will be there. Is he expecting to see other people during this break? I can't even open my mouth to ask the question.

"You know I love you, Dyl. This will be good for us," Max assures me with a confident yet pitying smile. I close my mouth with a snap and narrow my eyes at him but I don't protest. It seems like he's thought this through. I wonder how long this has been on his mind.

He leans over to kiss my cheek before getting out and grabbing his things from the back of the truck. He waves at me as he heads into the airport.

"Love you, Dyl! See you later," he throws out before the doors close behind him.

Watching him go, I have mixed emotions. It's so sudden that I feel shocked, but not as sad as I was expecting. I start the truck and drive back to my apartment in shock.

Chapter 29

Dylan

"Are you sure you can handle this meeting today?" Michelle checks again. Her eyebrows are knitted together, concern written all across her face.

Michelle is the only person I've told about Max breaking up with me. Or putting us on a break. She's been eyeing me every few minutes to make sure I'm okay. I keep reassuring her that I'm fine. I have too much to do to dwell on the breakup, or just break? I'm not sure, and anyway, I think I've been handling it well so far.

"Michelle," I whine like a child. "I told you I'm fine. I am focused on this meeting. I am prepared for the meeting. I've got this."

"Are you sure? I can go instead." Noah appears in my doorway, blocking Michelle from my view.

"Noah, you don't even know what we're talking about." Michelle bumps him out of the doorway and brings me the updated presentation folder. "Do you want to borrow my car? I know you left Shawn's truck at Vivian's house when you got back from the airport."

"No, I'll be okay. I actually preordered one yesterday and it should be here soon." I look around my office, scanning my desk for anything I might have forgotten.

"You have everything. You're ready," Michelle reassures me.

"Yes, thank you."

When the car arrives, Michelle walks me out and we double-check everything before I reluctantly shut the door and the car speeds off toward the restaurant. The restaurant is just a few towns over, about half an hour, and I am thankful Mr. Bonoventure is able to meet me halfway.

When I arrive at the restaurant, I give my driver a great rating and thank him before getting out and hurrying out of the cold and into the warm restaurant. The hostess takes my coat and hangs it up. I look around the restaurant and am pleased that I chose to wear one of my client dinner outfits that I brought from Dallas. This restaurant is chic, and my Dallas outfits fit the vibe better than my new, warm outfits.

I'm almost half an hour early but get seated quickly. I spend a few minutes looking over my proposal while I wait for the client to arrive. I can see the entrance from my seat so I look up every time the door to the restaurant opens to make sure I don't miss him. Although I am rather early, he shows up only 15 minutes later, early as well.

"Mr. Bonoventure, it's so nice to meet you," I say as I stand up to greet him. He's dressed in a nice suit sans a tie, his hair is sprinkled with gray and the lines around his eyes and on his cheeks tell me he's spent most of his life with a smile on his face.

He shakes my hand with a hearty pump. "Ms. Monroe, it is lovely to meet you." I am grateful that our communication before a face-to-face meeting included email, where I have a picture showing I am a woman. If he had gone into this meeting thinking I was a man, this might have turned out differently.

"Oh please, call me Dylan."

"Ah, Dylan. Please call me Richard." He grins at me, a smile filled with charm.

"Thank you for agreeing to meet me here, Richard." I return his smile as we sit down at our table.

"Oh, of course. I was visiting family a few towns away so it really wasn't too far from me," Mr. Bonoventure explains, picking up his menu to study it.

"Oh? You have family around here? Is this where you grew up?" I ask to get the conversation flowing. We can discuss business after we've ordered.

"It is. In Eagle Rock a few miles east of here," Richard explains. "I wasn't born there but my parents bought a farm when I was young and that's where I grew up. Much different than the city I live in now," Richard chuckles. "Well, part of the year. I actually live in Birch Lake during the school year, for my daughter," he explains and I nod, remembering what Michelle told me about his history.

"Oh yes! Michelle, my associate, told me that the big blue house across from the Sanitarium belongs to you," I say and he nods. "I love that house and property, it's just gorgeous."

"Thank you. It was my wife's house. Her grandparents passed it down and when I fell in love with her, I fell in love with the house. Unfortunately, I'm not there as much as I would like these days," Richard says, a frown appearing on his face thinking about his wife. He looks up and tries to smile. "I apologize for the sudden shift in mood. My wife passed away a little over a year ago and the house just holds so many memories for me, and my daughter. I could never give it up though.”

“Of course not. It's a beautiful house and part of her legacy. And I'm sure your daughter loves it,” I say and he nods his approval at my words. “But I can understand the city living versus country living dilema. I've lived in Dallas my whole life so the move up here to a wintery small town was quite a shock. Although, probably not as shocking as farm life,” I say which elicits another laugh from Richard and the sadness slowly melts off his features.

“Oh, it's definitely a change of pace. I think my daughter, Evelyn,” he says then chuckles. “Or, Evie, as she likes to go by now.”

“That's cute,” I chuckle.

“It suits her. But I think she likes the small town more than the city. Although, she hasn't complained about either. She just seems more like herself in Birch Lake. It's probably because it's her mother's hometown,” Richard says with a soft sigh before he clears his throat.

“It's an amazing town,” I offer. “I haven't been here long at all and I'm just blown away. Everyone is so nice and welcoming. The restaurants, minimal as they are, are delicious and homey.” Richard chuckles at my comment but he's nodding along, the fire back in his eyes.

“It's a great town. I can see myself spending more time there,” Richard comments.

“That's great,” I say. “Then our next meeting can be in our little office in town or one of the cute diners,” I add with a laugh.

“That sounds great.” Richard smiles at the idea and it makes me feel hopeful for our business relationship.

We lay down our menus as a waiter comes to take our drink orders, and shortly after, he returns with the drinks. After placing our orders, I turn to Richard and start to talk about our business and the portfolio that Michelle and I created. Richard is polite during the conversation, letting me do our basic spiel before I dive into more specifics for him.

Richard asks questions and seems genuinely interested and maybe even slightly impressed with all the work Michelle and I have done. I make sure to throw her name in a few times so she gets the credit she deserves.

As dinner is wrapping up, I promise to send him a file with the PowerPoint and a short PDF which he is eager to look over. We part ways and I can't help the giant smile on my face as I climb in a car to head home.

Chapter 30

Shawn

I hate that my truck smells like her. I hate that I love that it smells like her. The smell is fruity and makes my mouth water. I think it's apricot, or something similar, maybe I'm thinking too much about it and the smell is just oranges.

I need to stop overthinking this. I should roll the windows down and let the freezing breeze blow all traces of her out of my truck.

Honestly, I should go find her and apologize for what happened during dinner the other night but I still feel like I need some time to cool off. I know her boyfriend went back to Dallas but that's probably even more reason why I should stay away. She didn't seem happy with him but they're still together and I shouldn't interfere.

Huffing, I roll my windows down an inch or so, letting the cold wind whip inside, sucking out the smell of Dylan's perfume, shampoo, or whatever it is that is so intoxicating to me. Instead of getting her out of my truck, the wind whips up items in my truck, sending them swirling. Something from the backseat gets thrown forward and lodged in between the passenger seat and the center console.

The movement catches my eye. Something waves, bright and colorful. I pull into the parking lot on my left and put my truck in park before I reach over and pull out a scarf.

The sight of the scarf brings back memories of Dylan, of course. I press the scarf to my nose and inhale deeply before I realize I'm too far gone. I quickly toss the scarf on the seat next to me and lean back, closing my eyes. I take a deep breath before looking out the window.

A shiver racks my spine, either from the cold air or from the sight of Dylan, sitting in a restaurant across the street, with a guy who is not her boyfriend.

I narrow my eyes at the pair. They're both smiling and laughing and I can feel my stomach getting tighter.

Is she on a date? Right after her boyfriend left town too. Did they break up?

I make a note to check in with my mom. She and Dylan seem to have gotten close so maybe Dylan confided in her.

Before I can think about it, I find myself turning off my engine and getting out of the truck. My feet carry me to the restaurant. I can't linger outside without looking like a creep, staring into the restaurant, plus part of me wants to hear what they're saying. I'm not dressed appropriately for this restaurant but there is a bar area where I can place a take-out order. Walking over to the bar, I glance back at Dylan and her male companion. He's a bit older than I expected, there is some gray in his hair and smile lines around his face. They're deepening as he spends more time smiling at Dylan.

"Hi, can I help you?" I look back toward the bar and find the bartender smiling at me.

"What? Sorry." I shake my head and pick up the menu, scanning it and finding a couple of great options.

"I can give you a few minutes if you need some time," the bartender offers.

"Mm. No, I think I'm ready," I tell her.

"Are you going to be eating at this bar or is this To-Go?"

I debate eating here so I can have longer to see what Dylan and her date are discussing but I think twice and decide it would be better if I left. "To-Go please," I decide.

"Alright, what can I get for you?"

I place an order for a couple of items for myself and my mom and sit back to wait.

"Do you want a drink while you wait?" The bartender comes back after putting in my order. She slides a coaster across the bar and sets a glass of water on it for me.

"Ah, no. I shouldn't," I start to object but then she slides me their specials and one of the options catches my eye.

The bartender grins as I order one of the specials. I nurse the drink with occasional glances in the direction of Dylan. They're still exchanging smiles but I can't hear anything and the pit in my stomach isn't going away. I toss back the rest of my drink as the bartender comes out with a big To-Go bag.

With one look back at Dylan, I settle my tab and grab the bag before heading out to my truck. Her scarf sits waiting for me in my passenger seat. I drop the To-Go bag on the scarf and head to Mom's house.

Chapter 31

Shawn

"Mom!" I call out as I kick my shoes against the door frame, trying to detach the sludge of snow. I need to shovel her walkway again, I didn't realize how much snow we'd had since the last time I shoveled.

"Hey, what brings you by? Ooo what smells so good?" Mom rounds a corner and spots me by the door with the big bag. "What did you bring?" She takes the bag from me and walks into the kitchen to unpack.

"I hope you haven't eaten dinner yet. I may have gone overboard." I follow her into the kitchen and get plates out for us. She helps me dole out the food then we sit down at the kitchen table to eat.

Mom talks about her day and the new ideas she has had for her store but she also wants to hear input from Dylan, which apparently they have already scheduled a get together to go over everything. Mom glances at me every few minutes.

"Why are you looking at me?"

"Why are you so quiet tonight? What's on your mind?" Mom questions me, putting her fork down to give me her best 'Mom' stare.

"Mom," I start with a sigh.

"No, something is going on. Is it Dylan? I know you have a little thing for her." Mom winks at me and I practically choke on my food.

"What? No. No, I definitely do not," I protest but it falls on deaf ears. Mom just grins at me. "Mom, no."

"It's okay to like her. I know you haven't liked anyone in a long time. She is a great girl."

"Mom, she is… she is great, okay?" I relent, there's no need to deny it. "But she has a boyfriend, a pretty crappy boyfriend but still. And to make matters worse, I saw her at this restaurant tonight," I gesture to the food on the table, "with someone who is not her boyfriend."

"Were you spying on Dylan?" Mom's mouth drops a little and then she smacks her hand over her mouth to stifle a chuckle.

"Mom! I was not spying on her. I just happened to stop near the restaurant and I spotted her inside with somebody."

"And you decided to go into the restaurant," Mom pauses and narrows her eyes at me, "to spy on her."

I rub my hand over my face, feeling embarrassed. "No, that's not… Okay, that sounds bad but… It was not spying. I couldn't hear anything they were saying."

"So, you went into the restaurant to try to hear their conversation?" Mom questions, the little smirk on her face growing bigger as she teases me.

"Mom, stop," I groan.

"You have it bad for her, huh?" She teases me. I put my head down and focus on my food, ignoring her teasing smile.

"It's okay to like her," Mom says a few minutes later. "I shouldn't tell you this but she and her boyfriend are taking a break." I look up at that and Mom shrugs. "I guess the long-distance thing was taking a toll on them both."

"Oh, really? I guess she didn't really seem happy. She never talked about him that much either," I try to reason. "But does that mean the guy she was out with tonight was a new date, already? That's pretty fast."

"Well, we don't know the circumstances. You shouldn't be too quick to judge, dear."

"Yeah, you're right. You're right, of course." I nod and take another bite of my dinner. "So, what were you saying about the bookstore remodel?" I ask to switch subjects.

"Right. Well, I've been looking over the budget, and everything I want to do…" She trails off and I look up at her.

"And?"

"And… well, the budget does not really cover everything," Mom states.

"Do you need some money?" I ask and Mom waves her hand. "No, really. I can give you some. How much do you need?"

"Oh, no dear. No, I was thinking about your father's life insurance. I haven't done anything with the money as of right now but I was thinking we could use some of it, along with some of my savings, to fix up the bookstore. And the rest of the insurance we could set aside for your future," Mom tells me and it seems like she has thought about this.

"Oh, okay. Yeah. Do you need me to contact the insurance agency?" I start to ask questions about how to help but she waves me off again.

"Oh no. Your dad made sure I knew how to deal with everything but I was hoping that you could make an appointment with Dylan and set up a plan for the future of the business and you as well." Mom looks up at me to gauge my reaction.

"Oh. Yeah, I guess I could do that."

"Great! I already scheduled an appointment for tomorrow," Mom informs me with a grin, returning to her meal.

"Right, are you coming too?"

"No, I have to be at the shop tomorrow. Oh, make sure to ask if she has had a chance to look over the floor plan," Mom adds. "I know she's been so busy preparing for a big meeting with a potential client, so she might not have had a chance to go over it but I want to get started soon. Oh, ask her about that meeting too. She mentioned it was coming up soon and that was about a week ago so she might have had it already."

"Alright, I'll make sure to ask," I assure her.

"So, how have you been lately? I notice you seem a little more… a part of life," Mom says. I narrow my eyes at her.

"What does that even mean?" I question with a chuckle.

"Oh, you know." She waves her hand around. "Ever since your dad passed and you came back to town for good… You don't have to be here if it makes you so unhappy."

"Mom, it's not that it makes me unhappy. I love the business. I love this town. And I love you, of course." I finish my plate and bring it to the sink.

"Of course. But hun, I know you loved living in Minneapolis," Mom starts, her face lined with worry.

I cut her off. "Mom, stop. I wouldn't have moved back here and bought a house if I wasn't okay staying long term."

"But did you do that for you? Or for me?" Mom hums. "Or for Dad?" She adds.

"Mom," I sigh, putting my plate in the dishwasher.

"No, I'm serious. I can handle business here if you want to go back to Minneapolis." Mom places her hand on my arm, making sure my attention is focused on her. "I'm sure the guys can pick up the slack, or you can hire a couple of new people."

"No, no. This was Dad's business. It's my business now. I know how to run it, I know the guys. And with Benji gone… I can't leave too." The stress of Benji's move really affected my guys but thankfully, the years I worked at the business during high school and summers in college paid off. I know the business inside and out so taking over wasn't as hard as I expected. All the guys already knew me and respected me so it was easy to keep everything moving smoothly with the transition after my dad passed. "I like the work," I add.

Mom pauses, staring into my soul for a few seconds before she nods in acceptance. "You know you can talk to me about anything though, right?"

"Yes, Mom. I know. And I do." I lean down to kiss her cheek. When I pull back, she has tears in her eyes. "I promise that I am fine. *And*," I say with emphasis, "I will let you know if I need anything or if anything is bothering me."

"I don't know if you're just saying that to placate me but I'll accept it anyway." Mom pulls me down into a tight hug then she forces me to take the leftovers home for myself.

Chapter 32

Shawn

"Shawn! Sweetie, how are you?" Michelle pulls me into a big hug after I shrug off my coat. She takes my coat from me and hangs it up.

"Hey. Thanks, Michelle. I'm doing alright, how are you?"

Michelle chats with me as she leads me further into the office. She gets us both a cup of coffee while she talks. I look around the office and spot Noah sitting in his, chatting animatedly on the phone. Then I spot Dylan's office. I shift a foot until I can see her through the window to her office. She's focused on her screen and I can see her eyebrows are narrowed.

"She'll be right with you, dear," Michelle tells me and leads me back over to the little waiting area.

A few minutes later, right on time, Dylan walks out of her office. She stops short when she sees me in the waiting area. "Oh, hi Shawn. I thought Vivian was coming in today?" Dylan smiles in greeting but looks a little confused.

"Sorry, she sent me in her place."

Dylan chuckles. "It's no worries. Come on in." Dylan brings me to her office and I take a seat across the desk from her. "I started working on a portfolio for the business and one for personal as well. There are a few ideas I have."

Dylan spends a few minutes going over her ideas for the insurance plan money. She has already set aside a budget for Mom's bookstore project so she hasn't included that money in her other plans.

While she talks, I can't help but admire how great she is at her job, how passionate she is. She is so professional and confident. I trust her portfolio and have almost zero questions when she finishes going over everything. I'm a bit sad that our meeting is coming to an end. But then I remember that Mom sent me in with two other topics to cover.

"Oh, I am supposed to ask if you've had a chance to look over the floor plans for the bookstore yet. No worries if you haven't." Dylan's smile grows and she pulls out the floor plan that Mom gave her. Then she pulls up a file on her computer.

"I probably should not be using my work computer for this, nor doing it during work time. But hey, you're a client now, right? We love to go above and beyond here for our clients." Dylan winks at me and I chuckle.

Dylan shows me the ideas she has and multiple ways to change up the layout. "Hopefully, these layouts changes aren't going to mess with structural walls. I tried to differentiate but I'm not entirely sure how well I did. Here, I'll print them out for you to bring to your mom. It might be easier for her to look at them laying flat next to these original plans." She hits print before I can say anything and exits the room with a quick, "Be right back."

When she comes back she hands me a neat folder with all of the printouts tucked away.

"Thanks." I stand to head out but then I remember the other topic Mom mentioned. "Oh, Mom also said you have or had a big meeting with a potential client?" I ask and her face lights up. I smile back and return to my seat, eager to stay longer.

"Oh, my gosh. Yes! It was great. Michelle and I prepared this brilliant portfolio. We had dinner at this fancy place a couple of towns over, and he was so nice and seemed so impressed with my whole spiel. It went great! I already sent over the actual information to him and we have another meeting planned. It was great," she repeats with a big smile. "I only went into the meeting expecting to help out with one portfolio for him but the more we talked, I'm not sure about everything but he said he has a couple he might want to bring over!"

"That's great," I tell her, not entirely understanding how everything works but she is quite pleased so it must be great news. Her smile and energy are contagious, making me smile too. Then I pause, thinking about the dinner. "Wait you were out at dinner with a client yesterday?" I ask, for clarification.

"Yeah," Dylan says, telling me the name of the restaurant and complimenting the food. "Have you been there?"

"Ah, yeah." I chuckle, trying to hide my embarrassment. "Recently, actually," I admit, looking down.

"It's great, isn't it?" Dylan asks before going back to being excited about how well the meeting went. The relief I feel knowing that the date I thought I saw was just a client dinner almost outweighs the embarrassment and guilt I feel knowing I basically spied on her because I was jealous.

"Hey, are you free this weekend?" The words slip out of my mouth before I can stop them.

Dylan looks up a little surprised by my question. "Oh. Uhm, yes, I think so." She pauses to wait for the reason I asked. I hesitate because all I know is that I want to spend more time with her.

"Have you ever been ice fishing?"

Ice fishing? Really? That's the best I can come up with?

Before I can say 'Never mind' or change my mind and think of something better, Dylan's face lights up with excitement, replacing the initial confusion.

"Oh, my gosh. No, I have not been ice fishing. But I have always been sooo curious. Well, not always. I didn't even know it was a thing until I moved here. Heck, I've never even seen a frozen lake. Well, besides catching glimpses of Birch Lake, but I haven't been down to see it yet." She chuckles, her cheeks flushing. "What day were you thinking? Saturday or Sunday? What time? Is ice fishing an early morning thing, or afternoon, or evening?" She clamps her mouth shut, grimacing at all her questions.

When I don't respond right away, Dylan's smile flickers but she catches it. "Oh, I'm sorry. Was that presumptuous of me to assume you were offering to take me?" Dylan laughs an awkward laugh.

"No!" I say a little too loudly. She jumps a bit at my animated response but then she smiles a little, soft smile. "No, I mean, I was offering. That's what I meant." I try to recover from my outburst. "Yes, do you want to go ice fishing Saturday around 4:30? In the evening," I add quickly.

"Uhm, yes, please. I have a pair of boots and snow pants I haven't gotten a chance to wear yet!" She claims happily. "Is there anything I need to bring?"

"No, I'll take care of everything else we need. I already have a hut out on the lake that's mostly prepped. But I'm headed to the store anyway, I'll grab anything else we need tonight and then tomorrow evening, I'll come pick you up. Is that okay?" I ask just to make sure.

"Sounds good!" Dylan hops up with a smile on her face. I stand as well and she walks me to the front of the office. I say goodbye to Michelle and Noah nods at me and then I head out to the store.

Chapter 33

Shawn

I grab a few things from the store to make dinner while we're out on the lake and pick up a few extra items to make sure Dylan will be comfortable. I also texted the rest of the guys who use the hut to see if they were planning to go out Saturday evening. Most of them are busy with other plans but Xander and Kayson let me know they're heading out in the morning to drop a couple of lines but can make themselves scarce if needed. I debate telling them to get lost but it's their space too so instead I just give them a heads-up that I will be dropping by with Dylan. I shut my phone off before they can respond with anything annoying or teasing.

When I arrive at Dylan's apartment Saturday evening, I knock on her door and Dylan opens the door almost immediately and smiles up at me. "Hey, you ready to go?"

"Yes! Let me get my coat on. I've been all dressed up for an hour already. I'm a bit excited," Dylan admits with a grin, grabbing her coat off the hook by the door. She's been wearing her new parka lately and I miss seeing her in my old coat.

"Xander and Kayson are going to be there too if that's okay?" I tell her, in case she feels uncomfortable with the extra company.

Dylan just shrugs, her enthusiasm doesn't wane. She grabs her purse at the last minute before swinging the door shut behind us.

Dylan hops into my truck like it is the most natural thing in the world. I slide into the driver's seat and my heart flutters seeing her settle into her seat. As I start to drive away, I remember the scarf that she left behind.

"Oh, here." I pull out her scarf and hand it to her. Dylan's eyes light up as she takes it from me.

"Oh, my gosh! I have been looking everywhere for that." Dylan wraps the scarf around her neck and poses for me. I chuckle and nod my approval as I drive toward the lake. "Sorry, I guess I didn't clean up your car before giving it back," she adds with a chuckle, her eyes going wide as she stares at the lake. Her eyes glisten with wonder.

"It's fine. I didn't even notice it until the wind whipped it up here," I tell her.

Dylan presses the scarf to her nose, inhaling. I glance over at her and she blushes, looking away from the lake for a second to shoot me a bashful look.

"Sorry," she apologizes again. I quirk my eyebrow at her and her blush deepens while a little smile appears. "It smells good. Like you, or I guess your truck. Which also smells like you."

"Oh?" I shoot another glance at her, trying to focus on the road but enjoying the red creeping up her cheeks.

"Yeah. What? No one has ever told you how amazing you smell?" Dylan smiles, her confidence growing.

"Uhm, no." I drum my fingers on my steering wheel.

"Hm, I'm sure someone has mentioned it before," Dylan doubts me. I shake my head and focus on the road. Well, I focus on where the road ends and the lake begins. "Whoa, are you driving out onto the ice?" Dylan's voice sounds both excited and panicked.

"Yes."

Dylan looks out the window and bounces in her seat like a little kid. "Oh, my gosh. This is so cool. Wow, there are so many cars out here. And so many huts! Which one is yours?"

Instead of responding, I park my truck next to Xander's car and look over at Dylan. "Let's get out and I'll show you."

"Okay!" Dylan looks excited but she pauses as soon as she opens her door.

"What's wrong?" I ask as I pull on my gloves and hat.

"Am I going to fall? I don't know if I can walk across the lake. I've never done this before." Dylan's worries are cute. I chuckle, then get out of the car and walk over to the passenger door. I hold out my hand for hers. She hesitates only a second before sliding her gloved hand into mine. I almost wish that our hands were bare so I could feel her soft hand in mine.

Dylan grips my hand as she gingerly lowers herself to the snow-covered ice. She tests it with one foot first, sliding her foot back and forth, testing the stability. When she realizes there's a lot of snow covering the icy lake, she delicately lowers her other foot. She grips my hand and the truck pretty tightly as she gradually lets the ice take her full weight.

"See? You'll be fine. The layer of snow over the ice is pretty easy to walk on," I say and she looks down at her feet, stomping on the ground once, twice, before nodding in satisfaction.

Chuckling, I go to the back of my truck to grab the things I bought. I don't realize I'm still holding on to Dylan's hand until she follows me to the back of the truck. I drop her hand, reaching for my bag and swinging it over my shoulder.

"Heyyy!" Kayson greets us by swinging open the door to our hut, a beer already in his hand. "Welcome to our casa, Dylan." He steps back, spreading his arms to welcome her in.

"Wow," Dylan says, carefully making her way over to him and stepping into the small space. Kayson returns to his stool beside Xander and takes a swig of his beer. "This place is incredible. Gosh, I am so impressed."

"Are you being sarcastic?" Xander asks, then he looks at me. "Is she being sarcastic?"

"No, no!" Dylan protests. "This is awesome. This is like a little house, on ice!"

The guys chuckle. "Come sit, we left the couch for you two." Xander gestures to the comfiest spot, which also happens to be more of a loveseat than a couch. He winks in my direction. Dylan takes a seat and accepts the fishing pole that Kayson hands her. He helps her get the hole in front of her opened and sets up everything.

Kayson gets up to help me unpack while Xander and Dylan start chatting.

"You want us to head out soon?" Kayson asks with a smirk. I look at him out of the corner of my eye. I desperately want to say yes but I don't have any right to kick them out or be alone with

Dylan. "Ah, don't worry about it, we'll head out soon. We've been out here for too long anyway, not getting any bites either."

Kayson returns to his stool and I squeeze onto the couch next to Dylan. She smiles at me and tries to shift a bit to give me more room but I enjoy feeling her thigh pressed up against mine.

We chat for a few minutes, Dylan mostly keeping the conversation going. She's making my friends laugh and probably scaring away all the fish.

Eventually, Xander hops up and claps his hands. "Okay, Kayson, you ready to go? I need to get some dinner on the way home tonight. I promised Jamie she wouldn't have to cook because we'd catch something for her," he says with a big laugh.

"Ah, I guess that's what I get for letting you drive tonight. If I had taken my own car, I could have stayed longer and hung out with the beautiful Dylan here." Kayson winks at Dylan then claps me on the arm with a big grin. "Anywho, you two have fun."

"Oh, are y'all leaving already?" Dylan looks only slightly disappointed. "We didn't mean to kick you out. There's enough room for all of us here."

"No, no. We've been here since this morning, that's long enough. You two enjoy." Kayson and Xander quickly excuse themselves and hustle out of the ice hut with a wink back in my direction. I roll my eyes but turn my attention back to Dylan, who is still squished onto the couch beside me.

"So…" Dylan and I both start talking at the same time. We both chuckle and gesture for the other person to speak first.

"So, I should apologize." Dylan looks over at me with a slight frown. She looks guilty.

"Why would you need to apologize?"

"The other night, at dinner," she starts and I grunt, remembering that night. "Max's behavior was unacceptable and completely inappropriate."

"No, I'm sorry," I stop her before she can say anything else. "I reacted poorly to him being a dick to you. I shouldn't have. It's none of my business."

Dylan pauses. "He kind of was a dick, wasn't he?" A hint of a smile crosses her lips, I mumble my agreement. "Why did you get so upset?"

"I told you, I didn't like how he was treating you," I say again.

Dylan turns toward me, her legs pressing against me. "But why? Why did it matter to you?" Her eyelids lower slightly as she looks up at me.

I look at her, watching her for a few seconds, but she doesn't say anything. "I think you know why."

"Say it." Dylan places her hand on my leg, her eyes wide, her face animated. I stare back at her. Each of us testing the other.

"You have a boyfriend," I say, instead of what I really want to say. Dylan blinks but then slowly shakes her head. "No?" I ask, needing to hear her say it.

Instead of answering me, Dylan shifts on the small couch until her leg is sliding over mine and she is straddling my lap. She lowers her weight down onto me gently, all of our layers of clothing creating a barrier between us. In a short few seconds, she is straddling my lap, her hands are in my hair, knocking my hat off and her mouth attaches firmly to mine.

I only hesitate a second before I am kissing her back. My arms dart out and I grip her waist in my hands. I squeeze her gently, pulling her closer to me. Dylan moans into my mouth and I take advantage of her open mouth, deepening the kiss. Her hands tighten in my hair, making me grunt.

"Sorry," Dylan breathes out and I mumble a quick reassurance before our lips are pressed together again, leaving no room to talk.

I only release her to rip off my gloves so I can slip my hands under her heavy coat, needing to feel her bare skin. I have to pull up several layers to finally hit her skin and when I do she hisses a bit, my hands still slightly chilly since I wore my driving gloves rather than winter ones. I think about pulling away to apologize but she grips my hair, holding my mouth on hers.

My fingers move aimlessly across her back, up and down before sliding around to her front, touching her stomach gently. Her breath hitches again but I know it isn't because my hands are cold, they've warmed up from the heat of her body.

Instead of continuing north, I return my hands to her hips, then slip them lower to grab her ass. She moans again into my mouth and presses into me. I pick her up and she wraps her legs around me. I set her on the counter after a quick thought, the couch is too small to lay down on. I lean into her, pulling her to the edge of the counter, pressing into her.

After a few minutes of nothing more than our lips and tongues moving together, Dylan's hand pushes against my chest. It takes everything in me to break away from the kiss.

"We should probably... stop," Dylan says, breathlessly.

Disappointment grows in my stomach but I pull myself away from her. Her eyes are wild and her lips are pink and swollen. Dylan's cheeks are flushed a shade of pink and I don't know if it's from the heat between us or the cold that has seeped in since we separated.

"I'm sorry." I run my hands through my hair, embarrassed.

"Oh no. You have nothing to be sorry about. I literally jumped you." Dylan chuckles with self-depreciation.

"Trust me, the feelings were mutual," I grumble, adjusting myself awkwardly. Dylan tries to hide her little smile. "I'm sorry, do you not want to?" I ask, confused by the sudden change.

"Oh, no. Trust me, I do," Dylan says but it doesn't do a good job of making me feel better. "Sorry, that's pretty confusing, isn't it? I very much want to but Max and I… we just broke up. And I guess maybe we hadn't been doing well for a while but I just don't want you to think that you're just a rebound."

"Oh, I wouldn't be offended," I say immediately but that isn't entirely true. I like her too much to just be a rebound. Dylan chuckles at my response but luckily, she shakes her head.

"No, you deserve more than that." Dylan touches my cheek gently. "You know that, right?"

I don't know how to respond so I just give her a soft smile and kiss her once more, gently this time. It's just a quick kiss and then I help her off of the counter right as one of the fishing poles starts going crazy.

"Oh, my gosh! Shawn! I think we've got something," Dylan looks so excited that it almost distracts me from the tightening of my pants. I join her by the pole and we try to reel it in. It only lasts a few seconds before the line goes slack.

"Oh no, did we lose it?" Dylan pouts. I chuckle and nod.

"Here, let's pull it out and see if we need to put a new piece of bait on it," I say and she goes to work on reeling the line in. I grab a container from the counter.

Dylan squeals in shock when I open the container. "What is that?" She shrieks as I lift a wiggling creature from the container.

"It's a wax worm," I tell her with a chuckle, holding it out for her to see. She scrunches her nose in disgust but doesn't back away. "Do you want to put it on the hook?" I offer, curious to see her reaction.

"Uhm, I think I'll leave that to the expert," Dylan says, stepping out of the way so I can reset the hook and line.

"There, not too hard," I say after I've sent the line back down. Dylan scoffs and rolls her eyes at me. I chuckle. "Are you hungry?" I ask.

She looks up at me, her eyebrows raised but she smirks. "As long as you wash your hands," she retorts.

We spend the rest of the evening in an easy back-and-forth. She tells me about her life and family back in Dallas and asks about my life in Birch Lake, and my time in Minneapolis.

The line starts making noises suddenly and we both jump in out seats.

"Oh, my gosh. Did we get another one?" Dylan asks, setting her food aside and jumping up to check. I join her and watch as she tries to reel in the line. "Eek, help please," Dylan says, struggling with the line.

I step in behind her, wrapping my arms around her. She leans back against my chest and looks up at me over her shoulder. "Are you 'Ghosting' me?" She says with a giggle.

"What are you talking about?" I pretend not to know as I help her reel in the line. "Focus," I try to redirect her.

Dylan giggles again, seeing through me. I shake my head but don't admit anything. Instead, I focus on getting the fish in without loosing it again.

This time, we manage to pull the fish in. Dylan squeals again, seeing it dangling from the hook.

"My first catch!" She exclaims. I chuckle and take a step back to take in the moment. I grab my phone, snapping a picture of her celebrating next to the fish. "Hey!" She catches me taking the picture.

"Oh, sorry. I can delete it if you want. I just thought you should have a picture of your first catch," I explain, starting to feel embarrassed.

"No!" She giggles. "That's great, thank you. I'm not used to someone doing that" she says with a slight frown before the smile returns. "Can I hold it for a picture?" She asks.

"Of course," I chuckle. I help her pick up the fishing pole and hold the fish away from her while she decides how to pose, then I let the fish lay flat. "Okay, quickly. We have to throw the fish back soon," I tell her.

"Of course, sorry." Dylan grins and poses with the fish, shifting a few times to get a couple of angles too. I snap pictures while she moves. "Okay, let me see!" She hands me the pole and I detach the fish, slipping it back into the water while she looks through the pictures I took.

"Any of them good?" I ask, putting away the rest of the supplies to close up for the evening. I hadn't realized how late it had gotten until I grabbed my phone to take pictures and saw the time.

"So, many good ones. Please send me all of them," she laughs. "And thank you," Dylan says, a brilliant smile on her face as she hands the phone back to me.

"For what?" I ask. "It's not a big deal."

"No, it is. I really appreciate it. Taking pictures, and this whole evening. It's been so much fun." Dylan approaches me with a sweet, shy smile on her lips. She slips her arms around my neck, leaning into me. I grin down at her and wrap my arm behind her back, pulling her closer.

"I'm glad you enjoyed it," I admit.

"Oh, I did. All of it." Her smile turns seductive and I can't help myself. I lean down, pausing before my mouth hits hers.

"All of it?" I whisper against her lips.

"Mhm," she hums against my lips. I feel the vibration deep in my chest and I lean the rest of the way to capture her mouth with mine.

"I should get you home," I say a few minutes later, leaning my forehead against hers to catch my breath.

"You should," she agrees, equally breathless and not at all believable.

"In a few minutes," I amend, feeling her tongue on my bottom lip.

"A few minutes," Dylan agrees.

More than a few minutes later, Dylan and I finally detached from each other. We quickly bundle up in our coats and make our way back to the truck, which is warm thankfully, since I started up while we were pulling out coats on. Dylan holds my hand the whole drive back to her apartment and it's harder than I want it to be leaving her at her apartment and going back to my house alone. But it was a perfect evening.

Chapter 34

Dylan

I can't stop thinking about Saturday. I've been sitting at my desk for half an hour, staring at the screen and only thinking about Shawn and how amazing his lips felt on mine, and how disgusting wax worms are.

It's Monday morning and slow so I don't feel too bad daydreaming. A ping on my computer pulls me out of the memory. Looking down, I see that Kevin has sent me a message.

Kevin: Do you have time to chat? Update on that Dallas position.

Dylan: Free now.

My heart starts to beat faster as my mind races thinking about what the news might be. My desk phone rings a few seconds later and I have to take a deep breath before answering.

"Hey, Kevin," I try to keep my voice polite and as friendly as possible as I brace myself for whatever Kevin wants to tell me.

"Hey, Winter girl." Kevin sounds like he's grinning. I roll my eyes, thankful that we aren't talking face to face so I don't have to hide my annoyed facial expressions.

"'Winter girl'?" I shake my head.

"Yeah, 'cause you're in Minnesota, and it's winter," Kevin explains with a sigh.

"What is the update, Kevin?" I ignore him and press forward, needing to hear the news.

Kevin sighs, taking his time before finally telling me the update. "That position I mentioned? It's coming available soon."

"How soon?" I hold in my excitement.

"They're holding interviews this week so I'd say a couple of weeks before the start date," Kevin reluctantly shares the information with me. "I can get you an interview," he admits.

"When?" I ask, knowing there has to be some catch to his offer.

"Wednesday," he hums and I can hear that grin once again.

"Wednesday?" I repeat. Of course, there was a catch. "This Wednesday? Like in two days?" Tampering my annoyance is getting harder.

"Yep," the smack of his lips grates on my nerves and I can tell how pleased he is with himself. "So, you want the interview slot?"

"Yeah," I say without thinking about it. This is what I've been waiting for, of course, I have to go at least interview for the position. "What time is the interview?"

"9:30." Kevin's smirk is obvious. I'm sure there were other time slots available but he wanted to make it even more annoying for me.

"Great! I will be there!" I respond cheerfully. I can hear him grumbling on the other end of the phone. "Is there anything else, Kevin?"

"How's Minnesota? You got frostbite yet?" Kevin teases. I roll my eyes again. Michelle narrows her eyes at me from her desk, checking if I'm okay. I give her a thumbs up, shaking my head and gesturing at the phone.

"Thanks for getting me the interview, Kevin." I don't tell him that I actually did catch a cold. He doesn't deserve to know that.

I know I could have set up the interview by myself but since Kevin is my boss, it'll show that he supports the move.

Kevin mumbles a bit more, trying to think of something sassy to say but he takes too long so I cheerfully tell him goodbye and that I look forward to seeing him soon. I hang up before my voice turns too sarcastic that he can't miss it.

Once I hang up, the reality of the situation hits me. I've been here in Birch Lake for a month. I knew this position in Dallas was coming. I really wanted it, I deserved it. I told myself to stick it out for a month and then quickly get back to Dallas, but now that I've been living here and getting to know everybody, I'm a little bit less excited to leave.

"Michelle," I call out.

"Yes, dear?" Michelle comes over to my office, standing in the doorway. "Everything okay?"

"Yeah, I think I'm going to grab some lunch. Can I bring you back anything?" I get up and start putting on my layers.

"I'm okay. I brought some leftovers with me today." Michelle pauses and looks at me closely. "Are you sure you're okay, hun?"

"I just have to think over some things," I admit. She keeps looking at me with that same motherly-concern look. "I'm fine, really."

"You've been here a month," Michelle points out. I nod. "And I noticed there is a job opening in Dallas. Is that why you look so stressed?"

"I don't look that stressed," I return. Michelle gives me a look and I shrug. "Okay, maybe."

"Is that what the phone call was about?"

"Yeah," I tell her. "My boss is a tad annoying and this whole move and prospective job has made him even more intolerable. Well, you probably know about Kevin and his reputation."

"Ah. Yes, I do." Michelle nods in understanding. "I am here if you need someone to talk to, but I get it if you need time to think on your own," Michelle lets me know. I nod and give her a hug, which makes her even more concerned.

"Thanks, Michelle." I grab my purse and walk her back to her desk. "You sure you don't want me to bring you back anything."

"I'm good, dear. You go enjoy, go think over everything." Michelle waves me off and I head out into the cold. The wind whips my face as I walk down the street. It helps clear my mind.

Instead of going to get lunch, I swing by the bookstore, wanting to talk to Vivian. She's kind of become my confidant since I've been out here.

"Vivian," I call out when I open the door of the bookstore, the little bell jingling.

"Dylan?" Vivian pops out from the back and a wide smile stretches over her face when she sees me. "What brings you by?"

"I just got off the phone with my boss and that position in Dallas is available soon. They're starting to interview candidates and my boss set my interview up for Wednesday, this Wednesday," I let everything spill out as Vivian waits patiently.

"Oh. Okay." Vivian brings me over to the little sitting area in the store and we take chairs facing each other. "Explain."

"Okay," I start as we settle into our chairs. "Before I moved out here, my boss told me there was a position opening up in Dallas but I'd have to come out here first for a bit to see how I did out here in the position. You know, Michelle told me to give it a month, when I first moved out here. And I have, and now I have an interview back home…" I trail off, looking down at my hands in my lap.

"Do you want the job in Dallas?" Vivian asks the hard-hitting questions. "Or do you like the job here?"

"I don't know. The job in Dallas is what I've been working up to," I admit.

Vivian hums, thinking. She leans back in her chair and taps her fingers on her cheek. After a few seconds of silence, she leans forward, toward me. "I noticed you didn't answer my second question."

I sigh. "It's great. I love it. I love Michelle. Noah's okay. I love the freedom I have. Just recently, I had a great meeting with a new client and he transferred more money and accounts over to us than we initially expected. And this town," I gush. "I mean, come on. It is so beautiful and adorable and even though it is way too cold here, I love it." The smile on Vivian's face reflects my own. Her eyes sparkle. "And I love you too," I say with a pathetic little laugh.

"Oh, dear. You know I love you. This town is so blessed to have you here. But of course, we would understand if you needed to go back to Dallas for your career, or your personal life," Vivian adds and I frown. That's also true. I hadn't even thought about the personal life aspect.

My friends are back in Dallas. But I've made some great ones here too. Max is back in Dallas. But honestly, do I even want to get back together with him? Whether I go back to Dallas or not. I'm not sure getting back together is in the cards for us.

"What do you think I should do, Vivian?" I practically beg, my voice whiney even to my ears.

"Hun, it's up to you but if you want my opinion?" She asks and I nod eagerly. "I think you should go to Dallas for the interview. Just do the interview, maybe get lunch with your friends, and enjoy the sunshine. Honestly, you don't even have to worry about the situation unless you get the job offer," Vivian adds and then she shakes her head with a smile. "Which of course you will because you're great at your job."

"Thanks." I chuckle. "But you're right. I should at least go to the interview. Then we'll take it from there."

"Exactly." Vivian reaches over and pats my leg.

"Okay, I guess I am going to Dallas on Wednesday," I relent and Vivian smiles, nodding in approval. "Or maybe Tuesday night. Shoot, I need to check plane tickets."

"Oh, yeah. You definitely should," Vivian chuckles.

"Eh, I'll do it when I get back to the office." I chuckle and shrug it off, turning my attention back to Vivian.

"Oh! Do you have time right now to talk about the store?" Vivian asks with a grin.

"Yes! Oh, my gosh. I have so many ideas. Did Shawn show you those plans?" I ask

"Yes, he did. I loved them!" The little bell above the door goes off and we both turn our attention to the door. "Oh speaking of Shawn. Hi, honey!" Vivian calls out and waves him over.

Chapter 35

Shawn

Grabbing the lunchbox from my car, I head toward the back of Mom's bookstore. I hope she'll enjoy the lunch I made, and not question my motives for having lunch with her today.

When I enter the back door, I can hear voices in the distance. She must have a customer in the store. I take my time in the back, putting the food in the mini-fridge in the back then making my way out front. I spot Mom and Dylan sitting together, talking about something serious. A smile stretches across my face. I haven't seen Dylan since our kiss, which was only two nights ago, but I haven't stopped thinking about her.

I start to make my way over to them but then stop short when I hear them mention Dallas. I quickly step out of their line of sight and do something I'm not proud of, I eavesdrop, again.

"Okay, I guess I am going to Dallas on Wednesday." I hear Dylan say. She doesn't sound too excited but she also doesn't sound put out by the idea. I stop listening after that and head to the back of the store again.

Does she really want to leave? Will she leave?

My heart starts to beat faster. What will happen to us? Is there even an us? We only had one kiss, but it was a great kiss. Am I too late to ask for more?

There are so many questions that make my head spin. I step out the back door, letting the cold air sting my cheeks. Would she really leave without telling me? Why would she have to tell me anything? I scold myself.

I round the building, wanting to make my presence known so I don't have to eavesdrop again. I make my way to the front of the store and open the front door, the little tinkle of the bell indicating my entrance.

"Oh speaking of Shawn. Hi, honey!" Mom waves me over. I make my way over to them and my heart beats faster at Dylan's cute, sly little smirk. I can tell she's thinking about Saturday as well. I can still feel the heat of her against my fingertips.

"What brings you by, dear?" Mom asks when neither Dylan nor I say anything. She looks between the two of us but decides to ignore the obvious tension.

"I brought lunch." I gesture to the back of the store where I left the food.

"Oh, that's sweet. Let me go flip the sign then we can all sit and have lunch, and discuss some design ideas." Mom stands with a sparkle in her eyes.

I slide into the seat she vacated and focus on Dylan's face. She's smiling slyly at me. She leans in to keep her voice low.

"Hi. Thanks for taking me out to your ice hut Saturday. I had fun," her voice twinkles. "How are you?" Dylan asks when I don't say anything.

"You're moving back to Dallas?" I ask, ignoring her question and reminiscing about last night.

Dylan's facial expression changes from playful to confused, her eyebrows knit together and she tilts her head at me.

"I overheard you talking to Mom," I admit.

"Are you upset?" Dylan asks, sitting back in her chair, watching my expression closely. I try to fix my features to neutral but I came in too hot and she knows I'm upset.

"You didn't answer my question." I cross my arms, looking back at her. She pauses, evaluating me.

"I have an interview for a position in Dallas, in my old office," she clarifies. Her eyes scan my face and I struggle to hide my annoyance and disappointment. Her lips curve up in a smile, I narrow my eyes at her.

"What?" I growl.

"You'd miss me," she says as her smile grows. Dylan's eyes begin to sparkle as I shake my head, denying her statement. "Yes, yes you would. Don't deny it," she teases me, leaning toward me again.

Her smile makes my heart hammer and I want to smile back, I like her teasing. I felt heat rush to my cheeks because she's not wrong and I'm slightly embarrassed about how quickly I became attached to her.

"You're running away. Running back to your boyfriend," I practically spit at her with more venom than intended, trying to hold onto my slipping anger. Dylan's face pinches a little at my attitude.

"You know that we broke up. I'm pretty sure you were aware when you had your tongue down my throat on Saturday," Dylan throws back at me and I huff at her. She smirks, crossing her arms just as defensive as I am. "Not that I have to explain anything to you, but I knew about this job opening before I moved out here. My boss told me to stick it out up here for the time being and then when the position opened up… it was always the plan to go back to Dallas."

Dylan's explanation only makes me feel worse. I feel cheated. I want to spend more time with her. I want her to fall in love with this town, and with me, the way I've fallen for her.

No, I don't feel that way. It's too soon to feel like that. All we did was kiss. Well, it was more than kissing. And I wanted more. But it looks like I might not have the opportunity to.

"So, are you leaving?" I ask, point blank.

Dylan blinks at me then looks over my shoulder. I turn to see Mom coming back with our lunch on a tray.

"Are you leaving?" I ask again, needing an answer.

"For the interview. Yes, yes I am," Dylan says stubbornly, her eyes narrowed at me.

I stand up suddenly.

"Whoa, watch out, dear." Mom chuckles, moving the tray away from me, and setting it down on the little table between two chairs.

"I should leave you two. I didn't mean to interrupt," I say, needing to get away before I hurt Dylan's feelings or scare her off by confessing that I don't want her to leave.

Mom looks back and forth between Dylan and me. Dylan looks up at me for a few seconds before also standing. "No, it's okay. I should get back to work. Thank you for talking to me, Vivian," Dylan turns to Mom and gives her a tight hug. Then she turns to me, she hesitates like she wants to say something but she just gives me a sad smile. "Good to see you, Shawn."

Then she walks out the door of the shop, the little bell announcing her exit.

"What did you say to her?" Mom turns to me, swatting my shoulder before putting her hands on her hips.

"What? Nothing," I protest, reaching for my sandwich off the tray. Mom swats my hand, giving me a pointed look. "What? I can't have any of the food I brought?"

"No, you can't. Not until after you explain why she looked so dejected and left quickly when we had plans for lunch."

"I didn't know you had plans." I shrug, reaching for my sandwich again. This time, she let's me pick it up. I shove the sandwich in my mouth to avoid answering any further questions.

"It's just an interview, Shawn," Mom points out and I grunt over the sandwich. "She'll come back after the interview," she pauses, looking me over. Mom touches my arm gently. "You should tell her then."

"Tell her what?" I try not to choke on my sandwich. She hands me a water bottle to wash it down. She gives me another one of her pointed, motherly looks.

Chapter 36

Dylan

Wednesday comes quicker than I want and before long, I'm checking my phone for the tenth time since landing in Dallas. The plane delay is making me so anxious. We have been sitting on the runway, waiting for our gate to become available and I am stressing. I was already cutting it close coming in the day of the interview but now I won't have a chance to go to my old apartment before the interview. Although, that might be a good thing because I'm not sure if Max will be there, and I don't think I want to see him before the interview. I don't have time to deal with all that.

Finally, our plane lurches forward and we pull into our gate. There are a few annoyed cheers as the flight crew welcome us in and tell us where to find our bags. Thankfully, I did not check my bag and have access to it right away.

I wait impatiently for the rows in front of me to get off the plane before I grab my bag and hustle through the airport. My phone shows that I have 15 minutes before my ride share gets here so I weave in and out of the crowd and squeeze myself into a tight stall in the bathroom. I strip off my comfy plane clothes and pull on a blazer and pencil skirt. It may not be Minnesota but it is still winter and Dallas occasionally gets cold, so I leave on my sweater and thermal leggings. I'll probably regret that decision later but I don't have time to dwell on it right now.

As I leave the stall, I give a polite, apologetic smile to the next woman waiting in line. Primping in front of the mirror in a busy bathroom is not ideal but it's the best I can do right now.

With minutes to spare, I meet my car out front and gratefully let him take my bag to load it into the trunk. I sit back in the car and close my eyes. I should be prepping for this interview but I know my job and I love it. And I know I would be perfect for this position, so I take this opportunity to get my breathing and nerves under control.

"Miss, we're here," my driver tells me what seems like seconds later. I must have fallen asleep, whoops.

"Thank you." I get out of the car, take my bags with me, and head into the building.

Nothing has changed in the month that I've been gone. The office is still shiny and new, and very modern compared to the office I've grown used to in Minnesota. I take the elevator up to our floor and find Mary sitting at her perch behind three monitors with a phone in her hand. She hangs up when she sees me and gets up with a grin.

"Lyn! It's so good to see you!" Mary greets me with my infamous nickname. I try not to grimace and instead pull her into a hug.

"Mary, so good to see you too." I smile in greeting as she goes back to her desk.

She ignores the ringing phone as she pops a candy into her mouth. "You excited for your interview? I've seen some of the other candidates they've interviewed, yikes. You are by far my favorite option. Probably the best too," Mary adds with a wink.

"Thanks," I chuckle. "Hey, do you think I can store this behind your desk? My flight was delayed so I didn't have a chance to go back to the apartment." I hold up my bag and notice her smile has grown tight and forced.

"Oh, sure. No worries," Mary accepts the bag and tucks it under her desk. Her phone goes off again and this time she does answer. She nods, "Yup, she's here. Great, I'll send her in."

"That about me?" I ask and she nods.

"Yes, they're ready for you in Meeting Room 3. Don't worry, you're not off to your 'Doom', the other rooms were just booked first," Mary adds with a wink. "Good luck!"

"Thank you, Mary."

I make my way to "The Doom Room" and find Kevin waiting for me outside the room with a smirk on his face. I brace myself and try to smile politely.

"Hi, Kevin. Good to see you," I lie through gritted teeth.

"Lyn," Kevin says, letting the nickname linger. He chuckles at my annoyed look. "How's Minnesota?"

"It's great actually," I let him know with a shrug. His smile droops a little but then a thought hits him and he grins.

"So, does that mean you're not interested in moving forward with this interview?" Kevin looks too excited about the idea.

"No, Kevin. I am still interested in this position. That's why I flew in last minute to be able to attend this interview," I tell him with narrowed eyes. "Now, if you'll excuse me." I brush past him and head into the meeting room. Marvin, the Southern CFO sits on one side of the conference table, next to him sits our hiring director, Geraldine.

"Good morning, Dylan," Geraldine says, looking up from her paperwork to greet me.

"Lyn," Kevin comments, coming into the room much to my annoyance. He takes the seat beside me and I slide over to distance us a bit.

"Dylan is fine, thank you," I say quickly.

"How has Minnesota been treating you?" Geraldine makes small talk while Marvin continues to look over the papers in front of him.

"Well, I learned pretty quickly that my winter attire for Dallas was not nearly enough for the Minnesota weather," I admit with a laugh and Geraldine chuckles. "But it's been great. Michelle and Noah are great coworkers. It is a bit odd to only have two though."

"Oh, I'm sure." Geraldine chuckles again, nodding her head in agreement.

Marvin looks up from his paper and gives me a polite smile. There's almost zero recognition on his face. I guess he must have forgotten that we've met each other a few times.

"Oh, Dylan this is Marvin," Geraldine introduces us and I reach across the shake his hand.

Marvin shakes my hand and then he and Kevin exchange a nod. "Alright let's get this interview started."

"Thank you for flying in for this interview," Marvin says, standing to walk me out of the room.

"Of course. It's good to be back in Dallas," I say sincerely. As much as I've been enjoying Birch Lake, I have missed Dallas.

"Well, hopefully, we'll get you back here soon," Marvin says, glancing away from me in a way that lets me know he's just being polite. He probably doesn't even realize what he's saying.

"Thank you. I look forward to hearing about next steps," I say and then leave them to their after-interview discussions. I have a lot to think about as well.

"I'll be right out, wait for me," Kevin says over his shoulder to me. I nod and shut the door on my way out.

I walk around the floor, saying hi to my coworkers and going to grab a coffee while I wait for Kevin. I could probably sit down at an empty computer and do a little work but I don't plan on staying in the office too long.

Mary and a few of my other coworkers are in the kitchen area for a coffee break so I step in to join them.

"Lyn! It's great to see you," one of the men who I used to be an associate for says and I grimace but don't correct him. It's not worth it.

"Good to see you too," I say instead. I want to jump into their conversation but I see Kevin coming down the hallway.

"Let's do this quickly," Kevin joins the group, grumbling as he directs me to follow him to his office. I say a quick goodbye to the rest of my coworkers and hurry off down the hall after Kevin.

Once we're seated across from each other, Kevin clears his throat and looks up at me. "So, I think that went well. You should hear back later this week but it looks like it'll be good news."

"Really? That's good," I say but lack enthusiasm which Kevin notices and it annoys him.

"You're not happy about this?" Kevin calls me out with a heavy sigh, looking frustrated with me.

"Oh no, I'm pleased it went well," I say, still thinking it over.

Kevin narrows his eyes at me. "This is the next step in your career," Kevin points out.

"Technically, it's the same position I have now in Birch Lake," I remind him.

"Yeah, but that's there. This position is here, in Dallas," Kevin says with a smirk. "I would think you'd want the position here? There are lots of opportunities in the area and this is your home," he adds.

"I know. It's a lot to think about," I admit. I know what the job here means for my career but at the same time, I keep thinking about what Birch Lake might hold for my future.

"Are you seriously considering staying?" Kevin asks, incredulously. He's as shocked as me by my hesitation. When I was first shipped off to Minnesota just a few weeks ago, I had no doubt that I would accept the new job right away to keep me in Dallas but now, I have a lot to think about.

"I don't know, Kevin," I say with a sigh. "I guess, yes, I am considering all of my options."

"Wow," Kevin says then his computer beeps at him, indicating a new IM. He ignores me to stare at his screen. I guess I'm officially dismissed.

"Good to see you, Kevin," I say as I get up from the chair and head to the door.

Kevin grunts and waves his hand at me. "I'll let you know what they decide."

"Okay," I say and head out the door.

I wave goodbye to the people I pass on my way back to the lobby where Mary is back at her desk, blowing on a steaming cup of coffee.

"So, how'd the interview go?" Mary asks, looking up from her drink. She slides my bag to me and I swing it onto my shoulder.

"It went well, I think," I tell her, leaning on the counter to grab a mint for the road.

"That's great! So, we'll see you back here soon?" She asks and I shrug nonchalantly. "You better hurry home. I miss our nights outs. Especially after a long day of meetings, ugh."

"I know," I chuckle. "There are so many good places out here for after work drinks," I admit. I didn't think Mary and I were very close outside of work but I guess she was my closest friend in the office and it makes me happy to think that someone here missed me. I know Kevin sure hasn't, but the feeling is mutual.

"Right? Are there any good places in that small town in Michigan that they set you up in?" Mary teases.

"Minnesota," I correct then smile. "There's one pretty good bar," I tell her, thinking about the few times I've been.

"Only one?" Mary laughs and I don't like her mocking tone.

I laugh to cover my disdain for her tone. "Yeah, just the one. A great one though," I add.

"Dang, that town really is tiny." Mary chuckles, taking another sip of her drink.

"Yeah. Hey, I've got to run. Max is picking me up and I don't want to keep him waiting," I tell her.

"Oh, I ran into him the other night!" She tells me, tapping a well manicured finger on her chin. "He was wth some girl with an animal name. Guess they were meeting up with your friends. He was a bit rude though, like he was trying to get rid of me quickly," Mary relays the story with an eye roll. "Girl was real catty too. Oh! That might have been her name!" Mary exclaims.

"Oh," I say when I realize who she means. "Kitty." Duh.

"Yeah, sure," Mary says with a shrug. "Very friendly with the guys around her."

"Yeah, that sounds like her," I agree with an annoyed chuckle. I wonder if that's why Max was so keen on this 'break'. It should upset me but I guess I'm not entirely innocent either. "Alright, I'd better head out," I tell Mary.

She nods at me and wiggles her fingers as a goodbye as her attention returns to the phones on her desk.

I ride the elevator back down to the lobby and check my phone. I gave Max an estimate of when the meeting was going to be over and I make it out the front door just as his car is pulling up in front of the building.

"Thanks for picking me up," I say as I get in the car after an awkward hug. "And for taking the day off."

"Of course. I've had a lot to think about but I'm glad you're here now," Max says, driving away from the building and heading back to our apartment.

"Yeah, it's nice to be back home. Much warmer," I add with a chuckle. I want to bring up what Mary mentioned but I'd rather save that for when I have more energy.

"I'll bet," Max says, his eyes focused on the tricky traffic leaving the downtown business area and heading for our apartment.

Chapter 37

Dylan

"Wow," I comment as we step into our apartment. There's a musky smell in the air and dishes lining the counters.

"I've been busy," Max says with a shrug.

"Too busy to clean up after each meal?" I chuckle, my arms starting to itch at the uncleanliness of the apartment. The further into the place I go, the worse it gets. There are food containers on the coffee table and little gnats fly away with the sweep of his hand.

"You were always particular about how to clean and a great cook," Max explains as he shoves the trash into a trash bag he grabbed from the kitchen.

"Hm. Thanks," I say, noncommittally.

I watch as he does a general cleaning of the apartment while I stand by just watching. He glances at me every so often and I know he's waiting for me to jump in like I usually do, especially when he's cleaning so poorly. He's just picking up containers and used napkins but leaving the grime and grease rings.

The weaponized incompetence might have worked on me before but living in Minnesota and taking care of myself, and having Shawn come over to handle things when I couldn't, has really changed my perspective on my relationship with Max. I want to be a mother one day but not to my partner. It's really been a load off to only have to clean up after myself this past month.

Leaving Max in the living room, I walk to the bedroom and notice the state of things in here as well. It's not great. The bed is unmade and might be the same dirty sheets that were on the bed when I left. Max's clothes are strewn across the floor and I have to push them aside with my foot to get to my side of the bed.

Something about my side of the bed looks off to me but there's so much chaos in the room that I can't place what it is. I heave my suitcase onto the bed and go to the closet to find leftover packing boxes from when we first moved in together.

"What are you doing?" Max asks, coming into the room with an empty trash bag. He doesn't make a move to clean up though.

"Packing," I tell him as I begin to fill the first box.

"I thought the interview went well?"

Max drops onto the bed with gusto, enough force to jostle my moving box and suitcase. I stabilize my things before going to the dresser and digging through it. It seems like some of my t-shirts are missing but I can't say for certain if they aren't sitting in an unopened box in my apartment in Birch Lake.

"Well, it did. I think. But I'm not sure when the offer will be presented or the time frame for the start of the job, so I thought it was best to gather more things that I had forgotten and want with me in Birch Lake," I inform him and he squints at me, confused by the conversation. I sigh.

"Do you not want the job?" He asks, pushing his foot against the box to get my attention. I fold another shirt and set it inside the box. I don't know why I'm packing them but as soon as I stepped into this apartment, I got the sudden urge to get everything that belongs to me out of here. That might just be because it's pretty grim in here now that his maid and cook is gone.

"Technically, I have the same job," I point out. When Max looks even more confused, I explain. "The interview I had today is for the same job title as the one I got when I moved to Birch Lake. The position might be a little different because it would be out of a bigger office with more coworkers, probably more clients too but it's essentially the same job."

"I don't see how that could be. You told me you worked with two other people in Minnesota," Max points out.

"Well, yes. But my team here in Dallas wouldn't be much different. We would just be in an office with lots of other teams and other departments on the same floor or at least in the same building. In Birch Lake, it's just the one team," I try to explain to him but he's already looking bored. He was never very interested in my work. Which I don't blame him, if I didn't love finance, I probably wouldn't care to hear all the details either.

"Hm," Max replies, probably not knowing what else to say. Or maybe because he's stopped listening. "So, what do you want to do? I took the rest of the day off for you," he reminds me, laying back on the bed with what I'm sure he thinks is a seductive look.

"Yes, that was very thoughtful of you. I didn't expect it since you broke up with me the last time we saw each other," I point out, trying to hint that he's not getting any from me.

Max sits up, looking miffed. "That's not what I said. I expressed my desire for a break. I mean you ditched me to go live in Minnesota, that's basically Canada, which is a whole other country," Max whines a bit before shifting back to his seduction tactic. "But that doesn't mean I don't love you and stopped wanting you," he says but his words fall flat.

"Max," I say with a sigh as he moves to the edge of the bed, pushing my things away to get closer to me.

"Yes, baby?"

"You broke up with me, or wanted a break," I correct when he frowns at me. "I appreciate you picking me up and letting me stay here." At our shared apartment. "And for taking the day off for me. But I don't know what you're expecting out of this visit."

"It's just a visit?" Max asks. "I was hoping you would see how much better you have things here after a month in that dreary snowscape. Then you would come running back to my open arms," Max tries to entice me, putting on one of his charming smiles. And if I hadn't had Shawn's pouty smirk on my brain the last few days, or weeks, I might have fallen for it but I stay strong. Especially after Mary's story about Max and Kitty, I'm more than a little put off.

"I don't know," I admit. "I really like Birch Lake. I like the town. I like my coworkers. I like the people who live there," I say, a small smile growing on my face as I think about Birch Lake and all that awaits me when I fly back in a couple of days.

"Are you serious?" Max asks, affronted by my admission.

"I am serious," I tell him. "I wish you could have stayed longer and seen how wonderful the town is." Okay, now I sound a little dreamy. It isn't a fairy tale but it is close, in my honest opinion. And if Max hadn't been so moody and one-track minded, he might have actually liked Birch Lake.

"Dylan, please, be realistic. Your future is here, in Dallas," Max tries to persuade me. "I've had time to think it over and work on myself these last few weeks and I'm ready to move forward with our relationship and get back together, but that really only works if you're here too."

I sigh. It's not even noon and I'm already exhausted. "I'm still considering all of my options," I admit and he looks relieved, even though I most certainly did not say I was considering his idea of getting back together. I guess Kitty isn't doing it for him. The thought makes me chuckle. Before he asks why, I pat the box in front of me. "Why don't I take a pause on packing, you can take a pause on cleaning." I look around because he's been laying on the bed the whole time he's been in here and not one item has made it's way to the trash bag laying beside him. "Let's take a break and get lunch, okay?"

"Yeah." Max nods. "I think that's a good idea. And maybe we can go to some of your favorite places around Dallas. We'll get you to fall in love with this place all over again," Max says with confidence and I'm not sure if he's talking about Dallas or himself.

"Okay," I relent. "And maybe while we're gone, you can hire someone to come clean the apartment?" I suggest and he nods again. "I would have preferred if it was cleaned before I got here but better late than never," I add with a chuckle.

"Definitely," Max says, looking down at his phone, not at all understanding how disappointed I am that he left the place a mess and didn't think to clean up before my visit. "Okay, booked! That was easy."

"Okay, great. Let me change out of my interview outfit. I'll meet you in the living room," I say, trying to indicate that he should leave the room while I change.

"Sounds good," he says but he doesn't leave the room, he just continues to stare at his phone.

"Okay then," I mumble under my breath then grab a pair of jeans and a light sweater and go to change in the bathroom.

The bathroom is small enough that Max wasn't able to do too much damage thankfully. I hang up a dirty towel before setting my clothes on the toilet lid. I lean against the sink and look into the mirror. I thought I would look paler coming back from a winter up north but my skin is lightly tanned and I can only assume it's from the bright sun shining off the brilliant white snow.

I change quickly then reenter the bedroom where Max is sill laying in the same spot. "Ready?" I ask.

He glances up from his phone and gives me an appraising look. "I'm ready." He climbs off the bed and follows me out of the apartment.

Our first stop is for a delicious lunch at our favorite barbecue joint. I'm embarrassed to say how messy my face looks as I devour my meal quickly. It's delicious and one of the many things I've missed about Dallas while tucked away in Birch Lake. I might have to ask for a recipe or two to bring back with me, not that I'd ever be able to recreate the meal but I can always try. Maybe Shawn know how to cook meat.

Almost as if he can feel me thinking about Birch Lake, about Shawn, Max glances at me. He looks embarrassed as well. I grin at him and his annoyance fades a bit. "See? There's so many things you'll miss out on if you leave for good," he points out.

"I was just thinking about that," I say around a mouthful of brisket. I grimace at my garbled words and grab a napkin to wipe most of the sauce off my face. Thankfully, the order I get is best eaten with a fork so my hands are still relatively clean. I take a swig of my water to help clear my throat. "I love Texas barbecue but I'm sure they've got a restaurant or two near me," I say, my accent coming out as I take another big bite of my meal.

"Not the way Texas makes it," Max reminds me and I grumble a bit. It's true. I'm sure they have good BBQ but nothing beats my favorite Texas BBQ joint.

"You might have a point," I relent with a sigh but I don't let the thought get me down.

When we finish eating, mostly in silence, I clean my hands and stand up. "Where to next?" I ask, getting excited about revisiting the town I love and have lived in for so many years.

"Wherever you want to go," Max offers.

"An art museum?" I suggest.

Max looks displeased at this idea even though I didn't specify which museum. Of course, I should have realized that when he said 'wherever you want', he really meant wherever I want as long as it's something he's interested in too.

"Okay, so not the art museum, how about the Zoo?" I try another option. "It's nice enough out that it might be a little chilly but at least we won't be sweating."

Max smiles at the memory. One of our earlier dates was at the Zoo, during the dead of summer, and it was a nasty experience. The Zoo was awesome, but the weather was not. I'm surprised we continued dating after that cranky and hot day.

"An escape room?" Max asks.

"Not today," I say immediately. I cannot be locked up in a room with Max right now. Especially trying to solve clues to get out of the room, Max was never good at listening to directions. "I would suggest Sea Life but that's a bit far away, especially this time of day, the traffic wouldn't be good."

"So, home for a movie?" Max pushes.

I sigh. "Sure. I have some work I need to do so I guess that works for me," I say, standing up to leave the restaurant.

Once we're back at our apartment, which is thankfully clean now, I get my work bag from the bedroom and bring it out to the living room. Max sits down on the couch with me, bringing his computer out to do some work too. He puts on a movie without consulting me but I guess that gives me reason to focus on work.

"I think I'm going to go shower," I tell Max with a yawn, noticing the sun has gone down now, must be getting on dinner time.

Max nods, staring at his phone now even with another movie running in the background.

"Do I need to be quick?" I ask.

"Nah, I'll shower in the morning," he tells me, and I nod. I remember our shower schedules always worked well with each other.

"Do you want to order in for dinner?" I ask.

"Pizza?" Max looks up from his phone.

"Sure. The usual, please," I say. When he doesn't ask what that is, I have little hope for my dinner. I doubt he remembers my usual, but I would be pleasantly surprised if he did.

I go to the bedroom first and grab my travel kit and my pajamas then head to the bathroom, shutting the door firmly behind me. Glancing around the bathroom, I smile at the great job the cleaner did. Even though I had hardly noticed the grime earlier today, now the tiles sparkle and the air smells fresh and clean. I turn on the shower but stop short of withdrawing my arm as I notice products in the shower that weren't there when I left. I was gone a full month so it is possible that Max ran out of products but upon closer inspection, the additional conditioner bottle is for dyed hair, something Max does not have.

I frown, picking up the bottle. The label is not a brand I use but I've heard of it. Maybe he just grabbed it off the shelf at the store and saw the conditioner and bought it without looking at more information. I put the bottle back and sigh. I suppose it's always possible that someone other than myself and Max have used this shower recently. Although we have only been broken up for a few weeks, it wouldn't surprise me if Max has already had another girl here. It would be disappointing, and immensely hurtful but not altogether surprising. It is insane that this person felt comfortable enough to leave their conditioner here but maybe it was an accident or one of his family members stayed a few days. Honestly, it seems like the type of thing Kitty might do to stake her claim, or try to get a rise out of me.

I know I should feel a bit more devastated about finding the conditioner bottle but I choose to put the thoughts aside. If it keeps nagging at me, I will just ask Max. He's never been a great liar which doesn't bode well for his job. Instead of dwelling on it, I jump in the shower and dump a generous amount of the conditioner into my hand and use it with abandon.

Chapter 38

Dylan

When I come out of the bathroom half an hour later, already dressed for bed, Max is sitting in the living room with our food on the coffee table. He looks up when I enter and smiles before quickly opening his pizza box and loading up his plate.

"I waited for you," he tells me, proud of himself.

"Mm, thanks," I comment.

"You going to eat dinner in your pajamas?" He teases.

I shrug and sit down on the oversized chair beside the couch. "They're the only lounging clothes I brought," I tell him.

"I didn't remember what you liked so I just got you veggie pizza," Max says, flipping open the lid to the second pizza box.

"Okay, that's fine," I say, putting a piece of the veggie pizza onto my plate. I don't mind the veggie but it's definitely not my go to for the pizza place we usually order from. I take a bite and it's as good as I remember. We mostly eat in silence, finishing another movie. I eat almost half of my pizza before taking both boxes to the kitchen and put away the leftovers. I grab one more slice before going back to the couch.

"Oh, hey, some of our friends wanted to come over to see you while you're in town," Max informs me when I sit down.

I look up from my slice. "Like, tonight?" I ask.

"Yeah," Max says like it's no big deal.

"I thought we were in for the night," I say, gesturing to my pajamas. "Hence the outfit."

Max chuckles. "You can stay in them. Our friends won't mind," he tells me but I know he's wrong.

Our friends are all in similar professional industries and most are into high fashion. Everyone, even the men, will judge me for wearing my pajamas at a party.

"It's not a party," Max says, reading my expression. "Just our friends coming over to hang out."

"Knowing our friends, it will turn into a party," I say with a huff. "What time are they coming over?"

"Maryanne and Luis are at dinner now so the rest of the group decided around 9," Max informs me.

"9? That's so late," I mumble and Max laughs.

"Really? Small town life really messed up your schedule, huh?" Max teases and I narrow my eyes at him. He laughs.

"You're not funny," I tell him which elicits another laugh.

"I am. But seriously, no one will care if you're wearing pajamas. You look hot," Max comments and it makes me a feel a little gross when gives me a slow once over.

"Thanks, I'm going to go change." I stand up and go to the bedroom to change. I have to dig through the clothes I left behind to find something appropriate to wear, something that can be worn out of the house, just in case our friends decide a house party isn't enough and they want to go out. I'm just finished pulling on a nice t-shirt when there's a knock on the door.

I walk out of the bedroom to find that most of the group has arrived together.

"Dillie!" Cassidy launches herself at me and I easily catch her, letting her squeeze me in a big hug. "I've missed you!"

"Thanks, Cassidy," I say as I pat her back.

"Okay, let the rest of us say hello," Maryanne scolds Cassidy lightly, who reluctantly releases me and lets Maryanne have a turn. "Hey, sweets, how's Minnesota?" She asks as she gives me a quick hug.

"It's actually pretty great," I tell them as Luis gives me a side hug. "It's freezing, of course, sometimes below freezing, but other than that, it's pretty awesome."

"Really? I can't picture you handling cold weather," Kitty laughs, giving me a delicate hug before throwing herself at Max for a nicer hug.

"It took me a while," I admit with a chuckle. "But I'm handling it well now. I had to get a whole new wardrobe."

"Let's get some drinks then you can tell us all about it," Luis suggests, letting Max lead him to the kitchen to pour our drinks.

The girls join me on the couch while the guys prepare the drinks. I'm glad I changed because Maryanne is dressed too nicely for just an apartment hangout, I suppose they had dinner at a fancy restaurant. Kitty is always dressed in a tight little number, especially when Max is around, a fact that hasn't gone unnoticed. I've also noticed that she's recently dyed her hair.

"So, tell us all about your trip," Cassidy says, excited to hear more as she leans in. "How are you doing?"

"I'm good. It was an adjustment at first but it's been great," I say with a smile. "It's the cutest little town. I live right above a bookstore, the owner is actually my landlady," I tell them and Kitty waves her hand, cutting my story short.

"No, dear. Cassidy means 'how are you after Max dumped you?' And why are you staying in his apartment?" Kitty gives me a pitying look.

"Well, I mean I was asking about Minnesota," Cassidy starts but Kitty waves her hand again, silencing Cassidy this time. Cassidy pouts and I frown. Maryanne tries to ignore the tension.

"So, what's the deal? Quick while the boys are in the kitchen," Kitty insists.

"Oh, no deal, really. We've been friends for a long time and technically this is still *our* apartment but I am glad we both felt comfortable enough that I could stay here," I say with a shrug.

"Are you guys back together?" Kitty presses. "Are you moving back here? Is he moving to Minnesota?"

"Kitty!" Maryanne scolds but she also looks interested in my answer, not as desperately as Kitty though.

"Oh, uhm. Well, we haven't talked about it so no, I don't think we are back together. I mean, I haven't made any moves and neither has he," I say, uncomfortable with the conversation. Max did hit on me earlier today but nothing else has happened and I don't think I want anything to. "And we haven't discussed the move either. I'm still not sure what I want," I admit.

Cassidy pats my leg as the guys come out carrying drinks for us. "Well, let's just have fun tonight and you can make all those important decision tomorrow," she says with a giggle, taking a glass from Luis.

"To Dylan's return and hopefully tonight will get her to realize how much she missed us, enough to get her to stay," Max says with a wink, raising his glass to make a toast.

"Here, here," Luis agrees, lifting his glass as well.

The rest of the group echoes the sentiment, besides Kitty who grumbles. They are clink their glasses together. I grin and bear it, lifting my glass as well.

An hour into the get together, the day is wearing on me. I love my friends, and I'm glad to see them again but I've had a very long day and would love nothing more than to climb into bed, alone. Well, maybe not alone but certainly not with anyone here.

"You okay?" Max asks, leaning over with his hand on my thigh. Max has had a few drinks already and has started to get a bit handsy and not just with me. Kitty doesn't seem to mind it though but she does mind when his attention shifts from her and is on either Cassidy or myself. Max knows to stay away from Maryanne.

"I'm fine, just tired," I tell him, brushing off his touch.

Max leans in closer to me. "Why don't I get rid of our friends and we can retire to the bedroom?" Max offers, his voiced lowered with lust. He presses his lips against my neck, a gesture that used to make me fold instantly but not tonight.

"Max," I stop him, putting my hand on his chest. "I had a fun day but I don't think we should do anything tonight." I want to point out that it's his own fault but I remain civil. He broke up with me so I'm not sure why he thought he would get lucky tonight.

"What do you mean?" Max questions.

"Well, we're not together," I point out.

"Is this because of that Minnesota hillbilly?" Max asks, his voice turning rough.

"Ooo, there's a Minnesota hillbilly?" Cassidy butts into the conversation much to my annoyance. She has no boundaries but has always been sweet, if not nosy. And I can't be mad because we're sitting right next to her and Kitty. Kitty, on the other hand, looks downright peeved that Max is all over me. I have half a mind to push him in her direction.

"You're already seeing someone new? That's pretty low, Dyl," Kitty says with a smirk. She leans into Max and pats his arm. "Seems like you made the right decision to dump her."

Max pulls away from Kitty but not before I catch them exchanging a look. Kitty backs off a bit and I choose not to address the look that passed between them.

"He's not a hillbilly, but no there's not one and that's not the reason I'm saying no. And this is none of anyone's business beside Max and myself." I turn my attention back to Max and get up, dragging him with me into the bedroom for privacy. Cassidy pouts but doesn't follow us. Kitty watches us go with her arms crossed over her chest.

"What's going on between you and that," Max pauses to think of a word to call Shawn so I quickly jump in.

"Max, insulting him does not win you any favors with me," I tell him and he pouts. "You broke up with me," I say and he starts to protest but I stop him, "Okay, you put us on a break," I clarify.

Max grunts. "I didn't think you'd immediately find someone else to get with. It makes me think that something was already going on between the two of you," he says, looking defiant.

I sigh an shake my head. "Nothing happened between us while you and I were still together," I tell him.

"So something happened after we went on the break?" Max asks, jumping on my phrasing.

"No," I start but I can't lie. Something did happen between Shawn and me but I'm not sure what it means and it's something I want to discuss with Shawn rather than Max. It's none of his business. "Okay, not no," I admit. "But I don't know what's happening between us. Max, you wanted this break. I've been back for a few hours and we haven't talked about us at all. You even invited our friends over so we had even less time together," I point out and it makes him frown.

"Are you saying I don't want to spend time with you?" Max asks, his voice slurring more as his anger grows.

I step back, confused by his question and his tone. "No. Why would I say that? We're still friends, I think. Is there a reason you wouldn't want to spend time with me?" I ask as he shifts uncomfortably. I wonder if he'll confess about Kitty, and whoever has showered here, if it wasn't her.

"What? Like, you think I'm hiding something from you?" He says and once again I'm surprised, maybe he will confess.

"If you were hiding something from me, it was probably a bad idea to drink as much as you did tonight," I point out and he frowns. "Are you hiding something from me, Max?" I ask, stepping closer to him.

Max stares at the floor, his cheeks turning pink. "No," he says weakly and I can't believe him. "We're on a break," he says again, his voice stronger as he looks up at me.

I nod, accepting this statement. "We are on a break, so is there something you want to share with me?" He hesitates and I press on. "Is it about another girl?" I ask. He says nothing but doesn't deny it so I continue. "Is it about one of the girls here tonight?" I venture a guess and Max's head shoots up to look at me with wide eyes.

"How-how did you know?" Max asks, incredulously.

I sigh and sit down on the bed. Max reluctantly slinks over to join me. We sit side by side for a few seconds, letting the silence between us fill the room.

I can still hear chit chat outside our closed door so I know that Kitty and Cassidy have stuck around, even though the polite thing would be to leave. I'm sure Kitty convinced Cassidy to stick around so they can see the outcome of my talk with Max. I wonder if Kitty is expecting Max to tell me that he's chosen her over me. It doesn't seem like this conversation is leading that way but it might lead to him telling me he's been seeing her. I can only guess how long and I'm not sure if Max will be honest if his time with Kitty overlapped with our dating.

"I'm not mad at you," I tell Max, starting the conversation.

How can I be mad? I think our time away from each other showed me how different we are from each other. How much better my life could be. Max isn't a bad guy, he's just not the right guy.

"You're not mad?" Max asks.

"No." I shake my head. "It is a little annoying who you chose to move on with but I'm not really mad at you for it. It would be a bit upsetting if your relationship began before we ended things," I add, glancing over at him to see if he wants to jump in to admit what happened, but he doesn't say anything. "I found shower products that don't belong to either of us," I tell him and he has the decency to look embarrassed, and a touch annoyed.

"I told her she couldn't leave any of her things here," he grumbles. "It's still your apartment too and I felt guilty," he admits, finally opening up.

"Our lease ends soon if you want to resign with her," I offer and he shakes his head with a mirthless laugh.

"You are a great roommate. I'm not sure she would be though," Max comments. I chuckle. "So, what does this mean?"

"Well, we've both sort of moved on," I say and he looks upset but he knows he can't say anything to that so he just nods. "So, it doesn't seem that getting back together is an option. Plus, I think I'm going to stay in Minnesota," I say, surprising both of us.

Max looks over at me with an open expression. "I have to be honest, I was sure you'd come running back after the first week," he says and I laugh, he chuckles. "I'm pretty impressed that you lasted a whole month and want to stay longer."

"I'm sorry you didn't get to see how wonderful Birch Lake is," I tell him.

"I'm sure I would have liked it if it were about 50 degrees warmer," he says with another chuckle.

The tension in the room starts to melt away and I feel like I did when I first met Max. I knew from the moment I met him that we would be good friends, even if it didn't go beyond friendship. He has his bad qualities but the good far outweighs the bad and I know he'll make some other girl very happy.

"Maybe you can come visit in the summer," I offer. "If you need an escape from the Texas heat."

Max laughs now, a jovial sound and one I haven't heard in a while. I pat his leg, chuckling with him. "That's fair," he agrees.

"Just maybe, don't bring Kitty with you. I'm not sure I want to expose my friends up there to her antics," I say with a teasing laugh.

Max shakes his head and sighs. "I think hooking up with her was a bad idea," he admits and lays back on the bed.

"Oh, definitely," I tease and he glares at me but not in a mean way, it makes me laugh again. "You know how she is. She gets her sights set on a target and pursues it until she's got her claws in you. And then she won't let go until she's done with you." I shrug.

"Ouch," Max says. He lets out a breath and then sits up to face me again. "You're right though. I'm sorry if my actions hurt you," he apologizes and it sounds so sincere that I'm a bit shocked.

"Thank you. I'll admit it was upsetting but I've had some time away to think about our relationship and you were right to set us on a break. It was weird and new and kind of refreshing," I say, my tone shifting into one of excitement.

Max narrows his eyes at me playfully. "Wow, was I that awful?"

"Occasionally," I retort and wink when he snorts a laugh. "No, no. You were a decent boyfriend. I mean, you were great at first but things were definitely amiss these last couple months, maybe even a year or so. And I'm not saying I was perfect either," I quickly amend. "I don't regret our relationship but it is time to move on."

"So, does this mean I have to sleep on the couch tonight?" Max comments, making me laugh yet again. I bet all the laughing is really annoying Kitty.

"I think we can share the bed, for old time's sake," I add.

Max nods his approval. "Any chance I can get you to go out there and get rid of our guests?" Max asks and I laugh hard at that. "I guess that's a no."

"It is definitely a no. Nice try though." I pat his leg with mock sympathy. "That's your mess out there."

"I know, I know. You should at least come say goodbye to Cassidy, especially if you're leaving for good soon. She really does like you. It annoyed Kitty to no end when we all hung out and she kept asking about you," Max tells me as we stand up off the bed to leave the room.

"Oh, that's very sweet of her," I say and nod. "Okay, I'll come say goodbye to her, you handle Kitty."

Max sighs but opens the door for me and we walk out of the bedroom together.

Chapter 39

Dylan

Saying goodbye to Cassidy makes me realize how good a friend she's been to me. There are tears in both of our eyes as we wave goodbye. Kitty pouts in the hallway waiting for Cassidy to leave but she's slow to do so.

"Please come visit me," I say, standing in the doorway. Max has retreated to the bathroom to get washed up for bed and to give me space to say goodbye to Cassidy. "I don't mind if you wait until it's warmer," I add.

"Of course I will come see you," Cassidy weeps, wiping tears from her cheeks. "I don't care how hot or how cold. You're one of my favorite people." Cassidy launches herself at me and I catch her in another tight hug.

"I can't believe you're leaving us," she sniffles through her tears. "But, I am so so *so* proud of you!" She tells me with a brave smile.

"Thank you," I say, squeezing her tight. Kitty clears her throat and Cassidy and I glance her way. "I guess I should let you go now," I say and Cassidy rolls her eyes.

"She's just mad cause tonight did not go the way she thought it would. But I did warn her," she adds with a shrug. "Max would never chose her over you. I don't think he would chose her over anyone, to be honest," she leans in to say quietly. "As much as I love her, she's a little to clingy and desperate for most men."

I laugh and nod in agreement. "Maybe she'll settle down soon. Or maybe there will be a guy who's into that."

"True!" Cassidy agrees, ever the optimist. Kitty grunts her disapproval of her delayed departure. Cassidy rolls her eyes again but shrugs. "Okay, I guess I should go now. Don't stay away forever, and best believe that I will be visiting."

"I will count on it," I tell her, then give a wave to Kitty as Cassidy skips away down the hall. Kitty gives me a mean smile before turning on her heel and stabbing the elevator button.

I shut the door and find Max coming out of the bathroom. He has a towel wrapped around his waist with the workings of a six pack shown off but it doesn't even begin to compare to Shawn, not that I've seen him fully naked, or even partially naked but I've definitely felt his impressive chest and abdomen and I wouldn't be surprised if he sported a six pack.

"Cassidy finally release you?" He asks with a chuckle.

"Released, then caught again, then released, and caught again," I chuckle. "The cycle went on for a few minutes. But I didn't mind."

I start cleaning up the living room, falling back into my old routine of picking up after everybody. Max comes over and takes the empty glasses from me.

"You don't have to do that," he tells me as I hand them over. "I can do the glasses now and put away the rest of everything in the morning."

"Are you sure?" I ask.

He nods. "Yes. I know you've had a long day and you've spent too many years cleaning up after me. You shouldn't have to do that now that we aren't together and you're my guest, technically," he says and I'm impressed.

"I was a bit shocked that the apartment was a mess when I got here," I tell him. He looks embarrassed and shakes his head, bringing the dishes into the kitchen.

"Yeah," Max says, "I don't know what I was thinking. I got really busy at work and was studying a lot, enough that I started neglecting the apartment, and myself, as you can tell from all the take out."

"A lot of good places, though," I say and he chuckles, running his hand through his hair.

"I'm sorry the place was a mess though. I think that was one of the reason I was considering begging for you back," Max says with another nervous chuckle.

"You missed your house keeper and cook?" I offer and he nods.

"Exactly." We both chuckle. "That's another thing I should apologize for. I took advantage of you a lot in both of those departments. I hope you know how much I appreciated everything you did for me, and how much I suffered when you weren't around to help out," he adds as a reprieve. I smile.

"Thanks, Max. I've enjoyed living alone and only having to take care of and clean up after myself," I admit.

"I'm sure you do. A lot less work than living with me, huh?"

"Unfortunately," I say. "But it wasn't all bad."

"Are you hitting on me?" Max teases as he follows me to the bedroom.

"Oh, please," I throw back with a laugh. "If you start thinking that then you may well end up on the couch tonight," I threaten playfully.

"Okay, okay." He puts his hands up in surrender. "I promise no funny business tonight. "So, since you've made your decision, does that mean you're cutting your trip short?"

I think it over before nodding. "I think so. I might as well. I have a lot to figure out still, especially aout this job offer."

"Oh, did you get the offer?" Max asks, sounding excited for me.

"Not yet," I chuckle. "But I might as well reach out to decline, or withdraw my name from consideration."

"Good call," Max agrees. "So, do you need me to drive you to the airport tomorrow?"

"That would be great, thank you."

"No problem. Hey, how are you going to get your car up to Minnesota?" He asks as we climb into bed. It's a good question.

"Hm," I ponder. "I haven't thought about that. I don't really need a car at the moment. Most of the places I go are walking distance away, and if I need to go further, I've always found a way to get there."

"Ah, the hillbilly," Max says but this time there's no ill intent in his words so I let it go.

"That's true. He did let me use his truck but I doubt he would want to share it with me for the distant future. I could look into shipping my car up there but that's probably very expensive," I say and Max shakes his head.

"Yeah, I mean I could always drive it up for you, or help you sell it," he offers and I beam at him.

"Thanks, Max. I will look into all my options and let you know what works out," I say, feeling better about the idea.

"Sounds good," Max says, moving down in bed to get comfortable and stretching his arm to turn out his light, with a yawn that's contagious. "I'm glad we were able to talk about everything," he says in the darkness once I've switched off my bedside light as well.

"Me too," I say with a smile. "It went rather well. I didn't get to finish packing my things though," I remember. "I already talked to my parents and they are free for brunch tomorrow, I doubt I'll have time to do anymore packing before then and I'll have to catch my flight soon after. Depending on how long brunch is, you might have to pick me up and take me straight to the airport."

"Don't worry about any of it. I know you need to meet with your parents and tell them about your big decision so why don't I try to finish packing while you're at brunch with them and if I don't get everything finished, I can ship the rest out to you over the week," Max says with another yawn, putting together the plan quickly. "Or whenever."

"Are you sure?" I ask, again surprised by his generosity.

"Sure," he says. "I'll send you the invoice," he adds with a laugh.

"Actually, please do," I say, thinking it over. "I probably get a relocation package. I should check that out when I get home."

"'Home', huh?" Max asks. "It already feels like home to you?"

"It does," I admit, my smile growing in the darkness.

As much as I love Dallas and it will always hold a special place in my heart, Birch Lake just feels right to me. The people and the atmosphere are incredible, something I've never experienced before and it just feels like the perfect place for me.

"Dylan, time to get up," Max's voice slowly drifts into my sleep and my eye lashes flutter as I try to wake up. It feels like I barely slept at all but when I open my eyes, the sun is pushing through the curtains and it's time to get up.

"Mm, what time is it?" I ask, yawning and stretching as I sit up and swing my legs over the side of the bed. I look around and see that Max has made a pretty big dent in the packing that needed to be done.

"It is…," he trials off to check his phone, "9:15. I let you sleep in a bit but you still have plenty of time to take a shower and get ready for lunch with your parents."

"Whew," I says, getting up off the bed. "You did a great job packing. How long have you been up?"

"I woke up at 7:30 and wasn't able to fall back asleep so I decided to get to work," Max says, looking around the room, pleased with his work.

"Wow, looks great. Are you almost done? We can drop the first few boxes at the shipping store before heading to the airport," I offer and he looks around at the boxes.

"Yeah, I think I can get a few of these filled up and taped by the time you're done getting ready," he says, accepting the challenge set forth.

"Excellent. I'll leave you to it then," I say but he's already focused on packing the boxes.

I hope they're packed well and organized at least a bit. It'll make it easier to deal with when they arrive in Minnesota.

Although, I'm not entirely sure where I'm going to send them. I guess for now I'll send them to my current apartment but since I've decided to move permanently, I need to look for a more appropriate space. I do love the little apartment I'm in now, and I love my landlady but I'll need more space for all of these new boxes and space to grow.

I'm okay leaving Max with most of the big pieces of furniture because I was the one who compromised on those purchases when we moved in together. So, I'm not attached to anything here. There are a few decorative pieces I want to take with me but I'll worry about those later, maybe Max will pack some of them too but we'll see.

I leave him to continue boxing up my items while I go into the bathroom to shower. Using another generous helping of Kitty's products makes me chuckle with delight. I'm guessing these will sit in here until the next woman stays over but I don't expect Kitty will be back any time soon. Max seems like he regrets sleeping with her so I don't think he'll invite her over again.

When I'm dressed for the day, I head back to the bedroom to finish packing my suitcase. I need to make sure everything is ready for the airport just in case brunch is longer than expected.

Max has moved out into the living room and I can hear him busy packing out there. Which makes me think he might be getting my decoratie items packed. Hopefully, he's taking care to pack the fragile things with extra protection. I'm not sure if we have the proper supplies though, since this move is also last minute.

In the bedroom, four boxes have been taped shut. I'm impressed with his quick work.

"Okay, I'm ready! Can you take a break to drive me to the restaurant?" I ask with a hopeful smile. Max chuckles and nods his head.

"Of course," he responds, carefully setting a vase into one of the boxes.

"Yay, thanks!" I grab my purse and follow him to the car, bouncing on my toes with excitement. I want to give him some advice on carefully packing the vase and any other items but he's doing a great job and I appreciate his help, so I don't want to be too bossy.

Chapter 40

Dylan

"Dylan! Sweetie, it is so good to see you again. Wow, you look so tan," Mom says as she pulls me into her arms. Dad waits patiently for his turn then gives me a big bear hug that rivals Mom's.

"Hi, y'all," I greet them with a grin, feeling a sting in the corner of my eyes. I don't know why I'm crying, I guess I missed them. I don't know how I'm going to handle moving so far away from them. "Thank you for driving out to meet me today."

They may live in Texas but they're a few hours drive from Dallas so I am beyond grateful that they took the time to meet me for brunch today.

"Of course, sweetheart," my dad says, his arm still wrapped around me as we walk over to a table. We're sitting inside today, much too cold for us Texans to sit outside yet. "Your uncle keeps telling us we should visit for a weekend or so. It allowed us to see all of y'all." Dad grins at me and grabs the pitcher of water from the table, filling each of our glasses.

"Well, I'm so glad you did because I have big news," I say. I wanted to wait until we had ordered our food but it's too exciting to keep to myself.

Mom gasps. "You're pregnant?" She guesses but when she sees my face, she redirects with a chuckle. "You're engaged?" She tries again. Dad, thankfully, stay quiet.

I laugh. "Maybe I should just tell you," I offer.

Mom laughs and Dad chuckles his deep rumbling amused laugh. "Please," Mom says, gesturing for me to go ahead. "I keep putting my foot in my mouth. You do not look pregnant, by the way. And I'm assuming Max would be with you to make the engagement announcement. Or I guess, not Max anymore. I'm sorry, dear, I should have thought about it before making any guesses. I just got so excited, you look so happy," she apologizes with a slight blush to her cheeks.

"Thanks, I am happy," I admit.

Before I can tell them my news, a waiter comes over to get our orders. I order a big meal because I'm not sure when I'll get to eat next. I don't usually like to eat at airports, since I get too nervous to handle food before my flight, but it will be around dinner time when I land in Minneapolis so maybe Vivian and I can have dinner on our way back to Birch Lake. I feel bad that she's coming to pick me up. It looks like it snowed while I was gone so I hope the roads are okay for her to travel. I'll have to offer to drive on the way back, although, it might be safer if she drives since she has more experience.

"Okay, tell us the big news!" Dad interrupts my thoughts as the waiter walks away with our orders.

My parents sit across the table, beaming at me, trying to be patient while they wait for me to tell them. I feel the nerves in my stomach flitting around. I take a sip of my water to clear my throat.

"Is this about your interview?" Mom asks, her expression pinched in concern now. "Did it not go well?"

"Oh, honey," Dad says, his voice filled with sympathy.

"No, no," I stop them. "It went rather well," I admit.

"Then what is it, dear?" Mom asks, reaching out for my hand. I let her take it and she squeezes gently, a gesture I return. The tears pricking my eyes start to slide silently down my cheeks. "Oh, sweetie, it's okay. Oh… I think I know."

"What is it?" Dad looks a bit distraught. He hands me his napkin and I use it to wipe my cheeks and dab my eyes. I give him a wobbly smile and sniffle, trying to get ahold of myself.

"She's moving," Mom says. Her voice is soft and kind, her eyes become watery, and she squeezes my hand again. "Honey, it's okay. You want to start a new chapter of your life and we completely support you, 100 percent," Mom reassures me.

"But it's so far from y'all," I practically whine, sucking in a shaky breath to try to stave off the tears.

"I know but we are more than capable of traveling, dear," Mom reminds me with a chuckle. She squeezes my hand once more before pulling her hand back as our waiter returns to our table with our food.

"I would suggest going over the pros and cons of moving but it seems like you've made up your mind," Dad says, thinking analytically. "And I'm not saying that's a bad thing, nor disapproving. You're still young and have your whole life in front of you. I think it's okay to move for work. I certainly did, dragged your mother with me a time or two," Dad tells me with a smile at Mom.

"It was always an adventure. I loved it," Mom says, grinning back at him. Then she turns to me. "Texas will always be your home sweetie, but it's okay to venture out of state. For your job, or for love." She winks at me.

I blush. Dad looks between us. "Is there something I don't know?" He asks, narrowing his eyes as he takes a big bite of his tuna sandwich.

"There might be a boy in Birch Lake," Mom says with a teasing giggle. Dad raises his eyebrows at me but doesn't say anything, waiting for me to give any details.

I shake my head, my cheeks still feeling heated, and I focus on eating my lunch.

I had told Mom about Shawn when I first met him. I told her how annoying he was but also how hot he was, how good he smelled, how he helped me pick out appropriate clothes for the cold. She teased me then that I had a crush on him. And I had to remind her I was still dating Max. And of course, when Max broke up with me, she was the first person I called as I drove away from the airport.

"I don't know," I admit after a few minutes. They don't push me, letting me have time to eat and think about everything. "Mom was definitely right about me having a crush on Shawn, who knows where that will go, but more than anything, I fell in love with the town," I say with a sigh.

"That's incredible, sweetie," Mom tells me. "Well, like I said, you have our support. All the way. We'd love to come visit you when you're finally settled in. I don't think your father and I have ever lived in a small town."

"No," Dad agrees. "Well, there was that one town that was pretty small but it was still about 30 to 35 thousand people."

"Oh, yeah. I forgot about that place," Mom recalls with a thoughtful look. She turns her attention back to me. "So, has it been awkward around Max since you've been back?" She asks, taking another bite of her extravagant salad.

"It was at first," I admit. "But then we talked about it all and it was a good talk. Coming back, I didn't know if we would be able to be friends after this but honestly, I think we both saw that side of each other again in our talk."

"That's good, sweetie," Mom compliments me. "He's been one of your closest friends for a while. I'm glad y'all were able to repair that. And now you can happily move on with the next lucky Minnesota Viking!" Mom says, happily. She grins at me and claps her hands with excitement. Dad raises his eyebrows and my cheeks flush again.

"Mom," I whisper, scolding her.

"Oh please, having a type is nothing to be embarrassed about." Mom dismisses my concerns with a wave of her hand. "I like the athletic type," Mom says, laying her hand on Dad's arm with a flirty wink. Dad chuckles and shakes his head at her antics.

"Ugh, Mom, please," I groan, but I can't keep the smile off of my face. My parent's relationship is the reason I'm okay moving on from Max. I know he wasn't the right one for me but I also know that the right one is out there. I know what I deserve and I'm not going to accept less. Shawn better step up his game if he wants a future with me.

The thought about Shawn pops into my head before I can stop it. I don't know why he's the one person I thought of. And he hasn't necessarily done anything wrong, I just haven't indicated that I am open and willing to pursue something with him. I guess that's one of the things I need to add to my to-do list when I get back to Birch Lake.

"Eat your lunch, dear," Mom says with a laugh. "We don't have all day. You have to get ready for your flight to your new home." Even though she tells me to keep eating, Mom herself keeps chatting while occasionally taking a bite. I've only been gone for a month and I've spoken to them almost every day, but apparently I've still missed a lot. I laugh as I listen to her stories and regale them with my frozen lake and ice fishing adventures.

When we're finished eating lunch, we spend a few minutes hugging each other. Mom and Dad promise to visit me as soon as I get settled. We finish brunch early enough that they give me a ride back to my apartment. After another round of hugs, I wave goodbye to them as they drive away.

"Hey, I'm back," I call out when I open the door to Max's apartment. I look around the living room that's now filled with boxes, many labeled with room descriptions, all taped up. "Wow, you made a lot of progress while I was gone," I say, impressed, walking into the bedroom to find him.

"Yes, I did. I think I've got most of your things packed up and ready to go," Max says, looking up from the latest box he's finished taping. "How'd your parents take the news?" Max asks.

"Well, really well," I tell him with a satisfied smile.

"Good. I thought they would." Max smiles and looks around the room. "Okay, you have everything you need out of the bathroom?"

"Oh, good call," I say and dash into the bathroom. Max leaves the room, bringing a couple of boxes out into the living room. I gather up my toiletries and repack my little bathroom bag and then go to the bedroom to find a way to shove the bag into my suitcase.

"You ready to head to the airport? If we leave in the next half hour, we will have enough time to drop a few boxes to be shipped out today," Max says, coming back into the bedroom as I finish zipping up my suitcase.

"Sure, yeah. I think I'm done here. You can always ship anything I leave behind," I tell him then look around the room.

This was my home for a little over a year and it was a great apartment, aside from all the issues of cleaning up after Max. The apartment has a great view and a short commute to my office which made it perfect when Max and I decided to move in together.

"You okay?" Max asks when I don't move toward the door. He grabs my suitcase and my work bag and I follow him into the living room. I scan the living room one last time to see if there are any other belongings that I might have missed. Max did a great job gathering up everything that was mine.

"Yeah, everything is hitting me. I'm leaving," I say with a sigh and he gives me a sympathetic look.

"You're more than welcome to stay a few more days, or," he adds when I open my mouth to protest, "come visit whenever you want."

"Thanks," I say, pulling him into a hug. He hugs me back gently and we both linger longer than needed but it feels like our final goodbye. "I might take you up on that," I tell him with a small smile. "Feel free to look me up if you ever decide to come to visit Minnesota."

Max chuckles. I doubt he'll visit but who knows. "Will do. Now, let's get these boxes into the car and head out."

It takes a couple of trips to load the car but eventually, we finish and climb into the car to drop the boxes off. Thankfully, it's chilly outside today so I don't work up too much of a sweat hauling the boxes to the car.

"Do you know the address?" Max asks when we get all the boxes unloaded at the post office. He's gathered all the labels we need and is helping me fill them out, using our apartment, his apartment, as the return address.

"Yeah, I think I'll just send it to my current place," I tell him, rattling off the address. He nods, writing it down on one label then grabs another to copy it down as well.

"Are you going to move? I thought you mentioned looking for a different place if you decided to stay," Max comments and I smile. "What?"

"You listened," I say, pleased. Max chuckles and returns to filling out labels.

"That's something I do, on occasion," he says then gestures for me to keep working too.

"Good to know." I laugh. "And yes, I'll start looking for a place but the current place is working out well, for now. It's just a tad small," I admit, chuckling with a fondness for my apartment.

"Okay, let me know if you need any help going over contracts or anything," he says. "I'm sure someone at my firm will be able to help," Max grumbles a bit.

"Don't worry, you're going to finish law school and get that promotion. And if you don't, I just know that there will another firm that will scoop you up," I reassure him and he smiles gratefully.

"Thanks, I appreciate that."

"Of course. Okay, I'm done here. You done?" I ask as I slap the last label on and smooth it out.

Max nods. We bring the boxes over to the counter two at a time, filling the whole counter. Thankfully, there's no one waiting in line behind us. The worker moves through everything quickly and before I know it, I've paid and we're back in the car with my tracking receipt.

"Now, to the airport," Max says, putting the car into gear.

"Thank you so much for taking more time off to drive me to the airport," I gush as we hit the road.

"Today's a slow day," Max explains. "I have a test coming up and planned to spend the day studying so I don't have work today."

"Oh, okay. But still, I feel bad taking you away from your studying," I say and he shrugs.

"It's good to take a break," Max says and I agree.

"That's true. And please keep me updated on your law school adventures," I say with a smile.

"Of course," he agrees with a nod. "You were always great at making sure I studied. I might have to call you up when I finally take the bar."

"I would be honored to help," I tell him and we exchange a kind smile.

We fall into silence as we hit mid-day traffic heading toward the airport. After a few minutes, Max sighs and looks over at me before turning back to the road and frowning.

"What? What is it?" I ask, curious.

"I can't believe this is it. You're actually leaving. You're trading in this sunny paradise for that cold, barren desert," Max says dramatically but he's got his playful smirk on so I know he's just teasing me.

A laugh escapes my lips and his smile grows. "It's really quite beautiful there," I tell him and he shakes his head.

"Sure it is. Better than here?" Max gestures to the landscape around us and then frowns at our view. I laugh again because the drive from our apartment to the airport is not something that I would ever refer to as beautiful.

"The small town charm is just unlike anything you'd ever believe," I tell him with a dreamy sigh. He glances over at me and shakes his head with a chuckle.

"Alright. I guess I can't convince you to stick around," Max says, glancing over at me again.

I shake my head. "No. I've made up my mind," I speak slowly, my voice sounding confident and it makes me smile.

"I knew you seemed happier when I came to visit you," Max admits. "Maybe that's why I acted out," he adds. "Jealous. Of the town or of that guy... I should probably apologize to the hillbilly, huh?"

I chuckle. "He's not a hillbilly," I remind him.

"Yeah, sure. Lumberjack might be more accurate," Max amends. I pause, thinking it over then nod in agreement. "So, are you going to date him now?" Max asks. His tone sounds a little annoyed or jealous but he's trying to be polite.

"Honestly, I don't know. I think we both have some things we're working on. I enjoy spending time with him though," I tell Max and then grimace. "Sorry, probably shouldn't be saying that to you, huh?"

Max chuckles, stopping the car outside my terminal. He gets out of the car with me and gets my bags out of the trunk. "It's fine," he says. "We're still friends, and I want you to be happy," he tells me, handing over my bags and pulling me into a quick hug.

"Thank you, Max. I want you to be happy too," I admit and he smiles. His eyes are sad but we both know we're doing the right thing. "Okay, well, I'll see you around," I say with a little wave as I turn around to head toward the airport entrance.

"See you around," I hear Max call out after me. I turn back to wave to him then head inside with the rest of the passengers.

Chapter 41

Shawn

"Are you heading to the airport soon?" Mom asks, eyeing me as I pace in front of the counter where she's perched, ordering new inventory for the store.

"Why? Are you trying to get rid of me?" I tease.

"Yes. You're driving me nuts and you're wearing a hole in my floor," she points out, gesturing to my pacing pattern. I look down at the floor and notice tracks in the carpet. I rub my foot over the marks with a grimace.

"Sorry," I say, still trying to rub out the marks on the carpet. I'm sure that's not from me pacing just now but I'm glad she's going to be renovating the place soon. Hopefully, we can restore the old wood floors and get rid of this dingy carpet but we'll see.

Mom sighs, sitting back on her chair to give me her full attention, something I probably don't want but I've annoyed her enough today that I guess she deserves some answers. "Are you nervous to see her again?"

"Yeah," I admit and she nods her head in understanding.

"It was very sweet of you to offer to pick her up. I'm sure she'll be happy about the surprise. And I'm grateful I won't have to drive in this weather," Mom says, chuckling.

"I hope she won't mind. Maybe I should tell her I'm coming instead of you," I says and Mom shrugs.

"You can if you want but I think it'll be a romantic gesture that she will appreciate," Mom tells me with a dreamy smile. "Your father used to do so many romantic things for me."

"He did?" I ask. I never really noticed, I just thought everything he did was normal to do when you were in a relationship.

Dad was always kind to Mom; he always held her doors and brought her flowers once a month, sometimes more. There was more if I really think about it. Looking back, he was romantic. But growing up, I always saw him as my strong, masculine father. He ran a tight ship with his business and had the respect of everyone in town. And he taught me to never settle. Maybe that's why I've been struggling lately. I'm torn. I like Dylan. She's amazing, and I think my dad would have loved her. But I don't know what Dylan's future holds and I can't force myself to settle for following her around for the rest of our lives, if she would even want that. If she even wants me.

Mom notices the thoughtful look on my face and she taps her fingers on the counter. "He was a great man, your father," she says. "I've seen a lot of those traits in you."

"Really?" I ask and she nods. "Everyone in town loved him. Even neighboring towns too," I add with a chuckle.

"Honey, everyone loves you," Mom tells me, her voice sympathetic. "You've closed yourself off recently so you might not see it but this town respects you too. Your dad was certainly a staple of this town but you could be too, if you wanted," she adds. "And I know your dad's passing really affected you, I, of all people, can understand that. But I think your father would want both of us to start living our lives again. Not just coasting through. It's time to start living, hun."

Mom falls silent, gazing at me with love and hope in her eyes. It takes me a minute but eventually, I nod.

"I know you're right. Dad was one of the best people I've ever known. He would probably scold me for how I've been behaving lately. I don't know, I just always felt guilty that he was disappointed when I left," I tell her and her face falls.

"Oh, sweetie." Mom reaches for my hand. I let her take it and she squeezes it gently. "He was never disappointed in you. Sure, he missed you and was sad to see you leave but he wasn't disappointed. He was so proud of you. He knew that you had to go off and do your own thing. I know he always wanted you to take over his business but he knew that you needed to find yourself first. But I suspect he also knew that you would eventually find your way back here."

"And I did," I say with a sigh.

"Are you regretting coming back?" Mom asks, her voice filled with concern.

"No," I say firmly. "No, of course not. I love Birch Lake and I think it was time to come home."

"Perfect timing too," Mom says.

"What do you mean?"

"Well, with the new visitor. It was great timing that you came home and decided to stick around for a bit," Mom says with a wink.

"Oh, right." I chuckle.

"Speaking of!" Mom claps her hands. "You should definitely get going. And you know, it's a nice long drive, beautiful scenery, it would be a great time to talk to her. Ask her how she's feeling about everything. See if she wants to go out with you," Mom adds and I choke on a laugh.

"Mom! Wow," I chuckle.

"What?" She asks with a shrug. "Isn't that where this is all heading?"

"I don't know. What if she got back together with that boyfriend? Or what if she got the job in Dallas and is just coming back here to tie up some loose ends and ship all her stuff back?" I ask the important questions while Mom frowns at me.

"Wow, you really like her," she says.

"That's what you got from all my questions?" I chuckle.

"Yes. You wouldn't be so concerned if you didn't like her that much," she points out, giving me her best Mom look. "And like I said, it's a long trip from the airport. 3 hours, that gives you immense opportunities to get answers to those questions or even persuade her to stay if you have to!"

"Yeah, you're right," I relent with a sigh. I check my phone, Dylan texted my mom half an hour ago to tell her that she was at the airport and boarding the plane soon. "I should leave," I say, double checking to make sure her plane is on time.

"Yes, you should. You should have left an hour ago, especially in this weather," Mom scoffs.

The snow stopped falling early this morning and the roads are clear but with the sun out, Mom is probably worried about icy road conditions.

"I'll be fine," I reassure her. "I know the roads and I don't want to get there too early."

"But you also don't want to get there too late and make her wait around," Mom says and I sigh. She grabs my keys off the counter and tosses them to me. "Get moving," she instructs me.

"Fine," I say, glancing at my phone again. The flight is only about 2 and a half hours so I should probably get on the road. "I'll text you when I get her," I tell Mom, giving her a kiss on the cheek. She waves me out the door, not even letting me stop to zip up my coat.

I'm on the road before my truck even heats up. I can't wait to see Dylan. I want to hear all about her trip and her interview. I'm curious and nervous to hear about her decisions. I don't know if this is just her coming back to collect her belongings and tie up loose ends. I hope it's not.

My nerves are going crazy as I take the final exit for the correct terminal. The pathway is neatly plowed and lined with piles of snow. A few policemen are bundled up to make sure traffic is moving along. They're mostly huddled in a group but there's not much traffic, enough that they don't even glance while I idle at the curb.

I glance at my phone, checking her flight information again. It takes a few seconds to load but when it does, the website says the plane has landed so she should be getting off the plane and headed to get her bag, if she checked one. I do a quick scan of my truck to make sure it's not messy and there's room for her bags.

The doors of the airport exit next to my car open and a few people walk out, looking for their ride. I hop out of my truck and move around to the passenger side, waiting to open the door for

Dylan. It takes a minute but eventually, she walks out of the airport wrapped in a large winter coat with gloves and a hat on, chatting animatedly with an older gentleman.

A grin splits across my face as I watch their interaction. She helps him over to the car where what appears to be his granddaughter, is waiting for him. Once he and his luggage are safely tucked away in the car, Dylan steps back, waves goodbye then looks up to search for her ride.

When her eyes land on mine, I can see her smile growing. She bites her lip to stop the grin before walking quickly in my direction. I walk with long strides in her direction and we meet in the middle. There's a pause where we just grin at each other before she throws herself at me. I catch her in my arms and it feels great to hold her again. I give her a tight hug, breathing her in. The fruity smell that I now associate with Dylan, fills my nostrils.

Dylan giggles as we pull away from each other. "Did you just sniff me?"

My face heats up. "No," I deny but she giggles again, she knows I'm lying.

"Sure," she chuckles. I take her bags and lead her over to my trunk. "Thank you for picking me up, that was very sweet of you."

"Of course. I wanted to see you again and make sure you made it home safely," I say, hauling her bags into the second row of the truck then open the passenger door for her. She places her hand on my arm to help her get into the seat, then she gives my arm a squeeze before releasing it. I go around to get into the driver's seat and crank the heat when Dylan shivers.

"Thank you," she says, stripping her gloves off to hold her hands in front of the vent. "It was very thoughtful of you to pick me up. I told your mother that I would just order a car, or take the bus. I didn't want her to have to do this drive but she insisted," Dylan tells me and I nod.

"If I didn't like you so much, I would have made my mom cancel and force you to do that," I tell her with a chuckle.

"Oh, so you like me a lot, huh?" Dylan teases. I feel my face heating up again. My cheeks feel flushed.

"I just showed my cards right away, didn't I?"

"Yeah," she chuckles. "It's okay. I was going to wait to tell you I liked you after I shared my big news but I guess now is as good a time as any."

"Was that it?" I ask when she doesn't say anything else.

"What?"

"Was that you telling me you liked me?" I ask with a laugh.

"You didn't like it?" She giggles. I glance at her with a crooked smile and she grins at me. "Okay, okay. Fine. I like you. But I think you knew that."

"I might have had an inkling," I admit with another grin in her direction. She reaches over and lightly smacks my arm.

"Well, I guess I can't blame you. I didn't hide it very well."

Dylan chuckles, sitting back in the seat and turning the heat down so it's not blowing as hard. She shrugs out of her puffy coat and shoves it down by her feet.

"Wait, what were you planning to tell me before? What's the big news?" I look over at her again and her face twists with emotions, tears prick the corner of her eyes but she doesn't look sad, just reminiscent. "What's wrong?" I ask when she pulls down her sleeve to dab at the tears.

"Oh, nothing's wrong. I'm happy," she says with a soft sigh and a sweet smile in my direction.

"I'm glad you're happy," I tell her, glancing over at her and waiting for her to expand on it. What is her big news? Why is she happy crying?

Before I can ask and before she can say anything, Dylan's stomach growls and she jolts upright, placing her hand on her stomach, looking embarrassed.

"Are you hungry? I know a place in Clearwater, it's coming up soon," I tell her and she nods.

"I am hungry, yes, if you couldn't tell," she chuckles through her embarrassment. "Thank you, that would be great," Dylan says with a yawn, sitting back in her seat. I reach over and squeeze her thigh gently, an intimate gesture that I almost regret but Dylan rests her hand delicately on top of mine.

"If you want to take a nap, I can wake you up when we get there," I offer, shivers going up my arm as she lightly traces her fingers over the top of my hand. The pads of her fingers are gentle and smooth, tickling my skin.

"How far away is it?" She asks, thoughtfully.

"Another half hour, I think," I tell her, glancing at her sleepy face. She looks beautiful in the light of the setting sun. Her hair shines a golden color, the curls framing her face. She tucks a stray strand behind her ear, looking out the window.

"Then I shouldn't nap. I'm always cranky if my naps are too short," Dylan says when I glance over at her. She shrugs at her explanation and I chuckle. "You'll have to keep me awake with stimulating conversation," she teases.

"Yeah, I'm great at that." I chuckle. Dylan giggles and pats my hand, another yawn slipping out.

"You are. I like listening to you talk. I like your voice," Dylan tells me and I find myself glancing at her again. She's not looking at me but her fingers continue to trace the veins and callouses on my hand.

"Yeah?"

"Yeah. It's deep and sexy. And with your accent, mm," she hums her delight. "Like a Viking. Hey, maybe I do have a type," she adds with a thoughtful smile.

"Vikings are your type?" I chuckle.

"You know, I think they might be," she says, nodding. "My mom mentioned it earlier today. And obviously not like actual Vikings… well, maybe." I feel her watching me, looking me over, probably comparing me to a Viking. I guess I have some similar features. And especially in the winter when I let my facial hair grow out for warmth. And maybe I'm a little burlier this time of year, but most of it is muscle because of my job.

"I have an accent?" I ask and this makes her full on laugh. "What? Why is that funny?"

"Sweetie," she says through a laugh. The term of endearment makes my cheeks flush, I enjoy it more than I should, more than I care to admit. "You definitely have an accent. It's sweet. I like it. But it's there. You probably can't tell because you live here so everyone else around you has the same accent, but trust me, from an outsider, y'all have accents. Some heavier than others."

"Hm. You have an accent," I retort snippily which makes her laugh again. I love making her laugh. It's a beautiful sound and her smile lights up her face, the skin crinkling by the corners of her eyes. "Here we are," I say, taking the exit for the Travel Plaza I always stop at on the drive home from Minneapolis.

"See, such a stimulating conversation got us all the way here," Dylan says, climbing out of my truck, stretching from the drive.

"Talking about accents was a stimulating conversation?" I tease, following her to the building. "You're pretty easy," I add, teasing her back.

Her eyes sparkle with playful energy as she allows me to open the door for her. She brushes up against me as she walks into the building and lowers her voice to say, "Oh, I'm not too easy. You'll have to work for it a little bit harder."

My heart starts beating faster as I watch her walk away. She looks back at me with a wink and I quickly snap out of it and jog to catch up to her.

Chapter 42

Dylan

After my boldness with Shawn at the entrance, I run off to use the restroom and stare at myself in the mirror. Where did that come from? I'm not usually this bold. I'm feeling more confident after making the decision to move to Birch Lake. And being around Shawn makes me extra playful. He's usually pretty stoic so when he put his hand on my thigh and squeezed gently, I was a bit surprised, almost as much as he was, but it just made this even better.

I like being back in his presence. Just being near him is electric.

When I exit the bathroom, Shawn is leaning over a counter, looking at a display of massive donuts. I sidle up next to him and slip my arm through his, leaning against his side. He flinches a little but when he notices it's just me, he smiles.

"I'm getting us breakfast for tomorrow," he tells me. I quirk a brow and he frowns. "What?"

"And who said we're going to be together for breakfast tomorrow?" I ask him with a teasing smile.

Shawn blushes. "Oh, no. That's not...I didn't mean it like that," he tries to explain and I try to hide my smile, letting him dig himself out of the hole. "I just meant separate breakfasts. They have great donuts here," he changes tactics. "I wanted some for tomorrow and I thought you might like to try one."

My smile grows as he trails off. "I was just teasing you," I tell him, letting out a satisfied giggle. He shakes his head at me, his smile growing too.

"What kind do you want?" He asks, turning his smile back to the donuts, not addressing his breakfast together slipup.

"Mm." I lean into him again as I survey the donuts, picking out a giant, white-iced, sprinkled donut and an apple fritter at least twice the size of a normal one. "Wow, these look great," I say as Shawn pays the cashier. "But if these are for breakfast, what's for dinner tonight?"

"Ah, that would be this way," Shawn says and leads me over to a short line a few feet away.

The line is self explanatory, as most sandwich lines are, so I follow him down the line, ordering everything that looks delicious until my sandwich is piled high and the worker has to almost smash it down to get it wrapped tightly enough. Shawn pays once again even though I protest this time. I should pay for his meal, it's the least I can do since he picked me up from the airport. Shawn relents to letting me pay for our drinks and chips in the gas station side of the Plaza.

Once we're back in the car, I set up a little picnic for us so Shawn can eat his sandwich while he drives. There's silence as we eat, the only sound coming from the road and our chewing.

"Hey, Dylan," Shawn says after he's handed me his trash and I shove it into one of the bags that they gave us at the Plaza.

"Yeah?" I glance at him while munching on my sandwich.

"Since you were hitting on me earlier," he starts and I snort a laugh but gesture for him to continue. "I was wondering if that meant you and Max are officially done?"

I'm silent for a beat before I reply, "it does."

"Good, I never thought he deserved you anyway," Shawn responds quickly and I chuckle.

"You didn't know him very well," I point out and swat his hand away as he reaches for my bag of chips. He chuckles and diverts to grab a chip from his bag.

"The limited interactions I had with him were more than enough," he shakes his head with a dramatic sigh.

"Yeah, that wasn't great. For either of you," I say quickly so Shawn can't put down Max even further. He grumbles at my comment. "Neither of you were on your best behavior." I sigh. "I'll admit it was such a weird situation. Max and I hadn't been doing well and then he saw you and I together and he just assumed..." I trail off. Shawn glances at me.

"He assumed what?" He asks.

"It doesn't matter," I dismiss it and plow forward before he can ask again. "No one handled that night well. But while I was in Dallas, Max and I had a lot of good talks and no we are not together anymore. I think we might be able to be friends but it might take a while." I yawn, leaning back in my seat.

"We have about an hour and a half before Birch Lake, is that long enough for you to nap?" Shawn asks, teasing me. I roll my eyes and swat his arm gently. He chuckles.

"That sounds perfect," I admit, leaning the seat back as far as I can without squishing my bags in the backseat.

"I have a blanket back there if you're chilly." Shawn gestures to the back seat.

"Ooo, perfect." I reach into the back seat and yank the blanket out from under my bag. "You're prepared, huh?"

"Oh, yeah, you weren't taught that growing up. We tend to prepare for the winter by keeping blankets, water, snacks, in our cars, just in case," Shawn tells me. My jaw drops. "Yeah, it can get pretty cold out here in the winter. You need to be prepared if your car stalls or you hit a patch of ice and end up in a ditch. It can take a while for someone to find you if there's a bad storm."

"Wow, that's pretty scary," I admit, shivering at the idea of being stranded out in the cold. I yawn again, pulling the blanket around me as I snuggle into the seat. "Please drive carefully."

Shawn's laugh rumbles again. "You don't want to get stuck in the car with me for a few hours?" He asks, his voice teasing but the implication is there.

"Oh. Well, as much as we would heat up the car," I say and grin as the tip of his ears turn pink, "I feel like sweating in a car that's surrounded by snow, will make us freeze even worse."

"That's fair."

"I know," I say with another yawn. "Goodnight, wake me when we get close."

"Yes, ma'am." Shawn sounds like he's grinning but my eyes are already closed and I quickly drift off to sleep.

"Dylan," a deep, sexy voice infiltrates my peaceful sleep. I grunt and turn over, pulling the blanket over my chilly nose and snuggling down more. "Dylan, we're getting close."

"5 more minutes," I mumble but slowly lift the seat so I'm sitting up. Shawn chuckles at my comment. I yawn and rub at my eyes, blinking in the darkness before my eyes adjust and I see the sign welcoming us to Birch Lake.

Seeing the entrance to the town makes my heart flutter. I sit up and watch the sign pass by. The drive down the main street is quiet with the lamposts shining brightly against the fresh snow.

When we pull up in front of my apartment building, a sense of home settles over me. Shawn parks the car and while I bundle up again, he unloads my bags, carrying them to the foot of the stairs. He comes back to help me out of the truck. His hands grip my hips and he lifts me up before slowly lowering me onto the sidewalk. But he doesn't let go of me. We stand in the moonlight, looking at each other, both with small smiles on our faces.

"Do you want to come up?" I ask when he doesn't make a move.

"Yes," Shawn says, barely hesitating. We both laugh. "Sorry, was that too eager? I mean, yeah, sure, that would be alright."

"I think I liked the eager response," I comment, sliding my hand down his arm to hold his hand.

"Good." He leans in and I think he's about to kiss me. I want him to kiss me. But then he stops and narrows his eyes at me, a smirk playing at the edge of his mouth. "Wait, did you just ask me to come up so I'll bring your luggage up?" Shawn teases me and I giggle.

"That never crossed my mind," I reply with a polite and innocent smile. I release his hand and move toward the stairs, grabbing my smallest bag. "Oh, can you get those?" I say, pausing to glance back at him, biting my lip as I gesture to the rest of my bags, which is really just one larger bag, overstuffed with more items from Dallas.

Shawn shakes his head at me and lets out a grunt but he comes over to pick up the rest of my bags, following me up the staircase. I unlock the door and hurry into the warm apartment with Shawn close behind me.

Chapter 43

Shawn

The heat of the apartment is almost overwhelming compared to the chill of the winter night. I set Dylan's bags by the door as she nervously hurries to the heater and turns it down.

"Wow, I guess I left the heater on high while I was gone." Dylan looks back at me with a tight grimace. "I hope I didn't damage anything."

I shrug. "You weren't gone for too long," I tell her and she nods. "We can pop open a window if you're too hot?" I offer as she shrugs out of her coat.

"Oo, no. That would freeze us," she dismisses the idea and then reaches her hand out. "Coat, please."

"Are you asking me to stay?" I ask, taking off my coat.

Dylan blushes but takes my coat and goes to hang it with hers. She grabs her suitcases and wheels them to her bedroom. I watch her go.

"Make yourself at home," she calls out.

I take off another layer of clothing, still sweltering in the heat of the apartment. I lay my sweater over the back of the couch and drop onto it. I should have taken the small chair in the room but the couch has enough room that Dylan could join me if she wanted to. If she wants to be that close to me.

Dylan comes out of the bedroom, having also taken off a layer of clothing and is also now wearing fuzzy house slippers. I chuckle at them and she rolls her eyes.

"My feet get cold," she offers the explanation.

"They're cute."

"Oh, hush." Dylan giggles. "Do you want something to drink?"

"Whatever you've got is great," I say and she nods, going into the kitchen to retrieve two glasses for us.

"All I have is red wine. Is that okay?" Dylan calls from the kitchen. I glance back at her and she holds up the bottle.

"Works for me," I responds.

She comes back with two glasses filled with red wine. She hands me a glass before settling onto the tiny couch with me. I take up more than half of the couch, or rather 'loveseat', but she doesn't seem to mind. She sits with her legs crossed, her knee resting on top of my thigh. I pretend not to notice. She takes a sip from her glass then leans back to look at me. She smiles and taps her leg on mine.

"What?" I ask before taking a sip from my glass.

"Nothing," she says but I can tell she's holding back. "Oh, wait! I created a Pinterest board for your mom's store!" She hops up again, setting her glass on the coffee table and goes to dig her laptop out of her carryon then she settles back on the loveseat, our legs pressed together.

"A Pinterest board? What's that?" I ask, shifting slightly to be able to see her screen better. She turns for me, angling so her back is against my side with her computer in her lap.

"You ever heard of a vision board or a mood board?" She asks and it sounds familiar so I give a half shrug. She chuckles. "Well, Pinterest is like that. You have a board that you fill with pictures or symbols of things you want for your future. Some things can be literal or just aesthetics, in general," she explains, pulling up the website on her laptop. She clicks on one of her boards called 'Bookbound revamp'.

"And you made one for my mom's store?" I ask, intrigued. I look over her shoulder as she scrolls through the board.

"Yeah! I had a bit of time on my plane rides. I feel bad that I haven't done anything before now," she says with a grimace. "I haven't done a lot with the blueprints yet since I figured I might need your help with that, in case I want to move a wall that's structural."

"Good call," I say with a chuckle. Dylan glances back at me with a quirky smile. "Do you want to go over that tonight?" I ask.

"No, that's okay. I just wanted to show you this," Dylan replies, bouncing in her seat a bit. "Okay, hush and look."

"I wasn't talking," I start but she shushes me again and then directs my attention to the screen to show me her plans for the store.

"Okay, since this store is located in a small town right by the lake, we're going to go with a more beachy look. Well, lakey look," she corrects with a chuckle, reaching for her glass to take another sip before turning her focus back to the computer. "See these little knick knacks?" She points to the screen, pointing out little objects; a rowboat, a multitude of signs about lakes, paddles, tubes, and lots of other lake-related items. "Aren't they so cute? You can have them for sale too. But I wouldn't do too many items because then the bookshop just turns into a normal store, you know?"

"Okay," I say with a laugh, gesturing for her to continue.

"Oh! Here, look at these amazing bookmarks!" Dylan scrolls happily through more pictures, showing me the bookmarks. Some floral, some with water themes, and a lot with book themes. "I love these bookmarks. They're gorgeous. And we can make them with 'Bookbound' on them, and add details like the location, contact info, all that. So it's a business card and bookmark!" She seems pleased by this idea. I chuckle and she leans back into me.

"That's a great idea," I tell her. She shuts her computer and turns to face me, a difficult move on such a small couch, but now we're even closer together. "So, what's the big news?" I ask, her brow scrunches in confusion. "In the truck, you said you had news," I remind her.

"Oh! That. Okay, well, I have made a decision," she tells me, her lips turning up in a smile. She reaches for her wine glass again and gestures for me to lift mine.

"Are we toasting?"

"Yes, we are," she says, nodding her head.

"To what? Are we celebrating something?" I ask, my heart beating faster with anticipation to hear her news.

"Yes!" She exclaims, starting to frown like she's surprised that I'm not happier.

"Dylan, you haven't explained what the big news is," I tell her. Her eyes go wide and her cheeks turn pink.

"Oh, sorry. I guess I'm more tired than I realized," she explains before taking another sip of her wine. "I should probably stop. I think this is making me even sleepier," she adds with a giggle

"If you want, I can leave and let you get some rest," I offer. I need to be a gentleman here. Dylan reaches out and wraps her hand around my bicep, her brow raises when she gives it a little squeeze. I try not to flex for her, or at least, try not to noticeably flex.

"No, no. I want to share the news with you tonight," Dylan says, her other hand resting on my thigh as she leans into me. She's so excited to share her news, that must be why she's being so affectionate.

"Okay, tell me then," I encourage.

"So, you know how I was in Dallas for the job interview?" She asks, setting the scene for her news. I nod, not wanting to interrupt her rhythm. "It went well. They've already sent an offer letter. I just got the email when I landed today."

I frown. "Oh, that's great. I'm really happy for you," I say, trying to sound happy for her. But I'm not, in fact, I'm rather disappointed.

"No, shush. I'm not finished," Dylan dismisses my faux compliments, her smile morphing into a smirk as she shakes her head at me. "I made the decision to reject the offer and stay here in Birch Lake!"

It takes me a few seconds to process what she's just said and when I do, I can feel the smile on my face turning genuine. I shift in my seat, turning toward her more, accidentally shifting her hand on my thigh further into my lap. She doesn't move it but her cheeks flush. I'm sure they match my own.

"Really?" I ask, just to be clear.

"Yeah," she says excitedly, bouncing in place. She grips my arm and squeezes my thigh, excited. "I'm staying!" She squeals, leaping up from the couch and I instantly miss her warmth beside me. But I like watching her bounce around with happiness. "I'm so excited! I feel so at home here. And of course, it sucks to leave my friends and family behind but everyone has already promised to come visit me and have invited me back anytime I want so really, it's not so bad. Right?" She pauses and looks down at me. Worry is written across her face.

I reach out for her and she comes quickly, lowering herself onto my lap and letting me wrap my arms around her. "Of course not. I'm very excited for you, Dylan. This is amazing news. You'll have to find a bigger place to host all your out of town guests," I tell her with a chuckle. She looks around the room and nods in agreement.

"True. I have thought about that. I love this little place so much, so I'm really not in a hurry. Plus, I doubt any of my fellow Texans will want to come visit any time soon. Much too cold," she says with a giggle. She leans in my chest, snuggling close with a yawn.

"I'm glad you're staying," I tell her softly, trailing my fingers lightly down her arm. She shivers and I pull a blanket over us.

"Me too," she mumbles through another yawn.

"Do you want me to leave so you can go to bed?" I offer, reluctantly.

Dylan sits up. "I guess it is late," she says, standing up. I get up with her and fold the blanket back up, draping it over the back of the couch and grabbing my sweater. "But I don't want you to leave." Her words stop me in my tracks.

"You don't?" I ask, wanting to be sure.

She shakes her head, giving me a small smile. Dylan holds out her hand for me. While it's sweet and sultry, it isn't a seductive gesture. I place my rough, calloused hand in her small, soft one. Our fingers interlock and I follow her back to the bedroom.

"Make yourself at home," Dylan says with a cute wink. She releases my hand and I want to grab it back but I let her walk away. She goes to grab pajamas and leaves the drawer open for me. "There are oversized shirts if you want one to sleep in," she tells me as she walks past me to the bathroom. She looks me up and down and bites her lip, hiding a chuckle. "One of them might fit you," she doesn't sound very confident.

I laugh and paw through her drawer, appreciating her response to looking me over. I've had plenty of women check me out and it's often annoying or unwanted but I like Dylan's gaze on me. I push my shoulders back, standing up straighter. I glance over my shoulder and catch her watching me again. She blushes.

"Yes?" I ask with a smirk.

"Your mom stocked the bathroom with supplies for guests," she tells me once she winds her words and recovers from getting caught staring. "If you need to wash up," she offers.

"Thanks, I think I will," I reply and she nods, disappearing into the bathroom to finish washing up. I strip off my jeans, long johns, and my henley and quickly pull on one of Dylan's 'oversized' shirts. I let out a laugh when I finally get the shirt pulled down over my chest and stomach. It might be oversized on her but it's certainly form fitting on me.

"Why are you laughing?" Dylan asks, coming out of the bathroom. She's changed into her pajamas; a button up, long sleeved top with matching red pants. They look soft and comfortable and hang loosely on her body. She stops when she notices my outfit. I can see her fighting between laughing at my tight outfit or blushing at my state of undress.

"Alright, let's get the laughing out now," I instruct her, gesturing for her to go ahead with it. She bites her lip but a giggle slips out. "I know, I know. Not so 'oversized', huh?"

"No," she says and burst out into a fit of giggles. I stand through it, shaking my head at her. "But I was wrong," she says when she finally calms down.

"You were wrong?" I ask, my brows scrunching together in confusion. She nods, wiping the tears of laughter from the corners of her eyes.

"Yeah. I thought you'd have a six pack," she says and for some reason, it wounds me a little bit. I might have had a six pack back in high school and college but I haven't had one in years. I've never had any complaints though. My stomach is still tight and toned, but not with distinct lines for each ab.

"Are you saying you're not into the 'dad bod' look?" I ask with a rough chuckle. Dylan looks up at me and there's a spark in her eyes.

"Oh, trust me. You might not have a six pack but I don't think you could be labeled as 'dad bod', which I have to say, I wouldn't mind either. But that looks a lot like solid muscle," she says in awe, stepping toward me. She places her hand on my stomach, the material of the shirt pulled tight against me. "Firm," she mumbles.

I chuckle and she looks up at me from under her eyelashes. My laughter is cut off as our eyes meet. I clear my throat. "It's mostly muscle," I explain awkwardly. "From work. But I seem to pack on a few extra pounds during the winter."

Dylan bites her lip, looking back down at my chest and stomach. "You don't have to wear this, if you're uncomfortable. I don't mind." She blushes when she realizes what she said. "I mean, if you're okay going shirtless. I don't want you to feel uncomfortable." She glances down, her cheeks getting a deeper shade of pink on them when she notices I'm just in my boxers. She takes a step back.

"Are you uncomfortable?" I ask.

"No," she says quickly. I raise my eyebrows. "No, I'm not. I mean, you're very hot and I'm very attracted to everything," she gestures at my body, up and down, "you've got going on but I don't want you to feel like you're a rebound even though I am objectifying you," she admits.

"I don't mind," I tell her and she smirks, her confidence returning slightly. I pull the shirt off in one swift movement and Dylan stumbles back, gasping softly. "Have you never seen a naked man before?" I ask, teasing her. I'm, of course, not fully naked but her reaction is still amusing.

Her jaw drops and I chuckle. "Stop making fun of me," Dylan pouts. "I can't help that you're hot, that's your fault," she protests.

"Thank you?" I say with a chuckle. "I think."

"Go wash up before I can embarrass myself further," she instructs, fanning her face.

"I don't know. I'm kind of enjoying this," I tell her. I wink at her and she rolls her eyes before shooing me away.

Once I'm done in the bathroom, I go back to the bedroom and find Dylan under the covers, her curly hair spread across her pillow as she looks toward the window. She looks beautiful under the moonlight. Her face is fresh and a bit red from being scrubbed of makeup.

"I can feel you staring," she comments, bringing me back to my senses. She turns to look at me with a sweet smile. "Are you okay sharing the bed with me? I wouldn't want you to sleep on the tiny love seat. And I don't want to sleep on it either."

I chuckle. "I don't blame you." I walk over to the bed. Dylan pushes open the covers for me and I climb in. The sheets are cool against my skin but as I shift closer to Dylan, I can feel the heat from her body. "I'm comfortable here," I tell her when we're lying face to face. She nods, biting her lip with a smile.

I reach out and touch her check, sliding my hand across her jaw. She watches me with her delicate smile.

"Is this moving too fast?" Dylan asks.

"I don't feel like a rebound," I answer her, bringing up her earlier statement.

"Good. Because you're not," she tells me. Dylan reaches out and places her hand on my bare chest as I run my fingers down her neck and across her shoulder.

"Are you working tomorrow?"

"I am," she says with a sigh, closing her eyes when my fingers drop from her shoulder to her collarbone. "Are you?" She asks with her eyes still close.

I smile at her beautiful, peaceful face. "I am. We should probably go to sleep." My voice lowers and I speak softly.

"Are you sure?" Dylan peeks at me, her eyes fluttering as she struggles to keep them open.

I can tell she's both disappointed and grateful for my executive decision. I can tell she wants me just as badly as I want her but she's had a long day, and we're both very tired. I can wait a little longer for her. I nod and smile at her. Dylan's eyes close once again and a little smile is painted on her lips.

"Hey, Shawn?"

"Yes, Dylan?" I ask quietly.

"Your box of donation clothes is still in the closet," Dylan giggles at the revelation, pleased she got me into one of her tight shirts, and now shirtless instead.

I chuckle, shaking my head at her antics. "Go to sleep, Dylan," I say with a breathy laugh.

"Goodnight," Dylan mumbles sleepily.

"Goodnight, Dylan," I whisper as her breathing gets deeper .

Chapter 44

Dylan

When I wake up with a pounding headache, I groan, blinking to clear the sleep out of my eyes. The curtains let in a little light but it's really my alarm that woke me up. I reach over and slap at my phone. The room is filled with silence for a few seconds before I hear the sound of snoring coming from the living room.

I look over at the empty space beside me in bed and notice how messy my bed is but the spot isn't warm so it wasn't vacated recently.

I yawn and push back the covers. The room is warm so Shawn must have made sure the heater was on correctly whereas I have yet to make the timing workout where I don't wake up freezing. It's warm enough this morning that I don't need to put on my robe. But I still slip my feet into my slippers and pad my way out into the living room.

Shawn is asleep on the tiny couch and he looks so silly that I have to place a hand over my mouth to stifle a giggle so I don't wake him. He's sprawled on the loveseat snoring lightly with a pained expression on his face. His limbs are flung all over the place; an arm and leg thrown over the back of the couch, another leg half on the floor, and his head is tilted at an awkward angle on the arm of the couch.

I smile as I pass by him to go start the coffee machine. I need some caffeine to wake me up, especially because I have a full day of work today and need to formally reject the offer for the position in Dallas and state my intention to remain at the office in Birch Lake.

"Good morning," Shawn's deep, sleep-filled voice reaches me in the kitchen. I look up and see him stretching on the couch.

"Hi, when did you move out here?" I ask and he chuckles.

"You kicked me out of bed last night."

I gasp. "No! I don't remember that. I'm so sorry. I don't usually sleep talk. Well, maybe once or twice," I start to ramble and he laughs again, cutting me off.

"No, you literally kicked me out," he explains, standing up to join me in the kitchen. He kisses my forehead as I hand him a mug of coffee.

"Oh, no. Did I really?"

"Yep," he says, taking a big gulp from his mug. "That bed is too small for the two of us." Shawn grins at me and I laugh.

"Oh. I guess that means you won't be sleeping over again?" I ask, feeling disappointed.

"I didn't say that." Shawn grins at me, moving in closer and putting his hand on the counter on one side of me. He leans in and the smell of coffee fills my nostrils. "You're worth suffering for."

"Oh?" I say, blushing.

"Is that too forward?" Shawn takes a step back but I slip my arm around his waist.

"No," I say. "But don't you have a house for sleepovers?"

Shawn raises his eyebrow at me but a slow smile creeps over his face. "'Sleepovers', huh?"

"Yes." I laugh. "Do you not want me at your house?" I tease, poking his chest.

"I barely know you," he says, his voice lowering as his eyes flit to my lips then back up to my eyes.

"Do you want to know me?" I ask, my voice dipping too as I lay my palm flat on his chest. I feel his heart beating faster under my fingers.

"I do," he admits. "Let me to take you to work today," he offers, resting his hand on top of mine, giving it a gentle squeeze.

"Why? You know I work right up the street, right?" I chuckle.

Shawn shrugs as I step away from him to grab the bag with our donuts in them.

"Oh, yes! I forgot about those." Shawn snatches the bag out of my hand. I laugh and grab a couple plates for us. "And I want to drive you to work so I can spend more time with you."

I bite into my donut, thinking it over. "Hm. But you could just walk with me," I point out.

"Walk to work? Have you seen the weather today?" Shawn scoffs, shoving another bite of his donut into his mouth.

"No." I perk up and hustle over to the window in the living room. Looking out, I see the town is covered with fresh snow. The window is freezing to the touch so I pull my hand back quickly, my fingers getting too chilly. Shawn's phone is laying on the table near the window so I pick it up an swipe it open. "You should really have a password on your phone," I call out to him.

Shawn chuckles and joins me in the living room. He wraps his arms around my waist, looking out the window. "What are you doing with my phone?" He asks but there's not annoyance in his voice, only curiosity and amusement.

"Checking the weather," I tell him. "My phone was in the bedroom," I add.

"Ah. So, what's it say?" He asks, releasing me to go back to his donut.

"It says that you are driving me to work," I relent, huffing.

Shawn chuckles, his mouth full. "I'll pick you up after too," he tells me.

"Did you just finish my donut?" I ask, my mouth dropping open in shock. He narrows his eyes at me and then glances at the donut in his hand.

"No… We both got two donuts, right?" He glances at the bag on the kitchen counter and the remaining donut on my plate. "Wait, did I eat three of them?"

"Oh, my god. Did you?" I laugh, moving passed him to snatch the bag from the counter. "Okay, this one is definitely yours," I say, pulling the donut from the bag and pointing it at him accusatorially.

"Do you want the rest of it?" Shawn swallows his bite and holds out the half eaten donut to me.

I roll my eyes and shake my head, gesturing for him to eat it. "Go ahead, you're mostly done with it anyway." I laugh.

He winks at me and then shoves the rest of the donut in his mouth. "You can have my other one," he mumbles around the donut.

"Oh, I will," I tell him, putting the donut back in the bag and grabbing some fruit to pack for a lunch.

"That's a pretty lame lunch," Shawn comments, crowding me in the kitchen, and licking his fingers in my ear.

"Are you offering to bring me something better?" I ask, teasing him as I pack my bag for work.

"If you want me to, but I was thinking more along the lines of us getting dinner together. Tonight," he adds when I turn to face him. I raise my eyebrows. "Yes, I'm asking you out."

"Bold," I say.

"Considering I just spent the night," he starts.

"On the couch," I interrupt.

Shawn waves the claims away. "Considering I just spent the night, and picked you up from the airport."

"And ate my donut," I add and he laughs.

"Hush," he scolds me before continuing. "I think it would only be reasonable if we went out on a proper date."

"A proper date, huh?" I ask, thinking it over. He nods, waiting for my response. "And, driving me to and from work wouldn't count, right?"

"Correct," he says.

"Where would this date take place?" I ask, pretending to still think it over.

"Wherever you want it to be. Whatever you want to do," he adds. Shawn watches me with narrowed eyes but I can see amusement dancing in them. I sigh dramatically and shake my head, disappointed. "What? Why are you making that face?" Shawn asks.

"Well," I start, biting my lip. Shawn nods encouragingly. "I do like a man who makes plans. I mean, don't get me wrong, I also like spontaneity but since it would be our first date, I would like to see some initiative," I tell him and now he nods thoughtfully.

"That's a good point," he says then goes quiet.

"Are you rescinding the offer?" I ask after a few seconds of silence. Shawn glances up at me and grins.

"No, Dylan. I am still going to take you out. But don't worry, I will have something planned," he says with certainty. This puts a smile on my face. "Now, go get ready for work, please. I'll have to drop you off early so I can go home and change before my work."

"Only because you said please," I say before turning on my heel and heading back toward the bedroom. Shawn follows me so I continue our conversation. "So, what does this mean?"

"It means that I will pick you up after work and have plans for our first date," he informs me, waiting outside the bathroom door as I wash up. He leans against the doorframe and I look at him in the mirror. He's still shirtless and very tempting. I force my eyes back to my face and focus on my skin care routine.

"Hm," I hum as I paint my face with a light amount of makeup, Shawn watches me curiously but he isn't looking at my face, his eyes are a little lower. I glance down and notice a couple of my buttons have popped open and I'm showing a lot of cleavage. "So," I say, standing up and turning to face him. His face flushes as his eyes lift to meet mine, caught. "Would this date involve us coming back here afterward?" I ask, stepping closer to him. His eyes drop down to my cleavage once more. I trail my fingers lightly down the edge of the opening. His gaze follows my fingers. He swallows before looking up at me again.

"Only if you want," he says, his voice husky.

"What if you want?" I ask, stepping even closer, close enough that he's forced to look down at me, easily looking down my shirt.

"If I want…?" He stutters, clearing his throat. "What I want," he tries again, "can wait until you're satisfied and ready."

"Ready for what?" I ask, shifting my hand from my shirt to his chest. His body is warm under my fingers. His pulse quickens as my fingers slid down his chest, down his stomach, and come to a rest on the waist of his boxers.

Shawn sucks in a breath and we both look down to see the tent in his boxers. I bite my lip, looking back up at him with a teasing smirk.

"I know you're messing with me," Shawn says and I giggle. "But I am down for whatever you want to do. Now or later. Before work, skipping work, or if you're keen to punish me, after work."

"I should really go to work," I say, pushing my hand flat on his lower stomach. He sighs and backs out of the doorway for me.

"Yeah, alright. Let me freshen up while you get changed," Shawn says, but then he wraps his arm around me and pulls me against his chest. He presses his lips flush to mine and I react instantly, my mouth opening for his tongue and leaning into his embrace. I moan softly, not embarrassed by the noise as Shawn groans in response, pleased by my reaction.

When we finally pull away, we're both panting and flushed. His lips are red and raw with a touch of pink lipstick and I imagine my lips are similar but with smeared lipstick. Shawn grins at me and then sidesteps me to enter the bathroom like he hadn't just kissed me breathless. He winks at me before closing the bathroom door.

I wobble as I turn toward my closet and push hangers aside aimlessly, my mind still reeling from the kiss. My body still on fire. If he had any questions about me being ready, I hope my response to that kiss answered all of the questions.

Thankfully, I am able to pull on a coordinated outfit by the time Shawn comes out of the bathroom. And I'm mostly clear headed, enough so that I'm not tongue-tied at his still shirtless, and pantsless figure. I lick my lips appreciatively before my eyes reach his face. He grins at me, not mad at me checking him out. He's cleaned the lipstick off his face and looks fresh and happy. He looks me up and down, his eyes moving slowly. I pose for him and he chuckles.

"You know, I don't think I've ever seen a woman pull off a pantsuit better than you," he comments with a grin.

"Thank you." I smile back. "Wait, will I need to change for the date?" I ask. Shawn frowns, thoughtfully.

"I'll let you know. And if you do, I will bring you back here to change. So, don't think you're getting out of me picking you up after work," Shawn says, narrowing his eyes at me. I giggle but nod my head. He claps his hands. "Alright, let's go. I wouldn't want you to be late." Shawn gestures for me to get moving.

We pull on our layers of coats by the front door. Shawn helps me button up my coat and I'm a little shocked by how romantic it feels. I like it. Shawn smiles at me when he's done, then he hands me my hat and scarf, and mittens.

"Oh, come on. We're just walking to your car," I protest but he takes the hat back and yanks it down over my head. I glare at him.

"I'm not risking you getting a cold before our date," he tells me. I sigh. "As much as I enjoyed taking care of you when you caught a cold when you first moved here," he adds with a wink, "I would rather take you out on our first date tonight. Or if you want, we can just stay home all day, have a floor picnic, watch a bunch of movies, do whatever else we want to do… You've had a long week, I'm sure they'd understand if you didn't go into the office today," Shawn tries to entice me. "You can try again on Monday."

"Hmm," I pretend to consider it then shake my head, trying to hide a smile. "Nice try," I giggle, pulling the mittens on then looping the scarf around my neck. "But, I need to go into the office since I've been gone a couple of days. I have some work to catch up on." And I have to write a polite rejection letter. "Alright, I'm bundled up, let's go."

"You look cute," he says, opening the front door for me.

I grab my work bag and practically stomp out the door. I know I'm acting like a child but Shawn's eyes twinkle with amusement so I continue the dramatics.

"Shut up," I grumble as I hop down the stairs in my giant snow boots.

Shawn follows me, chuckling all the way to his truck.

Chapter 45

Dylan

Michelle is already at work when Shawn drops me off and she runs to greet me at the door. Her eyes are wide and her grin stretches across her face.

"Was that Shawn?" She asks excitedly as she ushers me into the office, closing the door between us and the cold wind. "Does that mean you two spent the night together? Not that it is any of my business," she adds quickly, raising her hands to apologize.

"It's okay." I chuckle, going into my office to take off my winter ware. Michelle stands in my doorway, eager to hear any details. I take my time taking my gloves off, hiding my little smile. Michelle waits patiently, her smile never wavering. I glance over at her and she raises her eyebrows.

"Okay, technically, he did spend the night, but there wasn't anything…" I trail off, trying to find the right words. "Nothing happened. I mean, we talked. It was nice," I admit with a small smile. I look up to find Michelle grinning at me knowingly.

"That's great, hun," she says sweetly.

"He's taking me out tonight," I tell her as my smile starts to spread. Michelle looks like she's holding back a squeal as I nod my head to confirm she heard me correctly.

"Aw, honey, that's just so great! Shawn is adorable. He's been moody lately and I can't wait to see him finally happy," Michelle comments with a clap of her hands, delighted. "So, where is he going to take you?"

"I don't know." Michelle and I walk over to get coffee and continue chatting. "At first he said wherever I want but I shut that down very quickly," I tell her with a chuckle. "Max, my ex, used to be good about planning dates in the beginning of our relationship but after a while he really stopped and didn't make as much of an effort. I know that I want a man who continuously puts in effort, to let me know he cares. Shawn knows this. Spontaneity is good but a first date requires plans. So, he promised to make plans."

"That's good. He has it in him, I think," she says and then sighs. "I've had a few relationships where the men stop putting in effort, it hurts. I wasn't always able to express that to them and just let it happen. I'm glad you nipped that in the bud right away," she adds with a chuckle. "Although, I'm sure he was probably just saying it to be polite."

"Oh, definitely. He was trying to be sweet, but as it's our first date, and since I'm still new to town, I do want him to make plans," I chuckle. "I'm excited."

"What are you going to wear?" Michelle asks as she fills up two mugs for us.

"I don't know. He said he'd let me know," I tell her, taking a sip from the mug, letting the hot coffee help me defrost.

"What are we talking about?" Noah sneaks up on us and I almost jump, but steady myself so I don't spill.

"Jeez, Noah," Michelle breathes out, clearly startled too.

"How did you two not notice me coming in?" Noah asks with a chuckle, reaching for a mug to get himself some coffee too. "The wind whipped open the door, it was pretty loud," he tells us as he pours out the remainder of the coffee. "Hey, Mr. Bonoventure is coming in today, right?"

"Wait, what?" My hand freezes with the mug halfway to my mouth. "Oh, my gosh, is that today?"

"This afternoon, yes," Michelle agrees with a grimace. "I guess that's what we should have been discussing," she adds with a chuckle. "Are there any updates we need to make to his proposal?"

"I'll go over everything now," I say, heading back to my office to get prepared.

"Let me know if you need anything from me," Michelle says as I walk away.

"Thank you. Check on me in an hour or so!" I call out, sitting down at my desk to get to work. I set my mug aside and pull up Mr. Bonoventures financial plans and proposal.

A few hours pass while Michelle and I work on finalizing the proposal for Mr. Bonoventure. We make a few tweaks and review all communication we've had with him. Michelle runs out to get lunch for her and Noah while I stay in my office, eating my donut and fruit and pouring over the plans. When she comes back she knocks on the doorframe of my office. I look up from my screen.

"You ready for the meeting?" She asks, glancing down at her watch. "He should be here in half an hour."

"I'm ready. Is the conference room ready?" I ask, gathering up any materials I need to bring with me.

"It's all set. Probably not as fancy as your conference rooms in Dallas but we do have the same technology," Michelle informs me as we walk to the conference room.

It's smaller than the smallest conference room in Dallas, with only one medium sized table with four chairs around it but she's right that all the tech is the same. Michelle has set out water bottles for us and notepads for any notetaking. I have my laptop to plug in for the presentation and Michelle printed out copies to have in hand in case Mr. Bonoventure prefers paper copies to the technological presentation.

"Everything looks great, thank you, Michelle. Will you be joining us?" I ask, setting my things down on the table.

"Oh, do you want me to?" She asks, a little nervous.

"Of course. Did you not attend meetings with the last FA who worked with y'all?" I look up from my computer and she's twisting her hands together. "There was an FA VP here, wasn't there? Wait, what about Noah? Have you ever joined him in his meetings?"

"Noah tends to take advantage of the credit card he has and takes his clients out to eat. And the other VP we had liked to have me set everything up and often called me in to 'fix' the presentation when he couldn't figure out how to work it, but he usually dismissed me quickly when he thought he had a hold on it," Michelle explains with a grimace and a shrug.

I chuckle. "Yeah, I worked for one of those too. Well, I would like you to join me if you're okay with that. You did a lot of the work and if I forget anything you can help me out," I say with a bright smile.

"Okay." Michelle smiles back. "Let me go get my laptop to take notes," she says cheerfully, scurrying off to get her things.

"Okay, I'm going to get everything pulled up on the screen," I tell her as she leaves the conference room.

Michelle comes back a few minutes later. She sets her things down. "I think I saw him parking," she tells me. "I'll go greet him and bring him back here."

"Thank you, Michelle." I turn my attention to the screen in front of me as she hustles out of the room again. I flip through a few things on the big screen to make sure everything flows smoothly.

I hear chatter in the lobby and look up to see Michelle and Mr. Bonoventure talking to Noah who has stepped out to greet him. I guess I should have talked to Noah about Mr. Bonoventure since he'll more than likely help out with everything if we're able to secure Mr. Bonoventure as a client.

Before I have a chance to go greet him in the lobby, Michelle leads him back to the conference room. Mr. Bonoventure walks in with a big smile on his face. He looks excited to get started.

"Dylan!" He greets me, thrusting his hand forward and shaking mine vigorously. "So good to see you again."

"Mr. Bonoventure, great to see you too," I reply with a delighted smile. My nerves evaporated the second his joyous energy filled the conference room.

"Ah, Richard, please," he reminds me.

"Yes. Richard, glad to see you. Please have a seat." I gesture to the chairs around me, free for him to choose. Michelle waits until he's chosen his seat before she takes one near me. "How have you been?" I ask once we're all settled in.

"I'm doing well. My daughter is loving the snow these days. I promised her I would take her sledding and then skating on the lake later today," Richard tells us.

"Oh. Well, then we will try out best to get you out of here quickly," I say with a smile. Richard chuckles and nods his head approvingly.

"I don't want to rush you if you have a whole presentation prepared," Richard jokes. Michelle chuckles nervously at this and Richard grimaces apologetically. "Oh, I'm sorry. I didn't mean that in a bad way."

"Oh no, it's fine," I assure him, giving Michelle a reassuring smile. "We will always have a presentation prepared but it's not always needed," I explain with a wave of my hand.

"Well, I have to be honest with you," Richard starts and I start to get a little nervous. "I've been thinking about your proposal and ideas for my business and personal accounts."

Richard pauses, clearing his throat and skimming the proposals in the folder in front of him. Michelle and I glance at each other. Her look is questioning, I shrug. Richard taps his fingers on the table as we wait patiently for him to continue.

"I think I've heard all I need to hear," he says and we're still on the edge of our seats, unclear where he's going with this. Then he smiles. "I love everything I've seen so far and think my assets would be in very capable hands here. I think I'm ready to move forward with your group and look forward to working with you both." Richard smiles at both of us and taps a pen on the table waiting for our responses.

Michelle chokes out a cough, earning a concerned look from Richard. I push a water bottle toward her and she smile gratefully before taking a couple of sips. I turn my attention to Richard and smile back at him.

"That's amazing. I'm very glad to hear it. We are very much looking forward to working with you to help you accomplish all of your business and personal goals," I tell him, genuinely excited to get started. "Did you have any questions or concerns, or just anything you want us to do moving forward?" I ask, sitting forward in my chair and grabbing my laptop to make any notes.

"Actually, yes. Thank you for reminding me," Richard acknowledges and he flips through his notes for the meeting. "I have already established an account for my daughter, Evie," he says and I nod, remembering. "But I was hoping to get your opinions about the account. I want to make sure I've chosen the right one. I know there are options for Trusts or specifically for school, etc. When I first set up the account, I hadn't fully done my research and my current advisor, well, there is a reason I'm choosing to find a new one."

"Ah, that's understandable," I tell him, making note of his request on my computer and adding Michelle to the document. "Yes, we will definitely look over the account, make sure it's the right one for you and if not, we will find the one that best fits you and your daughter," I inform him and he smiles, nodding in appreciation.

"That would be great, thank you." Mr. Bonoventure starts to stand, indicating the end of the meeting.

Michelle and I stand as well and we all walk out of the conference room. Mr. Bonoventure stops to shake our hands, offering a polite wave to Noah as he heads toward the door. Once he's gone, Michelle and I stand in the lobby for a few seconds, letting the silence swirl around us.

"Well, that was… good," Michelle finally says.

"Yeah. Short and sweet," I admit with a nod, then let out an awkward laugh. "Well, I should probably get started," I start to say but Michelle frowns at me. "What?"

"You don't want to take two second to celebrate?" She asks with a laugh, shaking her head at me.

"You're right, you're right. Sorry. Yay!" I say, a weak cheer but my excitement is channeled into my desire to get back to work, and get started on a new proposal.

"What are we talking about?" Noah says, startling us. "How did the meeting go?"

"Oh, it was great!" Michelle gushes.

I leave the two of them to discuss the meeting and slip off back to my office to begin putting together options for Mr. Bonoventure's daughter. There are a few options that I think he should consider but I try to go above and beyond with options and details. Then eliminate ones I don't think he would go with, although I'll have them on hand just in case.

While I work, my mind keeps slipping to my date this evening. A smile is permanently on my face as thoughts of Shawn float into my mind. He still hasn't told me where we'll be going tonight or what we'll be doing. I hope he'll let me know what I need to wear. I need to be prepared in this weather. And I like to be prepared for dates too. Even if I haven't gone on a real date in a while, and I have definitely not been on a first date in a very long while. I can hardly remember my first date with Max. I think it wasn't very impressive but we were both broke college students and we made the best of what we had.

Thinking of Max now makes me smile. I'm glad we were able to end our relationship on such good terms. I was a little worried after his trip out here. I think we weren't fully aware of how hard long distance would be and how difficult it would be to communicate. I think if we had really wanted to be together, it would have been easier, or at least worth it. But we were friends from the start and I can see us remaining friends.

"Knock knock," Michelle says as she knocks on the doorframe to my office. I chuckle and look up from my computer.

"Hey, is it that time already?" I ask, glancing back down at the corner of my screen to check the time.

"It is, but also, you have a visitor," she tells me with a wink.

"Oh?" I look out the window in my office to the lobby and spot Noah talking to the visitor, blocking my view. Noah shifts and I spot Shawn, smiling at Noah, and hear his laughter floating into my office.

"Good evening, ladies," Shawn's deep voice makes Michelle turn around and we both openly check out Shawn who is now standing in my doorway. He looks even more handsome than he did this morning when he dropped me off.

I stand up, tearing my eyes away from Shawn, a smile on my face as I start to gather my things. "Hey, handsome," I say with a grin. "I'll see you on Monday, Michelle," I toss Michelle's way with a little wave.

"Don't forget 'Around the Town' is tomorrow!" Michelle calls after me and I halt.

"Oh, my gosh. That's tomorrow?" I ask, thinking of everything that needs to get done for it. "I completely forgot! I've been so busy…" I start to ramble but Michelle smiles and it stops me.

"Don't worry," Michelle says, reading my mind. "I already have our little marketing goodies to hand out. Your Dallas office sent us a few boxes that arrived while you were gone. And I had some brochures and flyers printed with all of our contact information, including you. I know it was a little premature since it wasn't official that you were staying, but I had a feeling you'd fall in love with this town." She grins at me and gives me a thumbs up, and a sly wink.

"Oh, okay. Whew." I let out a breath, feeling the stress roll off my shoulders. I try to hide my smile, pleased that she was confident in me sticking around. "Thank you so much, I can't believe I forgot about it. What time do I need to be here to help set up?"

"It technically starts at 1 pm, but I think I'm going to come in around 12:00 or 12:15 to get everything set up," Michelle informs me. "You're going to the Spaghetti Supper at 5, right?"

"Yes, I'll make sure she's there," Shawn says, wrapping his arm around my waist to pull me out of the office.

"Bye, Dylan. Bye, Shawn. You two have fun," Michelle's voice sparkles as she and Noah wave us out the door.

Shawn holds the passenger door of his truck open for me and this time I don't even need a boost getting into it. I swing my bag inside, grab the handle and hoist myself up.

"How was work?" Shawn asks when he gets into the driver's seat. He cranks the heat even though I didn't have to walk too far in the cold.

"It was great!" I want to tell him all about it but our ride is short so I decide to save the details for later in the date.

"That's good," he says, pulling to a stop in front of my apartment building. "So, I thought I would let you go change and I'll stop in to talk to Mom while you get ready."

"That sounds good to me!" I reach for the door handle then pause. "Wait, what am I changing into?"

"Just something comfortable, and warm. And sexy," he adds then he frowns and looks me up and down. "So, anything."

"Oh?" I tease, raising my eyebrows. "That was not as smooth as you thought it was."

Shawn winces but he laughs. "I'm a little disappointed in myself as well. I'll try to think of something better while you get ready," he tells me with one of his charming grins. "Now, stay put."

"Oh?" I start but he shuts off the truck and hops out quickly, rounding the truck to open my door for me. "Wow, such service," I marvel as he reaches his hand up to assist me.

"I aim to please," he says, his eyes twinkling. I've not seen this playful side of him often but I love it, it's just another piece of him that I'm learning about and enjoying.

Shawn holds my hand all the way to my door and I almost feel like the date was the ride home and I already want to invite him in. But I also want to go out. Inviting him in can wait.

"I'll be down at Mom's. Do you want me to come pick you up when you're ready?" Shawn offers.

"Oh, that's okay. I'll just pop down when I'm finished. I won't hold it against you," I say with a teasing squeeze of his arm as I unlock the apartment door.

"So generous of you," Shawn responds as he leans in, his voice lowering. His gaze flickers to my mouth and mine drops as well. Both of us stand eerily still. "Do you want me to wait?" He asks after a few seconds of silence and zero movement.

"Should we wait?" I ask, almost breathless under his spell. I look up into his eyes and I can tell that neither of us want to wait any longer. This wouldn't be our first kiss so I don't know why we're being so cautious right now. So careful with each other. My body practically vibrates from anticipation. My hand still rests on his arm and I feel his thick sinewy muscles. The warmth from his body through his layers radiates against my palm.

"I don't want to wait any longer," Shawn admits, his eyes dancing between mine and my lips.

I lean my head back against my door, creating a bit of distance between him so I can look up at him fully. His eyes are hungry but tender. I slide my hand up his arm and behind his neck. With my movement, Shawn reaches for my face. He cradles my cheek gently, leaning down to close the distance between us.

When his lips find mine, I have to hold back a moan from the pure bliss his kiss gives me. He's so gentle but firm, claiming my mouth. His thumb strokes my cheek as his lips push mine open. I accept the taste of his tongue, deepening the kiss and leaning into him to take more.

We're both breathless when we finally pull apart. He rests his forehead against mine, his eyes closed as I peek at him. His hand drops from my cheek and rests on my collar bone as he tries to brace himself for recovery. I giggle and his eyes open, catching me admiring him. He pulls his head away from mine and smiles slyly at me.

"That should hold us over, don't you think?" He asks, his hand slipping down my arm until his fingers are locked in mine. He squeezes them gently.

"I think so," I say, my voice raspy.

Shawn reaches past me and opens the door of my apartment. My eyes widen but a small smile plays on my raw, probably messy, lips. Shawn chuckles and shakes his head at me. "I was just opening the door for you, like a gentleman," he adds, his tone a teasing scold.

"Mhm," I hum, stepping into the apartment, away from him.

"Don't tempt me though." Shawn watches me as I strip off my first layer, my winter coat. I wink at him but then slowly shut the door. I laugh at the amusement on his face and blow him a kiss before finally shutting the door.

When I hear his footsteps retreating down the staircase, I rush off to my closet to find an outfit to wear. Then, I strip down and hustle through a shortened shower routine. I debate going through with every step but it's only our first date, I don't need to be fully prepared. I don't think.

This gives me pause though. Shawn and I are both more than ready and willing to take our relationship to the next level but we also are just going on our first date. Maybe we should wait. I don't know if I can wait though, after such a delicious kiss.

I guess we'll just see how the night goes.

Chapter 46

Shawn

"So, where are you taking her?" Mom asks with a huge grin on her face. I knew it was a bad idea to leave Dylan to get ready while I stopped in to see my mom. Word has already spread around town that Dylan and I are hanging out, and going out on our first date tonight. And after that kiss, I should have stayed in with her. There's time for our real first date now that Dylan has decided to stay in Birch Lake.

"The only place you can go on a nice date around here," I remind her, tapping my fingers on the counter, impatient to see Dylan again.

She swats my hand away. "There are a couple places," she scolds me and I scoff. "There are," she replies defensively with a shake of her head, unamused.

"I want to make a good impression on Dylan," I say.

"I think you already have, dear." Mom smiles then returns her attention to the computer in front of her.

"So, do you like her ideas?" I ask, changing the topic and leaning on the counter to get a glance at the screen.

"I love them! These Pinterest boards are so good," Mom gushes. She clicks on another board and scrolls through the pictures that Dylan found inspiring. "I can't believe she had time to do all of this."

"I know, she's amazing," I admit, a small grin on my face.

"I know I'm amazing but what exactly are we talking about?" Dylan's voice fills my ears and her laughter sends shivers throughout my stomach. I turn around to see her wearing her giant coat, unzipped to reveal a beautiful teal sweater dress.

"You look great," I spit out without thinking. Dylan smiles and looks down at her outfit.

"Thank you, it's new." She winks at me.

"We were talking about your ideas for the store," Mom says, knocking me out of the moment. "They're great! I can't wait to get started."

"Whoa, you might want to work on the renovations before ordering new decorations," I point out and both Dylan and Mom chuckle.

"I guess he's right. Might be better to have a place to put everything instead of storing it while there's work being done," Dylan says with a shrug and Mom nods.

"I guess. But picking out the decor is so much fun," Mom says with a laugh. "Okay, you two should get going. I'll find another time to force you two into helping me with the layout and all those details." Mom waves her hand, dismissing all the tiny details like moving walls.

I chuckle then reach for Dylan's hand. "You ready to go?"

"I am," she says, accepting my hand. Her gloved hand sits warmly in mine. "All bundled up, I see."

"I wouldn't want a repeat of this morning," Dylan replies, her eyes sparkling with delight as she teases me.

"I don't know if I should be hearing this," Mom calls over to us and I've almost completely forgotten she was standing a few feet away from us.

"Oh, no." Dylan blushes intensely. "He just made me put on mittens, a scarf, and a hat. Even though he drove me to work so it's not even like we were outside for very long," she tries to explain.

"I'm just trying to protect you," I also explain, appealing to Mom. "Remember how ill prepared she was for the winter when she first got here? I don't want her getting sick again."

"Wow, you two already fight like an old married couple," Mom laughs. Dylan goes quiet, her cheeks growing pink again. I'm a bit embarrassed as well. This is only our first date, and it hasn't even started yet.

"Well, thanks for that," I say to Mom and then turn to Dylan. "On that note, we should head out before she says anything worse."

"Have fun you two!" Mom calls out as I lead Dylan out to the car. Dylan waves goodbye and promises to stop by later in the week to discuss potential floorplan changes.

"So, where are we going?" Dylan asks, reaching over to put her hand on my leg after she's comfortably buckled into the passenger seat.

"I'm taking you to the finest restaurant in town," I tell her, glancing over at her as I feel the heat on my leg.

"The only restaurant in town?" Dylan quips, squeezing my leg gently. I chuckle, trying to ignore the feeling of her hand.

"Ha, ha, very funny." I shake my head, chuckling. "There are multiple restaurants but only one that is best for a first date."

"Can I guess or should I leave it as a surprise?" She asks, her eyes dancing in the setting sunlight.

"Surprise," I say as I parallel park out front of the fanciest restaurant in town.

"Gloria's," Dylan says with a smile, looking out the window before turning her smile on me. "I've been wanting to try it."

"Good. Stay here," I instruct, getting out of the truck and moving to the passenger side to open the door for her. Dylan grins down at me and takes my outstretched hand to get out of the truck.

"Even though you were bossy, it was still slightly romantic," Dylan comments as her feet hit the ground. She slips a little and I'm quick to wrap my arms around her waist. She smiles up at me and I want to take her straight home but I shake the thoughts out of my head as I right her. "Now that, that was more romantic," she adds with shy smile.

"Thank you. I'll try to keep it up tonight," I tell her, trying to keep up our banter from earlier this evening too as I hold the front door open for her.

"I look forward to it," she replies, touching her hand to my chest lightly as she passes me.

We're led to our table and I follow Dylan with my hand on the small of her back. She smiles at me over her shoulder. I pull out the chair for her and am rewarded with an appreciative and impressed smile. I roll my eyes, trying to contain my smile. My cheeks are starting to hurt from how much I've been smiling lately.

The hostess sets down our menus and tells us to enjoy before leaving us alone. We're both hungry after a long day at work so we sit quietly for a few minutes, looking over the menus.

"Hi, welcome to Gloria's. My name is Charlotte and I'll be your server today. Do you all know what you want to eat or do you need a few more minutes?" The waitress says before she does a double take. "Shawn?"

I lift my head up from the menu and recognize Charlotte instantly. "Charlotte! Hey, how are you doing?" I ask before I remember my manners. "Oh, Charlotte this is Dylan, Dylan this is Charlotte. We've known each other since high school," I explain to Dylan who smiles up at Charlotte.

"Hi," Dylan says, holding her hand out to Charlotte. "It's very nice to meet you."

"Hi!" Charlotte responds brightly, shaking Dylan's hand a bit too long as she realizes who Dylan is. "Oh, my gosh. You must be the Dylan I've been hearing about."

Dylan's eyebrows raise. "Oh no, that doesn't sound good," she says with a nervous chuckle.

"Oh, my gosh. No, totally all good things. I mean, of course, newbies always get talked about and there's some speculation that's less than flattering…" She trails off, her cheeks turning pink. "I'm so sorry. Those were all rumors before you arrived. You know, small town, word gets around, not always correctly," she tries to explain.

I chuckle, looking back and forth between her and Dylan, who looks very amused.

"It's okay," Dylan interrupts, cutting Charlotte off from any more ramblings. She chuckles. "We have rumors in big cities too. But I'm glad there are good things being said too," she adds.

"Yes, of course. Sorry," Charlotte mumbles again.

"It's fine, really. And it's good to meet you. I'd love to hear all about how troublesome Shawn was back in school," Dylan lowers her voice conspiratorially before sending a wink in my direction. I chuckle, shaking my head at the two of them.

"Oh, I have stories," Charlotte admits.

"Anyway," I interrupt, clearing my throat.

"Oh, sorry again. I'm interrupting your date." Charlotte chuckles, lifting her pad and pen. "What can I get you two?"

We place our orders and Charlotte runs off to put them in and take care of her other tables. When we're alone again, I look up to find Dylan smiling at me.

"What?" I ask, a small smile spreading across my face.

"Nothing," she says. I narrow my eyes at her. "Well, you're just very handsome. You clean up nicely," she comments, her eyes looking me up and down.

"Oh, yeah?" I ask, enjoying her eyes on me.

"Mhm," she hums appreciatively. "I've never seen you in anything other than jeans and a sweater," she says, her eyes traveling across my shoulders.

"I'm still wearing a sweater," I tell her.

"Yes, but this one is so nice and looks so soft." Her eyelids droop a little as she admire my sweater, and probably what's underneath it. I flex for her and her cheeks heat up. Her gaze returns to mine and her blush deepens when she sees my smirk. "Oh, hush," she scold me, tucking her hair behind her ear.

"I didn't say anything," I respond with a wink, making her blush even more. I like this side of her. I've liked every side she's shown me and can't wait to see more.

Dylan reaches out and touches my arm that's resting on the table. Her fingers rub over the material of my sweater and I wish there wasn't material between us. I want to feel her hands on me and by the look in her eyes, she's thinking the same thing too.

Before I can suggest leaving the restaurant and heading back to my place, Charlotte arrives at our table with our food. Dylan pulls her hand away and its back in her chair so Charlotte can place the food in front of us.

"Alrighty, here you go," Charlotte says as she slides the plates in front of us. "How does everything look?" She asks, stepping back from the table. "Do you two need anything else?"

"Looks good," I say, watching the steam rise from my meal. Dylan licks her lips, admiring her food as well.

"It looks delicious!" Dylan says.

Charlotte chuckles, wiping her hands on the apron tied around her waist. "Good, I'm glad. Let me know if you need anything. I'll check in on you two in a few."

"Great, thanks," I say as Charlotte refills our waters and hustles off to another table.

"Wow, this is so good," Dylan mumbles around a mouthful and I smile, watching her devour her food. She slows when she notices me staring. "What? I didn't have much lunch today," she protests.

"I saw you pack your lunch," I remind her with a chuckle, digging into my own dinner. Dylan narrows her eyes at me and then points her fork at me too.

"Don't you judge me, sir," she reprimands me playfully.

"I would never." I wink at her.

"Good," she says, happily biting into another forkful of pasta. She lets out a breath and steam pours out of her mouth.

"Hot?" I ask with a laugh, blowing on my fork so I don't make the same mistake. She nods, fanning at her slightly open mouth.

"But sooo good," she says once she's able to swallow her bite. She smiles up at me and takes another bite, stopping to blow on it this time.

The pursing of her lips stirs something inside me and it seems like a very erotic act, blowing on her hot food. She smirks, noticing my reaction. I shift in my seat and shake my head at her. She smiles, pleased with herself.

"Oh, tell me about your meeting," I say, trying to find a safe subject so we can eat our dinner in peace.

"It was great!" Dylan practically bounces in her seat. "We had a great meeting the first time," she reminds me with a wave of her hand, "but this was so fast and he had already decided that he want to work with us!"

"That's incredible!" I tell her with a genuine smile on my face, happy for her.

"I know. I'm so excited. Michelle was a huge help, I really love working with her," Dylan gushes with pride.

"How's Noah doing?" I ask, curious how he's handling Dylan landing such a big account.

"Oh, he's fine. I think he's more than a little impressed. I've already told him that I'll need his help too. We're a team. All three of us," Dylan says with a nod, firm in her stance.

"Do you have a team name?" I ask and she smiles instantly.

"No, but oh my gosh, what a good idea. Although most groups go by the senior advisors name," she says, biting her lip as she thinks about it.

"Wouldn't that be you?" I question.

"It would," she admits, chewing as she thinks. "I don't think I would want that though. I think our group name should be something we all decide on. Maybe it could just be our location, since we're the only group in the area," Dylan says with a shrug.

"That's not a bad idea," I tell her and she nods.

"I'll bring it up with them tomorrow. Since I'm staying, I think having a group name will make it official," Dylan says with a laugh.

When our meals are finished, and I've paid the check, Dylan and I stand and walk to the door. Her hand fits perfectly in mine and we don't bother putting on our mittens as we head into the wind on the walk back to my truck.

"So, what's next this evening?" Dylan teases me, swinging our hands between us.

"Oh, you want more?" I ask, raising my eyebrows.

"I don't want the date to be over," she admits, her voice quiet as she looks over at me, almost bashful.

"Me either," I admit, making her smile. "I want to take you home," I say and she blushes more, "but, I do have something else planned. If you're up for it?" I ask.

"Well, as much as I wouldn't mind you taking me home," she says with a wink, as I open the passenger door for her. "I want to see what else you have planned."

"Good. Buckle up," I tell her, helping her into the car the rounding it to climb into the driver's seat.

Chapter 47

Dylan

"Where are we going?" I ask again. Shawn chuckles at my antics but shakes his head instead of responding to me. "Are we going night fishing?" I ask as Shawn pulls off the road and heads toward the lake. The idea sounds kind of exciting but Shawn is giving zero indication that I've discovered his plans.

I narrow my eyes at him but he ignores me with a big smile on his face. He navigates around ice house and other cars before coming to a stop in front of the hut he brought me to before.

"So, it is night fishing?" I ask, almost triumphantly, pleased with my guess but he just laughs again.

Shawn exits the truck and comes to my side to help me down. He takes my hand to help me. "Be careful," he instructs.

"Maybe you should just pick me up," I suggest with a sly smile. He laughs at me, rolling his eyes but his hands grip my hips without hesitation. He squeezes gently before lifting me out of the seat and setting me down on a pile of snow, covering the icy lake. I test the ground, still unsure of walking on a frozen lake. It's even more intimidating so late in the evening with little light to see where I'm stepping.

I'm a little huffy that he doesn't carry me to the hut but he does hold my hand, leading me into the warmish space.

The hut looks the same as it did when he first showed it to me but there are a few little new things. Now, on the little table sits a bottle of wine and two glasses. Beside them are a platter of mini desserts.

"I didn't know what you liked for dessert," Shawn says when I walk over to the platter, shedding my coat before reaching for a delectable.

"All of these," I say, waving my hand over the platter before finding one I want to try first, and popping it into my mouth. "I love sweets. These all look amazing."

"Local bakery," Shawn tells me. "But that's not the biggest surprise." He grins at me, pleased with himself. I turn back to face him, raising my eyebrows.

"Oh?"

"Look up," he tells me.

I do as he says. And when I tilt my head back, I see the stars sparkling in the sky. I'm blown away with how many there are, how bright they are. It's beautiful. I gasp and hear Shawn's deep chuckle.

"Again, not even the best part," he tells me when I drop my head to look at him. "Come here," he instructs, moving to sit on the cushioned seats, patting the place beside him.

I settle in next to him, leaning against his chest on the cozy seat. He's angled sideways to fit me comfortably against him. Shawn wraps one arm around my waist, holding me to him and then he reaches for the wine he must have poured as I gazed up at the stars. He hands me a glass then tilts his head back to look up at the sky. I must watch him too long because he smiles and touches my chin to tip my head back as well.

"We're just in time," he tells me, his voice lowered in a hushed tone. He takes a sip of his wine before returning his attention to the sky. I look up as well and I wonder how I didn't notice the clear roof last time. I don't think there was one, maybe he modified it for our date, or it just had panels to remove, or a skylight I didn't notice.

A flash of light interrupts my thoughts and I let out another gasp as the sky explodes into a symphony of lights. The colors seem to dance across the sky in such a mesmerizing display, I can't take my eyes off the sky. At first, I think it's fireworks but after a few seconds, I can tell this is all because of Mother Nature.

Shawn kisses the side of my neck, and I can feel his laughter again my back as it rumbles through his chest.

"This is amazing," my voice comes out as a whisper, filled with awe. I can't tear my eyes from the sky as I watch the lights dancing, twisting and turning.

We sit and watch for a few minutes before Shawn squeezes my arm. I sit up and he takes my hand.

"Come on," Shawn says, pulling me off of the seat. He hands me my coat and helps me redress for the cold night air.

Once we're both prepared, I follow him back outside. We walk around the hut and a few feet away before Shawn stops and pulls me into his arms, my back against his chest again as he points us in the right direction.

The lights are even more beautiful with the frozen lake in the foreground and the lights dancing along the horizon.

"Wow," I marvel, leaning back against Shawn's chest. He wraps his arms tightly around me, our body heat keeps me from freezing in the cold night air but it's still cold. Shawn pulls my hat down over my ears as I shiver. I snuggle back into him and he rewraps his arms around my middle. "This is beautiful. Wait, what is it?" I ask, suddenly realizing that I don't know what I'm looking at.

Shawn chuckles again, rocking me from side to side. "These are the Northern Lights," he tells me, speaking softly, his lips against my ear.

"Oh, my gosh. Really?" I squeal with excitement. "I've always wanted to see the Northern Lights. I didn't know Minnesota had them."

Shawn nods, squeezing me against him as we sway together under the lights. "It actually happens relatively often. I mean, not enough that it isn't still amazing every time I get to witness them," Shawn tells me and I glance over my shoulder to see his eyes wide, watching the lights move.

I turn around in his arms, facing him now. He looks down at me and something between us shifts. This night has been romantic and sweet. All that's missing is a big declaration of love. Although, it might be too soon for that, even if I'm starting to feel that way. But there are other ways of expressing one's affection. Shawn's eyelids lower as he reads the hunger in my eyes.

"Let's go back inside," Shawn says, reading my mind. I nod eagerly then giggle as he hustles me back into the ice house.

As soon as the door shuts, Shawn's hands are on me. He tugs at my jacket, almost breaking the zipper but I swat his hands away and easily slide the zipper down. He grunts and starts to undress himself instead. I giggle as his lips press against mine. We're leaning at an awkward angle, trying to undress ourselves while still kissing. We're struggling in the small space but eventually we lose a couple of layers and Shawn pulls me into his lap as he drops onto the cushion.

"Is it okay to do this here?" I ask, breathless as his lips move to my neck. His hands caress my back, my sides, moving around to my front.

"What do you mean?" His voice is rough and he nips at my skin. I gasp and work hard to stifle a moan when his hands slide up my stomach.

"Your friends," I manage to say as I suck in air, feeling his fingers touch the lace of my bra. "They won't…walk in?" I try to form the right question but my words are getting lost from the feeling of his hands and mouth on me.

Shawn chuckles, his hot breath on my neck. He plants a kiss there before responding, "No, it's all ours tonight," he assures me. His mouth returns to nipping at my neck and down to my throat. I lean back to expose more skin for him to kiss.

"Good," I say, my voice throaty and deep. "That's good," I try again but I still sound funny even after tyring to clear my throat. I suck in a breath when Shawn's lips work across my collar bone to the middle of my chest. He kisses down and I tangle my hands in his hair, holding him against me.

"Very good," he mumbles against my chest.

I shift on his lap and can feel him against me, even with a couple of layers still between us. His groan lets me know he's in just as much pain as I am, needing me as badly as I need him.

"Is it too soon?" He asks, looking up at me.

Too soon? Too soon after my breakup? Too soon after we got together? The questions fill my mind but they disappear when his hand grips me firmly.

"No," I respond with another gasp for breath. I trail my hands down the back of his neck and he smiles at me. His smile is soft and gentle, there's no pressure to continue. "It's not too soon. I want to. I've been thinking about this for a while," I say, bringing his face back to mine and kissing him softy this time.

When we pull back, there is a big smile on his face.

"Oh? Is that right?" Shawn teases me and I roll my eyes at him, a smile playing on my lips. "I have thought about you nonstop since I met you," he admits shamelessly, his voice lowering again, his eyes locked on my lips. I shift on his lap, pushing down gently as I move my hips, making him groan again.

"What have you thought about? Specifically," I add, trailing my fingers down his neck and dipping them below the collar of his undershirt.

"I've thought about how your lips would feel against mine," Shawn tells me, his thumb tracing my bottom lip.

"What else?" I ask, whispering against his thumb, our eyes locked on each other.

"I've thought about how your body would feel against mine, how your breasts would feel in my hands, my tongue on your neck," as he talks, his hands move over my body, gripping and touching each place he mentions, ending with a flick of his tongue against my neck.

"Please," I moan out, my eyes closing automatically, my head falling back. "I want you," I say with a heated breath. Shawn pauses his neck kisses and I whine.

"Open your eyes. Look at me. I want you to look at me when you say that," Shawn's voice is needy and dreamy.

My eyes fly open and my eye lids lower with lust. "I want you," I tell him, slower now.

I push my hands up under his shirt, bracing them on his stomach, maintaining eye contact. His eyes flash with hunger and delight. And I giggle as he lifts me up, standing with me and then spinning us around so I'm seated on the cushion and Shawn is kneeling in front of me. His fingers hook under the waistband of my thermal tights and I lift my hips to help him pull them down my body. He doesn't take his eyes off me until they're fully off. Then his attention turns to my legs, shaved thankfully. He plants kisses on my knee, working his way up one thigh then giving love to the other as well, squeezing both gently as he works. I lean back and sigh softly, running my fingers lazily through his hair.

Shawn looks up at me, asking for permission. I nod, biting my lip and he smoothly slips my panties down my legs before stretching up to kiss me again. Our mouths lock together and I open my mouth for him, kissing him deeper as I hear him rustling in his jeans. He pulls away briefly, grabbing a condom from his wallet. He holds it up triumphantly and it makes me giggle. He covers my mouth with his, swallowing my laughter with a deep chuckle of his own. Then our laughter is cut short, turning into moans as he pushes my legs wide, our bodies fitting together perfectly as he presses against me then into me.

"Are you too cold?" Shawn asks, pulling the blanket up to my chin after I shiver for the third time. "It won't get much warmer in here. We could get dressed and head back to my house," he offers.

I'm so comfortable nestled in his arms but the chill is getting to me. I shiver again even though I want to say I'm fine so I can stay in his arms a little bit longer. Shawn rubs my arms under the blanket trying to warm me up but he can feel the goosebumps on my arms.

"Okay, that's it. Time to get dressed," Shawn instructs. He moves me off of him and wraps me in the blanket before venturing out to grab our discarded clothes. He hops around, his feet probably freezing, quickly trying to get redressed. I giggle watching him and he shoots me an annoyed, playful look.

Shawn finishes dressing and grabs my clothes, coming back over to me, shoving them under the blanket for me. I maneuver under it, pulling on my clothes by wiggling around. I fold up the blanket and turn to find Shawn holding my coat out for me.

"Thank you," I say as I slip my arms into the coat. He helps zip me up and it's a very intimate act, my heart starts to beat a little faster as he tugs me closer to zip up to my chin. Shawn smiles at me and leans in to plant a kiss on my forehead.

"I don't know if this is too forward," Shawn starts and I raise my eyebrow at him. Too forward after what we just did? The thought makes me chuckle. "Do you want to come home with me?" Shawn asks, rolling his eyes at my look.

I place my hand on his chest, leaning in to kiss him softly. "I would love to come home with you," I tell him, my voice lowering as I look up at him from under my eyelashes.

"Good," Shawn says with a nod before he wraps me in his arms and hustles our huddled bodies out to his car.

Chapter 48

Shawn

Bringing Dylan home is another feeling of euphoria. And also panic because I don't remember if I cleaned up well enough to have a visitor, let alone Dylan.

We kick off our shoes in the entry way and I note that I should get a shoe rack or at least a basket. Although a basket would probably get wet and moldy when all the snow and ice melted off our shoes.

"Hey, what are you thinking about?" Dylan asks, reaching for my coat and tugging me closer to her. She's already lost a few layers while I was too busy in my head.

"Trying to remember if I cleaned up," I admit and she laughs, her hands working at the buttons of my outer coat. I shrug the coat off, taking Dylan's coat also to hang up in the coat closet by the door.

"I'm sure it's not too bad," Dylan assures me but I'm not convinced.

I watch as she walks into the living room, rubbing her arms a little, still defrosting. I make my way over to the fireplace, kneeling to shove a few logs onto the stack and striking a match, the fire lighting pretty quickly. Dylan gasps and I turn to find her staring at me, eyes wide and a small grin on her face.

"What?" I ask, chuckling as I stand and walk over to her, taking her into my arms.

She snuggles in close, her hands on my chest, smoothing across the fabric of my sweater. "That was incredibly hot," she tells me, no sarcasm in her tone.

"What? Me lighting the fire?" I ask with a raised eyebrow and another deep chuckle. She nods, her eyes still slightly wide, impressed.

"Uhm, yes," she states clearly. "I was tired from earlier but that just woke me up." I laugh, shaking my head at her. "Isn't it everyone's fantasy to make love in front of a roaring fire?" She adds with a wiggle of her eyebrows. She doesn't do it well though and ends up looking a little silly. We both chuckle.

"You know, I think I've heard something like that," I tell her with a bemused smile. She rolls her eyes at me now but pats my chest. "That's a common thing in old romance novels, right?" I ask. She eyes me with an appreciative smile. I shrug. "My mom owns a bookstore, remember?" I wink at her, releasing her from my arms and lead her into the kitchen.

"Ah, of course. I bet you've read every book in there," she teases me, leaning on the counter to turn on the coffee maker.

"Who's collection do you think it is?" I respond with a smile and she laughs out loud.

"Wow, very impressive." Dylan pushes off the counter and maneuvers her way in front of me, effectively trapping herself between me and the counter.

I smile down at her, leaning in for a soft kiss.

Only seconds later, the coffee maker starts spitting out fresh coffee, interrupting our moment. I lean back and tuck a stray piece of her hair behind her ear before grabbing a couple of mugs for us. I fill out mugs, handing one to Dylan then lead her back to the living room which is now significantly warmer with the fire going.

Dylan waits for me to sit down before she cuddles in close to me, trying to hide a yawn as she lifts the mug to her lips. I chuckle and wrap my arm around her waist, pulling her even closer to me.

When I kiss the top of her forehead, I breathe in the delicious fruity smell that I've come to associate with her presence. Soon, Dylan is breathing deeply and I notice her grip on her mug loosening. Gently, I take it from her hand and set it on the side table along with mine, trying my best not to jostle her.

Stretching, I reach for a blanket and pull it over us, making sure Dylan is tucked in so she doesn't get cold in the night when the fire finally goes out. I do have a heater in my house but I thought she would appreciate the fireplace, I prefer it too.

Before long, my eyelids start to feel heavy and the weight of Dylan on my chest, her heavy breathing, and the crackling of the fire luls me to sleep.

The next morning, I wake up to Dylan returning to the couch. She smiles, sitting down next to me, the edges of her hair wet and her face looks fresh.

"Good morning," I groan, stretching before struggling into a sitting position. I keep learning how uncomfortable sleeping on a couch is but I'm willing to suffer through it if it means being close to Dylan. Dylan rewards me with a smile, a bright, happy smile. She reaches for me and pulls me in for a good morning kiss.

"Good morning," she says when we pull away. The smile on my face makes her smile grow.

"You brushed your teeth," I accuse after tasting her minty fresh breath. I give her a knowing look. She blushes but her smile turns to a grin.

"I didn't use your toothbrush if that's what you're worried about," she informs me with a giggle, planting a little teasing kiss on my cheek. "I did the toothpaste on my finger thing," she explains, pushing off the couch to collect our cold coffee mugs.

I tread behind her, my limbs still stiff from the couch. One very satisfying stretch of my arm makes a popping noise that causes Dylan to give me a look of disgust and concern. I laugh and wave her hands away to take over making the coffee.

"Do you want me to drop you off at your office today?" I ask when we lull into a silence while the coffee brews.

"Yes, please," she says with a smile. "Should we talk about last night?" Dylan asks after I've handed her a fresh mug of coffee and she's taken her first sip.

"Are you having regrets?" The question slips out but I need to know. I have no regrets from last night but it might have been too fast for Dylan.

"Oh. Well," she starts, setting her mug down on the counter and I feel my heart drop into my stomach. Instead of interrupting to ask more questions or to try to reassure her about my feelings, I stay quiet and wait for her to continue. "No," she tries again, "I don't have any regrets. Part of me wants to feel guilty that I've moved on so fast, but I think that Max and I were over a long time before we officially ended things. And I think that you've been on my mind a lot longer than I care to admit."

"Is that such a bad thing?" I ask, moving closer to her and sliding my arm behind her back, pulling her to my chest. Dylan's smile turns cheeky. She leans into me, biting her lip, pretending to think over my question.

"Hm," she ponders. "Not necessarily. But what if you don't live up to my expectations?" She teases, batting her eyelashes playfully.

To lean into the moment and to tease her right back, I lower my head and start to plant gentle kisses down her neck and to the base of her throat. "What if I exceed all of them?" I ask, my voice thick with lust.

"Oh," she giggles, shivering in my arms. I can't tell if she's cold of if the shivering is from my mouth. "You think highly of yourself," Dylan tries to tease me but her voice wavers as my mouth goes lower on her skin, dipping under the tank top she stripped down to sometime in the night.

"Nah," I say, nipping at her skin to hear her gasp. "I just want to prove you wrong." I pause. "Or right. Depending on how you're looking at it."

Dylan chuckles but I can see her considering it. She runs her fingers through my hair, tugging my head back gently. When I look up at her, she touches her lips to mine softly and slowly, savoring the kiss.

"Are you doing this 'Around the Town' thingy too?" She asks, biting her lip, still considering things.

"Yes. My guys are setting up so I don't need to be at the gym until 1 pm," I say and Dylan's eyebrows knit in confusion. "Businesses that are not on the main street can set up booths in the school gym," I explain and she nods. "Why?" I ask, standing up and pulling her in close again, redirecting back to her question about the time. "Do you want to have a long talk about everything?" I ask, and then wince. "That sounded sarcastic but I promise that it was not meant that way," I promise her quickly but Dylan just laughs and pats my chest, reassuringly.

"It's okay." She bites her lip, looking at me carefully. "Do you want to have a long talk about everything?" She turns the question around on me but I can see her glance at the clock on the stove. It's not even 9 yet so we have plenty of time before 'Around the Town' starts.

I chuckle and my laugh brings her eyes back to me. "Worried that conversation would take too long?" I tease, tugging the ends of her hair. She bats her eyes at me and then licks her lips.

"Worried it wouldn't leave us enough time to do some other things," Dylan responds with a twinkle in her eyes.

"Should we have the talk later then? Maybe after the Spaghetti Supper? Which is going to be our second date," I tell her, taking her hand and leading her out of the kitchen. We didn't make it to the bedroom last night, and I haven't had the chance to give her a full tour, but all of that can wait.

"Asking for a second date already? And so soon too. Aren't you supposed to wait a couple of days before even speaking to me again?" Dylan giggles as I pull her along to the bedroom.

I shoot her a surprised look over my shoulder and she giggles again. "That's…" I can't think of how to respond to that. "Do people actually do that?"

"Oh, yeah. My friends complain about it all the time." She shrugs. "Dating is a sad, strange game."

"Ah, well… I want to go on a second date, and a third, and a fourth, and however many you will accept," I have no issue saying and this makes Dylan grin at me. "Starting with the Spaghetti Supper this evening."

"Let's see how this morning works out and then I'll get back to you," Dylan grins, her voice tittering as she holds back giggles. I shake my head at her, a smile playing on my lips.

Scooping her into my arms, she squeals and I bring her into my room. Thankfully, it's clean, and my sheets are fresh out of the wash (a couple of days ago). I lay her down on my bed and climb over her. She reaches up for me and pulls me down into a deep kiss.

Chapter 49

Dylan

After a lovely and fun morning, Shawn drops me off at the office and I hustle inside, eagerly accepting a mug of coffee from Michelle. The grin on my face must be unbearable but ever since I got back from Dallas and finally made up my mind, I've been deliriously happy. I'm also nervous but very excited for what the future holds in Birch Lake and with Shawn.

Shawn wanted to walk around with me during 'Around the Town' but I wasn't sure when I would get to so I promised to text him to let him know and if I got too busy, I'd just meet him at the Supper around 5 pm for our second date.

"You look happy this morning," Michelle comments, eyeing me with a sly smile. "Happier even than Friday," she adds, her eyes twinkling.

"It was a great date, and a great start to the weekend," I tell her. She raises her eyebrows, wanting to hear more. She follows me to my office as I take off my coat and tell her about our first real date together, leaving out a few sordid details. "We went out to dinner at Gloria's, which was delicious, and then he took me out to his little ice hut, ice house?"

Michelle shrugs her shoulders and waves away the question, gesturing for me to continue.

"Right, whatever they're called. And then," I pause to be dramatic, blushing a little as I think back on it. "Then, we got to see the Northern Lights," I tell her with a squeal. "It was so romantic and amazing, and apparently not super rare but still, it was incredible." I sigh, sitting down in my chair and leaning back with a dreamy smile on my face.

Michelle perches on the chair across my desk, sitting on the edge of the seat, eager to hear more. "Wow," she marvels, impressed with the date Shawn planned. "You know, I just knew he would go all out for the right woman," Michelle says with a nod of her head, proud that she was right about him. The thought makes me blush and makes me feel incredibly happy.

"What are you two chatting about?" Noah's voice makes me jump a little. Michelle and I both startle at his interruption, she puts her hand on her chest and chuckles. Noah leans against the door frame, eyeing both of us. "Are you guys just going to sit around all day and make me do most of the work?" He teases, shaking his head at us.

Michelle scoffs, rolling her eyes at him. "Honey, I've already gotten almost everything set up and it looks like you're just now rolling in." She eyes him, up and down. "Did you just wake up?" She asks with a chuckle.

Noah rolls his eyes as he tries his best to stifle a yawn. "It's Saturday," he says in his defense, shrugging. "Anything you need me to do? Maybe taste test that chili you brought?" He offers with a sly grin, rubbing his hands together, quickly waking up.

Michelle shakes her head, holding back a laugh. "Yeah, fine. It should be warm now. Go test it," Michelle says, waving him away. He happily pushes off the door frame and goes back into the lobby.

"Alright, let's finish setting up," I say, standing up from my chair with an excited wiggle. "Who is going to walk about first?"

"Eager for your chance to explore the town?" Michelle teases as she follows me into the lobby. Noah is greedily eating a bowl of chili, he gives her a thumbs up before digging his spoon in for another large bite. She chuckles and goes over to the table to organize things.

"I am eager to explore," I agree, helping her rearrange a few brochures and trying to make a pile of pens look cute. Michelle smiles and hands me a cute mug with 'Birch Lake Group' imprinted on it. "Did you make this?" I ask, holding it up to admire while I drop a handful of pens into it.

"Yeah," Michelle says. "I wasn't sure what our group name would be so I just went with Birch Lake since there aren't any other financial groups in town, yet. I hope you don't mind, but I did add your name to most of the marketing items," she adds with an embarrassed smile as she shows me the inside of the brochures. An old picture of me smiles up at me with my job description down below.

I chuckle. "No, I don't mind. It's funny that you knew I would be staying here before I even knew." Michelle chuckles and winks at me. "Although, I need to take a new photo. This picture was from my first year as a Financial Advisor."

"Ah, that's why you look so young and new, and full of hope," Noah joins in with a mouthful of chili. He steps aside to let us walk around the table, adjusting everything.

"Oh, hush," Michelle scolds Noah while I laugh. "Okay, doors open in ten minutes. I expect a full day since we have the new girl in town." Michelle gestures to me and I blush. "I debated getting a booth at the gym but I wanted you to get the full experience of 'Around the Town'," Michelle explains.

"Well, thank you. I'm excited."

"Oope, we can't forget our stamps," Michelle remembers, hustling over to her desk and grabbing three stamps and ink pads for all of us. She hands me a set and I grin at the cute design. "I didn't have a lot of ideas for financial related stamps," Michelle says with a grimace.

"Oh. Well, I like it," I assure her, testing the stamp on a notepad. The stamp comes away perfectly with our Birch Lake Group name and a couple of dollar signs,all inside a rectangle. I chuckle. "It's cute. Oh no," I groan.

Michelle looks over at me. "What's wrong?"

"I forgot to get a passport for myself," I pout.

Michelle, on the other hand, smiles at me. I raise my eyebrows at her. "Don't you worry about it. Bella stopped by while you were in Dallas and she dropped one off for you!" She tells me.

"Really?" I ask with a sigh of relief. Michelle nods, going back to her desk to grab the passport for me. I clutch it happily when she hands it over. "Oh, that's amazing. Wow, y'all really do look out for each other here, huh?" I chuckle.

"Yes, ma'am. That's what small towns are all about." Michelle beams at me.

Chapter 50

Shawn

"You look happy," Xander greets me from his kicked back, seated position behind our bare table.

I narrow my eyes at him and swat at his dirty boots that are dripping melted snow onto the table. "You couldn't have set up at all?" I try to reprimand but my mood doesn't work for scolding.

Xander narrows his eyes right back at me, suspicious of my mood this morning but he lowers his boots to the ground. "I brought the table," he protests, gesturing to the table. It's one that he built from some leftover wood and stains from the shop. When he asked me if he could build the table, he was worried that I didn't know he and my dad had a deal that he could take any left over things, that weren't needed or useable, to create beautiful pieces on his own time.

"It looks great," I say, running my hand over the smooth finish. "But, what about the things for our shop?" I clarify.

Xander shrugs. "Kayson has the rest of the stuff."

"I'm here, I'm here," Kayson says, out of breath as he comes jogging over to the table. He drops a couple of bags on the ground with a heavy thud before shucking off his coat. "Sorry I'm late boss. I thought I had everything packed up but I guess I forgot something." He reaches into one of the bags and pulls out the business cards carved into thick pieces of wood. "Nice touch, huh?" He asks, like it wasn't my idea.

"They look great. How many do we have?" I ask as I grab the other bag and lift it onto the table to empty it out.

"Hm." Kayson starts setting them out on the table, arranging them to look nice. "Well, with your 10, my 8, and Xander's 5," Kayson says, glancing over at Xander who shrugs. "We have 23," he continues. "But I think that should be enough since most people in town know about us. I still wish we could have put a QR code or something on the back but I get that would have been difficult to perfect by hand."

"Okay, cool, next time. Alright, now back to the, 'you look happy' conversation," Xander interrupts, pulling stuff out of the bag on the table.

"What are we talking about?" Kayson asks, dragging a chair behind the table to sit beside Xander.

I narrow my eyes at the two of them. "We're talking about our shifts for today," I say and continue before either of them can speak. "Xander, is your family stopping by at a certain time?"

"Yeah, around 2:15, is that okay?" He asks and I nod then look over at Kayson.

"Okay. Kayson, why don't you go first, then Xander you can head out whenever your family gets here," I instruct and both men nod.

"What about you, boss?" Xander asks, wiping the melted snow off the table.

"Yeah, you should go out this time. We can handle the table while you're gone," Kayson assures me.

"Fine," I say, giving in quickly. Last year, I stayed at our table the whole time but this year, I've got a few places I want to go to, to bring Dylan to. "I'll go later though but I'll be back before 5 so we can help clear the place and set up for the Spaghetti Supper."

"Works for me, boss." Kayson taps the table with a smile.

"How's everything looking over here?" Eloise stops by our table, causing Xander to sit up with a smile. "You guys ready for 1 to roll around?"

"There's our favorite 2nd grade teacher," Xander grins at her and she rolls her eyes at him.

"I'm the only 2nd grade teacher at this school," she replies as Xander stands to give her a quick hug.

"Still," Xander teases as she moves to side hug Kayson and then myself. "Marcus talks so highly of you that now Kaylee is begging to be in your class next year. I keep telling her she still has a few years before then but she made me promise to let her be in your class when she finally gets to 2nd grade."

Eloise laughs, fond of Xander's two children. "I can't wait, and Marcus is a delight to have in class. He was a little shy at the beginning of the year but he's been doing great and brought in some fun Christmas presents for Show n' Tell last week. Did you really make that moose for him?"

"I did," Xander says beaming with pride.

"He made this table too," Kayson points out, smacking his hand onto the table that has now been carefully decorated with our marketing materials.

"Oh, wow. It's beautiful," Eloise says, running her fingers over the smooth surface of the table.

"Thank you," Xander beams.

"Is this going home with you? I bet Jamie would love this," Eloise comments.

"Nah, the wife has a specific table she's designing," Xander tells her, pulling out his phone to show her the first few drafts she's made up. I've seen them before because both Xander and Jamie have sent me ideas to weigh in on. They have asked for my input and used my expertise to help design things in the past too, even when I was living in Minneapolis.

I move about the table, rearranging nervously while Eloise continues chatting with Xander and Kayson. After a few more minutes she pulls away and grins at our table.

"Alright, boys. Have fun! Don't forget to bring your passports with you when you start walking around." Eloise pats the table before hustling off, back to her room to prepare for all the parents that will probably file into her room to meet their kids' teacher. Although, the school does have an official 'Meet Your Teacher Day' before the school year starts in August, this Around the Town also gives the parents and students an opportunity to meet their upcoming teacher or check in with their current teacher.

Eloise's departing remarks remind me to grab our business' stamp. Hopefully, I brought enough ink pads. Setting up in the gym always brings lots of visitors.

Before long, Around the Town kicks off, and it starts with an official announcement from our town's Mayor with Bella standing behind him on the little stage in the gym. My mind immediately turns to Dylan, wondering how she's feeling about this town event.

Kayson heads out right away and then Mom is one of the first people to stop by our table. I hop up to give her a quick hug and Xander follows suit. She picks up one of our business cards and smiles at me while Xander grabs her passport for a quick stamp.

"This is gorgeous," she comments, rubbing her thumb over the smooth ridges of the wood.

"Thank you. It was Shawn's idea and design," Xander says, patting me on the back before handing Mom her passport back.

"Gorgeous," Mom repeats, still staring at the card. "Gorgeous table too," she adds, winking at Xander who beams with pride for his work as she accepts her passport back.

"Did you open the store today?" I ask her as she sets the card back on the table.

"I did. Got a couple girls working it right now while I'm walking around. Usually pretty slow to start so I figured I'd walk around first. I left them with our stamps. They're really cute this year," Mom explains and I nod. "I'm going to stop by and see Dylan," she says, her smile growing. "Are you going to see her?"

"Yeah, are you?" Xander asks, moving to stand beside my mom so it's like they're teaming up against me. I shake my head, trying not to roll my eyes at them.

"I would like to walk around with her," I admit but shrug. "But who knows if I our schedules will line up."

"Just text her. You've already got our schedule down so let her know when you're free," Xander suggests. Mom nods, agreeing with him.

"Yeah, I will," I say, but before I can pull out my phone, a potential customer walks over and I get pulled away to talk about the business.

"See you tonight." Mom waves as she leaves our table and heads to the exit of the gym, stopping at a booth near the exit to look over the knick knacks on the table.

Around 3:45, Jamie comes strolling over with Kaylee close by her side. Kaylee launches herself at me, wrapping her arms around my legs. She's so little that even jumping she barely reaches my knees. I have to squat down to pick her up.

"Uncle Shawnie!" She cries, wrapping her little arms tightly around my neck, squeezing a little too tightly with her baby super strength.

"Hey, kiddo," I greet her before Jamie hustles over to keep Kaylee from strangling me.

"Sorry, Shawn," Jamie says, detaching Kaylee from me and settling her on her hip. Kaylee gets distracted by Jamie's necklace, turning her attention away from me and toward the shiny stones. "How'd it go? You get any new business?" Jamie inquires.

I look down at the table, only five business cards are left, a few brochures are scattered across the table, and I've had to throw away two ink pads already. I pick up one of the brochures and smile at the picture on it. I hadn't thought to make new ones this year because I was so focused on making the business cards and taking over the business, but looking down at the brochures, my dad smiles up at me.

"Shawn?" Jamie brings me back.

"Yeah, sorry." I offer a polite smile and she gives me a knowing one back. "But to answer your question; yes, it went well and we have a couple of people who've said they want to reach out to us for a few projects. We're already pretty busy right now but I think some of them would be cool projects. Oh, got a lot of compliments on the table, and a few people making inquiries," I tell her and she grins with relief.

"That's great. It is a beautiful table," Jamie admits.

Xander and Kayson come back at the same time, little Marcus sitting on Kayson's shoulders. Jamie bounces Kaylee on her hip and shakes her head at the two.

"Look who I ran into on my way back from the can," Kayson says, groaning a bit under Marcus' weight. He may only be 7 but he's a chunky little guy. He's still got those cherub cheeks.

"Language," Jamie scolds. Xander laughs while Kayson hands over the kid to his dad, his eyebrows knit in confusion.

"What? I only said 'can', what's wrong with that?" He asks, shrugging at Marcus who giggles.

"We're back if you want to walk around," Xander turns to me with the offer. Jamie plops down in my chair and gives me a wink as she shifts Kaylee onto her lap to bounce her a bit.

"Are you two going to be okay if I leave for an hour or so?" I ask, turning back to fix Kayson and Xander with a firm stare.

Xander laughs at my insinuation and Kayson pretends to be offended. Marcus giggles again at his dramatic response.

"Yeah, yeah," Xander says. "We can handle it."

"I'll look after them," Jamie promises and Kaylee gives me a thumbs up. Jamie coos at Kaylee, complimenting her on her support, even though I'm pretty sure she has no idea what's going on.

"Alright." I grab two of the remaining business cards and stick them into my pocket before pulling on my coat. "I'll be back before 5 to help clean up," I tell them.

"Eh, we can handle it if you don't," Xander assures me.

"Yeah, go have fun with your girl." Kayson waves me away as Xander steps up to talk to one of our locals, interested in hearing more about our work. "Don't forget your passport!"

"Okay, I'll be back," I say again, quickly grabbing my passport and shoving it into my pocket before walking out of the gym. I step out into the cold once I exit the school and head directly to Dylan's office.

Chapter 51

Dylan

'Around the Town' starts and I feel my excitement rising as Michelle opens the door for any visitors. Michelle was right about people wanting to come meet the new girl because hardly five minutes passes by and people are already starting to trickle in. Although most are here to meet me, a few stop in to get our information for future business.

Michelle is chatting away with one of her friends from a nearby store who stopped in to meet me when Vivian walks in. A bright grin is on her face and she greets Noah with a quick hello before practically dancing over to me.

"How's it going, sweetie?" Vivian asks, giving me a quick squeeze before releasing me. She looks around the office and picks up a pen and brochure, tucking them into her purse, trading me her passport in return. I stamp it with ease after a few practice rounds, then hand it back to her.

"It's going well. Lost of people coming to gawk at the new girl," I tease, dramatizing the situation. Vivian laughs, her head falling back with joy. "It's been great though. Lots of invites to come see their stores soon. And we've already opened another set of ink pads," I add with a laugh.

"Oh, I'm sure. Everyone who hasn't met you but has still heard all about you so I don't doubt that they're stopping in," Vivian says with a chuckle.

"Wait, if you're here, who's watching your store?"

"I have a couple of part time workers who help throughout the week and two have graciously offered to work today," Vivian informs me. "Which is why I'm out and about early so they can both get a chance to walk around too. Do you get a time to walk around the town? I wasn't sure if you had gotten a chance to pop into any of the stores yet. I know you've been busy since you first moved here."

"Oh, I think we're going in shifts," I tell her, looking over at Michelle.

Michelle nods. "And it seems like Noah has disappeared so I'm guessing he's out and about right now. But I think I can hold down the fort if you want to go walk around with Vivian," Michelle offers.

"Oh, no. I wouldn't want to take her away from you," Vivian objects, waving away the idea. "I'm sure there are lots of others still waiting to come out to see you." She winks at me and I smile back.

"Yeah, I don't mind waiting until Noah gets back. I'm having lots of fun here anyway!" I tell Michelle with a grin on my face. She looks proudly back at me and gives me a happy nod.

"Alright. Well, I'll let you two get back to it. I have a few other stops I want to get to. I heard the hardware store is having a special sale for today! And with all the renovations I need to do,

I thought it might be a good idea to stock up," Vivian says with a chuckle.

"Do you need help with anything?" I ask as Michelle walks over to greet another person who scuttles into the office, stomping their boots on our mat to get the snow off.

"Oh, no it's okay I'm just going to order a few things. But Mr. Hagerty, he owns the hardware," she informs me before continuing, "he'll have everything either shipped to his house or to Shawn's. He helps Shawn with a lot of the supplies for his business," she explains.

"Wow, that's great. I'm so excited. Also I noticed you don't have any social media so I reached out to my friend in Dallas, Cassidy, she's great at that sort of thing. It's literally her job," I add with a chuckle. "I asked for her help, with ideas mostly because I can help you get your accounts set up."

"Oh, thank you. But dear, you do so much for me already," Vivian tells me.

"It's not too difficult, and I don't mind helping. I'm so excited to help out with renovations. Although, I'm more of a rearranging and organizing girl, rather than construction work," I admit and Vivian laughs.

"I'd love all the help I can get," Vivian confirms, reaching out to squeeze my arm affectionately. "Alright, well, I will let you get back to it!"

Vivian starts to back away as Michelle brings another person over to introduce to me. Before she reaches the door, she turns back to look at me. "I'll see you tonight at the Spaghetti Supper, right? I promise there's more than just spaghetti." she adds with a laugh.

"Yes! I'll see you there." I wave as she heads back into the cold to visit the next shop.

"Bye, Michelle!" Vivian calls out before the door closes behind her and I am once again surrounded by town's folk wanting to meet the new girl.

Close to 4pm, with one hour left before the Spaghetti Supper, our front door opens once again and Shawn comes strolling in. A smile lights up my face as I stand up to greet him. He pulls me into a tight embrace and I feel the cold lingering on his jacket.

"Come in, come in. Warm up a little," I say, pulling him away from the door.

Shawn unwraps his scarf from his neck and shucks off his coat. Noah comes out of his office to greet Shawn with a typical guy handshake and I point him in the direction of a newcomer who frowns and looks over Noah's shoulder at me but my attention is on Shawn now.

"How has your day been?" I ask, feeling a touch shy for some reason.

Shawn maintains a respectful distance even though I want him to pull me close. I smile up at him and he takes a step toward me.

"My day has been going well. I've been thinking about you," he admits with a devilishly handsome smile.

"Oh?" I ask, stepping closer to him, my smile growing.

"Get a room," Noah calls out as he shuts the door on the visitor. Michelle turns to him with a frown.

"Noah," she scolds.

"What?" He just shrugs and goes back to his office.

"He and Marlee still having some issues?" Shawn asks and I frown, sadly.

"Nothing new," Michelle says with a sigh.

"I told him he needed to talk to her," Shawn comments and Michelle shakes her head.

"Enough of that. I don't want to bring you two down. Why don't you go ahead and take Dylan around the town. I stopped in every store and almost everyone has a good sale running today," Michelle says with a bright smile.

"That's actually why I'm here," Shawn admits, turning back to me. "I was going to text you earlier to see if we could align our schedules but I got pretty busy. Do you have time now to go? Or did you already get to walk around?"

"I have not gotten to walk around yet. So, I would love to. If that's okay with you, Michelle?" I turn to ask her and she nods, clapping her hands with excitement.

"Don't you worry about me and Noah, we can hold down the fort here while you get to explore the town." Michelle grabs my coat for me and then ushers us out the door, slipping a couple business cards into my pocket, alongside my still empty passport.

"Is there a reason she was so eager to get rid of you?" Shawn teases as he reaches over to take my mitted hand in his.

"She's just eager for us to go out," I say, then blush, realizing what I said. "I mean, go out, like walking around the town. She knows I've been so busy since I got here that I haven't had a lot of opportunities to check out everything in town," I explain, rambling a bit.

Shawn watches me with an amused look and I clamp my mouth shut, rolling my eyes at him.

"A lot of people are eager for us to go out," Shawn teases, pulling me close against his side as he opens the first shop door for us.

We step inside as the bell rings and everyone looks toward the door at us.

"Shawn!" One woman hustles over and gives his arm a squeeze. "It's so good to see you. And who is this?" She quickly turns her attention to me.

"Ms. Lisa, this is Dylan," Shawn introduces us. "Dylan, Ms. Lisa."

"Hi, nice to meet you," I say as I'm pulled into a hug.

"Ah, Dylan! It is so good to finally meet you. I've heard so much about you," Ms. Lisa says then pulls us into the store, helping me shed my coat. "Come in, come in. Are you looking for anything in particular?"

I look around the store. It's a small boutique with lots of gorgeous items. "Wow, these are so cool," I say, walking over to a display with lake themed items. There's a little bracelet on display that has a few charms on it. I pick it up and look at each lake themed charm; a kayak, a fishing pole, a floaty tube, a snowflake for the season, flipflops as well. And around the display is a case of other charms as well.

"We like to change out the charms depending on the season but most of them are lake related," Ms. Lisa informs me.

"I love it," I tell her and she beams.

"Do you want one?" Shawn asks. I turn to him with a curious look. He gestures to the bracelet. "The bracelet, or a charm or two," he says, like he's offering to get one for me. "I'll get you whatever you want," he promises and I grin at him.

"That is so sweet," Ms. Lisa comments, putting her hand on her heart.

"The fishing charm?" I ask Shawn with a sly smile. His eyebrows raise as his smile grows, smirking at me.

"Oh, do you like fishing?" Ms. Lisa asks, oblivious to the tension growing between Shawn and I. She unlocks the charm box and picks up a fishing rod charm.

"I'm new to it," I admit. "But have fond memories and looking forward to making more."

Shawn grins at me as we follow Ms. Lisa up to the counter to check out. The girl at the counter smiles a polite smile at both of us, blushing when Shawn offers her one of his bright smiles. She ducks her head to focus on checking us out. I chuckle, knowing the effect of Shawn's smile. Ms. Lisa holds out her hands and Shawn and I hand over our passports. We each receive our first stamp.

"Don't worry," Shawn assures me. "By the end of the day, your passport will be filled."

"I'm counting on it," I tease. "And you didn't have to buy me anything," I tell him as the cashier hands us the bag with the little charm. Shawn smiles at me, tucking his wallet back into his pocket and leading me out of the shop. Ms. Lisa calls out a goodbye as we leave and we wave back at her.

"I know I didn't but I wanted to," he says, reaching over to zip up my coat while we walk to the next shop. He grins at me, causing butterflies in my stomach. "You picked a good one."

"Thank you," I say, standing up on my tip toes to plant a soft kiss on his mouth.

"Shawnie boy!" He's greeted the moment we step into the next shop. An older gentleman walks over to us, we meet him halfway and Shawn accepts a loose hug from him. Then the man turns to me with a big smile on his face. "Ah, and you must be Dylan."

"Yes, that's me," I say with a smile, shaking my head. Word gets around quickly in a small town.

"Dylan, this is Mr. Plum," Shawn introduces us when I shoot him a quick glance.

"Mr. Plum?" I ask, my eyes widening as I think back to the sign on above the entrance. "As in the 'Plum' from 'Plum's Pantry'?"

"That's me," he says with a proud grin. "But please, call me Henry."

"It's nice to meet you, Henry." I smile as he takes my hand and leads me deeper into the shop. The smell of fresh waffles fills the air. "Mm, what is that delicious smell?"

"Ah, that would be our homemade waffle cones," Henry explains, pulling me deeper into the shop. "We have a small station with candy and treats for the kiddos, including Stroopwafels." Henry points out the tables lines with candy and other goodies. Then we keep walking and he brings us over to the counter where others are lined up looking at ice cream flavors. "And my granddaughter, she's about your age, she just turned us onto this new trend of having alcohol infused ice cream."

"Hey, Dylan. Hey, Shawn," Diana greets us from behind the counter. She offers us little sample scoops of the alcohol options. "Here try it out. We just released the first test batch for 'Around the Town'. Let me know what you think."

"Thanks, Di," I greet her with the nickname and she smiles at me.

"Di is Henry's grandaughter if you hadn't guessed," Shawn explains before he takes a bite of the ice cream, then the alcohol hits him and his face pinches. Di laughs and I have to giggle as well. "How is it?" I ask through the laughter.

"It's…good," Shawn chokes out. He gestures for me to try my sample. I hesitate only a second before tipping the spoon onto my tongue and letting the cool, creamy ice cream melt on my tongue.

"Mm, wow! Okay, that was delicious," I tell Di and she grins. "Very strong but the flavor is so good!"

Shawn eyes me and I smirk at him. "That was weirdly impressive," he admits with an intrigued look.

"You want any scoops?" Di asks as she doles out a cup for the customer in front of us. She hands the cup over to her grandfather who has now taken up behind the cash register.

"I'd love to try one of the homemade wafflecones," I say with a bright smile. "Oh, wait, will that fill me up before dinner? I was excited to go to the Spaghetti Supper."

"It is pretty filling." Di thinks it over, tapping on the counter. "Hm. Oh, we just made a batch of Stoopwafels if you want to try it that way, if you don't want ice cream?"

"We can always stop by after the Spaghetti Supper, lots of people do," Shawn tells me and I think it over.

"Stoopwafel now then," I say with conviction. It's definitely the smarter choice, especially because we've just started walking around and I don't want to bring ice cream into any shops just in case it gets messy.

"Alrighty," Di says, hopping off a little step stool and skipping to the front window to collect a couple Stoopwafels for us. She comes back with them wrapped in wax paper and hands them to us over the counter.

"What do we owe you?" I ask, reaching for my wallet but before I can grab it, Henry steps in and waves it away.

"No, no. Free sample to get you hooked," Henry says with a grin. Di laughs but nods in agreement. "Don't forget the stamps," he chides Di. She rolls her eyes but has a smile on her face as she add another stamp to our passports.

"Thank you, Henry. Thanks, Di. See you later," Shawn says before I can protest. He's already got his hand on my back, starting to push me toward the door since we have a lot more stops to make before heading to the high school for the Spaghetti Supper.

"I will definitely be back!" I call out as Shawn ushers me out the door. "Bye, Di. Nice to meet you Henry!" I see them wave as the door shuts behind us.

"You're adorable wanting to talk to everyone for hours but we don't have a lot of time to chit chat at each stop," Shawn teases me. I frown and start to protest. "I told the guys I would be back to help clean up our booth and get ready for supper," he explains quickly.

"Oh, okay. Oops, sorry," I laugh, picking up the pace even though our next stop, small flower shop, is only about fifteen feet away.

Chapter 52

Dylan

I walk out the door of the flower shop with another stamp added to my growing collection and my face buried in a big bouquet of beautiful peonies that Shawn spared no expenses on. "You really didn't have to do that," I half complain as I get another whiff of the flowers.

"I like supporting local businesses, and they have local vendors who grow the flowers too," Shawn tells me as he takes the bouquet from my hands. I want to protest but I see him grip the flowers in one of his big hands, leaving both of mine free for him to capture one of mine in his free hand. I smile and swing our hands between us.

A lot of the stores on Main Street have signs directing us back to the high school so we make it through the rest of the shops and offices pretty quickly, my passport filling up. We even have time to stop at my apartment to drop off the flowers and other goodies we picked up before making it back to the high school a few minutes before 5pm. My stomach starts to growl and I start to get a little bit of a headache, two indications that it is time for me to eat again. Once we step into the school, all the delicious smells hit my nose and I inhale deeply.

"Oh no, are we too late to help set up?" I worry.

Shawn chuckles. "I'm sure there is still lots we can do. Let's go check out my set up," Shawn says, tugging my hand in that direction. We walk down a long hall before we come to the gymnasium. There are a few booths still set up but most are being packed up. We head over to the table where Kayson sits with a little boy in his lap and Xander clears the table.

"Hey, guys," I say, giving them a small wave as Shawn drops my hand to help them clean up.

"Dylan. What's up, girl?" Xander gives me a quick hug while Kayson makes the little boy wave at me. The kid pulls his hand away, old enough to hate being treated like a baby. I laugh and wave back anyway, making the little kid blush. "Oh sorry, you probably haven't met my kids, have you?"

"You have kids?" I ask, shocked.

Xander laughs as a beautiful woman with a little girl on her hip comes walking over to the table.

"He's got two kids, and a wife," she adds with an eyeroll at her husband. She hands off the little girl to Xander and pulls me into a hug. "You must be Dylan, I'm Jamie."

"Hi, Jamie. It's nice to meet you," I say the phrase for about the 100th time today but I've meant it every time.

"Nice to meet you too, dear. Oh, this is Kaylee," Jamie says, squeezing the little girl's foot much to her delight, she squeals happily, kicking her feet. "And that," Jamie points to the little boy on Kayson's lap, "is Marcus."

"Hi," the little boy gives me a shy wave.

"Hi, Marcus," I say back then turn to the little girl. "Hi, Kaylee." She gives me a bright yet shy smile.

"Named after her favorite uncle," Shawn comments, gesturing to Kayson.

"Yeah, kind of rude you guys named the girl after me," Kayson comments, making Kaylee pout. "Oh, sweetie. You know you're my favorite," Kayson says as a way of an apology, earning him and elbow to the ribs from the little boy in his lap. "Oof," he says, pretending to be hurt.

Marcus looks proud, his dad does too but Jamie scolds both of them. Jamie takes Marcus from Kayson's lap and tells him to help clean up while Xander goes to get their dishes from the car.

"Oh no," I say after Xander leaves. "Was I supposed to bring a dish?"

"Oh, don't worry about it, hun. There's plenty to go around. Food is provided by the town but we like to bring in our favorites as well," Jamie explains as Marcus wiggles around in her arms. She grunts before putting him on the ground. She lets him run off to play with his friends after she waves at one of the other moms to make sure they're watching him.

Kayson and Shawn quickly finish clearing off their table then leave us to go help set up the rest of the room. A woman hustles by and drops off a table cloth onto our table, giving us all a smile before she continues on to the next group.

"So, how was your day?" Jamie asks, tossing the table cloth over the beautiful table, which I think would look fine without but I guess this is better to protect the table from messy diners. I help her straighten it out and look around the room to see every other table being covered as well. When we finish, Jamie pulls me over to Kayson's vacated chair. She drops into the other with a loud sigh, sitting back to relax.

"It was great. We had a lot of foot traffic, mostly people wanting to meet me but I think we also got a few potential clients," I tell her as the boys work to clear the table off.

"Hey, ladies," Marlee comes over to our table and grabs an extra chair to join us. "How was everybody's day? You two hungry for some spaghetti?" She laughs loudly at that as she drops into the chair with an exaggerated sigh.

Jamie laughs at the sighing. "I literally just dropped and sighed too," she admits, making all three of us laugh.

"It's been a long day," I say in agreement, leaning back in the chair and not too subtly checking out Shawn as he bends over to pick something up off the floor. He catches me staring when he straightens up and winks at me. I roll my eyes, turning back to the girls. "When is food being served?" I ask, tactlessly.

Marlee checks her watch. "Should be soon. Mayor Bowen will give a little speech again before everyone can dig in but it'll be quick," she promises.

"Good. Mama is starving," Jamie says. Then she pauses, frowning. "Is it weird that I referred to myself that way when I'm not talking to my kids?"

Marlee laughs and I chuckle. "Nah, plus you're the only Mama here so it still fits."

"Good, thank you," Jamie says, rubbing at her sleepy eyes.

"So, still wanna stay in town after getting the grand tour of everything?" Marlee asks, leaning forward in her seat to meet my gaze.

"Oh, I love it," I gush. "It's honestly everything I hoped a small town would be. I've always heard about how cute and close knit small towns are but I never thought I would be able to handle it after living in Dallas. But I just love it. It's still way too cold for me but walking everywhere helped warm me up." The girls nod at my response.

"So, does this mean you're sticking around?" Marlee asks, raising her eyebrows and wiggling her shoulders excitedly.

I smile a small, mysterious smile, trying to contain the grin that wants to take over my face. Jamie raises her eyebrow as well and gestures for me to spit it out. I chuckle.

"What are you ladies talking about?" Xander asks, coming back over to us with his arms full, the little girl on his hip and a heavy looking bag that smells delicious.

Shawn comes over and drapes his arm over my shoulder, planting a kiss on my head. I'm a little surprised by his gesture but it also makes me smile. I look up at him and he gazes down at me before lowering his head to kiss me softly.

"Eeeew!" Kaylee cries out, pointing at the two of us. I pull back with a laugh and Shawn blushes. He excuses himself, telling us he's going to get more chairs for the rest of their group.

I wonder who all will be joining us. Probably the group Noah introduced me to when I first moved to Birch Lake. The thought of seeing everybody together again makes me smile.

Jamie laughs at Kaylee and Shawn and accepts Kaylee from Xander as Bella comes over to join the group. She says hello to everyone before dragging a chair between Jamie and Marlee. All three of them turn to me to get back to my decision but as soon as Jamie opens her mouth to ask about it, Bella's phone beeps and she looks down at it.

"Oops, hold that thought! Time to get things started." Bella hops up and scurries off. Kayson quickly takes her seat.

"When's the rest of everybody getting here?" Kayson asks.

"Soon." Eloise comes over to the table and says a quick hello to everyone before she takes a seat at the table.

A lot of people trickle into the gym and find tables to sit at and leave their coats at while the Mayor (explained to me by Jamie), Bella, and a few other staff get the stage ready for another speech.

Marcus finds his way back to his parents and crowds onto Xander's lap while he's chatting away with Shawn. There's a tap on the microphone to get everyone's attention and I turn to see the Mayor stepping up to talk.

"Alright, everybody settle down!" Mayor Bowen, a handsome older fellow, says into the microphone, creating enough of a static feedback that a few people groan and Bella flinches on stage. "Oops, sorry about that," the Mayor says.

There are a few seconds of feedback from the microphone before someone gets it settled. Bella gestures for the Mayor to step back up and try again.

"Okay! I don't want to waste any more time and chance the food getting cold so I'll keep it short," he starts. "Thank you all for coming out for 'Around the Town' and our Spaghetti Supper! And thank you to everyone who brought a dish or dessert," he adds. "We always have such a great turn out for every event in this town and today was amazing. I've heard from a few shops that their sales will continue over the weekend and it looks like the weather tomorrow will be as beautiful as it was today."

I chuckle. Sure, the day was beautiful but still cold. Shawn rubs his thumb over my hand and I lean into his side.

"Alright, I'll stop talking so you all can get on with the rest of the evening. Enjoy!" Mayor Bowen says and the room cheers before people start to get up to go over to the tables lined with dishes, including multiple big pans of spaghetti.

Shawn and I stay seated for a few minutes, chatting until the line dies down before we walk with the rest of our group over the dwindling line. He points out a pile of passports and tosses his in.

"For the tally, to see who will win the grand prize," he explains. I nod and toss my passport in the mix. Then Shawn hands me a plate and a bowl.

"Trust me, you'll need both," Shawn assures me.

I chuckle but as I make my way down the line, he's right. I might even need a second plate. Or just a second trip. There's plenty of food still waiting down the line as I load my plate up and of course, I let someone fill my bowl full of spaghetti. All of it smells and looks amazing.

Once my hands are full, I follow Shawn back to the table where some of our group is already digging into their food. The room is mostly silent as everyone focuses on eating, the sound of utensils scraping plates fills the room. When everyone starts slowing down, chatter fills the room, my table among them. Shawn slings his arm behind my chair and I lean back into him. He pulls my chair closer to him and gives me a bright smile.

"How's your food?" he asks.

"It's great!" I tell him after swallowing another bite of food. "I do feel bad though. I don't think I'll have room for ice cream tonight," I say with a frown.

Di laughs and Shawn chuckles. "No worries," Di says. "We're not going anywhere. You can always stop by tomorrow," she reminds me with a wink.

"Oh, don't tempt me," I groan, sitting back in my seat. Di chuckles and is pulled away into a conversation with Eloise and Conrad, who seem to be having a spirited debate about a TV show they watch.

Halfway through the Supper, the Mayor returns to the stage, tapping on the microphone to get everyone's attention. Bella rolls her eyes at the group before she hustles over to join him and the rest of her coworkers who are also scrambling.

"Alright, it's that time of the evening everyone!" Mayor Bowen calls out. "Time to give away the prizes!"

"Did they ever announce what the prizes would be?" Marlee asks with a glance around the table. She's mostly met with shrugs, no one knows.

"For third place, with 18 stamps!" The Mayor calls out.

"Wow, 18. That's incredible," I gasp. Shawn chuckles and squeezes my shoulder. "I only got 8, I think. Will we get our passports back?"

"Yeah, might take a while but I'm sure Bella can expedite the process for you," Shawn tells me with a wink. I lean into him and he lifts my chin to give me a soft kiss. "I'll help you win the grand prize next time," he promises me.

"Alright, I will hold you to it." I grin at him before turning my attention back to the Mayor who has already handed out the 2nd and 3rd place prizes. The 3rd place winner earned a dinner for four at Gloria's. And the 2nd place winner got a basket of free 'all expenses paid' weekend at the local Spa and Resort.

"And the winner of our 1st place prize, with a total of 32 stamps!" The Mayor announces, dragging it out to be dramatic. "Wow! That's a person who really supports their town!" He adds with a brilliant smile. There are chuckles among the crowd. "The winner is… Jamie Mason!"

"Oh, my gosh!" Jamie says with a gasp. "I won!"

"Babe! We did it!" Xander grins at her. Jamie rolls her eyes but hasn't stopped smiling.

"Who is 'we'?" Kayson asks with a laugh.

Marlee and Di start cheering loudly and I join in. Shawn chuckles but joins in with Kayson, cheering on their friend.

"Well, go get your prizes!" Di instructs, trying to take Kaylee off of Jamie's lap.

"Oh, my gosh," Jamie says again.

"The first place prize not only includes the dinner for four at Gloria's and the Spa weekend but it also includes gift cards and coupons for almost every store in town! And that includes childcare for the spa weekend!" Mayor Bowen adds with a wink as he watches Jamie try to detach the kids from her so she can collect her winnings.

Eventually, Jamie is released and she jogs over to claim a beautiful wicker basket with all her winnings. She grins at the room and blows kisses, much to everyone's entertainment. Then she runs back over to the table and sets the bounty before us. Not only does she get all the gift cards but the basket is also filled with candles, candies, and other little knick-knacks like bath and body products.

"Oh, I am soo jealous," Di says with a laugh. "This looks delightful."

"Please," Jamie says, gesturing to the bounty before her, "feel free to take whatever you want. Honestly, the coupons, gift cards, and free spa are more than enough for me."

"Oh, no. You deserve all of it… Oh! Actually, I do love this smell though," Di says, grabbing one of the candles and taking a big inhale. I giggle and Jamie shoots me a knowing eye roll.

Looking around the room at all my new friends as I'm nestled in the crook of my handsome man's arm, I can see how my future is going to be beautiful here.

"So," Marlee interrupts my daydreaming, "you never answered my question from earlier," she points out with a knowing smile.

"What question?" Eloise inquires eagerly. She spins her fork in a steaming bowl of spaghetti, I think her third bowl, as she waits for an answer.

"I asked if she had decided to stick around," Marlee informs everyone at the table since all eyes are now on me.

Shawn reaches over and takes my hand in his. I look at him and can see him holding back a smile, not wanting to steal the moment from me.

"So?" Noah asks, even though he knows the answer since I informed him and Michelle when I returned from Dallas. He's trying to suppress a grin as well, his arm slung delicately over Marlee's chair.

"Wait, what's going on?" Xander asks. Jamie shushes him and gestures for me to go ahead.

I grin at all of them and squeeze Shawn's hand.

"Everyone kept telling me to give it a month," I start and see eyebrows raising around me. "But I think I want more." Shawn smiles at me and I grin back at him. "Yeah, I think I'll stick around for a while."

Mairi Louise

Read on for a sneak peek into

Book 2 of the

Birch Lake Series

Chapter 1

Cassidy

"Cassidy!" Dylan squeals as she wraps her arms around me. I snuggle in, trying to hide from the wind.

"Wow, you weren't kidding about the weather here. How is this April?" I ask with a shiver. Dylan chuckles and quickly hustles me into the car, leaving my bags for Shawn to pick up.

"It's brutal," she admits, cranking the heat as we huddle together in the backseat of Shawn's truck. "But you'll get used to it, I swear. Well, I guess I can't talk yet. But I am getting there!"

"Yeah, that's why you added an extra blanket to my stash in the back," Shawn comments after he gets into the truck. "Hi, by the way, I'm Shawn." He reaches back to shake my hand before he notices that I've got all my extremities tucked under the blanket. He chuckles and withdraws his hand.

"Nice to meet you," I squeak. "I've heard so much about you."

Shawn looks at Dylan in the rearview mirror with a smile on his face and she rolls her eyes but has a matching grin.

"I'm so excited to see this bookstore," I say once we're on the road. "From what you've said about it, it sounds adorable.

And Vivian sounds like an absolute angel," I sigh, excited to get started on my next project.

When Dylan emailed me a few weeks ago asking for some social media expertise, I immediately jumped at the chance to see her again. My last project just ended and it was the perfect opportunity to fly out for a few weeks. She insisted I didn't need to drop everything but with my job, it's easy to travel and she's one of my best friends. I want to see the small town she fell in love with, and the man she fell in love with too. She hasn't admitted it yet but I know they've exchanged 'I love you's'. They haven't admitted to being 'in love' but I know they are.

"Oh it is and Vivian is amazing," Dylan gushes, leaning into me as I shiver again. I am starting to warm up but the wind was colder than I expected.

"I wouldn't say 'angel' though," Shawn teases. Dylan reaches up and whacks his shoulder. "Hey! I'm driving here."

"Be nice to your momma then," she scolds with a laugh. "I'm so glad you're here!" Dylan squeals again, squeezing me in a tight hug. I've never seen her this excited and energetic, usually I'm the outgoing and loud one. I'm not sure if it's the town, the boy, or the weather, but this place has really opened her up.

"I'm so happy to be here," I admit with a grin. "Thank you for picking me up."

"Oh, I wouldn't have had it any other way. Plus, it's a three hour ride so I figured we could get caught up and then maybe start going over some ideas for the bookstore." Dylan practically bounces in her seat with excitement.

"Don't you think the social media and design aspect is a little premature when the store is just getting started with renovations?" Shawn asks. Dylan pouts a bit but shakes her head.

"No, I think it's perfect," I step in to say, agreeing with Dylan. "This way we can be as involved in the whole process as we want. People love seeing the progress videos and updates on social media. And of course a the end we'll make a short video of everything that happened, for those who like the updates in one video," I add with a laugh.

"Oh that's me," Dylan admits with another happy laugh. "It's always so annoying to come across a renovation video and they're like two days in when it's going to take a month. Of course, I have to follow the account for any updates."

"Exactly," I nod in agreement. Shawn chuckles, shaking his head at us. "Plus, I don't mind getting my hands a little dirty when working on such special projects."

"Oh, really?" Dylan raises her eyebrow at me. "Wait, I want to help out too. I love 'Demo Day' on Fixer Upper. We can have a whole video dedicated to that!" She squeals with excitement over the idea.

"Dylan, honey, are you sure you want to be a part of the demolition?" Shawn asks from the front seat.

"Yes!" Dylan answers immediately. Shawn eyes her in the rear view mirror. He sighs, giving in pretty quickly.

"Fine, I will talk to the guys who are working on the project and see if they're okay with you two joining," Shawn informs us.

"Oh, who all is working on it?" Dylan asks, leaning forward to hear his answer.

"Kayson and Xander volunteered right away. We just finished a project so they were free. And I think Conrad might be helping out too. I'll have to check his latest project. His team is working pretty slowly but I think they might be finished," Shawn says, thinking everything over.

"Wait, are you the boss?" I as curiously.

Dylan laughs nervously and Shawn glances back at us with narrowed eyes. "Yeah, I am. Dylan doesn't know what I do, does she?"

"Uhm," I hesitate, not wanting to out Dylan.

"Hey, I know you have people who work for you and that you work with your hands," she says then blushes as Shawn raises an eyebrow at her.

"Mhm, is that it?" He asks. Dylan bites her lip and shrugs. "Yes, I'm the boss. I own the company, in fact. Well, it was my dad's and when he passed away, I took over."

"Oh, I'm sorry for your loss," I say, awkwardly as Dylan gives his shoulder an affectionate squeeze.

"It's been a few years," Shawn says. "And I'm grateful for the booming business he left me. We're a construction company," he goes on. "We take on projects of all sizes. From building houses, to decks, to docks. Lots of renovations lately since more and more young families are moving in and wanting to revamp their grandparents' handed down house. We'll do anything really. If the people of Birch Lake ask, we'll do it."

"Wow, that's pretty impressive. Do you ever have to turn down projects?" I ask, leaning into the conversation. The blanket slips from around me but I'm starting to warm up. Dylan takes the blanket and refolds it, tucking it back into a neat little basket with water bottles and snacks.

Shawn shrugs. "Well, one of our guys moved to Minneapolis a month or so ago. He had been with us for a while so it was a huge loss. I'm looking for new hires currently. If you know anybody," he adds.

"I know a few people who would excel but I'm not sure how they would feel about moving to Minnesota," I say and Dylan laughs.

"It's really great," she swears. "Oh, Clearwater is coming up, can we stop?"

"What's at Clearwater?" I ask, looking out the window. So far, the drive out of the city has been pretty typical. The city is just covered in snow.

"Bigger than your face donuts," Dylan states, giving me a wide eyed look.

"I think they're just 'big as your face'," Shawn corrects but Dylan waves a hand, dismissing his correction.

"They're huge! And they have amazing sandwiches. So, we are stopping for lunch and then probably have donuts for dinner?" She look at Shawn for confirmation. I can see him smiling in the mirror.

"Whatever you want," he offers.

"You'll love it," she promises.

Shawn takes the next exit and pulls up to a gas pump. Dylan flings open the door and pulls me out of the car. Thankfully, the wind isn't as strong here but I'm glad when she hustles us into the Plaza.

"Apple fritter?" Dylan calls over her shoulder as we jog toward the front door.

"Yes!" Shawn calls but his voice is cut off as the door shuts behind Dylan and me.

"Bathroom first and then food," Dylan instructs, pulling me in the right direction.

Once we're done freshening up, Dylan and I find Shawn already in the line for donuts. She snuggles up to him, planting a kiss on his cheek as he pays for all of our donuts then she turns back to me and pulls me into another tight hug.

"Yay, I am just so glad you're here."

"Me too." I wiggle with happiness. "And I cannot wait to see Birch Lake. Which is apparently so amazing that it made you leave Dallas. I mean, Dallas, Texas to Minnesota? That's so wild," I say with a laugh. Dylan tosses her head back and laughs loudly.

"It's crazy, right? You're going to love it," she swears. "Who knows, you might even love it so much you decide to stay too." Dylan shrugs nonchalantly with a little smirk on her face.

"You never know," I respond with a wink.

Author Bio

Mairi Louise has always had a love of reading and writing. From a young age, she would create adventurous little stories and devour every book she got her hands on. Now as an adult, she has found joy in turning her stories into novels that she is excited to share with everyone.

Mairi Louise invites you to visit her on Instagram @AuthorMairiLouise and X (Twitter) @MairiLouise2